PRAISE FOR

GINA WILKINS

"Gina Wilkins has penned yet another sterling story."
—*Affaire de Coeur* on *Countdown to Baby*

"Gina Wilkins's holiday keeper is like a Christmas stocking—
brimming with an endearing cast of characters
and stuffed with warm moments."
—*Romantic Times* on *Make-Believe Mistletoe*

"The power of Gina Wilkins's latest offering is found in her
richly drawn characters who move with ease to the cadence
of this heartwarming love story."
—*Romantic Times* on *Her Very Own Family*

"Touches the emotions and makes you
feel good all over. Don't miss it!"
—*Rendezvous* on *Full of Grace*

"This compelling love story is everything a
reader could want and more."
—*Romantic Times* on *Hardworking Man*

"Wonderful characterization makes this
engaging love story unforgettable reading."
—*Romantic Times* on *Fair and Wise*

"(She) twists and turns her intriguing plot in wondrous
ways to maximize our reading enjoyment."
—*Romantic Times* on *Loving and Giving*

Dear Reader,

The editors at Harlequin and Silhouette are thrilled to be able to bring you a brand-new featured author program for 2005! Signature Select aims to single out outstanding stories, contemporary themes and oft-requested classics by some of your favorite series authors and present them to you in a variety of formats bound by truly striking covers.

We want to provide several different types of reading experiences in the new Signature Select program. The Spotlight books offer a single "big read" by a talented series author, the Collections present three novellas on a selected theme in one volume, the Sagas contain sprawling, sometimes multi-generational family tales (often related to a favorite family first introduced in series) and the Miniseries feature requested previously published books, with two or, occasionally, three complete stories in one volume. The Signature Select program offers one book in each of these categories per month, and fans of limited continuity series will also find these continuing stories under the Signature Select umbrella.

In addition, these volumes bring you bonus features...different in every single book! You may learn more about the author in an extended interview, more about the setting or inspiration for the book, more about subjects related to the theme and, often, a bonus short read will be included. Authors and editors have been outdoing themselves in originating creative material for our bonus features—we're sure you'll be surprised and pleased with the results!

The Signature Select program strives to bring you a variety of reading experiences by authors you've come to love, as well as by rising stars you'll be glad you've discovered. Watch for new stories from Janelle Denison, Donna Kauffman, Leslie Kelly, Marie Ferrarella, Suzanne Forster, Stephanie Bond, Christine Rimmer and scores more of the brightest talents in romance fiction!

The excitement continues!

Warm wishes for happy reading,

Marsha Zinberg

Marsha Zinberg
Executive Editor
The Signature Select Program

MINISERIES

GINA WILKINS

ONCE A FAMILY...

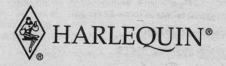

HARLEQUIN®

TORONTO • NEW YORK • LONDON
AMSTERDAM • PARIS • SYDNEY • HAMBURG
STOCKHOLM • ATHENS • TOKYO • MILAN • MADRID
PRAGUE • WARSAW • BUDAPEST • AUCKLAND

ISBN 0-373-21767-6

ONCE A FAMILY...

Copyright © 2005 by Harlequin Books S.A.

The publisher acknowledges the copyright holder of the individual works as follows:

FULL OF GRACE
Copyright © 1993 by Gina Wilkins.

HARDWORKING MAN
Copyright © 1993 by Gina Wilkins.

CONTENTS

Dear Reader,

A psychologist I once met at a party asked me if there was a recurring theme in my books. After some deliberation, I realized that many of my stories involve characters reaching a new awareness of the value of family. Perhaps they had previously taken their families for granted, or had become estranged from them. Or maybe they had been alone for so long that they had convinced themselves they didn't need, or even want, family ties. But by the end of their stories, all of them realized that there is nothing more precious than the love and support of a family—whether created by birth or by choice.

The FAMILY FOUND series has carried this theme through almost a dozen stories now, beginning with *Full of Grace* and *Hardworking Man*. Michelle Walker Trent sets the series in motion when she learns that she was separated as a toddler from six biological siblings. She begins a quest to find them, and in the process falls in love with a man from another huge clan.

The siblings have all led very different lives. Some belong to new families, while others have barricaded their hearts against the pain they endured when they were torn from their biological family. Oldest brother Jared Walker *(Hardworking Man)* remembers the trauma all too clearly, and it takes a very special woman to convince him to open his closely guarded heart again.

So maybe I do have a theme, after all—inspired, perhaps, by my own deep appreciation of family. The family I was born into, the one I married into and the one my husband and I have created together. I've been richly blessed, and it seems that I enjoy bestowing the same blessing on the characters I come to know and love in my books.

I hope you enjoy getting to know the Walker family in these first two books of the FAMILY FOUND series.

Gina Wilkins

FULL OF GRACE

Prologue

My dearest Michelle,

I want to take this chance to tell you one last time that you have blessed my life in so many ways. I could never have imagined the joy and pride I would find in the little girl who was given to me in answer to years of prayers.

Your father and I loved you from the moment we saw you. You were so small and frightened and vulnerable. You looked up at us with your big blue eyes filled with tears and your tiny mouth trembling and we knew our lives would never be the same.

Now your daddy has been gone for three years and I will be joining him soon. I know how lonely you will be, how empty this big house will seem to you. And I feel compelled to tell you something I have withheld until now because I couldn't bear to share you with those who may have had reason to feel you belonged more to them than to your father and me.

We told you that your real parents were dead and that you had no adult relatives who could have taken you in. I'm sorry, darling, but we kept one important bit of information from you. You do have a family, four brothers and two sisters, to be exact. All are older than you except one, a little girl only a few months old when your mother died when you were two.

I don't know what happened to any of them, but I will tell you that the last name was Walker. Your biological father was Hank Walker, your mother's name was Hazel. You lived in a rural area near Texarkana, Texas. You were born in Texarkana and given the name Shelley Marie Walker. Hank died while your mother was pregnant with your younger sister. When Hazel died so tragically soon afterward, there was no one else to provide for seven small children, so the decision was made to split you up and find homes for you. Perhaps a bad decision, but had a different one been made, your father and I would never have had you. I can't even bear to think of that.

Please forgive us for not telling you these things sooner, and try to understand our fears. We loved you so much. You were our life. We almost lost you once. We couldn't bear to risk losing you again. Remember us only with love, darling, and know that no child, no young woman, has ever been loved more than we loved you.

Mother

Chapter One

Tony D'Alessandro looked up from the letter in his hand to the young woman sitting absolutely still in a worn leather chair on the other side of his desk. With her rich brown hair swept into a neat coil, her blue eyes focused intently on his face, her seductive mouth unsmiling, her slender body clad in a suit that probably cost more than his monthly food allowance, the woman could have passed as a mannequin for a Rodeo Drive boutique.

When his secretary, Bonnie, had escorted Michelle Trent into his office less than ten minutes earlier, Tony had been struck speechless by the woman's beauty. Only after he'd closed his mouth and self-consciously cleared his throat had he become aware of the icy shell she maintained around her—invisible, but unarguably real.

He'd wondered if her lovely, porcelain-fair face ever warmed with a smile, ever softened with emotion. Now he knew that at least one person had loved Michelle Trent with an almost neurotic intensity—her adoptive mother, Alicia Culverton Trent, the late widow of immensely wealthy, near-legendary Dallas business tycoon Harrison Ellington Trent III. Tony knew of the family, of course, in the same way everyone else heard about them—through newspapers, magazines, gossip and rumors.

So what was wealthy, reclusive, incredibly beautiful Michelle Trent doing in the office of a low-profile, ex-cop-turned-private-investigator? With his usual straightforward approach to mysteries, Tony decided the only way to find the answer was to ask. "Why are you here, Ms. Trent? Why did you want me to read this letter?"

Her voice was as cultured and alluring as the rest of her. "I would think the answer is obvious, Mr. D'Alessandro. I want you to locate my brothers and sisters."

His left eyebrow rose as it always did when something intrigued him. "Why me?" he asked bluntly. "Surely you have attorneys who could initiate this search as easily as I can."

She inclined her head in an annoyingly regal gesture. "I have attorneys, of course, but I've chosen not to involve them. To be completely honest, you're the only one other than myself who has seen this letter or who knows about my search. I've been told that you are an honest, discreet investigator. I trust that your business ethics will ensure strict confidentiality in my case."

Piqued by the undercurrents of doubt in her voice, Tony scowled. "I've never gossiped about a client in my entire career, Ms. Trent, and I can assure you that won't change with you. I'm only trying to determine why you came to me with this."

She moistened her artfully tinted lips with the tip of her tongue, for the first time looking somewhat less imperturbable. "Eighteen years ago my father hired your father for an assignment that was highly sensitive and even involved physical danger to your father. It was important that the case be handled quickly, efficiently—and privately. My father was always grateful to yours for the skillful way he handled the job, and he told me that if I ever needed help, I should contact Vincent D'Alessandro."

"Who retired in '86," Tony finished for her. "I started the business back up two years ago."

She nodded. "So I found out."

Tony tried not to look surprised that his father had once handled a "highly sensitive" assignment for one of the wealthiest, most powerful men in Texas. He wasn't at all surprised, however, that the mysterious case had been handled well, or that it had apparently been kept utterly private. Vinnie D'Alessandro had never, in some thirty years in the business, broken client confidence, a record Tony had every intention of maintaining.

Michelle Trent crossed her long, silk-covered legs and subjected Tony to a thorough scrutiny. "Are you as good at your job as your father was, Mr. D'Alessandro?"

He crossed his arms over his chest and met her eyes, knowing if he looked down at those luscious legs he'd find himself stammering. "No one's as good as my father was, Ms. Trent. But I'm damn close."

It was a calculated risk, of course. If this insouciant attitude offended her, he'd lose what could turn out to be a profitable assignment. On the other hand, he intended to let her know that he didn't particularly care to be treated like a menial subordinate during their association, should there be one.

Her lips twitched in what he would have sworn was the beginning of a smile, and he felt his left eyebrow rising again. But she quickly suppressed the expression and nodded in response to his words. "I can depend on you to keep my business completely private?"

"You can trust me," he replied, too curtly.

"I trust very few people." Her tone was cool. Some might have called it icy. "Your father was one of them. I'm taking a risk that he trained you to be as honorable as he is."

Tony couldn't help but soften at her praise of his father. After all, his dad was a hell of a great guy. "I've always tried to be as much like my father as possible," he admitted grudgingly.

"Then consider yourself hired," she said. "I'll pay your usual rates, plus expenses, of course. I'd like to handle the transaction in cash, if that's agreeable to you. How much do you want up front?"

She opened the small leather bag resting in her lap.

Tony held up a hand, palm outward. "Now hold on a minute," he said quickly. "I haven't agreed to take the case yet. There are a few things I'd like to know first."

Michelle looked surprised that he wasn't jumping to take her money. "What things?"

He glanced back down at the letter. "This is dated five months ago."

"Yes. My mother wrote it six weeks before she—before she died," Michelle said, quickly masking the slight break in her voice. "I found it among her things the day after her funeral."

"And this was the first you knew of your brothers and sisters?"

"Yes. I'd always assumed that I was an only child for my biological parents, as well as my adopted ones."

Tony studied her shuttered expression, wondering if he'd imagined a note of longing in her words. He'd had cool customers before, had dealt with masters at concealing emotions and facts, but Michelle Trent confused him as few people had before her. Outwardly, she was cool, reserved, aloof. But there'd been something in her eyes when she'd talked about his father, something in that slight break when she'd mentioned her mother's death, something in her voice when she talked about her unknown brothers and sisters.

He couldn't help wondering if there was much more to Michelle than she allowed him—or anyone else, perhaps—to see. A veritable storm of emotions concealed behind a bank of impenetrable clouds.

It had been years since a woman had rattled his composure the way this one did, years since he'd felt as though all it would take was a fleeting touch to reduce him to tongue-tied incoherence. His reactions to her greatly annoyed him.

"Why are you so concerned with privacy?" he asked, though he suspected he already knew—the answer had to do with her money.

She proved his guess to be correct. "I'm a very wealthy woman, as I'm sure you know. Through unpleasant experience I've learned that there are many unscrupulous people who would leap at the chance to take advantage of me. Should word get out that I'm searching for my long-lost family, I'm sure I'd find impostors by the dozens lined up at my door."

Tony nodded. "Quite probably. Which explains, of course, why you want to keep your search out of the newspapers. But you said I'm the only one other than you who has seen this letter or who knows about your siblings. You haven't told your friends? Family? Your attorneys?"

She shook her head, avoiding his eyes for the first time since she'd entered his office. "I have only a few close friends, and I haven't seen the need to discuss this with them as yet. Not many of my adoptive family are left now that my parents are gone. Some distant relatives on my mother's side, my father's older brother and his son, both of whom live in California and whom I see only rarely. My attorney also happens to be my godfather. He tends to be overly protective, having known me ever since he handled the legal details of my adoption. He would be concerned about the financial risks of finding family members about whom I know nothing."

Tony wondered if such an attractive, obviously intelligent young woman could really be happy living as reclusively as Michelle apparently did. Her experiences must have been unpleasant, indeed, to make her this distrustful.

He scanned her mother's letter a third time. "How old are you now?"

"Twenty-six."

"So it's been twenty-four years since your family was separated."

"Yes."

"You don't remember anything about them?" He looked up at her as he asked the question.

She opened her mouth to answer immediately. But then she paused, frowned a bit and looked down at her lap before answering more slowly. "No, I don't remember."

"You started to say something else. What was it?"

In response to his tone—the one he'd used for interrogation back in his police officer days—she looked up quickly, her eyes widening. "I don't remember anything," she repeated. "I was only two. How could I remember?"

He didn't think she was being entirely straight with him, though he, too, wondered how she could possibly remember anything from that young age. Still, there'd been something in her voice when she'd answered….

Deciding to come back to that later, he nodded and changed the subject. "Your mother said the family was split up. I must assume that they were widely scattered, perhaps adopted, as you were. Most likely, their names will have been changed, as yours was. The younger ones, anyway. They're grown now, and the chances are slim they're all still living in Texas."

"I realize I haven't given you an easy assignment, Mr. D'Alessandro."

He gave her a cool, utterly confident smile. "I'll find them, Ms. Trent. Don't you doubt that."

Her answering smile was tentative, as though it was something she didn't do often enough. "I'm beginning to believe you will."

He cleared his throat abruptly, forcefully. "Which leads to the next question. What do you want me to do when I find them? Do you want to contact them yourself or would you like for me to make the initial contact on your behalf?"

"No!" She spoke too hastily, her knuckles going white from her tightened grip on her purse. Realizing her vehemence had startled him, Michelle took a deep breath and tried visibly to relax. "I don't want you to contact them. All I want is a list of their names and locations, if possible."

"So you intend to contact them yourself?" he asked carefully, still watching her face.

She hesitated only a split second before nodding. "Yes."

She's lying. Tony didn't know why, but he suspected that Michelle Trent had no intention whatever of meeting her long-lost brothers and sisters. So why was she hiring him to find them? Baffled, he stared at her in frowning silence until she squirmed in her chair.

"You'll take the case?" she asked.

What the hell. "Yeah, I'll take it."

If she was pleased or relieved, she hid it just as she hid her other emotions. With a brisk nod, she opened her purse and extracted a plain white envelope. "This contains a thousand dollars in cash," she told him, holding the packet out to him. "Will that be enough to get you started?"

"More than enough," he assured her, hesitating to take the money for some reason he couldn't quite understand.

When he didn't immediately reach out for it, she set the

envelope on his desk and rose gracefully from her chair. "I'll call you in two weeks for a report, around the first of May. Will that give you enough time to gather some preliminary information?"

"Well, yes, but why don't I call you if I—"

"No," she broke in coolly. "I'll call you. Good day, Mr. D'Alessandro."

Damn, the woman's attitude irritated him. Almost as much as her sexy walk aroused him. "Good day, Ms. Trent," he muttered, his gaze following the sway of her slender hips as she left.

He sighed rather wistfully when he was alone. And then he picked up the letter she'd left with him and read it one more time, slowly and thoroughly.

"Pat-a-cake, pat-a-cake, baker's man! Clap your hands, Shelley."

"Look, Shelley, Jerry's a horsey. Can you say horsey?"

Still hearing a distant echo of children's voices, Michelle woke with a start and peered blearily around her bedroom. The room was dark and quiet and, except for her, empty, just as it always was when she awoke.

She'd heard the voices again. Those laughing, high-pitched children's voices that had invaded her dreams for as far back as she could remember. Occasionally she heard them saying names—Shelley, most often, and Jerry and Layla. The dream voices, strange names, had never made sense to her, never seemed to have meaning. Since reading her mother's letter—and learning, to her great shock, that she'd been called Shelley for the first two years of her life— Michelle suspected that the voices weren't truly dreams, but snatches of memory.

She'd never told anyone about those dreams— memories—just as she hadn't told Tony D'Alessandro earlier that day when he'd asked if she had any memory of her brothers and sisters. She hadn't really thought he'd believe her. It had all happened so very long ago.

Her brothers and sisters. "Oh, God," she whispered, staring blindly into the shadows of her big, elegantly furnished bedroom.

So many years she'd longed for brothers and sisters. Gazed wistfully through the looming fences surrounding the fortress of a mansion in which she'd grown up, pampered and adored and so very lonely at times. Feeling as though she were the only child in the world. And all the time—all those years— she'd had four brothers and two sisters growing up without her.

Did they know about her? Did they, too, have bits of memory of playing together, laughing together? Had any of them ever looked for her, asked about her?

"Dammit," she whispered, rolling over to gather her pillow into her arms as though to comfort herself. "Why did she have to tell me? Why couldn't she have told me sooner?"

A week after her visit to the private investigator's office, Michelle threw open the door to her home in response to the doorbell, too eager to wait for her housekeeper to answer the summons. Only after opening the door did she mask her broad grin, turning it into a cool smile. "Hello, Taylor. Back in town so soon?"

A dark-haired beauty in khaki slacks and a multipocketed safari shirt sauntered past her into the entryway. "I've been gone four weeks, Trent."

Michelle lifted an expressive eyebrow. "That long? I hardly noticed you were away."

Taylor Simmons grinned and lightly punched Michelle's arm. "Yeah, right. So how are you?"

Michelle dropped the phony hauteur, knowing Taylor

meant the question seriously. "I miss Mother, of course," she answered candidly, "but I'm fine. You know me. I'm always all right."

"And even if you weren't, you wouldn't tell anyone," Taylor added with exaggerated exasperation.

"I'd tell *you*."

Pleased with the admission, Taylor smiled. "Yeah, I guess you're right. I wouldn't give you any other choice, would I?"

Michelle laughed and shook her head. "No." Taking Taylor's arm, she led her into the den. "Can I get you anything? Betty made your favorite cookies, of course. She started baking them the minute I told her you'd be here today."

Taylor groaned. "And I just managed to lose the two pounds I gained from the last batch of her cookies. Oh, well, it's back to grapefruit and cottage cheese tomorrow."

"Does that mean you want cookies?"

"Of course I want cookies. Dozens of them."

Amused, Michelle waved Taylor to a couch and pressed a discreetly placed button beside the wet bar in one corner of the large, pecan-paneled room. On the other side of the fifteen-thousand-square-foot Tudor house, a bell chimed in an enormous kitchen. After twenty-four years of such luxury, Michelle didn't doubt that the efficient Betty would respond almost immediately with refreshments.

"How'd the shoot go?" she asked, crossing the room to the couch where Taylor lounged with the ease of one who'd spent many hours in this same den. Michelle sat sideways on the opposite end of the couch, one elbow propped on the low-cushioned back, one leg tucked comfortably beneath her. For her friend's visit, she'd worn a short-sleeved peach sweater and ivory slacks, her chocolate-brown hair loose around her shoulders. Her peach flats lay now on the floor beside the couch, leaving her feet bare. There were very few people with whom Michelle could feel so comfortable. But Taylor had been her best friend since their first year of high school when Taylor's parents had moved to Dallas and into the exclusive social circle to which Michelle's family had belonged.

"The shoot went okay," Taylor answered in response to Michelle's question about her work as a much-sought-after professional photographer. "The usual hassles. Whining models, uncooperative weather, clothes that got misplaced or soiled, a few equipment problems. Other than that, I had no complaints."

Michelle laughed. "Oh, is that all?"

"Yeah. Same old stuff. And how about you? What've you done to stay busy for the past month? Lounge on satin pillows? Nibble bonbons? Foreclose on a few widows and orphans?"

"And don't forget my daily manicures," Michelle reminded her with a wave of one peach-polished hand. Polish she'd applied herself.

"That's understood, of course," Taylor replied gravely.

Her right elbow still propped on the back of the couch, Michelle rested her cheek against her right fist and fondly examined her friend. As she always did when hurried or in deep thought, Taylor had been running her hands through her short, almost-black hair, leaving it ruffled in spikes around her face. Not just anyone could get away with the style; Taylor's big, long-lashed eyes and classic bone structure made her a natural for the short, casual cut. "I'm going to say something sentimental."

Taylor sighed deeply and rolled her eyes. "Oh, Trent, do you really have to?"

"Yes. I'm glad you're back, Taylor. I've missed you."

Taylor's smoke-gray eyes warmed and softened. "I missed you, too. You're sure you're okay?"

"I'm sure." Michelle nibbled her lower lip, wondering

whether she should tell Taylor about the letter from Alicia, and about her visit to the private investigator. She really hadn't intended to tell anyone about her quiet search for her lost family. For one thing, she didn't know how she would explain that she felt driven to locate her siblings, but wasn't at all sure she ever intended to do anything with the information once she obtained it. How could she explain to anyone else what she couldn't understand herself?

She should have known she wouldn't be able to keep anything so momentous from Taylor. After one look at Michelle's expression, Taylor straightened abruptly. "What is it?"

Michelle blinked in surprise at the sharp question. "I— uh—what do you mean?"

"I want to know whatever it is you're debating telling me about," Taylor replied bluntly. "Something's happened, hasn't it?"

She really should have known. Sighing lightly, Michelle shook her head. "Why did I ever think I'd be able to keep it from you?"

"Keep *what* from me? What's wrong?" Taylor was beginning to sound worried. Like the others who cared most for Michelle, Taylor tended to be overprotective, despite her habitually brusque teasing. It had always touched Michelle almost as much as it exasperated her that her friends considered her fragile and vulnerable, just because of a couple of unpleasant experiences in her past.

Before Michelle could reassure Taylor that nothing was wrong, a heavyset woman in a red blouse and navy slacks wheeled in a serving cart loaded with a variety of refreshments, her famous raspberry-jam cookies taking the place of honor in the center of the cart. "Here you are, Miss Taylor. I made a double batch for you today since you've been gone so long."

"Betty, you shameless woman, you're going to turn me into a blimp yet, aren't you?" But Taylor was already reaching for a cookie even as she affectionately scolded the longtime Trent family employee.

"Hmmph." Betty eyed Taylor's figure with frank skepticism. "You and Michelle are both thin as rails. You think a man wants to cuddle a bundle of bones? No, ma'am. A man wants to know there's a woman in his arms."

Looking at Taylor's full bustline with unconcealed envy, Michelle murmured, "I don't think any man would mistake Taylor for another guy, Betty. No matter how she may be dressed," she added for Taylor's benefit, turning up her nose at Taylor's favorite army-surplus ensemble.

Unperturbed, Taylor laughed and shook her head, causing the soft indirect lighting to glimmer in her dark hair. "And no one could doubt that Michelle, here, is anything but a lady all the way down to her little peach toenails."

"That may be," Betty replied slyly, "but I notice that neither of you has a diamond on your left hand. No immediate prospects, either."

Taylor frowned as if in deep consideration of the older woman's words. "That's true, of course. You really think your raspberry-jam cookies would help us land Prince Charming?"

Betty tried without much success to mask a smile. Taylor had always been her favorite of Michelle's friends. "My cookies couldn't hurt."

Grinning, Taylor reached for one of the two Wedgwood dessert plates on the cart. "That just gives me even more of an excuse to pig out on them," she said cheerfully. "C'mon, Trent, dig in. Betty's cookies are going to bring us eternal love and devotion."

"Not to mention cellulite."

"No, let's not mention that," Taylor grumbled, defiantly adding another cookie to her plate.

"Want me to pour the tea, Michelle?"

Michelle shook her head and reached for the teapot. "No, thanks, Betty, we'll serve ourselves."

"All right. You just ring if you need me now, you hear? Good to have you back, Miss Taylor."

"Thanks, Betty. It's nice to be back." Taylor waited until they were alone again, an aromatic cup of tea resting on the low table in front of her, before turning determinedly back to Michelle. "Okay, spill it."

Michelle lifted a brow and glanced pointedly at the teacup in her hand.

Taylor sighed impatiently. "Not the tea, you airhead. What was it you were about to tell me when Betty came in?"

After only a momentary hesitation, Michelle set her teacup down, clasped her hands in her lap, and told Taylor everything from the moment she'd found the letter in her mother's possessions to the time she'd left Tony D'Alessandro's office. Characteristically, Taylor listened with intent concentration, nibbling on her cookies and sipping her tea without once interrupting or taking her gaze from Michelle's face. Only when Michelle had finished did Taylor finally speak. "You have six brothers and sisters."

Michelle swallowed and nodded. "Yes."

"Wow."

"I guess that's one way of putting it."

Taylor pulled thoughtfully at her lower lip. "You think this P.I. can find them?"

"He assured me that if it's possible, he'll find them."

"What are you going to do when he does? Are you going to try to meet them?"

Michelle looked down at her hands, which were clenched so tightly in her lap that her knuckles shone stark white. "I— I don't know," she admitted. "I don't think so."

"I see."

Risking a peek at her friend's unrevealing face, Michelle asked, "Do you think I should meet them?"

Taylor shrugged. "I don't know. I can see where you'd want to, of course, especially now that your folks are gone. But—"

"*But,*" Michelle broke in, "I'm a very rich woman and I don't know these people from Adam. They came from a presumably poor background, we have no idea how they've been raised, what sort of lives they live. I could be opening myself up to all kinds of trouble by acknowledging them as family."

Taylor nodded slowly, reluctantly. "As cold and cynical as that sounds when you say it, you're right, of course. I'd hate to see a bunch of strangers suddenly show up and start trying to sponge off you. It's not as though you haven't had reason to be cautious of the motives of others."

Bleakly, Michelle thought back to being a frightened, heartbroken eight-year-old crying for her mother in a dark, locked closet while a man she'd trusted wrote a ransom note to her father. And thirteen years later, at twenty-one, finding out that the first man she'd loved was much more deeply attracted to her wealth than her mind. "Yes, I definitely have reason to be cautious," she agreed, trying very hard not to sound bitter.

Taylor started to speak, hesitated, then changed the subject. "So tell me about this P.I. you hired. How'd you find out about him?"

"His father was the man who rescued me when I was— taken," Michelle answered. She'd never been able to say the word *kidnapped.* Taylor was one of the few people still living who even knew about the incident. Vincent D'Alessandro, Tony's father, was another. "I thought I'd be hiring the father, but he's retired. The son, Tony, started the business back up a few years ago. I understand he worked as a policeman before that."

"Tony?"

"Yes. Short for Anthony, according to his business card."

"Age?"

Michelle shrugged. "Early thirties, I think."

"Good-looking?"

It wasn't at all hard for Michelle to picture glittering dark eyes, a shock of jet-black hair, a bright smile and a sexy cleft chin, even a week after her brief meeting with Tony D'Alessandro. "Yes, he's quite attractive."

"Married?"

Michelle made a face at Taylor's increasingly avid questions. "Now, how would I know that? I hired him, I didn't date him."

"*Yet.* Here, eat a few more of Betty's cookies."

Michelle giggled—as Taylor had known she would. And felt incredibly better for it. "You idiot," she said mildly, but reached for her first cookie, anyway.

Looking entirely relaxed and accepting, Taylor lounged lazily against the cushions behind her. Only her eyes indicated she was at all concerned with Michelle's state of mind. "Do you want to meet your brothers and sisters?" she asked casually, sounding no more serious than she had when she'd asked about Tony's looks and marital status.

Fully aware that the question hadn't been in the least frivolous, Michelle took a moment before answering honestly. "I think—maybe—I do. But it scares me, Taylor."

"Then wait until you're ready, if ever," Taylor answered logically. "It's been twenty-four years, after all. There's no reason to rush now, is there?"

"No, of course not," Michelle answered. And even as she spoke, a niggling little voice inside her murmured that it might already be too late. The search had already been set into motion, and her safe, secure life might be changed irrevocably whether she wanted those changes or not.

Chapter Two

Michelle Culverton Trent was annoyed and she made no effort to conceal it as she took a seat in Tony's office and arranged the full skirt to her demure dress primly around her knees. Tony watched appreciatively, thinking again what fine legs she had, until Michelle cleared her throat abruptly to regain his attention.

"All right, Mr. D'Alessandro, you insisted on giving me information in person rather than over the telephone. Now that I'm here, perhaps we could get on with it?"

Because her snooty attitude brought out the worst in him, Tony leaned back in his creaky chair and slung his crossed feet onto his desk, his hands clasped behind his head, elbows out. He knew he was the very picture of lazy insolence, yet did nothing to counteract that impression. Damned if he was going to sit here and let Her Highness walk all over him just because she had more money than God and he happened to be working for her at the moment. "In a hurry, Ms. Trent?"

"I have other obligations."

"Oh? What is it today? A meeting of one of the many charity boards you belong to? An executive session at Trent Enterprises? Or is it your day to rock babies in the intensive-care nursery?"

Her reaction was satisfying; he'd wanted to see her lose a bit of that cool poise. Her blue eyes widening, she tightened her grip on the purse in her lap and leaned slightly forward. "I hired you to locate my brothers and sisters, not to snoop into my personal affairs."

He shrugged. "I like to know something about the people I do business with."

He'd been pleasantly surprised to discover that she was one of the favorite baby-rockers at Memorial Hospital. Somehow, she hadn't seemed the type to possess maternal instincts. Yet he'd learned that she'd been volunteering at that particular job for nearly five years, and that she refused any media credit or glory for doing so. He liked that.

Her eyes narrowing, she stuck her purse under her arm and rose from the chair. "Consider our business association terminated. Good day, Mr. D'Alessandro."

With that, she turned and headed for the door, slowly, decorously, not once looking back. And it was obvious that it took every ounce of willpower she possessed not to stamp out in fury.

Tony chuckled beneath his breath. So she had a temper. Maybe there was hope for Michelle Culverton Trent, after all. "Ms. Trent—"

She reached for the doorknob without turning to look at him. "I said good day, Mr. D'Alessandro."

"I have information about your brothers and sisters."

She became still, her hand remaining on the tarnished brass knob. Though she didn't turn, he knew he had her full attention. "Why don't you sit back down and I'll tell you what I found out," he suggested enticingly.

She gave him a long, considering look over her shoulder, obviously tempted but just as obviously still mad at him. "Exactly what did you find out about me? And why *did* you snoop into my personal affairs?"

He came very close to retorting that if she'd been having any affairs, she was damned discreet about them, since he hadn't gotten a hint of a serious relationship in her life. He knew that if he did say that, she'd be gone and he'd have seen the last of her. And he wasn't quite ready for that.

"I simply wanted to find out exactly how vulnerable you are to claims of relationship by impostors," he said soothingly, dropping his feet from the desk to sit straight in his seat and make an effort to look more professional. "As you pointed out, this is a very sensitive situation and I have to be careful, for your sake. All I've learned about you is the routine you've maintained for the past year or so. That gives me an idea of who you might come into daily contact with, in case word of the search gets out and anyone tries pulling a scam on us."

Okay, so it wasn't exactly the truth. It wasn't exactly a lie, either, he assured himself. And it *sounded* damned good.

Evidently she thought so, too. Looking half-convinced, she dropped her hand from the doorknob and turned to face him, though she didn't yet return to her seat. "You've found my brothers and sisters?" she asked warily. "All of them? Already?"

"I didn't say that," he reminded her, reaching for a file. "I said I have information about them. I can tell you all their birth names and their ages when you were split up. And I can give you current information about two of them."

Michelle moistened her lips, her eyes on the typed pages in front of Tony. He couldn't tell if her expression held more eagerness or dread. Perhaps an equal mixture. He tried to imagine how it would feel to be told that he had six brothers and sisters he'd never known about, to be given their names, details about a life with them of which he had no memory. He had to admit he wasn't sure how he'd feel about meeting those strangers who shared his genes.

"Why don't you sit down, Mich—uh, Ms. Trent." Damn, but it was getting harder to remember that he was her employee for the time being. He was all too eager to get beyond that ethical barrier. Not that he had a snowball's chance with her, anyway, he conceded fatalistically. But he'd never know until he tried, would he? And, for reasons he couldn't have explained had he made the effort, he seemed hell-bent to try.

He watched as she slowly crossed the room—oh, could this woman *walk!*—and sank gracefully back into her chair. "All right, Mr. D'Alessandro," she said, her voice only slightly less confident than usual, "I'm ready. What have you found out?"

Calling on years of professional experience, he kept his own tone brusque and impersonal as he began, knowing it would be easier for her if he did so. "Your biological parents had very little money and far too many problems. Your father, Henry 'Hank' Walker, had a hard time keeping a job during his twenties. At thirty-one, he died in an industrial accident in Texarkana when your mother, Hazel, was pregnant with your youngest sister. Accident reports said that he'd been drinking when the incident occurred, and it was believed that he'd been an alcoholic for years."

Michelle winced but said nothing. Tony noted sympathetically that her fair complexion had gone paler than usual.

"Your father had no family and your mother's family disowned her when she'd married him—she was seventeen and pregnant at the time—so there was no one for her to turn to after your father's death. Money was painfully tight, since the insurance companies weren't overly generous with an accident involving alcohol. She worked as a waitress as long as she was physically capable, just to pay rent on the one-bedroom apartment she'd moved you all into, and to put food on the table. Her prenatal care was almost nonexistent and she simply didn't recover quickly after your younger sister's birth just after you turned two. Eight months later she caught pneumonia and died."

"How old was she?" Michelle asked quietly.

"She'd just turned twenty-nine."

Michelle made a slight strangled sound, then fell silent again, waiting for him to continue. He took a deep breath, forcefully resisting the urge to walk around the desk and take her into his arms. Not in a sexual way, but simply to comfort her during what had to be a painful moment. She'd probably take his head off if he tried. Instead, he focused grimly on the notes in front of him.

"As you know, your parents left seven children. The oldest was a son, Jared, who was eleven when your mother died."

Michelle started, drawing his gaze back to her colorless face. "Jerry," she whispered, the word hardly audible.

Tony's left eyebrow rose sharply. "You remember him?" he demanded, though it hardly seemed possible that she would.

She shook her head, a bit too emphatically. "No, of course not. It's just—the name sounds familiar. Go on, please."

Skeptically, Tony nodded. "I was able to trace Jared through a series of foster homes until his graduation from a high school in Houston seventeen years ago, at which time he entered the military—the Navy, we think. It's going to take me a bit longer to find out where he is now."

"Did you—" She paused to clear her throat. "Did you find out anything in particular about him during those years? Was he happy? Did he get into trouble?"

"No. As far as I can determine, he was well-behaved, a

good student, but quiet and very withdrawn. According to the principal of his high school, Jared refused to allow anyone to get too close to him, had very few friends. After being separated from his family at eleven and then living in a number of foster homes, I can certainly understand why he'd be reluctant to get attached to anyone," Tony added pensively.

Her lower lip caught between her teeth, Michelle nodded for him to go on.

"Next was a sister, Layla, age ten." Again, he noted that Michelle seemed to react to the name, though this time he didn't question her.

"Like Jared, Layla was never adopted. She was, however, raised in only one foster home until her high school graduation and she seemed to be happy enough there, though she, too, was reported to be very introverted during her school years. She was also the easiest to find now. Ten years ago, she registered with a service that reunites families separated by adoption or other legal action, so that she could be traced if any of her siblings chose to initiate a search."

"I wonder why she didn't do so herself," Michelle murmured, almost as if to herself.

"Maybe you should ask her that," Tony answered gently. "Her married name is Layla Walker Samples, she's thirty-four, and she has three children, ages eight, five and two. I have their names here if you're interested. The family lives in Fort Worth, where her husband's an accountant and she sells real estate."

"You're very thorough, Mr. D'Alessandro," she said faintly.

"You're paying me to be, Ms. Trent."

She nodded. "Go on, please."

"Next in birth order was a brother, Miles, who was two years younger than Layla. Miles died in a car accident on his eighteenth birthday. He and his friends had been drinking beer to celebrate the occasion and three of them were killed in a head-on collision with another car."

Though he wouldn't have thought it possible, Michelle's face seemed to bleach even whiter. "He's—dead?" she repeated.

Seeing the stricken look in her eyes, Tony cursed himself for breaking the news so bluntly. It was just that he hadn't expected her to grieve for a young man she couldn't possibly remember. It seemed he'd lost sight of the fact that poor Miles had still been her brother, whether she remembered him or not.

"I'm sorry, Michelle." Her first name slipped out before he could stop it.

If she noticed, she didn't comment. "I'm fine. I'm just sorry to hear that he died so young, and so senselessly. Please continue."

"The five-year-old twins, Joseph and Robert—Joey and Bobby—were kept together. They went first to an orphanage and then into a foster home, where they got into some minor trouble at the age of nine and were sent back to the institution. They stayed in and out of trouble—nothing criminal, just reckless mischief—until they were sixteen."

"And what happened then?"

"They disappeared. They ran away from the foster home in which they'd been placed a few weeks before and they haven't been heard from since. I have inquiries out, of course, but so far I haven't turned up anything on them."

Michelle digested that news in silence for a few long moments, then took a shaky breath and looked back up at him. "That leaves only one. The baby."

"Lindsay was eight months old when your mother died. She was adopted, possibly by a family somewhere in Arkansas. She'd be twenty-four now. I haven't located her yet, but I've got quite a few inquiries out. There's a very good chance we'll find her."

Michelle straightened in her seat, raising one hand to brush a nonexistent stray strand into her neatly upswept dark hair. "You've been very efficient, Mr. D'Alessandro. And in such a short time. I'm impressed."

"Because I do my job well? Don't be." He closed the folder and extended it to her. "This file contains duplicates of everything I've learned to this point. I'll keep the original material here until the investigation is completed. You'll find the latest available addresses, the current information on your sister Layla, juvenile records on the twins."

Michelle took the file and held it gingerly, as though it might be explosive, he noted with a quick flash of sympathetic amusement. "Is that all for today?" she asked, on her feet once again.

He nodded, though he was tempted to stall for just a few more minutes with her. This interlude had convinced him that there was more to Michelle Culverton Trent—née Shelley Marie Walker—than she had allowed him to see before. Now he found himself irresistibly curious to discover more about her. But then, curiosity had always been his major weakness—or strength, depending on how one looked at it.

"You want me to continue with the investigation, then?" he asked carefully, not forgetting that she'd fired him earlier.

"I want you to find my family, Mr. D'Alessandro," she answered from the doorway. This time she turned the knob and opened the door. "I'll call you again in two weeks to find out what you've discovered. Oh…do you need any more money at this point?" she asked.

Shifting restlessly in his chair at the thought of taking more of her money—though he *was* working for her, he reminded himself impatiently—he shook his head. "No. Not now," he answered gruffly. "And I *will* find your family, though I can't promise I'll have all the information we need in the next two weeks."

"All I expect is your best effort. Good day, Mr. D'Alessan dro."

"Ms. Trent," he muttered in resignation, damned tired of the way she continued to address him so formally, almost as if the "Mr." erected a physical barrier between them. But she'd already closed the door behind her, so he had no opportunity to ask her to call him Tony. Not yet.

Jared Mitchell. Layla Renee. Miles Daniel. Joseph Brian. Robert Ryan. Shelley Marie. Lindsay Nicole. Seven children. Seven double names carefully chosen by a young woman living in poverty with the alcoholic husband she'd chosen over her family, a woman who'd driven herself so relentlessly that she died at twenty-nine. Had she fought to live, wanting to provide a future for her children? Or had she been too worn-out and defeated to care, perhaps thinking that they would be better off without her?

Swiping at an escaping tear, Michelle looked up from the file in front of her and thought with reluctant guilt of the luxury in which she'd been raised, the money she'd so often taken for granted because, for as far back as she could remember, it had always been there. Money that could easily have fed six more children.

As much as she'd loved her adoptive parents, Michelle couldn't help wondering why she'd been the one brought into this home. Why not the twins, or the baby? Why not all of them?

How she would have loved having brothers and sisters. She remembered childhood fantasies of having a big brother to watch out for her, play with her.

Jared. Eleven when they'd been separated. He'd remember

their time together, perhaps, remember a little sister named Shelley. *"Look at Jerry, Shelley. He's a horsey,"* the dream voices had said. Had Jared given her rides on his back, loved her and grieved for her when they'd been separated?

Layla. At ten, she would have been the little mother for her younger siblings. *"Play pat-a-cake, Shelley."* Had Michelle clung to her big sister as they'd been swept in opposite directions? Had they cried and futilely protested the separation?

Miles. Dead at eighteen. Had he been a reckless, mischievous boy? Had he had dark hair and blue eyes like her? Had he died missing the family he'd known until he was eight?

Joseph and Robert—Joey and Bobby. Five-year-old twins. Had they been identical? Closer to her age, had they tumbled and roughhoused with her, held her hands between them as she'd learned to walk?

And the baby. Lindsay. Had she been no more than another mouth to feed, another burden on an already-desperate situation? Or had she been welcomed with a wistful, hopeful love?

Michelle hid her face in her hands, thinking of the five children now grown to adulthood, as far as she knew, anyway. Would any of them want to see her again, want to be reminded of that troubled time in their young lives? Lindsay wouldn't remember that time, not even as much as Michelle did through her vague, haunting dreams. Would she want to meet a sister she'd never even known she had?

And did Michelle really want to meet these strangers who may share her hair color, her nose, her eyes? Who may well have come into her life much too late, and for no real reason?

Her deep sigh seemed to echo through the depths of the big, carefully guarded house surrounding her, empty except for her and the two employees who went about their jobs in other rooms. Would finding her lost family ease the loneliness she'd lived with so much of her life? Or only make it worse?

She really needed to talk to the one person who'd always been there for her, always cared about her, the only one who'd never let her down.

Taylor avidly studied the file spread out in front of her on Michelle's dining room table. "So you have at least two nieces and a nephew," she commented, reading from the top page. "Dawne, Keith and Brittany. I wonder if they look like you."

When Michelle didn't immediately answer, Taylor looked up from the file. "Michelle?"

Blinking at the sound of her name, Michelle focused on her friend, who sat across the table from her, sipping coffee and reading the file Tony had provided two days earlier. It had taken that long for Michelle to decide to share the file's contents with Taylor. "I'm sorry, Taylor, what did you say?"

"I was just wondering about your nieces and nephew. Where were *you?*"

Michelle cleared her throat and brushed busily at a non-existent bit of lint on her dark skirt. "Just—thinking," she answered vaguely.

"Did you ever find out if he's married?"

"I don't think he—Wait a minute." Michelle looked up abruptly, suspiciously. "If *who's* married?"

Taylor's smile was decidedly smug. "The guy you were just thinking about. The P.I. Tony, right?"

"How did you know I was thinking about him?"

"I didn't. It was a guess. You just confirmed it."

Michelle sighed. "All right, so I was thinking about him. Don't read anything into it. I was simply wondering if he's found out anything else since he gave me this information."

"It's only been two days, hasn't it?"

Michelle shrugged, trying to look nonchalant. "He got all this information—and more—in two weeks." The "more," of course, being the personal information he'd obtained on her. Why? she asked herself yet again. Why had he wanted to know more about her before beginning his search for her siblings?

"He sounds very good," Taylor murmured. "At his job, of course," she added mischievously.

"You can be such a juvenile at times," Michelle accused, falling into their habitual teasing insults to distract Taylor from the direction the conversation had taken.

"Honey, when it comes to attractive men I'm a full-grown woman," Taylor taunted with a toss of her dark head.

"Yeah, right. And if you've been on more than two dates with any particular guy in the past year, I'll eat a bug," Michelle retorted.

Taylor smiled. "Yuck. Lucky for you I haven't run into any Prince Charmings in the past year, isn't it?"

"How would you know if you had? You're still comparing all the men you meet to a memory of perfection." Michelle wasn't teasing now. Instead, her words were spoken with warm sympathy.

Growing abruptly serious in response, Taylor sighed faintly. "I guess I am. But it's not as if I haven't tried to get over Dylan. You know that."

"I know." Michelle wondered pensively if both she and Taylor had been fated to be unlucky at romance. Taylor had tumbled head over heels during a whirlwind Caribbean affair she'd been swept into while on a three-week photo assignment. And then her lover had been run down in the street by a hit-and-run driver. Taylor would have shared his fate had he not heroically pushed her out of the way at the last possible moment.

She'd spent a desperate night in a hospital waiting room,

only to be told the next morning that Dylan had not survived his injuries. His body had been returned to his family, whom Taylor had never met; Taylor had gone on with her life. But, Michelle thought sadly, Taylor had never been quite the same as before. Though she'd known Dylan less than a month, Taylor had truly loved him. Since then, she'd dated but, as she'd recently asked Michelle, what ordinary man could compare to a memory of a dream lover who'd given his life for hers?

Taylor swiftly turned the offensive back at Michelle. "What about you? Have you given any guy a fair shake since Geoff the Gigolo broke your heart?"

"He didn't break it, he only dented it a little. And I haven't met any man who interested me enough to take the risk that he's not like Geoff," Michelle admitted.

"So this Tony D'Alessandro doesn't interest you?"

Michelle couldn't answer that one. The problem was that Tony D'Alessandro interested her all too much. But why? Because he held the key to finding out about her long-hidden past? Or because she liked his smile and the spark of interest in his beautiful dark eyes? And *could* he be trusted?

She thought of his plain, functional office furniture and his neat, department-store clothing. It had been quite obvious that he wasn't exactly rolling in money. Was the interest he'd shown in her due to a mutual attraction or was he anticipating more reward than a one time fee for a temporary assignment?

Taylor began to look rather concerned at Michelle's hesitation. "Is he a nice guy?" she asked, making an unsuccessful attempt to mask the protectiveness in her expression.

Michelle thought of Tony's reaction to her unexpected distress at the news of her brother's death. His sincerely spoken promise that he'd find her family. "He seems very nice," she said. "But of course I hardly know him."

"Want me to go with you next time you meet with him? I could check him out for you, give you an objective opinion."

Michelle made a face. "Objective? I don't think so. And no, I don't need you to check him out for me. I'm quite capable of doing that myself, thank you."

Taylor grinned. "Are you politely telling me to butt out, Trent?"

"You got it, Simmons."

"Okay," Taylor agreed with a deep sigh. "But I surely would love to get a look at this Italian stud that has you so flustered."

"Why don't we change the subject," Michelle suggested uncomfortably.

"If you insist. Let's talk about your sister Layla, instead. She lives less than an hour's drive from here and she's made it clear that she'd like to be reunited with her family. Are you going to call her?"

Again, Michelle found herself at a loss for a definite answer. "I don't know."

Taylor propped her chin on her hand and studied Michelle thoughtfully. "I know we agreed you should be careful, but this woman sounds pretty respectable. A real-estate agent married to an accountant, living in suburbia with their three children. How dangerous could she be?"

Michelle automatically started to remind Taylor of the precautions inherent in wealth, but stopped because even she was aware what a shallow and mercenary excuse that was. She would have to start being honest sometime—with herself, if no one else.

It wasn't fear of losing her money that held Michelle back from contacting her siblings. It was fear of being hurt again. Taking the risks of caring, reaching out, needing someone again in the safe, comfortable routine she'd built for herself.

She'd have liked so much to see her nieces and nephew.

Dawne, Keith and little Brittany. She knew their names, of course. During the past two days she'd studied the file Tony had provided her until the edges of the pages had begun to crumple from handling. Just as she'd studied the names of her brothers and sisters, straining to remember any details to accompany those distant, barely remembered voices.

Jerry. Layla. "Play pat-a-cake, Shelley."

"I'm scared, Taylor," she said, hardly aware of speaking aloud.

Taylor's face softened sympathetically. "I know, Michelle. I know."

Tony was immersed in the computer research of Michelle's case late the next afternoon when Bonnie appeared in the open doorway to his office. A tall, beautiful black woman, Bonnie walked with a natural grace that inevitably reminded Tony of Michelle. But then, everything seemed to remind him of Michelle Trent these days, he thought with a faint sigh as he turned from the computer screen.

"The call on line one is for you, Tony," Bonnie said, setting a stack of correspondence on one corner of his desk. "He wouldn't give a name. I'm out of here for the day unless you need me for anything else."

"You go home and feed your family," Tony urged with a smile, one hand resting on his telephone.

"Hmmph. Today was Mick's day off. He'd darned well better have dinner on the table when I get home," Bonnie retorted, "or he might as well resign himself to eating out tonight."

Tony laughed. "You're a tough wife, Bonnie Kennedy."

She smiled brightly. "You should be so lucky to have one just like me."

Tony wasn't at all opposed to the idea of marriage and family. His happily married parents were the perfect example of how a loving partnership could enrich one's life. The problem was that Vincent and Carla D'Alessandro set a pretty high standard. Tony hadn't yet met a woman he thought he could love for the rest of his life with the same unfaltering devotion Vinnie had always given Carla. "I *would* be lucky to find someone like you," he assured Bonnie.

Both embarrassed and pleased, she shrugged him off. "If you think flattery will make me forget it's time for my annual raise, you're entirely wrong. But you'd better take your call now. I'll see you in the morning."

"Good night, Bonnie." Half his attention on her as she waved on her way out, Tony lifted the receiver. "D'Alessandro."

"I understand you've been looking into the background of Michelle Culverton Trent."

Frowning at the blunt, unprefaced remark, Tony automatically reached for a pencil to make notes if necessary. "Who is this?"

"My name is Carter Powell. I've been the attorney for the Trent family for over thirty years. Who are you working for, Mr. D'Alessandro? Who hired you to find her biological family?"

His eyes narrowing, Tony frowned at the hostility in the caller's voice, determined not to confirm anything without his client's permission. "If you're so convinced that I am working toward that goal, I'm surprised you don't already know who hired me."

Powell ignored him. "Did Michelle hire you herself? If so, how did she find out? Her adoptive parents never told her about her biological siblings."

"As an attorney, I'm sure you know all about client privilege, Mr. Powell. Surely you understand that I'm not at liberty to discuss my cases with you."

The attorney growled in frustration. "If you're working for

someone else, someone hoping to capitalize on her wealth, do your client a favor and tell him to forget it. Ms. Trent and her money are well-protected against opportunists. It won't work."

"I repeat, I cannot discuss my cases or my clients with you. Now, if there's nothing else—"

"Take a little friendly advice. Drop this case. If you *are* working for Ms. Trent, tell her you are unable to find out anything about her long-lost family and that you doubt anyone else could, either. Got that?"

Tensing in response to the barely veiled threat, Tony gripped the receiver more tightly. "Even if I were working on the case you've described, why would I want to take your advice?" he asked carefully, wanting the implicit warning spelled out. His pencil was poised to take the words down verbatim.

"I have some influence in this state, D'Alessandro, as I'm sure you'll find out if you ask around. Your own operation, on the other hand, is only two years old and still not firmly established in the business community. You would be wise not to work against me."

"Suppose I *am* working on the case you've mentioned. Suppose Ms. Trent is my client. How do you think she'd react if I mention this call to her?"

"I've known Ms. Trent for twenty-four years. You've known her a few weeks. I'm not worried about anything you have to say to her. Michelle knows that I have her best interests at heart, just as I always have. But for your own best interest, Mr. D'Alessandro, I suggest you tell her that the case is closed for lack of information. There's no need to make this any more unpleasant than necessary, is there?"

"Look, Powell, I—"

A firm click and a dial tone broke into Tony's angry retort. He slammed his own receiver into its cradle. Nothing made him more furious than threats, veiled or otherwise. Damned if he'd stand for being treated that way.

He snatched the phone back up and dialed a familiar number. "Dad?" he said a moment later. "I need to ask you a few questions about a former client of yours. Michelle Trent."

Chapter Three

Humming beneath her breath, Michelle cradled the tiny pink-blanketed bundle in her arms, stroking a downy soft head with her fingers. Her slow movements of the wooden rocker calmed her as well as the tiny infant she held.

Lakeisha was one of Michelle's favorite little patients in the intensive-care nursery. Three months old, the child still weighed less than five pounds, having been born nearly three months prematurely. Lakeisha's mother lived some distance from the hospital and wasn't able to make the trip more than twice a month, so Michelle was one of the volunteers who, along with the loving, caring hospital staff, made sure the infant didn't lack affectionate human contact.

Michelle had discovered the baby-rockers while investigating charity programs for contributions from Trent Enterprises. After the first session, she'd been hooked. Only in this busy, beeping, noisy nursery could she feel at peace, quietly content.

At first it had surprised her just how bright and noisy the nursery could be. Had she thought about it, she probably would have imagined the room to be shushed, dimly lit. Nothing could have proven farther from the truth. Babies cried, monitors beeped, crib alarms went off periodically, nurses worked, talked, laughed, visitors streamed in and out, doctors rushed in with orders and procedures, the janitorial staff mopped and scrubbed.

Somehow the babies had adapted to the carefully controlled confusion, learning to sleep through almost anything. Just as Michelle had learned to block out the noise and movements around her and concentrate totally on whichever fragile infant needed her attention at the moment.

Taylor couldn't understand Michelle's pleasure in the rocking program. "I'd get too attached," she'd admitted candidly. "It would devastate me to get close to one and then have it go home—or, worse, to have something bad happen to it."

Michelle had tried to explain that, yes, those were valid points, and yes, it hurt when babies she'd grown to love left her life forever, devastated her when a tiny infant lost its battle to live. But there were always other babies needing to be cuddled, crying for attention. Babies who needed Michelle's loving care as much as she needed to offer it.

With these babies, as with so few people, Michelle could freely offer the affection dammed up inside her without fear that her vulnerability would be exploited, her generosity abused.

Fifteen minutes later she carefully placed the sleeping Lakeisha in her constantly monitored high-tech bassinet, exchanged a few words with a smiling nurse, and headed for the scrub room to remove the sterile hospital gown she was required to wear over her street clothes when visiting the nursery. The gown halfway down her arms, she stopped in utter astonishment when she saw the man who leaned against a near wall, arms crossed carelessly over his chest, smiling at her. It wasn't hard to guess that he'd been watching her through the large observation window—but for how long?

"Mr. D'Alessandro," she greeted him warily, slowly removing the gown and tossing it into a nearby hamper. "What are you doing here?"

"We need to talk." He watched as she opened a small locker and pulled out her purse. "You look very nice today," he surprised her by saying then, his dark eyes appraising her thoroughly.

Still wondering what was so important that he'd had to track her down here, Michelle cleared her throat self-consciously at the personal observation. "Um—thank you," she murmured. She'd dressed professionally, almost sternly, for her two appointments with Tony. Now he was seeing her on a Saturday afternoon with her hair swinging soft to the shoulders of the pale pink sweater she'd worn with a full floral skirt and comfortable pink flats. It was obvious that he preferred this more casual look.

Trying to mask the awkwardness she felt at this unexpected encounter, she cleared her throat and spoke in a cool, brisk voice. "I still don't understand why you're here. I said I'd call you for news. Surely you haven't found anything so earth-shattering that it required you to track me down to tell me immediately."

"We need to talk," Tony repeated, not at all intimidated by her tone. He looked around, stepping aside for a scrubbed-and-gowned young father who was on his way into the intensive-care nursery. "But not here. Let's go someplace more private."

"Mr. D'Alessandro, I—"

"Michelle," he broke in firmly, his gaze holding hers. Startled by his use of her first name, she stared at him in silence when he continued. "I wouldn't be here if it wasn't important. Something's come up and I need to talk to you. Now. So cut me some slack, will you?"

She flushed at the unconcealed amusement lurking beneath the latter words. Perhaps she was overreacting to his sudden appearance. Maybe she *should* listen to what he had to tell her before reprimanding him. "All right, we'll talk. Where would you like to meet?"

He smiled. "I was sort of hoping you'd offer me a ride. I came here in a cab."

Since she was quite sure he owned a car, she couldn't help wondering why he'd arranged it so that he'd be riding with her when they left the hospital. Something else she intended to ask him when she found out exactly what it was that had brought him here. "Very well. We'll take my car."

His smile deepened. A passing nurse gave Tony a long, speculative look, then glanced at Michelle with obvious approval mirrored in her expression. Since Michelle was having a difficult time ignoring her own decidedly physical response to Tony D'Alessandro's sexy smile and knowing dark eyes, she quickly looked away from the other woman and headed briskly for the exit doors.

Michelle waited only until she'd navigated her two-year-old gray Lexus out of the hospital parking lot before glancing at the attractive man belted into the passenger seat. He seemed perfectly at ease as he lounged against the pale gray leather, giving her a smile that made her throat tighten. She cleared it abruptly. "So what was it you wanted to tell me?" she demanded, needing very badly to get back on a professional basis with him.

"I'd rather not discuss it in the car. I'll want your full attention. Take a right at the next intersection, okay?"

She sighed soundlessly. "Where are we going?"

"Someplace where we can talk without worrying about being overheard. I like your car."

Her eyebrows lifted at the change of topic. "Thank you."

"I've got a four-wheel drive. A Jeep Cherokee. Not as luxurious as this, of course, but it comes in handy when a case takes me onto country roads—or into places where there are no roads at all."

"Does that happen often?" she asked, intrigued despite herself.

"Often enough."

"Your job must be quite—interesting," she ventured carefully.

He laughed. "Yeah, sometimes. Other times it seems more like an endless stream of paperwork and computer research. I pawn as much of that off on the other guys as possible, but being the boss, I end up with most of it."

"The other guys?" she repeated curiously. During her two visits to his offices, she'd seen only Bonnie, his secretary.

"I have two full-time operatives. Bob and Chuck. Great guys. And one part-time employee, Cassie Browning. She's a bit overeager at times, but she shows a lot of potential. They do most of the legwork, while I concentrate on the computer and customer relations end of the business."

Michelle was rapidly revising her opinion of Tony's business as a low-level operation. Though he certainly wasn't in the big leagues of private investigation firms, he must be doing okay to employ three full-time employees and one part-time. She doubted that Tony made what most people would consider a fortune, but she was beginning to believe that he wasn't exactly penurious, either. Maybe he just liked wearing off-the-rack department store clothing—or jeans and knit shirts, as he was wearing today. Not that he didn't look wonderful in them.

She brought her thoughts sternly under control when he pointed out another turn. Obligingly, she followed his directions.

"So you like babies, do you?" he asked, catching her off-guard with another casual change of topic. "You looked very natural at the hospital. That was a tiny one you were rocking, wasn't it?"

Still bothered that he'd watched her without her knowledge, and at a time when she was admittedly more vulnerable than usual, she squirmed in her seat. "I enjoy the volunteer work I do at the hospital," she answered noncommittally. "It's quite satisfying."

"Quite satisfying," he repeated, that faint trace of amusement back in his voice.

"Did I say something funny, Mr. D'Alessandro?" she challenged.

"Forget it, Michelle. And by the way, could you drop the 'Mr.' stuff? The name's Tony."

Her fingers tightening on the steering wheel, she came very close to retorting that she hadn't given him permission to use her first name. Only the knowledge that the words would probably come out huffy and priggish—thereby providing him further entertainment at her expense—kept her from voicing them. "How much farther to where we're going?" she asked instead, ignoring his suggestion altogether.

"Turn right at the next traffic light. After that, it's only four blocks."

Since they had entered a middle-class residential neighborhood, Michelle suspected he was taking her to his home. She moistened suddenly dry lips and wondered if she should insist that they go to his office instead. And then she told herself that she could handle Tony D'Alessandro. Even trust him, to an extent. After all, he was a reputable businessman, a former policeman, the son of a man who'd once saved her life. The problem was, she wasn't entirely sure she could trust herself to continue to ignore her growing attraction to him.

The house Tony directed her to wasn't exactly what she'd expected. A sprawling red-brick ranch-style with white shutters and a neatly trimmed lawn, it looked too sedate, too average for the dynamic, wickedly attractive man beside her. "You live here?" she asked curiously, glancing at him as she parked in the driveway and turned off the engine.

"I did for fifteen years," he answered, already climbing out of the car.

So who lived here now? Puzzled, she followed him to the front door. He grinned at her as he pressed the bell. "Got you wondering, don't I?"

She frowned repressively at him, asking herself what had happened to the comfortable employer-employee relationship she'd established during their two former encounters.

The door opened before she could answer her own question.

An older man with weathered olive skin and steel-gray hair stood inside the house, smiling kindly at Michelle. Staring at him with a sizable lump in her throat, she could almost feel the past eighteen years fall away. Could almost imagine that she was eight years old, frightened, lonely, despairing of ever seeing her family again. Could almost hear his deep, comforting voice murmuring, "It's okay, Michelle, I'm a friend. You can just call me Vinnie. I'm here to take you home."

She'd never completely forgotten the horror of that time, though she'd tried. Tried so successfully that she *had* almost forgotten how kind her rescuer's dark eyes had been, how safe she'd felt when she'd burst into tears and he'd taken her into his big, strong arms. How he'd carried her out of that terrible place where she'd been held and hadn't let her go again until she'd been restored to her frantic parents. How she'd clung to him as the only good thing that had happened to her in five long, traumatic days. How he'd visited her several times afterward, bringing her little gifts, making sure she was coping with the endless questions of the police.

"Vinnie," she whispered, her eyes filling with sudden tears.

His creased face softened. "Hello, Michelle. It's good to see you again."

And then he held out his arms and she stepped into them without hesitation. And, as had happened on that evening so long ago, she was immediately warmed by a sense of being completely safe, utterly protected.

It had been a very long time since she'd felt that way.

Standing quietly behind them, Tony watched in surprise and rapidly growing fascination as Vinnie gathered Tony's formerly cool, seemingly unflappable client into a fervent bear hug. Other than confirming that he had once handled a sensitive job for the Trent family, Vinnie had refused to discuss the case even with his son, telling Tony that the details would be up to Michelle to discuss if she chose.

It had been Vinnie who'd suggested bringing Michelle here to tell her about the call Tony had received from her attorney. "You're still too mad," Vinnie had said bluntly—and entirely accurately. "You'll only set her back up if you go throwing accusations around about a man she's known nearly all her life."

Brimming with curiosity about Michelle's emotional reaction to seeing Vinnie again, Tony followed impatiently when his exuberant father ushered her inside the house. They entered the wood-panelled den where Tony had spent so many hours in his youth. And then Vinnie turned back to Michelle, studying her flushed face in approval.

"Look at you," he said. "All grown-up and prettier than

ever. No wonder your father bragged about you the way he did while you were off at college."

Obviously a bit flustered by her impulsive greeting, Michelle stopped straightening her hair and looked at Vinnie questioningly. "You stayed in touch with my father?"

Tony was as surprised as Michelle by Vinnie's reply. "Your dad and I had lunch together once a month for nearly fifteen years. In fact, I saw him only two days before his heart attack. I came to the funeral. A real crowd turned out, didn't they? Your father had a lot of friends."

"A lot of people claimed friendship with my father because of who he was, not because they genuinely liked him," Michelle answered with a trace of bitterness. And then she gave Vinnie a smile that made Tony fully aware that he'd never received one like it from her. "It must have meant a great deal to him to know you weren't that type."

Vinnie was clearly pleased. "Your dad was a fine man," he said gruffly. "We had some good long talks. I miss him."

"So do I," Michelle whispered huskily. And then she crossed her arms at her waist, making Tony fancy that she'd suddenly gotten smaller and more vulnerable. "I didn't know my father had stayed in contact with you when you stopped visiting us at home."

Tony wondered if the hurt in her voice was as obvious to Vinnie as it was to him. His left eyebrow lifted as he looked toward his father. Vinnie cleared his throat and glanced at his son before looking back at Michelle.

"I wanted to keep visiting you, Michelle," he explained gently. "It was your mother's idea for me to stop. She thought you'd be able to put everything behind you quicker if I wasn't hanging around to remind you. Maybe she was right."

Michelle obviously didn't agree, though it was just as obvious—to Tony, at least—that she was reluctant to criticize her mother's decision. "I felt so safe when you were around," she said instead. "And you always made me laugh. I missed you when you stopped coming by."

Vinnie sighed. "I'm sorry if I unintentionally hurt you. We were all only trying to do what was best for you, of course."

"Yes, of course." Michelle smiled again, her practiced, social smile this time. Tony wondered if it annoyed Vinnie as much as it did him. His curiosity was rapidly growing about the case his father had taken on for the Trent family. Obviously, Michelle had been involved. The most obvious possibility, of course, was kidnapping. The very thought made Tony's blood run cold. He could only hope he was wrong.

Suddenly tired of being left out of the conversation, he cleared his throat. "Why don't we sit down?" he suggested when he had their attention. "Dad and I want to talk to you about a new development in your case, Michelle."

"Where are my manners?" Vinnie scolded himself, immediately taking Michelle's arm to lead her to a deep, comfortable sofa. "Please, sit down. I wish my wife was here to meet you, but she's working on a case this afternoon. Did you remember that she's an attorney with the D.A.'s office? Tony, why don't you get us something to drink. There's iced tea in the refrigerator. Or would you prefer coffee, Michelle? My son makes a decent pot of coffee—taught him myself."

Michelle glanced at Tony with amusement lighting her blue eyes, making him shove his hands quickly into his pockets to keep them from reaching out to her. Damn, but this woman could take his breath away! he thought in dazed amazement. What was it about her that did this to him?

"Iced tea will be fine, thank you," she murmured, drawing her gaze from Tony's with a touch of heightened color in her cheeks.

As he headed for the kitchen, Tony wondered if that faint

blush indicated that Michelle could possibly be attracted to him, as well. Or was he being hopelessly optimistic to imagine that these feelings weren't entirely one-sided?

Chapter Four

Oddly shaken by that exchange of glances with Tony, and still embarrassed by her uncharacteristically emotional greeting of Vinnie, Michelle clasped her hands in her lap and looked down at them, her thoughts whirling. Of everything she'd learned in the past few months, discovering that it had been her mother who'd put an end to Vinnie's visits shook her most profoundly.

Michelle had adored the gruff, kind-eyed man who'd rescued her from her kidnappers, had looked forward to his visits with the eagerness only a lonely eight-year-old could have known. She still remembered those visits so clearly—Vinnie had admired her toys, played games with her, brought her funny, inexpensive little gifts, told her stories about his three boys that had made her long to meet them, play with them.

She remembered hearing Vinnie talk exasperatedly about his oldest son, Tony, the ringleader, the one who'd so carefully planned and executed the pranks his younger brothers had gleefully followed him into. Funny, she'd forgotten that until now. Her mouth quirked into a slight smile as she could almost hear Vinnie sighing and saying, "Don't know what I'm going to do with that boy."

And then her smile faded when she remembered telling Vinnie that she'd love to meet his sons. Vinnie's dark eyes had softened as they'd rested on the lonely little girl in her huge, toy-filled bedroom. His hand had been warm on her shoulder.

"My boys would like to meet you, too," he'd said sincerely. "They'd treat you like a pretty little princess it was their privilege to entertain. And my wife would just love to know you. She was always disappointed we never had a little girl for her to pamper. Maybe you'll join us for Sunday dinner sometime, okay?"

But that invitation for Sunday dinner had never materialized, and Vinnie's visits had ended soon afterward. Now Michelle knew that they'd stopped at Alicia's request. Why? Hadn't her mother known how much Michelle had enjoyed those visits, how she'd longed to meet and play with Vinnie's children?

Feeling guilty that the thought even crossed her mind, Michelle wondered for a moment if Alicia had stopped the visits precisely for that reason. Alicia had always been so overprotective of her adopted daughter, so lovingly, if almost neurotically, possessive. Particularly after the kidnapping. It had been a long time after that before Michelle had been allowed out of her mother's presence. Alicia had even wanted to hire a tutor and pull Michelle out of the private school she attended, but Michelle's father had firmly vetoed that idea, asserting that the child needed playmates.

"I was sorry to hear you lost your mother recently," Vinnie said from the nearby chair he'd settled into. "I know the two of you were very close."

Michelle pulled her gaze from her hands to glance up at him, noting the genuine sympathy in his dark eyes. "Yes, we were."

"You doing okay?"

She managed another polite, distant smile. "I'm fine. Thank you for asking, Mr. D'Alessandro."

Vinnie scowled, the expression darkening his usually pleasant face, drawing his heavy, dark brows into a pronounced V. "'Mr. D'Alessandro?' You called me Vinnie before."

"Michelle tends to hide behind formality whenever she feels that she's losing control of a conversation," Tony said blandly, returning to the room with a tray holding three glasses of iced tea. He smiled when Michelle glared at him. "Just as she's tempted to fire me every time I step out of line."

"Like now," Michelle muttered, refusing to dignify his unrequested analysis of her with the heated denial that obviously trembled on her lips.

"Undoubtedly." He set the tray on the coffee table, then sank onto the sofa beside Michelle, ignoring the vacant chair across from his father. He offered Michelle a tall glass, smiling at her expression. "Tea?"

Innately reserved, properly raised, studiously dignified Michelle Culverton Trent would never have considered dumping a full glass of iced tea over anyone's head, he thought as she accepted the glass. Never, that is, before now. He waited to see if she'd follow through on the urge that was written so clearly on her lovely face. He wasn't surprised when she tilted her chin and gave him a cool nod. "Thank you."

"Don't you just love the way she gets all haughty and royal when she's displeased?" Tony asked his father. "Princess Di couldn't do it better."

Thoroughly irritated, all traces of sadness gone, Michelle

frowned at him. He was quite pleased with himself for taking the pain out of her eyes. For some reason, it bothered him a great deal to see Michelle Trent looking sad and vulnerable.

"You had something to discuss with me about my case? Something that involved your father?" she asked brusquely.

"Actually, I don't know if Dad's involved or not," Tony admitted. To Michelle's obvious relief, he stopped smiling so cockily at her and chose to accept her switch to business. "I had a call yesterday afternoon that I thought I should discuss with you. I discussed it with Dad first to get his professional opinion on how this should be handled. I often consult with my father on my cases."

"You had a call? Concerning me?"

"Yes. It was your attorney, Carter Powell."

"Carter?" Looking thoroughly confused, Michelle set her tea glass on a coaster and turned to face Tony more fully. "Why would Carter call you? How in the world did he know you were working for me?"

"That's what I thought I should ask you," Tony explained. "I understood you'd told no one but me of your search for your family."

"Only you and my friend, Taylor Simmons," Michelle confirmed.

"Taylor Simmons?" Tony frowned as he repeated the name. "Would this Simmons guy have talked to your attorney?"

"Taylor is a woman and no, she wouldn't have talked to Carter," Michelle corrected him coolly. "She would never discuss my personal business with anyone, even my attorney."

"A woman, huh?" Tony nodded in approval, though he didn't pause to examine his reasons for being rather relieved by the information. "So why did Carter Powell call and order me to stop working on your case? Why would he be so opposed to you finding your family that he'd resort to threats against me?"

"Threats?" Michelle stared at Tony in disbelief. "Oh, surely not."

"I'm telling you, Michelle, the man threatened me."

"With what? What, exactly, did he say?"

Tony scowled. "They weren't direct threats, of course. He had more discretion than that. It was all implied."

"Then you were surely mistaken. Carter has always been protective of me, particularly since my father died, but he would never threaten anyone."

"Dammit, Michelle, I know when I'm being threatened," Tony retorted heatedly.

"I'm quite sure it's happened often, given your personality, but trust me, this time you're mistaken."

Vinnie intervened when Tony would have told her exactly what he thought of her opinions of him. Looking rather amused by the younger couple's squabbling, Vinnie leaned toward Michelle. "You really don't know how your attorney could have found out about your search for your family, Michelle?"

She shook her head. "I really don't. Unless Tony, during his search, somehow tipped him off?"

"I didn't," Tony inserted curtly. "I know how to do my job."

Vinnie nodded, his lips twitching with the smile he held back. "Then perhaps you should contact your attorney and ask him yourself," he suggested to Michelle. "It's up to you to determine whether the man is exceeding his authority as your attorney in trying to protect you."

"Yes, I agree. I will certainly contact Carter immediately." Michelle shot Tony one quick, so-there look.

"Michelle, is there anyone else who may have cause to feel threatened by your search?" Tony asked thoughtfully, searching her face for a reaction to his impulsive question.

Puzzled, she asked, "Why?"

"Humor me, okay? Who stands to benefit if something happens to you?"

She shrugged. "My uncle, I suppose—my father's brother. He and his wife live in California. I don't see them very often, since they weren't particularly close to my parents. Uncle Richard and his son, Steven, run the California branch of Trent Enterprises."

"What's your uncle like?" Tony asked.

"Distant," Michelle replied slowly. "Rather snobbish, I'm afraid." Reluctantly, she added, "He tried to talk my parents out of adopting me. I found out years later, by accident, that he thought they were making a mistake to take in a child who'd been raised for two years by people he considered socially inferior. He warned them that they didn't really know what to expect from such questionable breeding."

"He told you this?" Vinnie demanded, looking appalled at such cold insensitivity. Tony's hands had clenched around his tea glass. He knew they would have made fists had they been empty.

Michelle shook her head, an old pain coloring her voice when she explained. "I found a letter he'd written them in my father's things after Mother died. It…hurt."

She hadn't meant to add that, Tony realized when she abruptly stopped speaking, looking annoyed with herself. Immediately concealing the vulnerability, she smiled faintly and shook her head when Vinnie would have reached out to her. "I got over it. As I said, I was never particularly close to my uncle, anyway."

But she hadn't gotten over it, Tony decided, not really. Had that old letter given her one more reason to feel alone and lost after her mother's death? Had it been one more reason for her to begin a search for the family she'd once had and lost?

And then she seemed to realize why Tony had asked about her uncle. She looked at him when she spoke again. "As I explained, Uncle Richard is a snob, but I can't imagine him giving you veiled threats through my attorney. It just isn't his style. He would be much more likely to make his objection in person. Forcefully, but openly. He's never been one to mince words or conceal his opinions."

"What about your cousin? Steven, wasn't it?"

"I don't know him very well," Michelle admitted. "We rarely saw each other, since he was raised in California. He's five years older than I am. All I really know about him is that my father called him an irresponsible playboy. I think he has a weakness for pretty, not-very-bright women, even though he's been married for several years."

Tony cleared his throat, wondering how to approach the next subject. "I have one more question."

She gestured in resignation. "Go ahead."

Glancing from Michelle to Vinnie and back again, Tony asked bluntly, "What happened to you eighteen years ago? Why did your father hire mine under such secrecy?"

Michelle flinched. "That isn't relevant."

"How do you know it isn't?" Tony countered. "You don't even know how your attorney became involved in this."

Michelle looked to Vinnie, her expression somewhat pleading. "Is it really necessary to rehash that old case?"

Vinnie sighed and gave his son a look that held both censure and understanding. "Probably not. But my son likes to know all the angles when he takes a case, particularly when problems crop up. I told him it was up to you whether you wanted him to know about that other incident."

Michelle was quiet for so long that Tony was convinced she would refuse to tell him. And then she sighed, pushed back her hair and gave him an annoyed look. "I was—I was kidnapped when I was eight years old. Your father found me and rescued me five days later."

Tony made a massive effort to conceal how appalled he was at having his guess confirmed. He couldn't understand why he so violently hated the thought of Michelle in danger—then or now. "What happened?" he asked, his question more harsh than he'd intended.

Michelle looked down at her hands, seemingly relieved when Vinnie answered for her, as though understanding that she didn't like to talk about that time. "The kidnapper had been a trusted family employee," he explained. "A security guard who'd worked for Harrison Trent for three years. During that time, he befriended Michelle, teasing her and playing with her and talking to her to earn her trust. One day he tricked her away from her family by telling her he wanted to show her a litter of kittens he'd found in the garage. He drugged her and drove away with her in the trunk of his car."

Tony swallowed a string of vicious curses, setting his tea glass down with a thump that splashed liquid over the rim. "I hope you got the bastard."

"I got him," Vinnie confirmed grimly. "Beat the holy hell out of him, too, when we were supposed to be making the ransom drop. Let's just say by the time I was through with him, he couldn't wait to tell me where he had Michelle stashed."

"I was in a closet," Michelle murmured, "for the greater part of five days. It was dark and hot and sometimes I thought I'd smother."

Tony couldn't withstand her lost-little-girl tone. Without thinking, he reached out to her, covering her hand with his own. "I'm sorry," he said, holding her eyes with his when she looked at him in surprise at his action. "I wish I didn't have to make you relive this. But I have to know if there's anyone besides your attorney who has reason to want to stop me from doing my job."

He'd half expected her to snatch her hand from beneath his. It pleased him when she didn't. "I still think you're over-reacting to Carter's call," she murmured, though without accusation this time.

"Believe me, Tony, I followed up all leads eighteen years ago. The jerk wasn't working alone, but I was satisfied that everyone involved was apprehended. I checked out Michelle's uncle, but I found no evidence that he'd participated in any way. As for the lawyer—well, all I can tell you about him is that he was Harrison Trent's attorney for years without any problems that I know of."

"I don't like being threatened," Tony grumbled, still angry when he remembered the obnoxious tone the attorney had used during the call.

Michelle did move her hand then, sliding it from beneath Tony's to reach for her tea glass. "I'll let Carter know that I don't appreciate him trying to interfere in my business without my permission," she said. "He won't bother you again."

Tony was far from satisfied, but it was obvious that he'd get no further with Michelle at the moment. After all, she'd known Carter Powell most of her life, and Tony for less than a month. How could he expect her to trust his gut feeling that something just wasn't right with her family attorney?

"I understand Tony's located one of your sisters," Vinnie said, smoothly changing the subject.

Still rather pale from the pain of rehashing her traumatic childhood experience, Michelle nodded. "Yes, he has. She lives in Fort Worth."

"Now isn't that a coincidence? You're practically neighbors."

"Yes."

"I guess you're really looking forward to meeting her."

Tony watched as Michelle moistened her lips with the tip

of her tongue. They glistened enticingly and it was with some difficulty that he focused on what she was saying in answer to his father's comment.

"I haven't actually decided whether I should contact my sister," Michelle said vaguely.

Vinnie started to question her further, only to be interrupted when Carla D'Alessandro entered the room. "Sorry I'm late," the slender brunette apologized to her husband. "This Harmon case is such a headache. Hello, darling," she added for Tony's benefit, smiling fondly at him as she sank into the vacant chair.

"Hi, Mom," he greeted her, standing. "You look tired. Want a glass of iced tea?"

"That sounds wonderful. Thank you."

"No problem." He gestured at Michelle. "This is Michelle Trent, a client of mine. Can I get you anything else, Michelle?"

"No, thank you." She looked to his mother as Tony headed for the doorway. "It's very nice to meet you, Mrs. D'Alessandro."

Michelle found it hard to believe this woman was Tony's mother. Slim and attractive, Carla D'Alessandro looked ridiculously young to have a son in his early thirties. But her smile was warm and genuine, her eyes kind. Michelle suspected that Carla was a mother who'd always be available when her sons needed her.

By the time Tony returned with his mother's drink, Michelle had heard about his younger brothers—Michael, an attorney in Austin and Joe, a medical student in Houston— and about the scrapes the three adventurous brothers had gotten into during their youth. As he had years earlier, Vinnie again insisted that Tony had always been the ringleader.

"Don't believe it," Tony refuted mildly, handing Carla her glass along with a loving kiss on the cheek. "I was just the one who always nobly took the blame. To protect my little brothers, you understand."

Michelle gave him a look she hoped fully expressed her disbelief. "Of course."

"And if I *did* come up with the majority of the ideas, it was only because I was the most intelligent," Tony added, dropping back onto the couch beside Michelle.

"I believe your brothers would take issue with that," Carla murmured.

"If you'd had brains, you'd have done like your brothers and gone into respectable professions," Vinnie added sternly. "Instead, you had to follow in my shoes and be an ex-cop-turned-P.I. I tried to talk you out of it, but you never would listen to any advice I had to give."

"Of course I listened to you, Pop. I just didn't always agree with you. And besides, whoever said law was a respectable profession?" He grinned at his mother as he taunted her about her career.

Quite calmly, Carla took off her shoe and lobbed it at him, murmuring something in Italian that didn't sound particularly flattering. Laughing, he caught the shoe deftly, chiding his mother for throwing things at him that could accidentally hit Michelle instead. Smiling as Carla defended her throwing aim, Michelle thought wistfully that this seemed to be a happy, loving family. How she missed the good times she'd spent with her parents. How she longed for a family of her own, despite her lingering fear of taking such a risk.

Michelle waited only a few minutes longer before announcing politely that she really had to go. Both Carla and Vinnie urged her to come back anytime, so warmly that she felt she really would be welcome should she visit again. Not that she expected to do so. After all, why should she?

"How about giving me a lift home, Michelle?" Tony asked casually. "It's not far out of your way."

She couldn't graciously refuse, of course, not in front of his parents. "All right."

Tony managed to hide his amusement at her expression. He knew full well that if it had been up to Michelle, they wouldn't have been leaving together. He chose not to take it personally. He'd already decided that the toughest part of this case would be convincing his beautiful client that he could be trusted—as an investigator and as a man who was growing more personally involved every minute he spent with her.

He kissed his mother, then lingered at the front door with his father for a few moments after Michelle had gotten into her car. "What do you think, Dad?"

Vinnie shrugged. "She obviously trusts her attorney. Maybe you *did* misinterpret the call."

"Carter Powell knows information about Michelle that he shouldn't know. And I didn't misinterpret his instructions for me to drop the case and try to convince Michelle to drop it, as well. Something's going on."

"You may be right, Tony. I'll point out that all you've been hired to do is to locate Michelle's brothers and sisters, but I don't expect you to drop this other thing."

"The problem is that I don't really expect Carter Powell to drop it. I'll hear from him again."

"Then I'll just tell you to be careful."

"I always am, Dad." Tony glanced toward the car, where Michelle waited with apparent patience. "What do you think of her? Did she turn out the way you'd expected she would?"

"She's a lovely, well-mannered, intelligent woman. But in her eyes I still see a lot of the lonely little girl I knew."

"Yeah. Maybe I can do something about that."

Vinnie narrowed his eyes. "What did I tell you about getting personally involved with your clients, boy?"

"You told me it was dangerous and ill-advised," Tony replied without hesitation. "You also told me that if you hadn't done so yourself thirty-five years ago, you never would have married Mom."

Vinnie sighed gustily. "Don't keep the lady waiting, Tony. It's rude."

"Right. I'll call you later, Dad, okay?"

"Mmm. And Tony?"

Tony had already started down the steps. He looked over his shoulder. "Yes?"

"Watch yourself."

Knowing that Vinnie referred to Michelle as well as to her aggressive attorney, Tony nodded. "I will. Ciao, Dad."

Tony waited until Michelle had backed out of his parents' driveway before glancing at his watch. "Damn," he muttered, shaking his wrist as if it would help, "stupid watch has stopped again. I'm going to have to break down and buy a new one." As though it had just occurred to him, he added, "It's getting late, isn't it? Why don't we stop somewhere for dinner?"

"Dinner?" Michelle glanced at him warily. "Now?"

"Yeah. Unless you have other plans?"

"Well, no, but…is there something else about the case you want to discuss with me?"

He shifted in his seat to face her, watching her profile as she drove. "To be honest, no. This has nothing to do with the case. It's purely personal."

He watched as her fingers tightened on the steering wheel. "Personal?" she repeated, as though she wasn't quite sure she'd heard him correctly.

"Yes. Will you have dinner with me, Michelle?"

She moistened her lips as she had earlier. Again, the gesture drew his full attention to her soft, lush mouth, making him wonder exactly how those lips would feel beneath his. "I don't know, Tony. I'm not sure that's such a good idea."

"It's a dinner date, Michelle, not a lifelong commitment.

No big deal, right?" It was a big deal, of course, at least to Tony. But he thought it best not to let Michelle know exactly how much her answer meant to him. He didn't want to frighten her away by pushing for too much, too soon.

"I don't think it's wise for us to date while you're working for me," Michelle explained carefully.

"Does that mean you'd go out with me if I *wasn't* working for you?"

Again, she hesitated. "Maybe."

"So what's the problem? I'm not going to stop looking for your brothers and sisters, and I won't suddenly decide to raise my fees. Nor lower them, for that matter. As far as business goes, it's strictly professional. But, after hours, I'd like to get to know you better."

"Why?" she asked bluntly, taking advantage of a red traffic light to look fully at him.

"I like you," he answered simply. And then he smiled. "I don't know why, exactly, but I do. So why don't you give me a chance to try to convince you to like me, too?"

"If I say yes, it's only to dinner," she warned, her fingers still flexing nervously on the steering wheel.

"Of course. That's all I expect." *For tonight, anyway.*

She seemed to reach a sudden decision. "All right. Where would you like to eat?"

He couldn't quite believe it had been that easy. He knew there was still a long way to go before Michelle fully trusted him, but this was one hell of a start. "Ever been to Vittorio's?"

"Yes. It's very good."

"My uncle—Mom's brother—owns the place. There's always a table for me there."

In response to an impatient honk from behind them, Michelle pressed the accelerator, passing beneath the light that had turned green without her noticing. And then she reached for the car phone built into her dash. "I'll just let my housekeeper know I won't be home for dinner," she explained. "She worries if I don't show up when she's expecting me."

Tony settled back in his seat and pretended not to listen while she made the call. He was also trying hard not to think about Michelle's wealth, which only made him nervous when he dwelled on it. His family had been comfortably middle-class, nowhere near Michelle's social or financial standing. But after finding out about bits and pieces of her childhood, he was sincerely grateful for his own normal background. Loving parents, brothers to play with, enough money to provide a few luxuries in addition to the necessities, but not nearly enough to cause his family to live in constant fear of kidnappers or fortune hunters.

At the moment, Tony was feeling considerably richer than Michelle. He wondered if she wouldn't agree with him.

Chapter Five

"So anyway, after he'd begged for weeks to be quarterback, we finally told Joe he could try it for a couple of plays. First pass he made to me sailed right through the neighbor's window. Old lady Winter," Tony added with an expressive grimace. "Meanest old biddy ever to haunt the state of Texas. Not only did she demand that we pay to fix her window, but she refused to give us back our football. And it was a good one, too. Real leather."

Michelle smiled, thinking of the younger Tony's indignation—an indignation that still colored his deep voice. "Did you get into trouble with your father?"

Tony grinned. "Nah. Dad couldn't stand old lady Winter, either. He grumbled a little and told us to be more careful, but we knew he thought it was kinda funny."

That didn't really surprise her about Vinnie. Michelle would have bet he'd have been a great father for a trio of boys. Again, she found herself envying Tony his memories of growing up with his brothers, with whom he was obviously still close.

"Did you always want to be a private investigator, like your father?" she asked.

He shrugged. "Actually, I was a cop first. Dad was a cop, too, you know. He quit the force after being injured on the job—he was shot during a holdup attempt. While he was on medical leave, he started doing some background research on a couple of Mom's cases. He liked it so well he went into the business."

"How old were you when you joined the police department?"

"Twenty-one. Right out of college."

"You didn't like it as much as you'd thought you would?"

"No." Without elaboration, he finished his linguine, then abruptly changed the subject. "So what about you? We've been talking about me ever since we got here. What were you like as a little girl? I'll bet you were a perfect child, right? Never mussed your dresses or lost the bows from your curls. Straight-A student, the kind teachers just love."

Flushing, Michelle looked down at her half-eaten vegetable lasagna. Tony had just pretty well summed up her childhood. She tried to remember an incident in which she'd rebelled against her parents' sometimes suffocating rules. "I did get into trouble once," she remembered. "I was at Taylor's house and I stayed forty-five minutes past my curfew. We'd been watching old movies on TV and lost track of time. My parents were worried sick. I was grounded for a week."

"Forty-five minutes?" Tony repeated. "How old were you?"

"Sixteen," Michelle admitted.

"I see."

Feeling oddly as though she needed to defend her unadventurous adolescence, Michelle murmured, "My parents were always rather overprotective. Especially after—well, you know."

"Didn't you ever feel the need to cut loose and do something daring? Something your parents wouldn't approve of?"

"I did once," Michelle answered quietly, picturing a young man with a devilishly charming smile and bright, hungry eyes. The problem was that she'd misinterpreted that hunger as a desire for her, rather than for her money. It hadn't helped that her father had been unable to resist the urge to say "I told you so," when the truth had come out.

She'd spent the past five years living carefully, cautiously, pouring her energy into her obligations to Trent Enterprises, her heart into her hospital volunteer work. She'd even managed to convince herself that she was happy—most of the time.

Tony waited a few minutes for her to expand on her answer. When she didn't, he changed the subject. "Why are you having such a hard time deciding whether to contact your sister Layla? I've checked her out, as well as her husband, and they seem like perfectly respectable, apparently likeable people. We know Layla wants to be found or she wouldn't have registered with the reunion service. So why don't you call her?"

"I wouldn't know what to say to her," Michelle admitted, risking total candor. "She may be my biological sister, but she's still a stranger. I don't know her, I don't remember her. What would we talk about?"

"You haven't known me very long, but we haven't had any trouble talking tonight," Tony pointed out with a smile of understanding. "Of course, I've carried the brunt of the conversation, but maybe Layla's a talker, as well. Maybe you'd end up finding a new friend as well as a sister."

"You make it sound so easy," Michelle accused him, pushing her plate away, her appetite gone. "How would you feel if you suddenly discovered that you had brothers and sisters you'd never met, never known about? Would you want to rush out and find them?"

"I've asked myself that question since I took your case," Tony confessed. "And I've decided that, yes, I would want to find them. Maybe they'd be strangers, but there's something special about knowing you share the same ancestry, the same genes. Blood relationship is certainly no guarantee that you'll be close, or even *like* each other, but how can you not make an effort to find out?"

Though she was surprised that it was so easy to talk to this man about something so personal, Michelle realized that she really wanted his opinion. "Sometimes I think I'd really like to meet her," she said, watching Tony as she spoke. "I think about how nice it would be to have a sister, to know my nieces and nephew. But what if we meet and it's awkward and uncomfortable? What if we end up just staring at each other and trying to think of something to say? Or worse, what if one of us has expectations the other just can't fulfill?"

That was one of her biggest concerns, that Layla would expect her to immediately experience some bond, some connection that she may never feel. Ten at the time they'd been separated, Layla probably had memories of her younger sister, whereas Michelle had nothing but half-heard voices from dreams. "I wouldn't know what to do," she murmured, hoping Tony would somehow understand what she herself was struggling to comprehend.

It seemed he did. His smile softening, he reached across the small table and took her hand. "I can see why you'd be nervous. But I think you owe yourself a chance to meet her, just to satisfy your own curiosity. I think that curiosity is going to haunt you until you do something about it. Am I right?"

Michelle sighed, leaving her hand in his, though she refrained from returning his warm squeeze. "Probably."

"If it would help, I'll go with you when you meet her. Maybe it would be easier for you with someone objective along to keep things moving if the conversation drags."

Michelle was surprised by his offer. But she was also pleased, particularly since she sensed he genuinely wanted to help her. Because he cared?

She brought herself up short at that thought, quickly pulling her hand from his. It was much too soon to be thinking that way, she reminded herself sternly. Much too risky to start trusting another man with a charming smile and hungry eyes. To think that maybe this time the desire *was* for her, and not for her wealth.

"Thank you for offering. I'll think about it," she said, stirring sweetener into her freshly refilled coffee to avoid his eyes for the moment.

"You do that."

Tony might have said something more on the subject, but they were interrupted by yet another member of the restaurant staff stopping by to make sure their dinner was satisfactory. And didn't they want dessert?

Tony had explained with a rueful smile that being the nephew of the owner had always guaranteed him very prompt and personal service when he dined at Vittorio's. Sometimes *too* personal, he'd added when his uncle had asked a few pointed, matchmaking questions about Tony's relationship with Michelle.

It amused Michelle to note that the laid-back, Texan-down-to-his-boots private investigator subtly changed when he was with his family. When she'd first met him, she'd thought the only thing particularly Italian about Anthony D'Alessandro was his name. Now she could see that his ancestry was more a part of him than she'd previously suspected. She also hadn't expected that he could switch without hesitation from lazily drawled English to rapid, flawlessly accented Italian, as he did when he spoke to one of the older restaurant employees, who was obviously delighted to be able to converse in her native tongue.

Michelle had found Tony much too attractive when their association had been nothing more than professional. Now, seeing him under more personal circumstances, she was drawn even more strongly to him. Which played utter havoc on her peace of mind. She had no intention of getting personally involved with the man she'd hired to find her long-lost family!

Michelle drove Tony straight to his apartment building after dinner. She was relieved that he didn't press her about contacting Layla, choosing instead to keep the conversation light and amusing. "I enjoyed having dinner with you, Michelle," he said when she parked in a space he'd pointed out by his apartment. "We'll have to do it again."

"Perhaps," she said, still trying to be cautious.

He smiled and slid a hand behind her head. "Definitely," he corrected, his mouth already lowering toward hers.

Michelle stiffened, but it was too late. Tony's lips covered hers deftly, warmly. And she melted into the kiss as though she'd been starving for it.

Tony lingered over the kiss just long enough to make her want more. And then he pulled slowly, reluctantly away. "Drive carefully, Michelle."

He opened his door and had one foot outside before Michelle found her voice. "Tony?"

He glanced over his shoulder. "Yes?"

"I still think it would be wiser to keep our relationship on a professional basis. At least for now," she added a bit shyly.

His smile melted whatever was left of her prudence. "Maybe it would have been wiser," he agreed. "But it's much too late for that now, *cara*. Goodnight."

"I—uh—goodnight." She waited until he'd closed the

door behind him before putting the car into reverse and backing out of the parking space.

Cara. The word echoed repeatedly in her mind as she drove home, Tony's husky voice as clear as though he still sat beside her. She spoke no Italian, but she knew that word. Dear. Did Tony toss out such endearments easily, or was he really beginning to care for her, as he'd implied?

And was she being an utter fool to wonder if she'd found more than a chance of locating her long-lost family when she'd stepped into Tony D'Alessandro's office?

Tony lay sprawled on his back in bed, his hands crossed behind his head, eyes focused intently on the ceiling, as though he'd find some answers in the acoustic tiles above him. He chewed thoughtfully on his lower lip, then released it when he fancied he could almost still taste Michelle, though it had been hours since he'd kissed her. Hours since he'd made himself pull away from her when what he'd really wanted to do was to carry her into his apartment and find out everything there was to know about Michelle Trent. Like what it would take to release the passion he sensed smoldering behind her prim-and-proper veneer.

Since thoughts of that nature proved more uncomfortable than productive, he turned his attention to his lingering misgivings about her attorney. Despite Michelle's conviction that Powell had only the best intentions where she was concerned, Tony suspected otherwise. Carter Powell hadn't sounded like a kindly family attorney loyally looking out for the welfare of a valued young client. He'd sounded very much like a man willing to resort to threats to protect his own best interests. Why? What was he afraid of if Michelle continued her search?

In sudden decision, he stretched toward the nightstand beside the bed, snagging the telephone receiver. He punched in a number and waited impatiently for an answer. "Chuck? It's Tony. Sorry I woke you. First thing tomorrow, I want you to turn over your notes on Jared Walker to Cassie. Let her take the search from here…

"No, you haven't done anything wrong. I've got a new assignment for you. I want you to find out everything there is to know about Carter Powell, an attorney here in Dallas. I particularly want to know about his work for Trent Enterprises. Michelle Trent, in particular. And, Chuck—I'm not going to ask a lot of questions about how you do your research. Just get me everything you can find. Soon."

Michelle hung up her telephone with a sigh of frustration. She'd been trying to reach her attorney for nearly a week—since Tony had told her about Carter's call to him. Each time she'd called, Carter had been in court or in a meeting or out of the office. She hadn't even been able to reach him at home.

Already annoyed with him for calling Tony without her authority, she decided she was going to have to be very firm when she did speak to him. He was going to have to acknowledge that she was an adult now, not the child he'd known since toddlerhood, and that she was quite capable of handling her own personal business. And she didn't appreciate having to go to so much trouble contacting him when she needed to speak to him.

She was working at home that day. Though she'd never been interested in the corporate operation of Trent Enterprises, and had no need to earn a living, she'd wanted something productive to do with her time. It had been her father who'd suggested a job for her, not long after the fiasco with Geoff, when Michelle had been desperately in need of something to do besides brood about the disastrous ending of her first serious love affair.

Since that time, Michelle had taken on all responsibility

for the sizable charitable contributions made by Trent Enterprises, Dallas. She was the one who investigated charitable organizations, responded to pleas for funds, approached the board of directors with yearly budgeting proposals and requests for increases as needed during the year. Every week she received stacks of mail containing requests for donations; she diligently read and researched each one. Not only did the task give her something worthwhile to devote herself to, but it also served a legitimate purpose, one she could be quite proud of.

She was reading a form-letter request from a national charity organization in the home office that had once been her father's when she heard the front doorbell ring. Knowing Betty would answer it, she didn't pull her attention from the paperwork until she heard a sound from the open doorway. She looked up expecting to see her housekeeper, only to find Tony D'Alessandro leaning casually against the doorjamb, arms crossed over his chest, watching her with obvious amusement at her surprise.

"Hi," he said.

"Tony! What are you doing here?"

"I don't suppose you'd believe I just happened to be in the neighborhood."

She laid the letter on her desk. "Try again."

He dropped his arms and sauntered into the room, looking around with interest at the rich wood panelling, the crowded shelves of books, the framed hunting prints, the comfortable leather furniture, the glossy cherry desk. "Nice. I've always wanted a study like this."

"You still haven't told me why you're here."

"That housekeeper of yours is quite a watchdog," he remarked, walking around to her side and resting a hip on the desk, his jeaned leg only inches from her hand. "You wouldn't believe what I had to tell her to convince her to let

me in to see you unannounced. I'd already had a hard enough
time getting past the big guy working on the front gate."

"That's Betty's husband, Arthur. He's been with the family
as long as Betty has. He was my mother's driver, though now
he primarily handles general maintenance of the grounds
and vehicles, since I prefer to drive myself," Michelle explained, pulling her hand away to clasp it with the other in
her lap. "Did you find out something new about my family,
Tony? Is that why you're here?"

He shrugged and reached out to brush a strand of hair
away from her cheek. "There is a lead on your oldest brother,
Jared. We've confirmed that he entered the Navy straight out
of high school and served for several years. Nothing on his
most recent whereabouts yet, but we'll find him."

Her cheek tingling from that all-too-brief contact, Michelle
looked up at him. "You could have told me that over the phone."

"Mmm," he murmured in agreement. "But I couldn't have
done *this* over the phone." And he leaned over to kiss her, his
mouth covering her surprise-parted lips with the same seductive skill he'd displayed the last time he'd kissed her.

He really was going to have to stop doing that, Michelle
thought, her eyelids drifting downward. Or else she simply
couldn't be held responsible for her actions.

Again, it was Tony who brought the kiss to an end. "I've
been wanting to do that again for the past six days," he
murmured, touching a fingertip to her lower lip. "Have I
mentioned that the shape of your mouth makes me crazy?"

Michelle cleared her throat. "Oh, is that what does it?" she
managed to say fairly evenly.

He chuckled. "Are you ever at a loss for a put-down?"

"With you it seems to come naturally." To avoid talking
about the kiss, she immediately turned the conversation back
to business. "How long do you think it will take you to find
Jared?"

The smile in his eyes told her he knew exactly what she was doing, though he answered cooperatively enough. "I've turned the case over to Cassie Browning. She's been working part-time for me for nearly a year," he reminded her. "She's young, but eager. Goes full tilt into any assignment I give her. I think she's got her eye on a partnership. D'Alessandro and Browning Investigations. Or, knowing Cassie, she'd probably prefer top billing."

Michelle tried very hard not to be bothered by the fond indulgence in Tony's voice when he talked about his employee. It was really none of her business if this Cassie had her eye on more than a professional partnership with Tony, Michelle reminded herself sternly. So why was she suddenly feeling suspiciously—almost primitively—possessive?

"I have a few more things to do this afternoon," she said pointedly. "Was there anything else you wanted to discuss with me?"

"I've got a couple of tickets to a play tonight. I know this is short notice for a Friday evening, but how about it?"

Michelle had been momentarily distracted by the chime of the front doorbell. Who was it *this* time? "How about what?"

He sighed his exasperation with her deliberate obtuseness. "Will you go to the play with me tonight?"

That got her full attention again. "Tonight?"

"That's when the play is," he replied patiently. "I'll pick you up at seven, okay?"

"Come on, Michelle, tell the man yes before someone else does. Someone like me," Taylor added, strolling into the room with a speculative look at Tony. She held out her hand to him across Michelle's desk, her smile full of mischief. "Hello. I'm Taylor Simmons. You must be Tony D'Alessandro."

Rising to his feet, Tony briefly took her hand, returning her smile. "As a matter of fact, I am. How did you know?"

"You're the only handsome Italian-type Michelle has mentioned lately," Taylor quipped, grinning unrepentantly at Michelle's groan of embarrassment. "So, Michelle—are you going out with him tonight or not?"

Resisting the urge to hide her face in her hands in the hope that both of them would just disappear, Michelle stood and shoved her hands into the pockets of her full cotton skirt. "I guess I will."

"You'll have to forgive her. She's usually much more courteous," Taylor told Tony with laughter warming her husky voice. "In fact, Michelle cut her teeth on the social graces. So what have you been doing to annoy her, hmm?"

"I seem to do that without even trying," Tony answered.

"That's not so bad. She needs to be challenged occasionally. It wouldn't be good for her to get too complacent, you know?"

"I *am* still in the room," Michelle reminded her friend peevishly.

Taylor laughed. "So you are. Have I annoyed you so greatly that you'd never consent to loan me that great sequined jacket you bought at Neiman's last month? I've got a date tonight and I don't have a thing to wear."

"What? No grubby jeans or safari jacket?" Michelle asked in mock surprise. "This must be someone special."

"Well, no," Taylor admitted ruefully. "But I've been wanting to try that ritzy new restaurant since it opened last month, and this guy just happened to have reservations for tonight."

Tony cleared his throat. "I'll leave you two to your comparisons of notes about your dates tonight. It was nice to meet you, Taylor. See you at seven, Michelle."

"You haven't told me what play we're seeing," Michelle

reminded him quickly as he headed for the door. "I won't know what to wear unless you tell me where we're going."

"Robert F. Kennedy High School," he answered over his shoulder. "It's my cousin's senior-class play. A comedy, I understand, though I'm not sure whether the author intended it to be. I think it's safe to assume the dress will be casual."

With that, he was gone, leaving Michelle to stare after him in half-amused disbelief. He was taking her to a high school senior play? That was his idea of a date?

Taylor waited only until Tony was out of hearing before making a fist and jerking it downward in front of her in a sign of approval. "All *right!* Michelle, he's delectable. Why didn't you tell me?"

"I told you he was nice-looking," she murmured, still rather distracted.

"You didn't say he was gorgeous. And you didn't say what a great smile he has, nor how funny he is. I really liked him."

Michelle frowned. "You did?"

Taylor laughed and shook her head. "No, not like that. I liked him, but I don't think he and I would ever have any real electricity. Not the kind I felt bouncing around between *you* and Tony, anyway."

Flushing, Michelle pushed her hands deeper into her pockets. "Don't be ridiculous. I hardly know him."

"So how does he kiss? I'd bet he's damned good at it."

"What makes you think he's kissed me?" Michelle hedged, knowing her deepening flush gave her away.

"There was a smudge of pink lipstick at the corner of his mouth, right beside that cute little dimple. The same color you're sort of wearing, by the way. Unless he's into cross-dressing, there's only one way I can think of that your lipstick ended up on his mouth."

"So he kissed me. It was just a kiss."

"Just a kiss?" Taylor asked, her eyebrows lifting skeptically.

Michelle sighed. "Okay, it was an incredible kiss. An award-winning, bell-ringing kiss. But," she added when Taylor grinned, "that doesn't mean anything else is going to happen between us. I don't intend to rush into anything."

"Nor am I suggesting you should," Taylor replied promptly. "I'm simply suggesting that you give Tony a chance. Forget about Geoff and judge Tony on his own merits, all right? Maybe the two of you will turn out to be perfect for each other. It's been known to happen."

Michelle nodded, unconsciously tracing her lower lip with one fingertip. "I know he's not Geoff, Taylor."

But those old scars couldn't be put aside as easily as Taylor made it sound. It was going to take time for Michelle to decide for herself whether Tony was a man who could be trusted with her wary heart.

Chapter Six

Michelle might have had more fun on other dates than she did with Tony that night. But if she had, she couldn't remember. She might have laughed more some other evening during her life. She just couldn't have said when. She might have had more attentive, more charming, more irresistibly entertaining escorts. If so, those men had long since slipped her mind.

Surrounded by Tony's aunts, uncles, cousins and parents in the high school auditorium, she should have felt shy, out of place. Instead, she felt welcomed and appreciated, part of the group that laughed so good-naturedly at the antics of the enthusiastic young people on stage. And when Michelle commented that Tony's cousin Dominic showed signs of real acting talent, the others were so pleased and flattered that one would have thought the praise had come directly from Steven Spielberg.

It was probably one of the most successful dates Michelle

had ever had. Which didn't explain why she grew more nervous and unsettled as the evening drew closer to an end. Nor why, by the time she and Tony lingered over grilled chicken sandwiches at his favorite fast-food restaurant after the play, she'd become quiet and introspective, avoiding his eyes as she pretended to concentrate on her fries.

"Michelle, is something wrong?"

"No, of course not. How's your sandwich?"

"How *was* my sandwich, you mean," he said, motioning toward the empty wrapper in front of him. "I've been finished for ten minutes."

Startled, she realized she'd withdrawn more than she'd been aware. She couldn't even remember the last thing she'd said to him. Had they been talking about the play? His family? The weather?

"Sorry," she murmured, clasping her hands in her lap. "I was thinking about something else."

Like how very much she was growing to like him. How much she enjoyed being with him. How badly she wanted him to kiss her again. And how the very thought of a relationship with him had her breaking into a cold sweat.

Tony rested his elbows on the plastic-laminated tabletop, still watching her more closely than she found comfortable. "I've been avoiding talking business this evening, but I did want to ask if you ever talked to your attorney about his call to me."

Michelle shook her head. "I've tried to call him, but he's been hard to reach this week."

"I bet," Tony muttered.

She ignored him. "I left a message for him to call me as soon as possible. I'm sure I'll hear from him tomorrow."

"Mmm." Tony's skepticism was quite obvious in the quiet murmur and the lift of his eyebrow. In response to the look she gave him, he sighed and let the subject of her attorney drop. "Have you thought about my offer to go with you to meet your sister? Would you like me to set up a meeting?"

Her stomach contracted with a new set of nerves. "I don't know, Tony. I—"

"Michelle. Let me call her for you. We both know you want to meet her."

"Do we?" she muttered, giving him a resentful glare. "Since when do you know so much about what I want?"

He didn't answer. Instead, he gave her a smile that held so much cockiness and sympathetic understanding that she couldn't decide whether to squirt ketchup on him or burrow into his arms. Since neither action seemed particularly appropriate at the time, she took a deep breath and said, "Give me more time to think about it. If I decide to take you up on your offer, I'll call you."

"You'll think about it? Seriously?"

"That's what I said, wasn't it?" she snapped. "If you're so convinced this is what I want, why question my decision?"

"I'm well aware that you don't particularly value my advice, but I still think you'll be sorry if you don't do this. I'd hate for you to have any regrets later."

He just couldn't resist getting in a little dig. Why was it that Tony seemed to like her best when she was more than a little annoyed with him?

"Finished with your dinner?" he asked, abruptly changing the subject. "Want a fried apple pie or an ice-cream cone for dessert?"

"No, thank you."

"Then I'll bus the table." He reached for her empty paper cup, giving her a grin. "Can't say I don't take you to the best places, can you, darlin'?"

"I think you look quite natural busing tables," she retorted, doing her best to hide the little shiver that coursed through her at his lazily drawled endearment. "Perhaps you missed your calling."

"I'll keep that in mind if people suddenly stop wanting incriminating photographs of cheating spouses."

Michelle smiled with a vain attempt at cool amusement and handed him her empty French-fry wrapper.

Tony insisted on walking Michelle to her front door when he took her home. With amusingly old-fashioned courtesy, he helped her out of his four-wheel drive and kept one hand at the small of her back as they walked up the four steps to her door.

Keys in hand, she looked up at him with a polite social smile, assuming he would kiss her again, aware that she wanted him to. "I enjoyed the play, Tony. And the meal. Thank you for taking me."

Leaning one shoulder against the door, he touched her cheek, stroking the line of her jaw with one gentle finger. "I enjoyed having you with me. In fact, I think it would be all too easy to become addicted to being with you."

It seemed so easy for him to say things like that. Could he really mean them? She moistened her lips, wondering what to say in return.

Tony drew his finger across her damp lower lip. Her mouth parted slightly in reaction, and he ran the tip of the same finger just along the inside of her lip. She shivered, imagining his mouth on hers, his tongue tracing the path his finger had taken.

"Have I told you that I think you're the most beautiful woman I've ever known?" Tony murmured, sliding his other hand into her hair so that her face was cupped between his palms. She felt his unsteadiness with a sense of wonder. "That I've never met anyone who affected me quite the way you do?"

Her eyes closed when he kissed her, her hands rising tentatively to rest on his chest. The kiss was long and deep and thorough, and Tony was breathing rapidly when it ended. Michelle wasn't sure she was breathing at all.

"Michelle," he whispered, his lips moving against her temple, his arms drawing her closer. "Tell me I'm not the only one feeling these things. Tell me it's not all one-sided."

Her fingers clenched convulsively into his soft cotton shirt. "I don't—I don't know what you want from me," she managed, lifting her eyes slowly to his face. "What you want me to say."

He sighed and rested his forehead against hers. "You really have a problem with trust, don't you?"

"I've had reason to."

"Men who said they wanted you when what they really wanted was the Trent money?" Tony asked perceptively, lifting his head.

She nodded stiffly.

"I could tell you that isn't the case with me. I could tell you I couldn't care less about your money. That it's only you I want—very badly. But I know it's going to take time for you to believe those things. Time for you to get to know me, to know you can trust me. I won't rush you."

"I—" She cleared her throat of a large, near-painful lump. "Thank you."

He shook his head, his smile crooked. "I foresee a lot of cold showers in my future. But, just to hold me over…" And he kissed her again, until her knees were weak, her ears buzzing, her lungs burning from lack of oxygen. She clung to the doorknob when he finally released her, not at all sure that her legs would support her without the assistance. "Will you see me tomorrow?" he asked.

"Yes," she whispered, her voice barely audible.

"I'll pick you up tomorrow afternoon—say, two o'clock? Dress casually. You do own a pair of jeans, don't you?"

"Of course," she replied, hoping she was right. When *was* the last time she'd worn a pair of jeans?

He dropped one last, quick kiss on her still-trembling mouth. "Good night, Michelle."

She could only nod in response. He smiled with a mixture of satisfaction and frustration, then loped toward his Jeep. Michelle pulled in a much-needed breath and opened her front door, ready to be inside where she could hide in the security of her bedroom.

By the time Tony picked Michelle up Saturday afternoon, she'd begun to wonder if she'd lost her mind during the evening before. She hadn't acted at all like herself, hadn't maintained any sort of professional distance between herself and Tony. Just the opposite, in fact. She'd encouraged him to believe she was interested in more than a professional liaison with him—and it was much too soon for her to even speculate about anything of a more intimate nature.

Pressing her cool hands to her flaming cheeks, she stood before the mirror in her bedroom, trying not to relive the kisses they'd shared when he brought her home. Unable to completely block them out of her thoughts. They'd haunted her dreams during the night, replayed themselves over and over in her mind all day—and, desperately as she might try to believe otherwise, she knew full well that she was not only expecting, but *hoping* he would kiss her like that again today.

What had ever happened to that cool, cautious reserve she'd cultivated so carefully during the past five years?

Aware that it was nearly two—the time he'd said he'd be picking her up—she concentrated on the reflection in the mirror again, wondering if she'd dressed correctly. It would help, of course, if she had some idea of where he'd be taking her, but she was already learning that there was no predicting what Tony D'Alessandro might do.

Since he'd suggested jeans, she'd found a pair—though it had taken twenty minutes of searching. She didn't remember the last time she'd worn them, but she'd obviously gained a couple of pounds since. The soft denim fit her like a second skin, molding her slender hips, hugging her thighs, shaping her long legs. They sported a designer label on the back pocket, though she couldn't have said whether that particular designer was the "in" one at the moment. She'd chosen a short-sleeved floral cotton T-shirt and white leather Keds to complete the casual outfit, pulling the top section of her hair into a barrette and allowing the remainder to fall loose to her shoulders. Studying her reflection, she decided wryly that she looked about twelve years old. And she was having severe doubts about leaving this house without changing into something more tailored and respectable.

Downstairs, the doorbell chimed discreetly. Michelle wiped suddenly damp palms on the legs of her jeans and reminded herself that Tony was doing a job for her—but that he had become a friend, in a way. After all, he was the son of a friend of her father's. At least until this search for her siblings was completed, she had no intention of allowing it to go further than that. She was feeling too vulnerable, too unsettled just now. Too susceptible to a brilliant smile and warm masculine charm.

"So watch your step, Trent," she told the denim-clad figure in the mirror. And then she turned on one sneaker and headed downstairs, settling her face into the polite social smile she reserved for employees and casual acquaintances.

Hands in the pockets of his faded jeans, Tony waited impatiently in the antique-filled parlor to which the ever-efficient Betty had directed him. Frowning at the expensive accoutrements surrounding him, he wondered what it would have been like to grow up amidst so much luxury, waited on hand and foot by loyal servants. Having been taught from an early age by his liberated, career-minded mother to make his own bed, iron his own shirts and cook his own meals when necessary, Tony couldn't picture himself in Michelle's place.

Not that he didn't appreciate the nice things around him now. Tony had a healthy respect for money and the luxuries it could provide—he'd just never considered it the primary ingredient for happiness.

Just as well, he thought with a grimace, remembering the current shape of his bank account. Admittedly, the new large-screen TV he'd recently purchased had left a major dent in his finances. But watching the basketball play-offs on fifty-two inches of viewing screen had made the investment seem worth it at the time.

A sound from the doorway made him turn to find Michelle watching him silently. She was wearing jeans, he noted immediately—and, boy, did they look good on her! How he'd love for his hands to mold her hips as caressingly as that soft denim did. But her expression…

He almost shook his head in exasperation at the cool smile she gave him. She might as well have been wearing a sign warning him to keep his distance. Whatever progress he'd made on their date last night had apparently dwindled during a night of second thoughts.

Which only meant, of course, that he was even more determined to regain lost ground.

Without giving warning of his intentions, he took two steps toward her and drew her into his arms for a fervent kiss of greeting. "You look great," he said when he drew back, pretending he didn't notice the startled reproval in her expression. "Ready to go?"

The soft hollow of her throat was exposed by the scooped neck of her flowered T-shirt, her rapid pulse clearly visible there—evidence of her reaction to the kiss. Had Tony not been trained to be so observant, he might have accepted at face value her brisk nod and detached tone. "Yes," she said evenly. "Where are we going?"

She was good, he'd grant her that. Indulging himself with one last, quick look at that telltale throbbing in her throat, he took her arm. "How does a picnic sound?"

"It's a lovely day for one," she commented, her arm stiff in his loose grasp. "Very warm for this early in June."

"Yes, it is, isn't it?" His smile mocked her formality, but he didn't push, knowing she still had a long way to go before she learned to trust him the way she should. After all, he counseled himself, she still hardly knew him. Something he intended to remedy as quickly and as thoroughly as possible during this day together.

It amused Tony that Michelle settled into his Jeep as gracefully as though she were sliding into a limousine, smoothing denim as carefully as she would silk. He told himself it was a good sign that she was behaving so formally—it meant he was making her nervous. Which beat the hell out of being ignored altogether, he decided, whistling between his teeth as he rounded the front of the Jeep and climbed beneath the wheel.

He lifted a friendly hand to the heavyset middle-aged man wielding hedge clippers on the bushes beside the massive front gates of the Trent estate, which Michelle had explained were usually kept open during the daytime, closed at night. The man glared back at him. "I think I'm making progress with Arthur," he commented. "He didn't shake the clippers at me today."

"Arthur doesn't trust strangers easily," Michelle replied.

"Then it seems he has a lot in common with his employer."

She shrugged delicately.

Tony cast her a thoughtful, sideways glance. "Will you tell me about him?"

She returned the look in question. "About Arthur? What do you want to know?"

"No, not Arthur. The guy who hurt you so badly. The one who made you so suspicious of my motives and my interest in you."

Her brows drew downward into a frown. "Oh. Him."

So there had been a "him." Tony had been taking a stab in the dark, half hoping he was wrong. His hands tightened on the wheel. "Who was he? When did it happen?"

She looked out the window beside her, concealing her expression from his searching looks. "He wasn't anyone important. Someone I met in my senior year of college. I was naive, he was smooth. I'd fallen for him before I realized how deeply attracted he was to my money. He didn't even bother to deny it when I finally confronted him about it—as though it amused him that I'd ever thought he'd want me for any other reason. I got over him easily enough, but I'm no longer naive. I suppose I owe him that one."

"What was his name?"

She looked at him then, obviously startled by his harsh tone. "Why?"

"So I can smash his teeth in if I'm ever lucky enough to run across him. I owe him one, myself. Because of that jerk, I've got to somehow convince you that I'm not mentally counting money every time I kiss you, that I don't see dollar signs every time I look at you. I've never had to defend myself against being a gigolo before. I can't say I much like it."

Michelle flushed. "I never said I thought you were a gigolo," she muttered.

"Isn't that what they call guys who court women for their money?"

"It may be," she retorted with renewed spirit. "But that hardly applies here, does it? It's not as if you're…courting me."

He lifted his left eyebrow. "Is that right?"

"You're doing a job for me. I'm paying you to find my brothers and sisters."

He swallowed a curse. "Right," he said coolly. "But that's all you're paying me for, got that? After hours, I'm on my own time. Which means I hope you like hamburgers and pizza, lady, because my budget doesn't often run to chateau briand. *Capisce?*"

To his surprise, she giggled. "You can cool the Italian temper," she said with more genuine emotion than she'd shown since he'd picked her up. "I happen to like hamburgers and pizza just fine."

He didn't quite know what he'd said that had set her at ease, but suddenly she was talking as easily as she had during their date the night before, her smile the real one now, not the fake social expression he'd grown to dislike so intensely. "I don't see a picnic basket," she said, looking over her seat to the back of the vehicle.

Tony was glad he'd spent an hour that morning cleaning the debris out of his Jeep and vacuuming the formerly grubby flooring. "I didn't bring a picnic basket."

"Are we stopping for takeout?"

"No."

Michelle waited a moment, then sighed gustily. "Picnics generally include food," she informed him. "You did say we're going on a picnic?"

"A barbecue, actually. It's at my cousin Paul's house. He and his wife, Teresa, have invited us over for a cookout and softball game with some mutual friends."

"We're going to someone's home?" Michelle repeated. He watched as she plucked discontentedly at her jeans. "I should have worn something nicer."

"Sweetheart, it's a barbecue, not high tea. You look fine." She looked sexy enough to stop traffic, of course, but he didn't see any need to elaborate at the moment.

"I don't remember meeting your cousin Paul last night. Was he there?"

"No, he and Teresa had other plans and couldn't come to the play. They sent Dominic a good-luck telegram before the opening. He got a kick out of it."

"Just how many cousins do you have?"

He grimaced. "Mom's side or Dad's?"

"Combined."

"Heaven only knows. They're spread out from New York to California, not counting the distant relatives still in Italy. Dad's got seven brothers and sisters and they've all got kids—Paul's a D'Alessandro, by the way—and Mom's one of five girls, no brothers. We have a major reunion on one side or the other every two or three years, usually here in Dallas since it's sort of halfway for those at opposite sides of the country. Grandfather D'Alessandro was the one who first settled here—he had some vague dreams of being a cowboy like the ones he'd seen in the American movies when he was a kid in Italy."

"And was he a cowboy?"

"Nah. Ended up selling shoes in a department store. But he never missed the rodeo when he had the chance to go to one. He took me a few times before he died when I was ten."

Michelle looked dazed by the size of his family. "How do you keep up with everyone?"

"The aunts keep us well-informed," he answered in amusement at her expression. "The family hotline's probably been busy all morning about you after last night."

"About me?" she repeated weakly.

He laughed. "Yeah. Aunt Marie probably called Aunt Angelina first thing." His voice changed to an exaggeratedly accented falsetto. *"You should meet the lovely girl Antonio brought to Dominic's play. So pretty. So refined. Much too good for our Tony, of course, but maybe she won't notice until*

*after they're married. He's almost thirty-three, you know.
We'd almost given up on him finding a nice girl."*

Though she'd flushed brightly at his mention of marriage,
Michelle laughed. "Surely, it's not that bad."

"Are you kidding? It's almost a sin in my family to be
single past thirty. Especially for the girls. My cousin Anne-
Marie's going on twenty-eight now and still not married.
The aunts are spending a small fortune lighting candles for
her. Her mother, Aunt Lucia, has stopped nagging her to find
an attractive young doctor and started hinting about any
single guy with a pulse."

"So how did you get away with being single so long?"
Michelle asked, twisting in her seat to look at him. "You've
never been married, have you?"

"No. I was involved with someone for a while, but
whatever we had wasn't strong enough to weather some
personal problems I had a couple of years ago," he replied,
wincing as he thought of how badly he'd treated Janice just
before they'd broken up.

Angry and embittered with his job at the police department, caught in the midst of a political turmoil, he'd taken
his frustration out on her with impatience and emotional
neglect. Had there really been anything serious between
them, she'd have knocked some sense into him and
demanded that he treat her with the respect she'd deserved.
Instead, she'd decided he wasn't worth the effort and she left
him just before he left the department. He'd been too caught
up in his own problems to miss her for long. "She's married
now, I hear."

"Does that bother you?" Michelle asked just a little too
casually.

"No. It's been over a long time."

"Oh."

Unable to read her tone, he glanced over at her. She was

looking out the windshield at the road ahead, her hands clasped loosely in her lap, her beautiful face composed, her thoughts hidden from him. Disliking the distance between them, he reached out and took her left hand in his right one, raising it to his lips. He noted in satisfaction that her breath caught audibly when he flicked the tip of his tongue across her knuckles.

All in all, the day was going quite well so far.

Michelle liked Teresa D'Alessandro from the moment she met her. Dark-haired, dark-eyed, seven months pregnant and unabashedly pleased with her condition, Teresa welcomed Michelle to her modest countryside home, warmly claiming that Tony was one of her favorites of her husband's many cousins. "I'm from a small family myself," she confided to Michelle soon after they'd arrived. "I have one brother and he has only one child. The first few times Paul took me to D'Alessandro gatherings, I was overwhelmed."

"I know the feeling," Michelle confided, glancing around the large, acre-and-a-half backyard of Teresa's home, where some twenty people—more than half of them claiming kinship with Tony—laughed and teased and talked familiarly. Tony was right in the middle of the group, his voice raised as he defended himself against a good-natured gibe of some sort, talking rapidly and with a great deal of gesturing. Again, Michelle noted that he suddenly became very Italian when surrounded by his family. Definitely fascinating.

"I was raised as an only child," she explained to Teresa, trying to keep her mind on their conversation rather than Tony, "and I have only one cousin, whom I don't know very well. I'm not accustomed to such large, extended families, either."

Teresa nodded, then smiled. "You get used to it quickly," she assured her. "The D'Alessandros are a very loving, very supportive clan. Any one of them would be here in a minute if we needed them. It's a nice feeling, you know?"

"I'm sure it is," Michelle replied, though she wondered if Teresa thought her relationship with Tony was more serious than it actually was. Teresa talked as though Michelle, too, would be a part of that clan soon. Michelle considered explaining that this was only her second real date with Tony, that it was much too soon to be thinking seriously about a relationship with him, but then she decided to just let it go.

Some things only got more complicated with explanations.

Breaking away from the group of men with whom he'd been talking, Tony rejoined Michelle and Teresa. "How are you at softball, Michelle? We're about to get up a game, now that everyone's here."

"I've never played," she admitted.

Both Teresa and Tony stared at her in surprise, to her discomfort. "You've never played softball?" Tony repeated. "Ever?"

"No. Never. But don't let that hold you back," she added hastily. "I'll enjoy watching while you play. I'll talk to Teresa."

"No way. It's long past time you had your first lesson," Tony argued flatly. "You're on my team."

Michelle shook her head. "I'm not going to make a fool of myself in front of your friends. Really, Tony, I'd rather just watch."

"Tough," he answered succinctly, his grin daring her to continue arguing with him. "You're playing. We need you," he added. "The teams will be uneven if you don't play, since Teresa's sidelined by her delicate condition."

"Delicate condition, my behind," his cousin-by-marriage retorted indelicately. "If Paul weren't so concerned about the ball hitting me in the stomach or something, I'd show you I could run circles around you—even in my 'delicate' condition!"

Tony laughed and gave Teresa a quick, affectionate hug. "You probably could, but let's not try it today, okay? Paul's nervous enough about his first baby."

"No kidding. The man has all but wrapped me in cotton during the past couple of months," Teresa muttered in exasperation. "He's even fetching his own beers these days."

"That *is* a miracle," Tony agreed solemnly, his eyes smiling.

"You guys aren't talking about me again?" Paul, a few years younger than Tony but very similar in appearance, joined them on the brick patio, tossing a softball from hand to hand. He smiled at his wife, his love for her apparent in his softened expression. "You're not trying to make me look bad in front of Tony's girlfriend, are you, *amore?*"

Teresa slid her arm around her husband's waist. "Of course not, Paul. You usually do that so well yourself."

Paul growled. Michelle laughed, even though she wasn't quite sure how she felt about being referred to as Tony's girlfriend. Not that it seemed to bother Tony. He slid an arm around her waist. "Hey, Paul, Michelle's never played softball before. I think we need to do something about that, don't you?"

"Definitely," Paul agreed enthusiastically. "Hey, everybody! Tony's girlfriend's a rookie! We've gotta show her how this game is played, right?"

Michelle's face flamed as the others immediately and teasingly agreed. Tony laughed, earning himself a poke in the side from her elbow. He grunted in response, but leaned over to brush his lips across her cheek. "Trust me, *cara.* This is going to be fun."

Chapter Seven

"'Trust me. This is going to be fun.' Hmmph!"

Tony laughed at Michelle's disgruntled mutter, glancing across the console to where she sat in the passenger seat of his Jeep, glaring at the streak of dirt that decorated her clothing from neck to knees. "I never said you had to try to slide home during your first game, Michelle. That was your idea, remember?"

"I wasn't trying to slide home," she retorted. "You know perfectly well that I tripped over my shoelace."

He grinned. "Oh, is that what happened? To be honest, I thought you were starting the slide a little early. After all, you'd just left third base."

"And I would have made my first run if I hadn't tripped," she sighed, remembering her disappointment in being tagged out. She'd been so pleased just to hit the ball and make it to third base. When the next batter had connected, she'd started to run without noticing that her shoelace had come untied during the game.

Full of Grace

"Don't worry about it, darlin'. You did fine for your first game. After all, our team won."

She made a wry face. "I really don't think that had much to do with my being one of the team members. But your friends were very patient with me."

"They liked you."

She was warmed by his words, pleased that she'd managed to fit in again with his family and friends. Though she still tended to be rather shy in such large, exuberant crowds, she'd enjoyed herself immensely today. She couldn't help comparing his casual family gatherings to her own past family functions, when a few impeccably dressed relatives gathered for dinner at one home or another. Food served on the finest china and crystal, self-conscious manners, conversations centered around politics or topical events, polite air kisses as opposed to the smacking embraces Tony's family exchanged.

"Do all your family members speak Italian?" she asked to distract herself from more comparisons. She'd been highly entertained by the occasional good-natured squabble during the exuberant ball game, conducted in amusing combinations of Italian and English slang. And again, Tony had slipped into emphatic Italian as easily as his cousins, to Michelle's secret delight.

Tony shrugged. "It's habit to fall into it when we get together. Besides, it pleases the aunts that we haven't completely lost touch with our heritage—or with each other."

Michelle thought fleetingly of her six brothers and sisters—would they have had barbecues and played softball together had they not been separated so young? If she were to contact them now, was there any chance that her children, if she ever had any, would grow up knowing and enjoying their cousins as much as Tony seemed to enjoy his?

"What are you thinking?" Tony asked suddenly, making her look up to find him watching her as he drove.

She pushed a strand of hair away from her face. "I was thinking about my brothers and sisters," she admitted. "Wondering if it's too late to ever feel like a family with them now. Whether they'd even be interested in trying. Maybe they have all the family they need now."

"And maybe they're as lonely as you are, wishing they had brothers and sisters to share their lives with," Tony returned. "Maybe Layla would give anything for a sister to talk to and go shopping with and whatever else sisters do together. Let me call her, Michelle. Let me set up a meeting."

Her throat tightened, her fingers clenching in her lap. "I don't—"

"Say yes."

She took a deep breath. "All right. Set it up."

The Jeep swerved fractionally before Tony straightened it. "Was that a yes?"

"Yes. You'll still go with me to meet her?"

"Of course. If you want me to."

"I want you to."

"Then I will." He waited a moment, then gave her a smile. "Was that really so hard?"

Her own smile felt shaky. "Yes."

He reached over the console to touch her cheek. "I don't think you'll regret it, Michelle. This first meeting was inevitable from the time you hired me to find them."

"I know," she admitted. "But I'm still nervous about it."

"I understand."

Oddly enough, she believed him. It was as if Tony understood exactly what she was feeling, in a way no one else had before him. Not even her adopted parents. Or Taylor. She'd never felt quite as close to anyone else as she did to Tony at this moment. And that realization was as terrifying as it was exhilarating.

Tony walked Michelle to her door, but refused her polite

invitation to go in for a drink. "I'd better go. I'm sure you'd like to clean up and get some rest."

"A hot bath does sound nice," she agreed with a smile. "I think I used muscles this afternoon I didn't know I had."

"You'll feel them tomorrow." He rested one hand on the doorjamb beside her head, looming over her as she turned to face him. "I'll give you a call tomorrow, okay? We'll set up the meeting with your sister."

"All right. If she's agreeable, of course."

"Something tells me she will be." He lowered his head to kiss her, his hand still propped above her head. "Did you have a good time today?" he asked when he released her mouth, his head still bent to hers.

"Very much," she murmured, aware that his lips hovered only an inch or so from her own, wanting him to kiss her again. When he didn't immediately move to do so, she took the initiative and lifted her mouth to his.

Tony didn't let her effort go unrewarded. Crowding her against the door, he wrapped both arms around her and kissed her until her ears buzzed, her knees quivered, her heart raced frantically in her chest.

He groaned when he pulled away. "If I'm going to stick by my resolution to give you plenty of time to learn to trust me, I'd better go now. You could tempt a saint, Michelle Trent, and I'm no saint."

No, Tony was no saint. He was a devil in tight denim—and Michelle had never been more tempted in her life. But she sighed and nodded, putting another prudent three inches between them as she stepped sideways and reached for the doorknob. "Goodnight, Tony."

"Buonanotte, tesoro." He touched her cheek as he turned to leave. She opened her door and stepped into the house, uncertain whether her heart had melted in response to his seductive murmur or the incredible tenderness in that fleeting

touch of his fingers against her face. She covered her still-warm cheek with her hand as she headed dreamily up the stairs to her bedroom.

Michelle was awakened early Sunday morning by the ringing of the telephone on her nightstand. Still half-asleep, she groped for it, knocking a paperback book to the the floor before successfully finding the phone. Pushing her hair out of her eyes, she croaked, "Hello?"

"Did I wake you?"

"Tony?" She rubbed her eyes and sat up.

He laughed, the low, rich sound making her shiver. "I'm sorry. You must have really been out of it."

"I'm awake now. Good morning."

"Buon giorno, carina."

"I like it when you do that," Michelle murmured, lingering remnants of sleep making her forget to guard what she said to him.

"When I do what?"

"When you speak Italian. Very sexy."

His voice deepened. "In that case, I'll have to speak to you in Italian more often."

"Oh, I think you're quite dangerous enough as you are," she said, coming fully awake with the unmistakable meaning in his tone. "Why did you call?"

"I just wanted to start my day out with the sound of your voice. I couldn't think of a nicer way to wake up."

"Oh." She blushed, though she knew it was silly.

"We'll have to do this more personally sometime."

"Tony…"

He laughed again at her mutter of reproval. "Sorry, *tesoro*. It's not fair of me to take advantage of you when you're still in bed. Um—let me rephrase that. It's not fair of me to take advantage of you when you're in your bed and I'm still in mine."

"You're incorrigible."

"So I've been told. How are those muscles you were complaining about after the ball game? Sore this morning?"

Michelle stretched lazily. "No. They're fine."

"Good. I'll make a ball player of you yet."

"Is that right?"

"Mmm. It was fun, wasn't it?"

She smiled, knowing her smile carried through her voice. "Yes. Very much so. Thank you for taking me."

"We'll have to do it again."

They talked for nearly an hour, chatting about nothing in particular, laughing frequently, until Tony reluctantly informed her that he had to go. He was having lunch with his parents and youngest brother that day and hadn't even showered yet, he explained. He promised Michelle he'd be in touch with her again very soon. She knew from his tone that he would follow through on that promise.

When her doorbell chimed Sunday afternoon, Michelle answered it, half expecting to find Tony on the other side, even though he hadn't said he'd come by. After talking to him that morning, she'd hung up the phone with a dreamy smile and a funny little buzz of excitement somewhere deep in the pit of her stomach. A buzz that hadn't quite gone away since.

She had never been courted quite so intriguingly—nor so successfully.

She hadn't at all expected to find her attorney on her doorstep.

"Carter!" she greeted him. "This is a surprise."

He stepped across the threshold, his distinguished face grave, his faded brown eyes focused intently on her face. In his early sixties, Carter Powell kept himself in good shape, only a hint of a paunch beneath his hand-tailored suit, his hair gray but still thick and stylishly groomed. "Hello, Michelle. I hope this isn't a bad time for you."

"No, of course not. Come into the den. Betty's not here this afternoon, but I'd be happy to make you some of the herbal tea you like."

"No, thanks. I can't stay long."

"You've been very busy the past week. I've tried to reach you."

"Yes, I know. I'm sorry I couldn't get back to you sooner. As you said, I've been busy."

Sitting across from the wing-back chair he'd selected, she dropped the polite chitchat. "You seem to have found the time to check up on me. Why did you call Tony D'Alessandro and ask him to drop my case, Carter? How did you find out that I'd hired him?"

"You know that I've always kept an eye on you, Michelle," Carter returned stiffly, lowering his gray brows in apparent offense at her tone. "I promised your father before he died that I would, and I have done so."

"You haven't answered my questions," she reminded him patiently. "What possible reason could you have for ordering Tony to call off the search for my siblings? And why would you do that without contacting me first?"

He sighed and patted his hair as though to make sure it was still neatly styled. "Perhaps I was out of line not to call you first," he admitted. "It has become such a habit to see to your best interests that I sometimes do so without considering whether you'd approve of my methods. But you have to understand, I was shocked when I found out that you'd embarked on this foolish, dangerous quest. I simply wanted to put an end to it as quickly and as painlessly as possible."

"Foolish? Dangerous?" Michelle shook her head in confusion. "I have no idea what you're talking about, Carter. I'm simply trying to locate the brothers and sisters I was separated from when I was a toddler."

"Michelle, you know nothing about these people, about the way they've turned out, how they've been raised. They're strangers, not family. What could you possibly have in common with them?"

"Genes, for one thing," she replied dryly.

He made an impatient gesture of dismissal. "An accident of birth. The important thing is that you've been raised as a Trent, given the responsibilities inherent with that name. Why would you want to risk being at the mercy of a bunch of strangers claiming a kinship you don't even remember?"

"I don't expect to be at anyone's mercy," Michelle answered calmly, though his words had renewed her own nervousness at the risks inherent in the quest she'd undertaken. "Tony is checking out my brothers and sisters very carefully. The one sister he's already located is a real-estate agent, married to an accountant, the mother of three young children. Very respectable, very safe, apparently."

"You've located one of your sisters?" Carter repeated sharply. "You've already been in contact with her?"

"No, not yet," Michelle replied. "Though I've authorized Tony to set up a meeting with her."

Carter shook his head. "I think you're making a grave mistake, Michelle. How do you know this woman won't expect you to help her put those kids through college?"

"Carter, you're overreacting. I have no intention of supporting any of my brothers and sisters or their families. I only want to meet them. Is that so hard for you to understand?"

"Yes, I'm afraid it is. You have friends, you have family. Why didn't you come to us if you felt something lacking in your life?"

Michelle wondered if Carter had been hurt that she hadn't consulted him before hiring Tony. After all, he had taken care of her for years. "My uncle and cousin live in California, Carter. I hardly know them. And as fond as I am of you, you have your own family, your own very busy life. This decision is already made, the search already started. You're just going to have to accept that. I promise you I'll be very careful. I'm not even going alone to meet my sister. Tony's going with me."

"Is that right? And what's in it for him?"

Michelle bristled at his tone. "Nothing's in it for him. He offered out of kindness when he sensed that I was nervous about the meeting."

"Yes, well, I assume you haven't been billed for his services as yet. I can assure you he isn't motivated entirely by the kindness of his heart. Private investigators don't make their money by offering free babysitting services to their clients."

"Babysitting services?" Michelle repeated slowly. She couldn't believe Carter was talking to her this way. He never had before. And then she realized that this was probably the first time she'd ever gone against his recommendations.

Something in her voice or her expression made Carter clear his throat and hold up a conciliatory hand. "Now, Michelle, I didn't mean to insult you. I simply meant that I think you should be wary of this man and his motives."

"I want you to leave Tony out of this," Michelle snapped. "Leave him alone, Carter. No more calls, no more interference. Is that clear?"

"There's no reason for you to take that tone, Michelle."

"Isn't there?" She stood. "If you'll excuse me, I have several things to do this afternoon. You know the way out, of course. If I have need for your legal services, I'll contact you."

Carter stood, shaking his head, looking unexpectedly amused. "If that didn't sound just like Harrison Trent when he was in a temper. You may have been adopted, but you are very much his daughter. He loved you very much, you know. It was important to him that I promised to watch out for you."

She couldn't help softening. "I know he loved me. I loved him, too," she murmured. "I miss him, and Mother. But I'm perfectly capable of looking out for myself."

"So I see. You've grown up on me, Michelle. It's very hard for me to realize that you're not the little pigtailed girl I used to ride on my knee."

Her temper cooling, Michelle reached out to the man she'd known all her life, touching her fingertips to his arm. "Thank you for being concerned about me, Carter. But trust me to know what's best for me. Believe me, I've learned the hard way about being too naive or trusting. I'll be careful."

"I hope so. By the way, Michelle, how did you find out about these siblings of yours?"

"Mother told me about them in a letter she left me. I found it in her things a few weeks after she died."

"Oh. That surprises me."

Michelle cocked her head thoughtfully. "You knew about them all along, didn't you?"

He hesitated only a moment before nodding. "Yes. From the beginning. And, to be honest, I agreed with your parents' decision not to tell you about them. I couldn't see that there was anything to be gained by doing so."

"Obviously my mother changed her mind."

Again, he nodded, his expression grave. "Yes. I hope she didn't make a mistake." He was almost to the door when he paused and looked back at her. "Michelle, will you do me one favor?"

"What is it?" she asked cautiously.

"Let me look over the final bill from this investigator before you pay it, just to make sure everything's legitimate.

Instruct him to itemize. And don't give him any money in advance without a fully detailed statement, all right?"

Thinking half-guiltily of the thousand dollars she'd already paid Tony in advance, Michelle shifted her weight. "I'm sure your concern is unnecessary, Carter, but if it makes you feel better, I'll have you examine the bill before I pay it. I'm convinced you'll find it quite reasonable."

"Yes, well, we'll see. It doesn't hurt to be cautious. After all, you've only known this man a few weeks." *And you've known me twenty-four years,* his eyes added, just a touch of hurt still visible in their depths.

"All right. Thanks for coming by, Carter. I'll talk to you soon."

Michelle waited until she'd heard the front door close behind him before sinking bonelessly back down in her chair. Carter had seemed so utterly convinced that she was making a mistake in contacting her long-separated family.

What if he was right? Hadn't she worried about that for weeks before hiring Tony to find them? Hadn't her concerns been the reason she'd hesitated about contacting Layla once she'd been located?

What if she was only setting herself up to be hurt again?

She chewed unconsciously on her knuckles as her thoughts turned to Carter's warnings about Tony. She desperately wanted to believe Tony's assurances that he was interested in her, not her money. But, as Carter had reminded her, she really hadn't known Tony very long. And he *was* being paid to help her find her brothers and sisters.

Hadn't she known from the beginning that it was unwise to let personal feelings interfere with a professional relationship?

"…so then we piled the guy's intestines onto a tray and reached in—"

"Joe, please!" Carla D'Alessandro protested faintly, looking rather green at her youngest son's gory description of a surgery he'd recently assisted with. "Must you go into such gruesome detail?"

"Oh, sorry, Mom," the handsome young man apologized with a smile. "I didn't mean to gross you out."

From a chair nearby in his parents' den, Tony snorted. "Yeah, right. Like everyone sits around talking about abdominal surgery. You're going to lose a lot of friends if you don't change this new habit of talking shop to civilians, Joe."

"Your brother's going to make a fine doctor," Vinnie put in sternly, looking up from the Sunday sports section he'd been scanning. "You should be proud of him, not criticizing him for his dedication to his work."

"So there," Joe muttered, giving his older brother a smug grin.

"Yeah, well, just keep your needles and scalpels away from this bod," Tony retorted, patting his flat stomach. "I only trust my organs to a guy who knows what he's doing."

"I'd be happy to recommend a good veterinarian," Joe tossed back.

"Now, boys," Carla interceded patiently before Tony could respond. "I'd hate to have to send you to separate corners at your ages."

Tony laughed, knowing that she'd probably do so if she deemed it necessary, even though he was almost thirty-three and Joe twenty-four. Knowing as well that he and Joe would probably go.

Still grinning at the thought of sitting in a corner at his age, muttering and sucking his thumb, he stood and stretched, then tucked his knit shirt back into the waistband of his faded jeans. "Mind if I use the phone in the kitchen? I need to make a call."

"Bet you're calling a girl, right? And we all know your

taste runs to blond, busty and borderline bright. So who's the bimbo-du-jour, Tony?"

Tony scowled at his grinning sibling. "Someday someone's going to rearrange that pretty face of yours, Giuseppe D'Alessandro. And it may just be me."

Joe cocked a dark eyebrow and made a show of flexing his biceps. *"Che cosa?"*

"You heard me, *fratello.*"

"Anytime you want to try it, brother."

"Boys," Carla murmured again, not bothering to look up from the business section of the Sunday newspaper.

Chuckling, Tony headed for the kitchen. Though he carried Michelle's number on a slip of paper in his wallet, it wasn't necessary for him to pull it out. The numbers came as easily to him as his own when he lifted the telephone receiver and pressed the buttons. He smiled in pleasure when Michelle, rather than her housekeeper, answered at the other end. "Hi."

"Tony."

Something about the way she said his name made his brows draw sharply downward. "Something wrong?"

"No, of course not. How are you?"

How are you? He frowned quizzically at the receiver, wondering why she'd gone back to the rather distant formality she'd projected the first few times they'd been together. "Okay," he answered cautiously. "I wanted to ask you if you're free tomorrow afternoon."

"I—uh—why?"

"How'd you like to go meet your sister?"

"You've talked to her?" Michelle asked quickly.

"Yeah." He smiled a little as he remembered the other woman's tearful excitement when he'd talked to her not long after he'd called Michelle earlier. "She's really looking forward to seeing you, Michelle. She sounded very nice."

"You're still going with me, aren't you?"

The faint trace of anxiety in the question pleased him. Whatever was bothering her today, at least she still wanted him with her for this meeting with her sister. She wouldn't want just anyone with her at such a personal time—would she? "Of course I am. Didn't I promise I would?"

"Thank you."

"No problem. So what are you doing this afternoon?" he asked casually, hoping for some clue to the sudden change in her behavior since their pleasant, hour-long call earlier that morning.

"Paperwork. And I just had a brief visit with my attorney."

Tony stiffened. "Powell?"

"Yes. He won't be bothering you again."

So that was it. Her longtime attorney had been preying on her old insecurities. "What did he say about me?"

"He's simply concerned about me, Tony. I told you that from the beginning. He's worried that my brothers and sisters will try to take advantage of me, and that…" She stopped abruptly.

Tony had no trouble completing the sentence. "And that I'll take advantage of you."

"He's just overly cautious."

"Did he try to talk you into firing me?"

"Of course not. He knows I intend to make my own decisions. He simply asked to see your final bill before I pay it. Itemized, of course. I assured him that he wouldn't find any problems with it, but if it made him feel better, I'd let him look it over."

Fingers clenching the receiver, Tony swallowed his fury. It wouldn't exactly look good for him to throw a fit over Powell's request to see his bill, he reminded himself. Michelle would wonder if he *was* trying to hide something, when the truth was that Tony was angry that Carter had done so much damage to the fragile trust Tony had established with Michelle during the past two days.

It was all he could do to keep from blurting out that he had no intention of taking money for anything he did for her. Theirs had long since stopped being a professional relationship. She probably wasn't ready to acknowledge that, either.

"All right. When it comes time to bill you, I'll send an extra copy," he forced himself to say evenly.

"Thank you for understanding. And, again, I'm sorry Carter bothered you. He was only trying to protect me."

Was he? Pushing aside his lingering doubts about the attorney's motivation, Tony abruptly changed the subject back to the plans for the following day. "I'll pick you up tomorrow afternoon—say, one o'clock?"

"I have some things to do tomorrow morning," Michelle countered. "I'll pick you up at one at your office."

His scowl deepened at the subtle but unmistakable power play. Why was it so important that Michelle drive tomorrow? he wondered disgruntledly. "Fine," he muttered, deciding to go along with her. For now. Until he had a chance to remind her in person that she had no reason to be suspicious of him.

"I'll see you tomorrow, then."

"Right. 'Bye, Michelle." He couldn't help hanging up with more force than he'd intended.

"Damn," he grumbled, slamming his fist on the kitchen countertop.

"Problems?"

Tony looked up to find his father watching quizzically from the doorway. "Where are Mom and Joe?"

"Your mother is helping Joe pack to go back to Houston," Vinnie replied dryly, rummaging in the refrigerator. "Sure hope that boy finds an old-fashioned sort of girl to marry. Your mother has him badly spoiled. Want a beer?"

"Yeah. Thanks."

"So does this suddenly lousy mood of yours have any-thing to do with Michelle Trent?" Vinnie asked, handing Tony a cold bottle.

Tony sighed and twisted the top of the beer, taking a long swallow before answering. "Yeah," he said finally. "She's been talking to her attorney today. He's got her questioning everything from my integrity to my fee scale."

"He's a cautious man. We warned you of that."

"Michelle should know by now that I can be trusted not to take advantage of her."

"Tony, she's known you a few weeks. She's known Carter Powell nearly all her life. Don't be too hard on her."

With a resigned nod, Tony set his beer on the counter and stared glumly at it. "I guess I'm just discouraged that I've still got such a long way to go to gain her trust. I thought we'd made some progress. Thanks to Powell, it looks like we're back to the starting line."

"Is it really so important for you to have Michelle's un-conditional trust?" Vinnie asked quietly.

Tony looked at his father, trying to decide how to answer. Before he could form the words, Vinnie lifted one heavy eyebrow. "I see that it is," he said.

His face warming, Tony looked quickly away. "I'll admit I'm falling for her. Hard."

"After spending time with her again, I certainly understand why. But—be careful, Tony. She's been badly hurt. You can't rush her into trusting you before she's ready."

Tony thought of the old fear in Michelle's eyes when she'd talked of her kidnapping, the old pain when she'd mentioned the man who'd wanted her money more than her. Would it be so hard for her to believe that all Tony wanted was to make sure no one ever hurt her like that again?

"I won't rush her," he promised his father. He only hoped he'd be able to keep that pledge.

Chapter Eight

Expecting to go into Tony's office Monday afternoon, Michelle guided her car into a parking space at exactly one o'clock. But before she could even reach for the door handle, the passenger door opened and Tony leaned in. His black hair was attractively wind-tossed, his dark eyes gleaming. He wore a white shirt, a navy-and-burgundy floral tie, a sport coat and jeans. He was probably the most naturally sexy man Michelle had ever known.

"Hi. You really should keep those doors locked, you know. Some weirdo could climb right into the car with you."

"So I see," she replied, watching him slide in and reach for his seat belt. She hoped her casual tone hid the unexpected burst of excitement that rushed through her at seeing him again. "Perhaps I *should* be more careful."

"Smart aleck." He leaned across the console and kissed her lightly before she'd been aware of his intention. "You look especially nice today. Did you dress up for me or your sister?"

Resisting the impulse to touch the tip of her tongue to her tingling lips, she cleared her throat and restarted the engine, suddenly pleased that she'd selected the becoming jewel-tone print dress. "For my sister, of course. Why should I go to this much trouble for you?"

"More insults, *cara?*" He sounded absurdly pained.

Biting her lip against a sudden grin, she nodded. "I told you it just seems to come naturally around you."

"I'll have to see what I can do about that."

But he didn't sound particularly disturbed, Michelle noted, turning a quick look at him as she guided the car out of his parking lot. In fact, he sounded quite pleased with himself about something. "You know where we're going, I assume?"

"Of course. Your sister gave me very clear directions."

"You wrote them down?" Michelle asked pointedly, looking at his empty hands.

He tapped one forefinger to his temple. "I assure you they're in a safe place."

She gave him a skeptical look. "I hope you mean they're pinned to the inside of your jacket."

He laughed. "You don't give an inch, do you, darlin'? Just drive toward Fort Worth and I'll let you know when to turn."

More relaxed than she'd been since Tony had called to tell her a meeting with Layla had been arranged, Michelle obligingly headed west. Did he know how nervous she'd been when she'd dressed that morning? How her stomach had clenched into knots at the thought of meeting this sister she didn't know? How close she'd come to calling the whole thing off?

"I talked to Bob O'Brien this morning—one of my operatives," Tony added in explanation. "He's got a lead on your sister Lindsay."

"He's found her?" Michelle asked quickly, wondering if she were ready for another meeting so soon.

"No. But we have learned that she was adopted. We think we may even have found the adoptive family's name."

"You don't know where she is now?"

"No," Tony replied again. "Not yet. But there's a strong chance we'll find her with the leads we have now."

"When you do," Michelle said slowly, accepting his ability to achieve the results he promised, "I don't want her—or her family—contacted. Not yet. I don't want anyone pressuring her either for or against meeting me. And…I'd like to wait and see how this meeting with Layla goes before I decide whether to try to make contact with the others," she admitted.

"I understand." He twisted in his seat and draped an arm over the back, his hand dangling close to her shoulder. "Are you nervous?"

"Not as much as I was earlier," she confessed, slanting him a smile that felt just a bit shy. "I'm glad you're going with me."

His eyes darkened in satisfaction. "So am I, Michelle."

Michelle quickly turned her attention back to the road ahead. "Feel free to turn on the radio, if you like," she offered. "Or there are CDs in the console."

Obviously curious about her tastes in music, Tony opened the console and rummaged inside. "Interesting," he murmured a moment later.

She smiled. "Why?" Though, of course, she knew. Her music collection ran from Barry Manilow to Bob Seger, Prince to Garth Brooks, Rachmaninoff to Miles Davis, Barbra Streisand to Tanya Tucker. Tony wouldn't be the first to point out that it was an eclectic mix, to say the least, and one not generally expected of her.

"Rock, pop, jazz, country, classical, show tunes. About the only types missing are rap and opera."

"I have to draw the line somewhere. No offense to your Italian heritage, of course."

Chuckling, he selected a disc and slid it into the dash-mounted player. "So we have a taste for country-and-western music in common. I didn't expect that. You're just full of surprises, aren't you, *cara?*" His tone caressed her almost as effectively as a physical touch.

She swallowed hard and tried to answer coherently. "I've told you my parents tended to be overprotective when I was growing up. I spent a great deal of time alone with only my dolls and my stereo for company. I wasn't choosy about which stations I listened to, as long as the music was good."

"Bet your mother wouldn't have liked this at all," Tony guessed as Garth Brooks belted into "Much Too Young (To Feel This Damn Old)."

Michelle laughed. "You're right. She hated country. And rock. And pop and jazz. She gave only borderline approval to show tunes, telling me I should enrich my mind with the classics rather than wasting time with popular garbage."

Though he looked as though he would have liked to comment, Tony only nodded. They rode for a few minutes without speaking, yet they weren't uncomfortable. And then Tony asked, "Do you ever think about having a family of your own? You talk about being lonely as a child, but don't you still feel that way sometimes?"

"Sometimes," Michelle admitted cautiously. "I have my work now, of course. And my friends."

"You like kids?"

"I wouldn't spend four or five days a month rocking babies if I didn't," she pointed out.

"Want any of your own?"

She cleared her throat. "Eventually. Being adopted, I used to worry about any medical conditions I might pass along to my children. Now I suppose I'll find out whatever I need to know from the records you've uncovered."

He shrugged. "I didn't see anything in your family history to be concerned about."

"How about my father's alcoholism?" Michelle asked with a bitterness she couldn't quite conceal.

"Lots of people have alcoholism in their families," he reminded her. "There is evidence that the tendency is inherited, but it's not inevitable. After all, you don't seem to have a problem with it."

"No. But I'd be very careful to make sure my children knew there was a possibility they'd inherited the tendency," she added. "My adoptive parents weren't heavy drinkers and they always stressed moderation to me. I would do the same for my children."

"Children? Plural?"

She nodded. "I know from experience how it feels to be an only child."

He touched her cheek, his finger tracing a line down her jaw. "I think you turned out just fine."

She shifted in her seat. "Thanks."

He dropped his hand, though it still rested so close to her shoulder she could almost feel its warmth. "I like big families myself. I've always wanted a houseful of kids, once I found the right woman to have them with."

Since the conversation was becoming a little uncomfortable, and more than a little too personal, Michelle swiftly redirected it. "You'd mentioned that you were planning to spend Sunday with your parents. Did you have a nice visit?"

"Yeah. Joe drove up from Houston, so the only one missing was Mike. He couldn't get away from Austin. The rest of us had a good time, though. Joe's a real clown."

"He's doing well in medical school?"

"Oh, yeah. He's the genius of the family," Tony admitted with unmistakable affection. "Going to make one hell of a good doctor."

"You sound quite proud of him."

"I am. Just don't tell him I said so."

Which, of course, sounded as though Tony assumed Michelle would be meeting his brother. She was having enough trouble dealing with the possibility of getting to know her own family, much less more of Tony's, she thought edgily.

In automatic reaction to the opening piano notes of one of her all-time favorite songs, Michelle turned up the volume.

"'The Dance,'" Tony murmured, indicating he'd recognized the tune, as well. "I like this one."

"It's one of my favorites. Such beautiful accompaniment."

"Nice lyrics, too."

They were quiet during the poignant ballad of a man who looks back at his life and wonders if he would have missed the pleasure to avoid the pain had he been able to predict the future. The song had appealed to Michelle from the first time she'd heard it, had been the reason she'd purchased this CD.

In a country western twang, the singer concluded that life is better left to chance. If anyone's life had been subject to the whims of chance, Michelle figured hers had. The trip she was making now was certainly a prime example.

Michelle parked her car and then sat with her hands clenched around the steering wheel, staring at the house in front of her. Though modest, it was nice, brick-and-vinyl siding with window shutters and flowering bushes just bursting into bloom along the front. The lawn was neatly trimmed. A tricycle and a small red wagon sat under a greening pecan tree at one side. The place was a far cry from Michelle's own impressive mansion, but looked very much like a home.

And inside, her sister waited to see her again for the first time in twenty-four years.

"I'm not sure this was such a good idea," she heard herself saying, her voice sounding rather small.

Tony's left hand covered her white-knuckled right one on the steering wheel. "Everything's going to be fine, Michelle," he assured her quietly. "I don't think you're going to regret doing this."

She took a deep breath and looked at him. "You'll help keep the conversation going if I can't think of anything to say?"

He smiled and leaned over to kiss her lightly. "You bet I will. But if you run out of things to say, you can always start insulting me again. As you've pointed out more than once, that comes naturally for you."

He began to draw back, only to stop in surprise when Michelle reached out to clutch his lapel. "Tony," she whispered, drawing him closer. "Thank you for being here with me."

"Anytime, darlin'," he murmured, and kissed her again, more lingeringly this time.

Rather flustered, Michelle made Tony wait until she'd quickly repaired her lipstick before they stepped out of the car. He took her hand as they started up the walk. She didn't resist.

Tony pressed the doorbell. The door opened before the chimes had faded away inside. Staring at the woman who'd opened the door, Michelle had the oddest feeling that she was looking at an image of herself in ten years or so. She hadn't really expected to see so many resemblances between herself and Layla Walker Samples.

Eyes the same color blue as her own filled with tears as Layla raised one hand to her throat in a show of emotion. "Shelley?"

"Michelle," she corrected, her right hand tightening in Tony's left. "And this is Tony D'Alessandro."

"We spoke on the phone yesterday," Tony said, offering his free hand. "It's nice to meet you, Mrs. Samples."

"Please call me Layla. Come in."

Surreptitiously studying her sister as she released Tony's hand and stepped into the entryway, Michelle noted the strands of gray in thirty-four-year-old Layla's glossy brown hair, the faint lines at the corners of her eyes. Had their mother looked like this when she died? Would the other sister and brothers share so many resemblances to herself?

A comfortably rounded, sandy-haired man who looked to be in his late thirties stood when the quiet threesome entered the inexpensively decorated living room. "This is my husband, Kevin," Layla explained, stepping close to Kevin's side. "The children are playing at the neighbors' house this afternoon, so we can talk."

Michelle glanced at a large studio portrait on one wall. Two dark-haired, blue-eyed little girls sat primly beside a grinning little boy who looked very much like Kevin. "They're very attractive children," she offered tentatively.

Layla smiled and waved Tony and Michelle to a plain blue sofa. "Thank you. Could I get you something to drink? Iced tea? Coffee?"

"No, thank you," Michelle answered, clasping her hands in her lap.

"None for me, either, thanks," Tony seconded. He glanced from Michelle to Layla and said, "It's surprising how much the two of you look alike. Was there a strong resemblance between all the children of your family, Layla?"

Grateful for the opening, Layla nodded and reached for a faded old photograph on the table beside her chair. "This is the only thing I have left from that time," she explained, passing the photograph to Tony. "My foster mother helped me keep up with it, because she thought it was important for me to remember my family."

Michelle hesitated a moment before looking at the photo. When she did, she spotted herself immediately, looking much as she had in the early portraits Alicia had commissioned of her. She was sitting on the lap of a girl of perhaps ten—Layla, obviously. Studying the picture more closely, she saw that Layla still looked much as she had then. An older boy stood behind Layla. His hair was darker, his features less delicate, but the resemblances were there, particularly in the blue eyes. Jared, she thought.

At Layla's left sat a chubby boy of seven or eight, his broad grin showing several missing teeth, his pug nose freckled, his hair lighter than his older brother's, though his eyes were as blue. That would be Miles. Michelle's throat tightened at the thought that she'd never had the chance to know the boy with the mischievous grin. And now she never would.

At the far right of the photograph stood two eerily iden- tical boys in matching clothing, their dark brown hair combed exactly the same, sticking up with the same cowlick in front, their blue eyes fixed on the camera. Only their expressions were different—one serious, the other smiling. Which was Joey, Michelle wondered, and which Bobby?

Finally she made herself look at the woman in the center of the photo, the woman she'd avoided looking at until now. Her mother. A woman who looked older than her late twenties, whose thin face was already lined with weariness, her pale eyes mirroring the hard times she'd known. A baby, no more than eight weeks old, slept in her arms, tiny features indistinguishable from most babies of that age. Michelle realized that Hazel had already been widowed by that time and would live only a few months after the portrait had been taken.

"She won a family portrait in a draw held at the local su- permarket," Layla explained softly when Michelle had been silent for several long minutes. "She was hoping for the grand prize of a month's worth of groceries. God knows we could have used them more—but I've treasured this photograph."

Michelle looked up at her sister. "You remember her."

"Yes."

"What was she like?"

Layla hesitated, then moved her hands in a frustrated, vulnerable gesture. "Tired," she said. "Sad. Quiet. But sometimes she laughed at something we said and she looked so different. I always thought she was beautiful when she laughed. And sometimes she sang when she rocked one of you little ones to sleep. She had a lovely voice."

Michelle gazed at the photo and tried to remember being rocked in those arms, longed for just a vague echo of a pleasant voice singing her to sleep. But when she thought of a mother's voice comforting her in the night, it was Alicia Culverton Trent she remembered. Feeling uncomfortable, as though she should apologize to the woman in the photograph, she turned her attention back to her sister. "I didn't know I had brothers and sisters until my adopted mother died a few months ago."

"I know. Tony explained when he called me." Layla tucked a strand of hair behind her ear and sighed. "Maybe it was better for you that way. Better that you didn't remember. It was a long time before I could stop missing my brothers and sisters and get on with my own life."

"Layla wanted so much to find you again," Kevin interceded when his wife's voice broke. "It was my idea for her to register with the service that helps reunite families separated by adoption. We hadn't been married very long and we couldn't really afford to hire someone to search for everyone. And Layla was always afraid to intrude on her brothers' and sisters' lives, worried that they wouldn't want her to show up and remind them of those hard times."

"We don't know if the others will feel that way," Michelle said, glancing again at the photograph. "But we have some leads on them. I think I want to contact them, see if they want to meet us again."

"Oh, I wish you would," Layla murmured wistfully. "I'd love to see them again. Jared and the twins and the baby. If only Miles…" She pressed her lips together and shook her head. "It's so hard to believe he's dead. I still think of him as the happy little boy he was before."

Tony had broken the news to Layla during the call. Michelle was relieved that he'd taken care of that already. Obviously, Layla had taken the news hard. "You haven't mentioned our father," she made herself say, though she wasn't sure she wanted to know. "What was he like?"

Layla made a face. "That's not an easy question to answer. He was gone so much, none of us really knew him. When he was home, he sat in a chair and drank and our mother waited on him hand and foot. I don't know where he went when he left and I don't know why he kept coming back. I don't know why they kept having children together when they could hardly feed the older ones. To be honest, our lives didn't change that much after he died, though Mama got even quieter than she had been before."

"You must have been the one to take care of the rest of us when she worked or when she was sick," Michelle guessed.

Layla smiled a little and nodded. "Jared and I did. Sometimes I felt like the mother of the family. I usually cooked the meals and did the laundry, gave you your baths and tucked you in bed. Maybe that's why I've been so comfortable with my own children—the routine was very familiar to me. I enjoy it."

She smiled at her husband, and Michelle watched with a faint touch of envy. This was obviously a close, happy home, she thought, unable to avoid comparing it to her own big, empty house. She pushed the unbecoming thought away and urged her sister to tell her more about their time together.

Layla cooperated happily, entertaining them with anecdotes of childhood pranks and adventures, obviously remembering those years quite clearly. "You loved jelly sandwiches, Michelle. You asked for them all the time. It was one of the few things we could afford. Do you remember?"

Michelle shook her head, unable to remember ever having a jelly sandwich. Certainly not after she'd gone to live with the Trents. She decided that, though the times must have been hard for the troubled Walker family, there had still been love in the home, and the laughter of children. It was nice to know.

As he'd promised, Tony participated in the conversation, making it easier for Michelle to join in as well. And Kevin was a pleasant, good-natured man with a contagious smile who seemed pleased to meet his new sister-in-law. It was glaringly obvious that he also adored his wife.

"…and there you were, sitting in a rocking chair with the baby in your lap, singing 'Old Mcdonald' while she stared up at you with her big blue eyes," Layla was saying, laughing and shaking her head in remembered exasperation.

Realizing her attention had strayed, Michelle listened more closely.

"I just about had a heart attack. You were so little yourself and you could have hurt her, but you were being so careful. I put her back in her crib and fussed at you for taking her out and you looked up at me and said, 'You was busy, Layla.'"

Startled, Michelle frowned. "But Mother—my adopted mother told me I was a late talker. I was nearly three when she got me and she said I didn't say more than a word or two for the next six months. She even took me to doctors who said there was nothing wrong with me and that I'd talk when I was ready—which, obviously, I did."

Layla looked puzzled. "But you talked early, Shel—um, Michelle. By fourteen months you were already using complete sentences. We all thought you were a genius or something."

"Obviously your silence was in reaction to the changes in your life," Tony suggested.

"I suppose so," Michelle murmured, unable to remember how long it had taken her to adjust to her new home, her new parents. It seemed now as though they'd always been in her life.

Perhaps that was the reason she couldn't remember anything else of her natural family, she mused. Maybe it had been easier for a confused child to pretend she'd never known a home other than the one she'd ended up in, never known a mother other than the one who read her to sleep every night until she was eleven and pronounced herself too old for the ritual.

A burst of noise from the back door to the house made all four adults look around just as three children scampered into the room. "We're home, Mama," the oldest child, Dawne, announced unnecessarily.

"So I see." Gathering two-year-old Brittany into her lap, Layla looked at Michelle. "These are my children. Dawne, Keith and Brittany."

Finding herself fascinated by Brittany, who could have doubled for herself at the same age, Michelle smiled. "Hello."

"Who are you?" Keith asked bluntly.

"I'm your Aunt Michelle," she answered, turning her smile toward Layla. "Your mother's sister."

Her eyes going bright, Layla returned the smile, her own notably unsteady.

The visit lasted another forty-five minutes before Michelle realized it was time to go. By that time, she was thoroughly charmed by her nieces and nephew, as well as her newly found sister and brother-in-law. She decided to thank Tony as soon as they were alone for persuading her to allow him to arrange this meeting.

"We really must be going," she said, rising from the couch. Tony did the same.

Pushing herself out of her chair, Layla shook her head in admiration. "You're still full of grace," she murmured.

At Michelle's look of puzzled inquiry, she smiled. "You wouldn't remember, of course. It was a family joke that each child was born on a different day of the week. Mama used to recite that poem to us. You know, 'Monday's child is fair of face.' I was born on Monday. Jared loved to make me blush by teasing me about that line."

"Michelle must have been Tuesday's child," Tony commented, smiling at her. "I noted how gracefully and socially correct she was the first time I met her."

Michelle made a face at him, then frowned at her sister. "How could we each have been born on different days of the week? What about the twins?"

Layla laughed. "Joey was born at 11:55 Thursday night, Bobby ten minutes later, which made it 12:05 Friday morning. Jared was Saturday's child, and Lindsay was born on a Sunday. Miles was Wednesday's child."

She paused for a moment, her expression reflective. "The lines of the poem seemed to fit everyone but him. He was supposed to be full of woe, yet he was the happiest, best-natured little boy…"

She sighed and shook her head as if shaking off echoes of the past. "I'm so glad you found me, Michelle. I hope we see each other again soon. I haven't stopped missing you—any of you—for twenty-four years."

Michelle took a tentative step toward Layla. "I've always wanted a sister," she said. "I don't intend to lose you now that I've found you."

With a small, choked sound, Layla threw her arms around her, hugging tightly. Michelle returned the hug, her eyes burning, her heart full. She didn't know how it had happened, exactly, but this felt so right, so natural. She had found her sister.

She drew back with a shaky smile. "You'll bring your family to my house for dinner soon? I'll call you."

"We'll be there," Layla promised. She turned to Tony and held out her hand. "I don't know how to thank you."

He took her hand in his larger one. "I'm afraid I can't take credit for finding you. Thanks to your foresight in registering with the service, it only took a couple of telephone calls."

"But you're still looking for the others," Layla argued, "and I think you'll find them. It means so much to me to think that I may get to see them all again after so many years. If Kevin and I can help with the expenses…"

"I'm taking care of that," Michelle interrupted firmly, noting Tony's suddenly uncomfortable expression. "I began this search, remember? The expense isn't a problem."

Kevin took Michelle's hand. "You've made my wife very happy today."

She smiled at him. "I'll see you again soon, Kevin."

"Of course. We're family."

The children all politely bade Michelle and Tony goodbye. Michelle's throat tightened when little Brittany raised her chubby face for a kiss and said, "'Bye, Aunt 'Chelle."

"'Bye, sweetheart." Michelle looked half-pleadingly toward Tony, needing to get away quickly before she burst into tears. He reacted as though he'd read her mind, courteously bringing the visit to an end and escorting Michelle to the car.

"Want me to drive?" he offered as they approached the Lexus.

She nodded and handed him the keys. "Thank you."

Michelle was grateful that Tony didn't press her to speak during the first fifteen minutes of the drive. She needed that time to steady her emotions, to come to terms with the changes that had occurred in her life with this reunion with her sister.

When she did begin to talk, it was about Layla and Kevin and the children, how nice they all seemed, how happy and comfortable their home was, how glad she was to have found them. Tony listened with a satisfied smile, adding little more to the conversation than an occasional agreement.

Over halfway home, Michelle suddenly realized how much she'd been talking. She stopped with a self-conscious laugh, wondering at her uncharacteristic lapse of manners. "I'm sorry. You must be ready for me to be quiet."

"Not at all," he countered without hesitation. "I'm glad you're so happy about the meeting. I'd hoped it would turn out this way."

She nodded. "It could have been so different, of course. We could have been stiff and uncomfortable with each other, found nothing in common, no reason to continue seeing each other."

"True." Tony made a show of wiping his brow with one hand. "You have no idea how I worried about that, since I was the one who nagged you into meeting them."

She laughed and shook her head. "I don't think you lost any sleep over it."

"Don't bet on it," he replied, sounding suddenly so serious that she wondered if he really *had* been as worried as he claimed. Before she could ask, he changed the subject.

Though she went along with the ploy willingly enough, Michelle found herself wondering wistfully if she was really becoming more than just another case to Tony. Or did he give such personal, supportive service to all his clients?

The problem was that he had become so much more than

just a business associate to her. He'd become a friend. Maybe more than a friend. And she wasn't at all sure how she felt about that.

Chapter Nine

Tony's emotions were uncomfortably mixed as he listened to Michelle talk about her sister. He was pleased, of course, that the meeting had gone so well. He hadn't entirely been joking when he'd said he'd felt a certain responsibility for the outcome. And he was happy that she and Layla seemed to have the potential to build a lasting, mutually supportive relationship. He never wanted Michelle to be lonely again.

The simple, rather painful, decidedly unbecoming truth was that he found himself jealous of the ease with which Layla seemed to have earned Michelle's affection—and even her trust. With Layla, Michelle had eased down the barriers she kept between herself and everyone else, barriers Tony had only managed to peek through once or twice.

He wanted those barriers between them gone.

Turning into the parking lot of his office, he parked Michelle's Lexus beside his Jeep. "Have dinner with me?" he asked without preface.

She blinked at his abrupt tone, then nodded. "Why don't you follow me home. My housekeeper's baking fish for dinner. There's always enough for a guest."

"Sounds good. I've got a few things to wrap up here first. How about if I see you in—say, an hour and a half?"

"Fine." She reached for her door handle. "Thank you again for going with me, Tony."

He opened the driver's door and climbed out from behind the wheel, not bothering to respond to her repeated gratitude. He waited beside the open door until Michelle rounded the car and joined him there. "Drive carefully."

"I wasn't planning on hot-rodding home."

"See that you don't." He tilted her chin up and pressed a kiss to her smile.

"You seem to be making a habit of that," Michelle observed when he released her.

He studied her expression, unable to quite read her eyes. "Was that a complaint?"

She thought about it a moment, then smiled and shook her head. "No."

"Good. See you later."

All in all, he decided, his hands in the pockets of his jeans as he watched her drive away, the day hadn't gone badly after all.

And it wasn't over yet.

Tony was due to arrive for dinner in less than half an hour when Michelle's phone rang. Thinking it might be him, she snatched up the receiver of the den extension. "Hello."

"Hi. It's Taylor."

"Oh, hi. How was the date Friday night?"

"The food was fine. The conversation definitely needed spice. How was yours?"

"We had fun. But I really want to tell you about what I did today."

"Yeah? What'd you do?"

Michelle smiled, anticipating Taylor's excitement. "I met my sister Layla. As well as her husband and her children."

"You met her? Really?"

"Yes. Tony went with me. We spent several hours visiting with them. Oh, Taylor, you'd really like her. She's so nice— and I look so much like her! It was sort of strange at first to look at her and see so much of myself, but after a while it felt really comfortable. And the children are adorable, and so well-behaved. I'm having them over for dinner soon. I'd love for you to meet them."

"Michelle, this is wonderful!"

"I know. I never would have imagined it would turn out like this. I was so worried. Tony kept trying to reassure me it would work out, but I didn't really believe him until I met Layla."

"Layla must have been thrilled to see you again. She remembered you, of course."

It wasn't a question, but Michelle answered it anyway. "Yes. Clearly. She said she would have recognized me right away because of the family resemblances. She told me so many stories about when we were little, in such detail that I almost felt as though I remembered the incidents she described. Tony told me on the way home that he could tell Layla had never really gotten over being separated from her brothers and sisters and that he thinks it meant the world to her for us to contact her."

"So how did it really feel, Michelle? Was it like making a new friend? Or did you really feel as though you were talking to your sister?"

"Both," Michelle answered after a moment of thought. "At first, she was a nice stranger. But the more she talked about the games I enjoyed as a baby and the toys I played with and the foods I liked, the more I felt a real connection, you know? Tony said—"

Suddenly aware of just how often she'd brought Tony's name into the conversation, Michelle paused self-consciously. "Well, um…"

"Sounds like things between you and Tony are getting very interesting."

Michelle cleared her throat. "I like him," she admitted. "He's been very good to me since I hired him, gone beyond my expectations of finding my family and reuniting me with them."

"You don't really think he's done that just because he's dedicated to his career, do you?"

"What do you mean?"

Taylor laughed. "Michelle, I saw the way the man looked at you Friday. He's definitely besotted. And you were looking back at him exactly the same way."

"Oh, I—"

"Don't try to deny it. I think it's great. You deserve a relationship with a nice guy for a change."

"It's a little too soon to be talking about a relationship," Michelle said cautiously. "Tony and I have only known each other a few weeks."

"But you're giving him a chance, right?"

"We're…seeing each other," Michelle admitted, thinking of his imminent arrival for dinner.

As though in response to her thoughts, the doorbell rang. She knew Betty would let Tony in, but she didn't want him to catch her talking about him with her friend. "I'd better go, Taylor. Betty has dinner ready."

"You wouldn't be evading the issue, would you?" Taylor demanded with mock severity.

"No, of course not. Why don't we have lunch one day this week and we'll talk more."

"I'd love to, but I can't. That's why I called—to tell you I'll be out of town for a couple of weeks. A client wants some fashion shots taken on Galveston Island, and they're flying models in from New York. It's going to be a big job—a little more notice would have been nice. But the client's always supposed to be right, you know. At least, that's what they keep telling me."

"Then we'll get together when you get back in town," Michelle said, smiling at Tony as he strolled into the room. He'd changed, she noticed, into a dark green cotton shirt and charcoal-gray slacks. He looked slim, dark and entirely too handsome for her peace of mind. It was suddenly difficult to keep her mind on her conversation with Taylor.

"I'll call you when I get back," Taylor was saying. "I'd love to hear more about your sister. I can't wait to meet her."

Michelle's pulse shot into overtime when Tony took her hand and raised it to his mouth, his lips warm and soft as they brushed her knuckles. "Oh, yes, of course, Taylor," she said quickly, giving Tony a repressive frown. "We'll talk when you get back."

"Right. Guess I'd better let you go. Sounds like you've got something better to do than talk on the phone."

Michelle tried to speak normally, though it wasn't easy since Tony had turned his attention to her neck. "I—uh—what do you mean?" she asked just as he kissed the soft, vulnerable spot beneath her left ear. Her breath caught in her throat.

Taylor's laugh was embarrassingly knowing. Michelle had the strangest feeling that her friend knew her neck was being nibbled as they spoke. "Tell Tony I said hi," Taylor murmured. "Have fun, Michelle."

Michelle's cheeks were flaming when she hung up. "I can't believe you did that!" she accused Tony, rounding on him.

He stepped back, looking absurdly innocent. "Did what?"

"Kissed me—like that—right in front of Taylor!"

He laughed, his dark eyes sparkling devilishly. "Michelle, you were on the phone. I really doubt that she could tell I was kissing you."

"Trust me. She knew," Michelle muttered.

"And would it matter if she did?" he asked, his tone casual but his eyes suddenly watchful. "Does it embarrass you to have your friends think you're getting involved with a lowly P.I.?"

"What an awful thing to say," she scolded him, planting her fists on her hips. "As though there's anything wrong with what you do for a living. Or as if I'd be snobby enough to care."

His smile deepened. "Then why are we wasting time arguing? How about giving me a real kiss?"

"How about if you…"

Her decidedly indelicate suggestion was muffled into the depths of his mouth. Michelle resisted for all of thirty seconds. And then she put her arms around his neck and kissed him back exactly the way she'd been wanting to all day.

In immediate reaction, Tony tightened his arms around her, pulling her as close to him as physically possible. He deepened the kiss, his tongue slipping between her eagerly parted lips. Michelle closed her eyes and tilted her head back to give him better access.

It seemed like a very long time before Tony lifted his head to give both of them a much needed-chance to breathe. Michelle wondered dazedly if her eyes looked as glazed as his did.

"Whoa," he murmured, his voice husky, his smile shaky. "Now, *that* was a kiss!"

Her arms were still around his neck. Suddenly self-conscious, Michelle dropped them and stepped back. To hide their unsteadiness, she pushed her hands into the pockets of the pleated white slacks she'd worn with a teal silk blouse. "I'm sure Betty has dinner ready. Are you hungry?" she asked, trying to sound somewhat normal. Knowing she failed miserably.

"Honey, I'm ravenous," he answered deeply. It was clearly obvious that he wasn't talking about food.

Her blush deepening, Michelle cleared her throat. "Behave," she ordered him, somewhat desperately.

He laughed. "Yes, ma'am. Maybe we'd better eat. Before I get—um—distracted again."

Betty served dinner with her usual efficiency, coming in frequently to check on them and refill their drink glasses, occasionally giving Michelle a look to signify approval of her guest. "How about dessert?" Betty asked Tony after noticing that his Sevres dinner plate had been cleaned of the baked fish served in her own delicate sauce. "I've made a cheesecake with a mixed fruit topping."

"Sounds good. Thank you." Tony took a sip of the excellent white wine served in Waterford crystal, then smiled across the table at Michelle as Betty hurried away for the desserts. "Do all your guests get such luxurious treatment?"

She met his eyes over the low flowers-and-candles centerpiece artfully arranged on an octagonal beveled mirror. "They do when Betty likes them."

"Then I'm glad I passed the test," he murmured, glancing around at the antique cherry furniture and heavy crystal chandelier. "It wouldn't be hard to get used to this."

Following his gaze, she tried to see the dining room through the eyes of someone who hadn't grown up in the house. She supposed it was quite elegant. But to her it was home, for as far back as she could remember.

Thinking of Layla's much more modest surroundings, she wondered how her sister would feel the first time she saw Michelle's home. She hoped it wouldn't intimidate her. "I really would like to have Layla and Kevin over for dinner soon. Do you think they'd be comfortable here?"

Tony shrugged. "I don't know why not. You and Betty have certainly made me feel welcome tonight." His smile reminded her of the kisses they'd shared before dinner.

Michelle was relieved when Betty entered with their desserts, promising to bring in coffee when they were ready. Not that Michelle had much appetite left. Though normally she would have thoroughly enjoyed the excellent cheesecake, tonight she was all too aware of Tony sitting across the table.

Studying him from beneath her eyelashes, she watched the candlelight dance in his black hair, admired the ripple of muscles beneath his dark shirt when he reached for his wineglass. His firm, beautifully molded lips closed around a bite of the creamy dessert and she had to swallow a low moan as she instinctively imagined those lips on her skin. It wasn't at all hard to imagine herself in bed with him, his dark head bent to her breasts, his tanned, callused hands caressing her body. In fact, at the moment it was very hard to think of anything else.

Tony glanced up to find her watching him. Whatever he saw in her eyes made him stop eating. Very slowly, he set his fork on his plate. Michelle looked quickly down at her own barely touched dessert, though she knew it was too late to hide her reactions to him.

It had never been so difficult before to conceal her feelings. She'd learned early in life to don a protective social mask whenever it seemed prudent to do so. So why couldn't she keep that mask in place whenever she was around this man?

"Michelle?" His voice glided over her like satin—smooth, seductive.

"What?" she whispered without looking up from her plate.

"Would Betty be terribly insulted if we didn't wait for her to serve coffee?"

"I'm—" She stopped to moisten her lips. "No, of course not."

"Then would you mind taking me on a tour of the rest of the house now? I'd really like to see your room," he added huskily.

Her eyelashes flew up, her gaze meeting his across the table. She didn't have to ask what he meant, or to wonder at his sudden interest in her home. It was quite clear that he wanted to make love with her. Now.

Her throat tightened in sudden panic. She knew that all she had to do was say no, or change the subject. Tony wouldn't push her into something she wasn't ready for. Sometime during the past few weeks, she'd learned to trust him that much.

The real reason she was suddenly trembling, suddenly petrified, wasn't because Tony had indicated he wanted to make love with her. The truth was that she wanted him, too— so badly she could almost taste it—and she simply didn't know what to do about it.

It had been so long since she'd been intimately involved with anyone, so long since she'd trusted any man enough to get that close to her. Was she really ready to take such a step with a man she'd known such a short time?

"Or," Tony said easily, forcing a smile as he picked his fork back up in response to her silence, "we could always finish dessert and have our coffee. Betty's certainly a good cook. How long did you say she'd been with you?"

"Long enough to understand if we don't wait around for coffee." Michelle laid her Irish linen napkin on the table and rose from her chair. For once in many years of caution, she was taking a risk, reaching out for what she wanted. And she wanted Tony—as she had never wanted anyone before.

Tony stood quickly and stepped toward her, rounding the end of the table, his eyes locked with hers. "Michelle?"

She smiled shakily and reached out her hand to him. "You said you wanted to see the rest of the house?"

"I'd like that," he murmured, his fingers closing tightly around hers.

She clung to that large, strong hand as she led him from the dining room.

Michelle's bedroom was large and romantically decorated. A marble-framed fireplace dominated one end; Victorian chintz chairs and a delicate lamp table formed a sitting area in front of it. A four-poster antique cherry bed was covered with a delicate hand-crocheted spread of antique lace and piled with throw pillows. A matching triple dresser held a silver hairbrush and mirror, photos of her parents in heavy silver frames, and five fragile hand-blown perfume bottles. A heavy, carved armoire hid a television and VCR. Impressionistic prints and paintings adorned the fabric-covered walls.

Michelle noticed that Tony barely glanced around him as they entered the lovely room. His attention was focused solely on her.

"You are so beautiful," he murmured, his hands coming up to frame her face. "I've wanted you since the first time I saw you."

She felt the unsteadiness in his hands and it pleased her to know that he wasn't taking this lightly. She wasn't, either. She covered his hands with her own, giving him a smile that felt decidedly shaky. "Tony."

He lowered his head, very slowly, his lips hovering for

just a moment before closing over hers. Michelle tilted her head back and closed her eyes, her entire concentration focused on the kiss. He didn't hurry the embrace, didn't immediately deepen it. Instead, he lingered. He savored. He nipped and nibbled until she clung to him bonelessly, aching for more.

His teeth closed lightly around her lower lip, and then his tongue soothed the nonexistent marks he'd left. He parted her lips with the very tip of his tongue, then drew back just as she opened to welcome him. Growing frustrated with his taunting, she pulled his mouth more firmly to hers and thrust her tongue between his lips, deepening the kiss herself.

Immediately, Tony's arms went around her, crushing her to him as he reclaimed control of the embrace. One hand at the back of her head, he held her still for a sensual invasion and exploration that left her on fire, burning for him as she'd never burned before. She strained against him, arms tight around his neck, breasts crushed against his chest, her hips pressed to his hardened thighs. She wanted—*needed*—him so desperately that she didn't think she'd survive if he stopped now.

She almost cried out in protest when he tore his mouth from hers and lifted his head to stare down at her, his dark eyes glittering, lean cheeks flushed with color. He held her away from him with his hands on her forearms, his hold gentle but firm. "Michelle," he muttered, and his voice was raw, gritty. "Are you sure? Really sure?"

"I want you, Tony," she murmured, touching his hot cheek with her cool, trembling fingers. "I want you so much."

Though he quivered at her words, he seemed to force himself to hold back. "It's been an emotional day for you. I don't want you to confuse your feelings. I don't want you to have any regrets tomorrow."

"You think I'm feeling grateful to you?" she asked in sudden comprehension.

"Yes," he answered bluntly. "And I want it to be more than that."

Touched, she wrapped her arms around his neck once more, rising on tiptoes to bring her face close to his. "It's not just gratitude, Tony," she murmured, letting her sincerity show in her eyes and color her voice. "I don't—I'm not sure what it is exactly, but it's not gratitude. I want you. I've wanted you almost from the beginning."

"Michelle." Visibly shaken, he drew her closer, burying his face in her hair. "Oh God, Michelle. I need you."

"Then why are you waiting?" she whispered.

He made a choked sound deep in his throat. And then he turned to sweep the crocheted spread from the bed, heedless of the throw pillows that tumbled to the floor around them. He lay Michelle on the snowy sheets as carefully as though she were made of fragile glass, and his tenderness brought tears to her eyes.

It must be important to him, she thought hopefully, drawing him down with her. Surely he couldn't look at her this way, touch her this deeply, if it were only casual sex to him.

Though Tony's fingers weren't steady, they were quick. Michelle's clothing seemed to fall from her body as he swept his hands over her, leaving her nude and shy in the light from the crystal bedside lamp. And then Tony shrugged out of his shirt and she forgot to be shy, too caught up in admiration of the perfect male body revealed to her.

His shoulders were broad, tanned, his chest firmly muscled beneath a sexy mat of curly black hair. His stomach was flat, his hips lean, and he slid his charcoal slacks down legs that were long and taut. He paused a moment before removing his black briefs, as though giving her one last chance to change her mind. When she only watched him in silence, he took a deep breath and removed that last barrier between them, revealing himself fully aroused and hungry for her.

Michelle held out her arms.

Gathering her into his arms, Tony buried his face in her neck, planting a string of moist, arousing kisses from the tender spot below her ear to the pulse pounding in the hollow of her throat. Only then did he turn his attention to her breasts, his hands shaping her almost reverently before he lowered his mouth to the pointed, exquisitely sensitive tips. Michelle caught her breath and arched mindlessly when he pulled one pebbled nipple firmly into his mouth, suckling with an intensity that drew an overwhelming hot response from deep inside her.

"Tony! Oh, Tony." She buried her fingers in his thick, wavy jet hair, her smooth legs tangling with his rougher ones.

"Michelle. *Cara*." Tony slid his hand between her thighs, filling his palm with the crisp curls there, his fingers stroking, inciting. He murmured approval and encouragement in an intriguing mixture of wickedly smooth Italian and sexy Texas drawl. Michelle thought there had never been a more fascinating combination.

And then his fingers moved again and she couldn't think at all.

By the time Tony slipped inside her, she was lost. She'd never known it could be like this. Never experienced such a heady combination of fire and tenderness, giving and sharing. She'd never dreamed that a man's hands could be so clever and so gentle, his lips so skillful and yet so vulnerable. She'd never heard her name murmured with such an entrancing combination of pleasure and pain, demand and request, exhilaration and entreaty.

He was everything she'd ever dreamed of in a lover,

sweeping her into passion with a reckless fever she'd never known, yet taking the time to make sure there would be no unwanted repercussions from this glorious interlude.

It wasn't gratitude and it wasn't just desire. It had to be something very close to love.

She cried out against his lips as an explosion of sensation accompanied the disquieting realization, and heard as if from a distance the harsh sound Tony made when he stiffened in her arms with his own release. Afterward, Michelle pushed away any lingering questions about her feelings for Tony, choosing, instead, to give in to the heavy lassitude creeping through her. She burrowed into his chest, his arms snugly around her as she closed her eyes and savored.

She thought she heard him murmur something in Italian as she slid into an exhausted, satiated sleep. She didn't even try to guess what he'd said. At the moment, it was enough to be held close to his warmth, his ragged breath ruffling the damp hair at her forehead, his lips just brushing her skin. His heart beating strongly, reassuringly against hers.

She didn't know how much time had passed when she was roused by Tony's movements as he tried to slip from the bed. "Where are you going?" she asked groggily, her hand tightening on his arm, holding him still.

"It's after midnight," he answered, tenderly brushing her hair away from her face. "You need your rest."

He'd turned off the bedside lamp, she noted sleepily, so that the only illumination came through the lace at the windows, making him look big and mysterious in the deep shadows. Her fingers tightened on his arm.

"Don't go. Stay with me," she murmured. For tonight, she couldn't bear the thought of being left alone in the bed where she'd spent so many lonely nights.

"If I stay," he said, and his voice was suddenly gruff, "you won't get much rest."

She slid her hand slowly up his arm to his shoulder. "Neither will you," she murmured, tugging his head down to hers.

He didn't complain.

Chapter Ten

Michelle's alarm went off at the usual time Tuesday morning. As usual, she groaned, turned off the alarm without opening her eyes and sank deeper into the pillows, stretching lazily beneath the covers. What *wasn't* usual was the solid, hairy leg her toes encountered on the other side of the bed.

Her eyes flew open. "Oh."

Propped on one elbow, the white sheet draped over his hip looking very bright against his tanned skin, Tony watched her with a smile in his dark eyes. "Do you always wake up so reluctantly?"

She smiled. "Yes. But I rarely have such a nice reason to open my eyes."

"Mmm." He bent to brush a kiss against her sleep-softened mouth. "That was a nice thing to say. Careful, Michelle, or you might get into the habit."

She gave in to an impulse to brush a heavy lock of hair

off his forehead. "I'm sure you'll give me a reason to insult you again before long. Maybe during breakfast."

"Was that an invitation?"

"You're so bright."

He chuckled. "It's already starting, I see. And I'd love to have breakfast with you, if you don't think your house-keeper's husband will be waiting downstairs with a shotgun."

"I think I'm old enough to have an overnight guest without answering to my staff," Michelle assured him.

"So they don't usually say anything?" The question was asked just a bit too casually.

She avoided his eyes by reaching for the quilted satin robe draped over a nearby vanity chair. "The situation has never come up. I'm not in the habit of having overnight guests here."

"I see." He sounded so smugly pleased with her answer that Michelle was tempted to throw something at him.

"I think I'll take a quick shower before breakfast," she announced, standing and belting herself into the robe, her back to the bed.

His arms went around her before she'd even realized he'd gotten up. "I think I'll join you," he murmured, his lips moving against the back of her neck.

Not surprisingly, it was the longest, most delightful shower Michelle could ever remember taking.

The breakfast table had been set for two. Limoges china, this time, with heavy crystal glassware holding pulpy orange juice. Fresh flowers at the center of the table gave off a welcoming scent, blending with the aroma of fresh-baked muffins in a linen-covered basket, and coffee kept hot in an insulated carafe. Michelle flushed lightly at the raised-eyebrow look Tony gave her.

"Do you always dine so elegantly in the morning?"

"No," she answered with a sigh. "Betty's obviously showing her approval again."

He grinned. "I like her, too."

The door to the kitchen opened and Betty bustled in with a tray, greeting them as naturally as though Tony were a regular at the breakfast table. "Good morning, Michelle. Mr. D'Alessandro."

"Why don't you call me Tony," he suggested, giving her one of his charming smiles as he took his seat.

Betty flushed like a schoolgirl, to Michelle's amusement. "Thank you, Mr. Tony. Help yourself to a muffin. I've got fresh fruit here and bacon, and there's homemade jam on the table if you want it with your muffins. Would you like me to cook you some eggs?"

Tony assured Betty that muffins, bacon and fruit were quite sufficient, explaining that he rarely ate eggs. "Cholesterol, you know."

"Cholesterol," Betty muttered. "Now you sound like Michelle, always counting calories and fats and cholesterol. And not an extra pound on either of you. How are you supposed to put in a good day's work without fueling up at breakfast?"

Dancing with suppressed laughter, Tony's eyes met Michelle's across the table. And held.

Neither of them noticed when Betty suddenly grew quiet and slipped from the room, her own smile tremulously pleased.

Some time later, Tony sighed with audible reluctance and set his drained coffee cup on the table. "I guess I'd better go. I'm expected to make an appearance at the office today."

"And I have a budget meeting at Trent Enterprises this afternoon," Michelle said, equally disinclined to bring the lovely morning to an end.

She walked Tony to the front door, where he kissed her

lingeringly. "I'll call you tonight," he murmured, when he finally raised his head and stepped back.

Michelle nodded, and then watched until he'd climbed into his Jeep and started out of the driveway before closing the door behind him. Leaning back against the door, she closed her eyes and allowed herself one long, delicious moment of reminiscing before beginning her usual weekday routines.

Tony D'Alessandro was irrevocably, unresistingly, head-over-heels in love. The utter certainty of the realization should have made him nervous, should have at least had him making an effort to protect himself from the vulnerability of the condition.

Instead, he found himself grinning like an idiot, leaning back in his chair with his hands behind his head, feet crossed on the desk as he replayed every moment he'd spent with Michelle Trent. From the day she'd walked into this very office and annoyed almost as much as she'd aroused him— to the night before, when she'd taken him into her bed and her body with such artless, honest passion that she'd all but brought him to his knees in overwhelming pleasure.

He loved her as he'd never loved another woman. And, at the moment, life looked very good indeed.

"You suppose he's been drugged?" a man's voice asked wryly from the open office doorway.

"Could be," a woman answered with exaggerated concern. "What else could make him look that smug and sappy?"

"Oh, I don't know," yet another man contributed, "he always looks kinda sappy. Don't think I've ever seen him smiling quite that contentedly before, though. Maybe he's brought us all in to fire us."

"Or cut our salaries," the first man mused. "Yeah, he'd like that. More money left for him, you know."

Tony sighed and dropped his arms and feet, straightening in his chair. "Would you jokers knock it off?" he complained to his employees, waving them into the office. "Glad to see you're all on time for our meeting, for a change."

"Tony, there's a call for you on line one," Bonnie announced, standing in the doorway her three co-workers had just vacated.

"Who is it, Bonnie?"

"Mike Halloran."

"Tell him I'll get back to him, will you? And hold all my calls during this meeting…" He hesitated, then added, "Unless it's Michelle. If she calls, put her through."

"Right." Bonnie closed the door to his office behind her as she went back to her own desk.

Tony glanced around to find his staff seated around his desk—and looking at him with identical curiosity. "Shut up," he growled, knowing the effort was futile even as he spoke.

"Michelle, huh?" It was blond, blue-eyed Chuck Johnson who spoke first, his wholesomely freckled face split with a grin. "Who was it told us never to get personally involved with the clients, hmm?"

"So that's why he looked like the post-canary cat when we came in," petite, red-haired, green-eyed Cassie Browning murmured. "Tony's in love, guys."

"Well, hell, I'm half in love with Michelle Trent myself, and all I've seen are her bank statements," Bob O'Brien drawled, his sharp eyes typically cynical.

Tony scowled. "Leave Michelle's money out of this."

Bob shrugged. "You're the one who told me to look into her finances, find out exactly what she's worth and how she's spending it. Just doing my job, boss."

"Yeah, well, keep your opinions to yourself from now on. All I need from you is the information I assigned you to get for me."

"Right." Not noticeably fazed by Tony's tone, Bob tossed a folder onto his disgruntled employer's desk. "There you go."

A second report landed on top of that one. "That's all I could find so far on Carter Powell," Chuck explained. "Other than the mistress he's got set up in Houston, he looks clean enough."

"Mistress?" Tony's left eyebrow rose. "He's married, isn't he?"

"Very. Wife's one of those big-time society types, involved with just about everything. A real asset to his career, if you know what I mean."

"Nothing unusual about a man keeping a piece on the side," Bob muttered. "And what's that got to do with Michelle Trent, anyway?"

"Probably nothing," Tony admitted. And then glanced back at Chuck. "But don't stop yet. Keep digging, okay? If there's anything else to know about Powell, I want it."

"What's this vendetta against the guy? What do you think we're going to find?" Chuck asked curiously.

"Call it a hunch," Tony answered more lightly than he felt. "You know how I hate getting threatening phone calls."

"Speaking of mistresses," Cassie interjected, pulling a manila envelope from a battered briefcase, "Martin Hurley definitely has one, as well. I've got a name, address and photos. *Now* can I work full-time on finding Jared Walker? I've got a lead on a Jared Walker in Tulsa who could be the one we want. And I've got a hunch…"

The three men groaned. Cassie scowled. "All right, I know how you feel about my hunches" she grumbled. "But this time, I'd put money on it. I think I'm close to finding Michelle's brother, Tony. If you'd just put me on the case full-time…"

Tony pulled thoughtfully at his lower lip, weighing the

next month's payroll against Michelle's anticipated pleasure in finding her oldest brother. "All right," he conceded finally. "I'll give you a couple months, Cassie. Full-time. But I'll need something more solid from you than a hunch."

"You'll have it, Tony. Soon." Smiling her satisfaction with the small victory, Cassie sat back in her chair.

Tony turned his attention to Bob. "Anything on the twins?"

Bob shook his head. "Nothing. It's like they no longer existed after they ran away at sixteen. For all we know, they didn't."

Tony didn't want to have to tell Michelle that she'd lost three brothers before she'd had the chance to know them. He frowned. "Stay with it, Bob."

"You're the boss."

Uncomfortably aware that Michelle wasn't his only client, Tony directed the meeting into other business matters, though he knew Michelle would never be far from his thoughts. For once, Bob, Cassie and Chuck cooperated easily, as if sensing that they'd teased him enough for the time being about his obvious feelings for Michelle Trent.

Tied up with other responsibilities, it was nearly an hour after his staff meeting ended before Tony had a chance to open the file Bob had brought him on Michelle's financial status. He took one look at the neatly typed report and choked on the sip of lukewarm coffee he'd just taken, the beverage splashing over the rim of his mug when he set it abruptly on the desk. He blinked, as though to clear his vision, and checked the numbers again.

Damn. He ran a hand through his hair, his eyes locked on the figures. He'd known Michelle was well-off, but her relatively simple lifestyle—even considering her luxurious home—had deceived him as to her true worth. Her father and grandfather had been shrewd businessmen and clever financial planners. Michelle could live quite comfortably for the rest of her life without ever touching the principal of her inheritance. No wonder she hadn't found it necessary to establish a career other than her charity work.

His hand was shaking a little when he closed the file. Her money shouldn't make a difference in the way he felt about her, he told himself—and it didn't, really. But still he felt the gap widen between them.

He wouldn't lose her, he thought with a scowl of determination. Whatever it took, he wouldn't lose her.

Michelle frowned down at a computer report on her desk. The figures in front of her represented the monthly profit-and-loss statement from Trent Enterprises, Dallas. It was simply a formality for her, as major stockholder, to look over the reports; the excellent management staff her father had assembled during his later years ran the corporation smoothly and with little interference from Michelle. Despite her efforts to stay involved with the corporation by monitoring reports and statements and seeing to the responsibilities her father had given her for charitable contributions, she knew she really made little impact on the company's operations.

For the past few years, she'd been content with her part, feeling safe and comfortable in her routines and reclusion. Content with her charity work, her few friends, her rare social functions. Now something was changing. For the first time in years, she found herself wanting more. And more than a little nervous at the thought of the risks inherent in reaching out.

She thought of the risk she'd taken two nights before making love with Tony. Not a physical risk, but an emotional one—opening herself to a heartache infinitely more devastating than Geoff had inflicted. The youthful, infatuated feelings she'd had for Geoff were nothing when compared to the way Tony made her feel. Would she survive this time if their new, so-fragile relationship ended disastrously?

Though they'd talked on the telephone, she hadn't seen Tony since he'd left after breakfast Tuesday morning. He'd explained that he had to work on a case Tuesday night and Michelle had been committed to a civic organization meeting Wednesday evening. Now it was early Thursday afternoon and she missed him so much she ached with it. Should she have allowed herself to get in this deep, this fast? Was she being a total fool?

The telephone at her elbow rang, interrupting her deep musing. Rather relieved at the distraction, she answered it.

"Michelle?"

"Yes?"

"Hi, it's Teresa D'Alessandro."

Pleasantly surprised, Michelle smiled. "Teresa! How nice to hear from you."

"I hope I'm not calling at a bad time. And I know it's short notice, but I have an invitation for you for tomorrow night."

"An invitation? To what?"

"Tomorrow's Tony's birthday. Did you know?"

"No," Michelle admitted. "He didn't mention it."

"That doesn't surprise me. Anyway, he'll be thirty-three, and Paul and his brothers have impulsively decided to give him a surprise party. We want you to help us out."

"A surprise birthday party?" Michelle repeated, intrigued.

"The party's going to be at Vittorio's—we've reserved the private dining room in the back. Maybe you could help us get Tony there without him suspecting anything?"

"I can try," Michelle replied. She'd never been involved in a surprise party before. It sounded like fun.

"Great. I knew you'd want to be involved," Teresa enthused. "We could tell how crazy Tony is about you. Everyone thinks you make a nice couple."

"Well, I—uh…" Michelle flushed deeply at the confirmation of Tony's warning that the family had probably already discussed their relationship and given opinions. She wasn't accustomed to having her private life conducted so openly—and certainly not used to the well-intentioned prying of a large, close, demonstrative extended family. And yet, rather than being annoyed, she found herself pleased that the D'Alessandro clan had approved of her.

Teresa laughed in understanding. "I know. I'm starting to sound like a real D'Alessandro, aren't I? Already sticking my nose in. But you might as well get used to it—and keep in mind that we're pretty good-natured about being told to mind our own business."

"What do you want me to do for the party?" Michelle asked, somewhat desperately redirecting the conversation.

"Just tell him you're in the mood to eat at Vittorio's—tell him you're craving Vittorio's linguine, or something—and have him there around eight o'clock."

"But Tony and I don't even have a date for tomorrow night," Michelle protested, feeling rather presumptuous at being involved in the scheme. "What if he has other plans?"

"He won't have other plans," Teresa said confidently.

Michelle hoped she was right. "All right. If I can, I'll have him there at eight. But be prepared with Plan B if this doesn't work out, okay?"

"I'll give you my phone number and Uncle Vinnie's, just in case," Teresa promised. "This is going to be so much fun. Paul and Joe and Mike have been wanting to do this forever. No one's ever managed to catch Tony by surprise before—but this time, we're getting him! We're hoping by getting it together so quickly there won't be time for anyone to spill the beans."

"I hope you're right. I think I'd like to see Tony caught by surprise," Michelle murmured, smiling in anticipation.

Michelle was still smiling several minutes after her conversation with Teresa ended, feeling as though she'd found another new friend. She thought of all the people who'd probably be at the birthday party, some of whom she'd already met, others she hadn't. She'd certainly found a lot of people she hadn't expected to when she'd hired Tony D'Alessandro to find her brothers and sisters, she thought rather dazedly.

A sudden chill ran through her as she pictured going back to a life of lonely days and even lonelier nights. And, again, she wondered if she'd made a mistake in trying to change her safe, insulated life.

Tony and Michelle had made plans to see a movie Thursday evening. Tony called twenty minutes before he was due to arrive and said he'd gotten tied up at work and was running late. "Would you mind if I pick you up on my way home and then stop by my place to change?" he asked.

"Of course not," Michelle assured him. "In fact, if you're too tired tonight, we can—"

"Don't even think it," he ordered gruffly. "I've been looking forward to seeing you all day. I'm showing signs of severe Michelle withdrawal."

"Guess we can't have that."

"I knew you'd understand. See you in a few minutes, honey."

Michelle was waiting by her front door when he arrived ten minutes later. He pulled her into his arms and kissed her as though it had been two years rather than two days since he'd last seen her.

"Whew!" he said, when he finally released her. "Just made it. Another few minutes without a kiss from you and I'd have been a goner."

Breathless and disheveled, Michelle laughed at his foolishness and reminded him that they were going to have to hurry if they were going to have time for him to change before the film began. Tony took her hand and hustled her to his Jeep, teasingly complaining about having had to wear a sport coat and tie for a professional meeting that day, making her laugh at his exaggerated distaste for the clothing.

She couldn't remember ever beginning a movie date with more eager anticipation.

"You look very nice this evening, by the way," Tony informed her when they were underway.

She smiled, automatically smoothing the taupe slacks she'd worn with a delicate short-sleeved eggshell silk sweater. "Thank you."

"Did I ever mention that you're the classiest lady I've ever dated?" he asked, still in the teasing tone he'd greeted her with.

"I'm not sure I know how to take that," she replied with wry humor.

He chuckled. "It's just that you wear your jeans like silk and the casual clothes you have on now like an evening gown. There's something about you that's—well, classy. Maybe it's because of that poem Layla was talking about—you know, full of grace. You're like that."

Michelle flushed and squirmed self-consciously in her seat. "You're embarrassing me."

"Sorry. It was meant to be a compliment."

"Then I'll thank you and change the subject. How was your day?"

"Busy," he admitted. "I've spent the past two years complaining because the business was building so slowly and now all of a sudden I've got more work than I can keep up with. I'm thinking about putting Cassie on full-time, maybe hiring another part-time apprentice."

"That's good, isn't it?"

"Oh, sure. As long as it doesn't interfere with seeing

you," he added, catching her hand to give it a squeeze. "I'm not one of those workaholics who puts the job ahead of personal relationships."

"That's nice to hear," she murmured, caught off guard.

He released her hand and guided the Jeep into the parking lot of a large apartment complex. "This is where I live."

Michelle looked around curiously. The complex was big and professionally landscaped, one of those sprawling, mid-priced areas planned for working-class singles and young marrieds. The parking lot was filled with economy cars and pickup trucks, the identical buildings marked with large metal numbers. Tony parked in front of building number twelve.

"I'm in apartment B," he explained, opening his door. "Come on in. It'll just take me a few minutes to change."

The apartment was furnished in "early department store"—boxy blue-and-green-plaid furniture, wood-veneer tables, brass-plated lamps. A pair of dark socks lay on the floor beside an empty Pepsi can, an untidy stack of newspapers scattered close by. The adjoining kitchen was similarly cluttered. Tony cleared his throat. "I—uh—wasn't expecting company when I left this morning."

She smiled. "Don't worry about it. It looks just the way I'd expected it to."

He frowned. "I'm not sure how to take that."

She gave him a little shove. "Go change. We'll be late for the movie."

"Yes, ma'am. Make yourself comfortable. I'll be right back. There are canned drinks in the fridge if you want one, but don't touch the fuzzy green things in the plastic bowls. I'd swear one of them snapped at me this morning."

Laughing, Michelle wrinkled her nose, hoping he was exaggerating. He disappeared into the apartment's only bedroom, leaving her to look around the living room, curious about the personal things he'd set around. A framed photo-graph of his parents, another of Vinnie and Carla surrounded by three teenaged boys. Michelle touched a finger to Tony's face in the photo, entranced by the glimpses of the man he'd become in the youth he'd been.

There was a sport trophy on the table with the photo-graphs. Football, she noted. Most Valuable Player. Judging from the year engraved into the metal, Tony would have been a senior in college when he'd earned the award. She hadn't even known he'd played football.

A built-from-a-kit bookshelf beside the couch overflowed with paperback novels. Michelle noted without surprise that Tony's taste ran to adventure and thrillers. On top of the bookshelf, two goldfish swam lazily in a bowl decorated with blue aquarium gravel and a plastic pirate skeleton.

Framed posters hung on the wall—colorful, tasteful, unusual. Michelle studied them with interest. They weren't inexpensive. Neither was the large-screen television, nor the state-of-the-art VCR and stereo system. Despite his off-the-rack clothing and department-store furniture, Tony didn't scrimp on things that were important to him, it seemed.

Two strong arms circled her from behind, startling her. "Okay," Tony said into her ear, "so the place won't ever be featured in one of those ritzy decorating magazines. But I've got big plans for moving up someday."

"Is that right?" she asked, turning in his arms to drape her own around his neck. He'd changed into soft-washed jeans and a short-sleeved, band-bottomed white pullover that con-trasted appealingly with his dark coloring. His ebony hair was slightly mussed, as if he'd hastily combed it with his fingers after donning his shirt. He looked wonderful.

"Tony," she whispered, lifting her face to his. "Kiss me."

He made a sound somewhere between a laugh and a groan

and pulled her closer. "It would be my pleasure," he murmured, just before his mouth covered hers.

The first touch of their lips seemed to enflame both of them. Tony pulled her roughly against him, crushing her breasts to his chest as he deepened the kiss, claiming her mouth with painstaking thoroughness. Michelle didn't protest his sudden intensity, but threw herself wholeheartedly into the embrace, as hungry as he for more.

His hands swept her body, stroking down her back, cupping her bottom, pulling her tightly against him. She felt his arousal, hard and swollen against her stomach, and she trembled in reaction. She buried her fingers in his hair, holding his mouth to hers. The kiss grew frenzied, feverish, his hands avid, demanding.

His groan came from deep in his chest, reverberating against her. "Michelle," he grated, his voice hardly recognizable, his lips still moving against hers. "How badly do you want to see that movie?"

She closed her eyes and took a quick breath when his mouth moved to her throat. "What movie?" she whispered.

The words had hardly left her before she found herself caught into his arms, being carried swiftly through the living room toward the open bedroom door.

Tony dropped her without ceremony onto the unmade bed, following without hesitation to cover her mouth and her body with his own. She gathered him into her arms, their legs tangling, her mouth moving hungrily beneath his lips. Their breathing had grown harsh, rapid, their movements frantic, clumsy with need. Michelle's formerly neatly coiled hair tumbled around her face, the pins lost, unnoticed. Her tailored clothing fell carelessly on the floor, followed immediately by Tony's jeans and pullover.

His mouth was hungry at her breasts, his fingers searching out the tender, swollen skin between her legs. He murmured broken words of desire, of need. Of love. Incapable of answering, Michelle held him more tightly, silently urging him on. And when he thrust inside her, she cried out, his name trembling on her lips, her love for him swelling inside her until she shuddered with a release more powerful, more devastating than anything that had come before it.

And still he drove her on, shifting, rocking, stroking until she exploded again, sobbing with the incredible beauty of it. This time he was with her, his lips at her ear, his voice raw and husky and tender. "Michelle. Oh, love."

And then he, too, was unable to speak coherently for several long, heart-stopping moments.

Chapter Eleven

Muffling their giddy laughter, Michelle and Tony slipped furtively through the front door of her house, well aware that the night was more than half over. "I've got to go," Tony murmured between kisses as they lingered in the entryway. "You need your rest."

"I'll miss you," she murmured, holding his face between her hands as she returned his kisses.

"I'll miss you, too, but I have an early meeting in the morning."

"It *is* morning," she reminded him, nibbling lazily at his lower lip.

"Mmm." He kissed her, then set her resolutely away. "Go to bed, Michelle."

She sighed. "If you insist."

"Sorry about missing the movie."

She smiled wickedly. "I'm not."

His eyes warmed, but he managed not to reach for her

again. "Let me make it up to you tomorrow—uh, tonight. We'll try again."

Michelle suddenly remembered the assignment his family had given her. She moistened her lips, hoping she didn't ruin their scheming. "Um—would you mind if we went back to your uncle's restaurant for dinner?" she asked, her fingers twisting behind her back. "I really enjoyed eating there last time."

Tony looked surprised, but pleased. "Of course. Uncle Vittorio will be delighted to see us. I'll call him and make sure he has a table ready for us."

"All right." She knew his uncle would handle his part much more smoothly than she had hers. "Good night, Tony."

He risked one last, quick kiss, then stepped back with a sigh. "Good night, Michelle. Sleep well."

"You, too."

He grimaced ruefully, one hand on the doorknob. "I'd sleep better if you were in my arms," he murmured. And then he laughed quietly. "Then again, maybe I wouldn't sleep at all."

"Maybe you wouldn't," she agreed huskily, her eyes locked with his.

He groaned and opened the door. "You could test the will-power of a monk, *tesoro.* Good night."

The door closed with an abrupt click behind him. Michelle automatically turned the lock, then brushed her tousled hair away from her face and walked dreamily toward the stairs, feeling very much like a woman in love.

Michelle checked her appearance in her purse compact, frowning as she patted a stray hair into place in her neat chignon. She touched the corner of her mouth with her little finger, making sure no lipstick was smudged there. She hoped the jewel-toned floral silk dress she wore was appropriate for the evening.

Tony sighed gustily from behind the steering wheel. "Michelle," he said, drumming his fingers on the wheel, "you look beautiful. *Bellisima. Perfetta. Now* can we go eat?"

Michelle flushed and put the compact away. She was really lousy at this surprise party bit, she thought ruefully. She'd been so nervous ever since Tony had picked her up that he'd asked twice if something was wrong.

"Sorry," she said, reaching for her door handle. "It's just that I know we'll be back on the family hotline tomorrow, and I want to look nice for the inspection."

Tony laughed, accepting her explanation as logical. "You're the one who wanted to eat at my uncle's restaurant tonight," he reminded her, climbing out of the Jeep.

"Yes, I was, wasn't I?" She took a deep breath as he caught her hand in his to escort her inside.

Tony seemed puzzled when his uncle immediately ushered them to the private dining room. Michelle was watching his face when what seemed to be hundreds of people called out in unison as she and Tony were led into the room. "*Buon compleanno,* Tony!"

His eyes wide, his face split with a grin, Tony looked to Michelle. She smiled back at him, pleased that he'd obviously been caught off guard. "Happy birthday, Tony."

"You were involved with this?" he demanded, sliding an arm around her shoulders as they were surrounded by laughing, chattering members of his family.

"I was just assigned to get you here," she answered.

"Which you did very well," Teresa complimented, giving Tony a hug, made awkward by her pregnancy. "Were you surprised, Tony?"

"Are you kidding? I can't believe you guys did this!"

"Hey, *old* man!" A dark-haired young man who had to be one of Tony's brothers punched Tony's arm. "Got you!"

"Yeah, you did. Now I owe you one, *fratello.* Joe, this is

Michelle Trent. Michelle, my youngest brother, Joe. He's not real bright, but we're fond of him, anyway."

Smiling, Michelle held out a hand to Joe. "Don't worry, I never believe anything he says. You're the doctor, aren't you?"

"I'm working on it," he replied, leaning over to kiss her cheek as naturally as if he'd known her for years. "Nice to meet you, Michelle. The family's been telling me nice things about you."

Michelle sighed faintly, then smiled and shook her head. Apparently she was starting to get used to the D'Alessandro clan. It didn't even particularly bother her anymore to know that she and Tony were the topic of so many family conversations.

Tony was practically engulfed by family members—his brother Michael, his parents and cousins—all of whom wished him a fond happy birthday, then turned to include Michelle in their midst. A tiny, very old woman was led to Tony by a solicitous relative whom she waved aside as she kissed the cheek Tony leaned over to offer her. She spoke to him in a rapid spate of Italian. He answered easily in the same language, his tone soft with affection. And then he glanced at Michelle.

"*Ah, scusami, Tia Luisa. Ti presento Michelle Trent.* Michelle, this is my father's aunt Luisa Sanducci. She keeps the rest of us in line."

"I only try," Luisa retorted, the words heavily accented but clear. Her faded dark eyes warm, she patted Tony's arm with a frail, spotted hand. "With this one, it is difficult. *Mio Dio,* he is such a handful!"

"*Io?*" Rounding his eyes in mock innocence, Tony placed a hand on his chest as though shocked at the accusation. "*Tia,* you wound me."

Luisa chuckled and shook her head, looking at Michelle with a wry smile. "You see? He is incorrigible."

Tony laughed and hugged the older woman. *"Ti amo, Tia Luisa."*

"Anch'io ti amo, caro. Now stop wasting your time with me and enjoy your party."

The next two hours passed in a blur of laughter and teasing and affection that was almost visible between the people in the room. On the rare occasions when she wasn't involved in pleasant conversation, Michelle watched in delight as the others traded good-natured insults and swapped bits of gossip. A heated political quarrel broke out between two of Tony's uncles, swiftly and efficiently interrupted by their wives. Minutes later, the same two uncles stood side by side and toasted Tony's birthday with yet another new bottle of wine.

As always, it fascinated Michelle to watch Tony with his family. He was so different with them, she mused, watching his hands fly as he gestured to illustrate something he was saying to his brothers. So Italian. So utterly irresistible. And she was rapidly beginning to love his close-knit family almost as much as she was beginning to love him.

As the hour grew later, Tony was led to a table holding a pile of gifts in brightly colored packages. While he opened them and exclaimed over each one, Michelle nervously pulled a square package out of her purse, her heart pounding. She'd spent all morning looking for the right present for Tony, and now she questioned her choice.

Was it too much? Should she have chosen something less expensive, less personal? Yet they were lovers, deeply involved in an affair that was growing more important to her with each passing day. Did that make her choice more appropriate?

Tony's eyes met hers and held as she handed him the package. The rest of the family watched avidly when he tore off the silver paper to reveal the jeweler's box beneath. Tony caught his breath at his first glimpse of the thin, elegant gold-and-steel watch.

"Michelle," he said, looking from the watch to her flushed, anxious face. "This is beautiful. Thank you."

"Well—you needed a new one," she reminded him, uncomfortably aware of the many eyes focused on them. "I hope you like it."

He'd already removed it from the box to discover the words engraved on the back. "Happy birthday, Tony." It was dated and signed only "Michelle." She had been tempted to have the jeweler add "With love," but knew it was much too soon for that.

"I love it," Tony murmured, taking her in his arms without regard for their audience. "Thank you, Michelle." And then he kissed her, lingeringly and thoroughly, to the obvious approval of his family.

Michelle was totally embarrassed when he released her, but couldn't manage to be annoyed with him. She felt oddly comfortable with Tony, with his friends and family. For the first time in so very long, she wasn't at all lonely, didn't feel like an outsider.

Even as the thought warmed her, an ominous frisson of warning slid down her spine.

You're getting in too deeply, Michelle. You're setting yourself up for heartbreak.

Pushing the depressingly pessimistic thought away, she resolved to enjoy every minute of the remainder of the party. She refused to let her cowardice ruin such a wonderful evening.

Tony's hand was in her hair, his body warm and heavy against hers. Limp and pleasantly exhausted from their love-making, Michelle lay beside him, her eyes closed, her slightly swollen lips curved into a contented smile. She felt his lips graze her temple and opened her eyes to look at him, savoring his smile. "I thought you'd fallen asleep."

"No." He dropped another tiny kiss on the end of her nose. "Just recuperating."

She ran a hand up his chest, fingers burrowing into the crisp dark hair. "I understand the stamina begins to go as you get on in years," she murmured commiseratingly. "You really should get some rest, poor dear."

Tony choked on a laugh and tugged her into his arms. "Witch," he muttered with mock ferocity. "Give me five more minutes and I'll show you stamina."

"Gee, I don't know, Tony. I wouldn't want you to strain yourself."

"You didn't have many spankings when you were growing up, did you, *cara?*"

"I was shamelessly spoiled."

"I noticed." He nuzzled her hair. "So how did you manage to turn out so perfectly, hmm?"

"Oh, I wouldn't say perfect."

"I would," he murmured, no longer teasing. His lips moved against hers. "Perfect." And then he kissed her, almost reverently, the beauty of the embrace bringing a lump to her throat.

They held each other in silence for several long moments after the kiss ended. And then Tony drew back, only to stop immediately when she winced at a sharp tug on her scalp.

"Oh, sorry, honey. My watchband caught a strand of your hair," he explained, gently extricating it. "There. Better?"

"Better," she assured him.

Supported on his right elbow, he lifted his left wrist to admire the watch again. "It's a beautiful watch, Michelle. Thank you again."

"You really like it?" she asked, oddly shy.

He smiled. "I really do. You shouldn't have been so extravagant, of course, but I appreciate the gesture."

Had she spent too much? Michelle wondered with a fresh surge of anxiety. Was Tony concerned about her motives in buying the watch?

"I wanted to get you something you needed," she explained seriously. "And I wanted to get a good watch that wouldn't wear out too quickly. It's not as if I couldn't afford it, Tony."

"Michelle, it's a great watch," he repeated firmly. "And I know you could afford it."

She searched his face gravely. "Does that bother you?"

He hesitated, then shrugged. "Sometimes," he admitted. "I worry that you'll think I'm like that jerk you knew before—the one who only wanted you for your money. That's not true this time."

Touched, she pressed her fingertips to his cheek. "I know you're not like Geoff, Tony. You're nothing like him."

"No." He caught her hand and pressed a hot kiss in her palm. "Oh, Michelle, I—"

He broke off whatever he'd intended to say to kiss her hand again. Unnerved by the sudden intensity of the moment, Michelle spoke quickly. "Tell me how to say 'Happy birthday' in Italian," she requested. *"Buon...?"*

"Buon compleanno," he completed, seemingly as relieved as she to ease the tension between them.

"Buon compleanno, Tony," she repeated carefully.

He smiled at her accent. *"Grazie."*

"Teach me something else."

His left eyebrow rose wickedly. "All right. Repeat after me. *Ti desidero.*"

"Ti des—Ti desi—" Michelle paused and looked at him in question. "What am I trying to say?"

He pulled her closer, his legs tangling with hers, and she realized that he'd grown hard and aroused again. He covered her breast with his hand, his slow kneading making her swell into his palm in heated response. "You're telling me you want me," he murmured, his lips moving against hers.

She wrapped her arms around his neck, arching into him. "Then let me say it my way," she whispered. "I want you, Tony. I want…"

His mouth covered hers, smothering the unnecessary words.

"Dad? Dad, are you out here?" Tony looked around his father's large backyard late Saturday afternoon, searching among the many flowers, bushes and vegetable plants with which Vinnie had amused himself since his retirement.

Vinnie's gray head popped up from behind an enormous azalea bush he'd been pruning. "Tony! I wasn't expecting to see you this afternoon. What's up?"

Holding two cans of beer he'd brought out from the kitchen, Tony waited until his father approached him, then motioned toward a couple of wrought-iron lawn chairs and matching table. "Got time to sit down a minute? I need to talk to you."

"Sure." Vinnie set his gardening tools on the table and took one of the beers. "Thanks. I was just about to stop for a cold drink. Already getting hot, isn't it?"

"It tends to do that around this time of year," Tony replied, settling into one of the chairs.

"Mmm." Vinnie tilted the can for a long swallow before lowering it to look at his son. "Okay, now. What did you want to talk about?"

"Michelle."

"Why doesn't that surprise me? You've gone and fallen in love with the girl, haven't you?"

Tony flushed and cleared his throat. "Well, yes," he admitted. "But that's not the problem."

"Good. I wouldn't mind having her for a daughter-in-law. I picked her out for you a long time ago, you know."

"So why didn't you do something about it long before this?" Tony demanded with a skeptical grin.

Vinnie shrugged expressively. "If I'd introduced her to you, you'd have resisted her just to prove you didn't need me interfering in your love life."

Tony snorted, looking down at his opened but untouched beer. "I doubt it. Even if I'd tried, I'm not sure I could ever have resisted Michelle."

Vinnie smiled reminiscently. "That's the way I felt about your mama."

"Yeah. I know." Tony only hoped his own love affair worked out as successfully as Vinnie and Carla's.

"Chuck called me at home a couple of hours ago," he said, getting to the real reason for his visit. "He's found something on Carter Powell that disturbs me. I'm not sure what to do about it."

"It concerns Michelle?" Vinnie demanded, straightening abruptly in his chair.

"Very much so."

"Have you talked with her?"

"No. I don't have any proof yet, Dad. I'm afraid she wouldn't believe my suspicions. After all, she's known the man most of her life."

"Then get your proof."

"That's why I'm here," Tony agreed grimly. "I need some professional advice from the best on how to go on from here."

Vinnie set his beer down, all business now. "Okay, son. Start from the beginning. What have you got?"

Michelle hummed beneath her breath as she turned her car through the gates of her driveway Saturday afternoon. After Tony had left that morning, she'd dressed and headed for the hospital to spend time with the babies, their tiny bodies cradled in her arms as she'd rocked them and crooned to them. At one point she'd found herself daydreaming about rocking an infant of her own, picturing it with silky ebony hair and mischievous dark eyes.

She'd caught herself short, sternly chiding herself for throwing away all caution in her infatuation with Tony, but still the fantasy had enchanted her.

Her contented smile faded when she saw the car parked in front of her house, one she recognized immediately. Carter Powell. There'd been a time when she'd enjoyed his visits; now she worried that they'd only quarrel again over her involvement with Tony and the search for her remaining brothers and sister.

"I'd given you another five minutes before I left," Carter said without preamble when Michelle joined him in the parlor where Betty had served him tea and cakes.

"I'm sorry, Carter. Did we have an appointment for this afternoon?" Michelle waved him back into his chair as she seated herself near him.

"No," he admitted gruffly, setting his teacup and saucer on a convenient coaster. He reached down to the floor, where he'd set his Italian leather briefcase. "I have some things to show you."

Her stomach tightened, as if in forewarning that she wouldn't like what he was going to tell her. "What is it?"

He held out a manila folder. "This is a copy of a report that Tony D'Alessandro requested from one of his employees. He received it this past week."

Mechanically, Michelle took the folder, though she didn't immediately open it. "What is it? And how did you get it?"

"How I got it doesn't matter," Carter replied coolly. "My job is to watch out for your welfare the best way I know how. As for what it is, I suggest you see for yourself."

Very slowly, Michelle opened the folder and looked down. The numbers printed on the pages made her catch her breath. "I don't understand—"

"I see you know what you're looking at," Carter said with audible satisfaction.

She stared at the pages, dazed by their implications. "It's a financial statement of some sort. On me."

"Yes. Everything you're worth is printed on those pages, Michelle. Bank accounts, stock holdings, investments, assets. It's all there."

"And you say Tony asked for this?" Michelle asked, raising her eyes to his, knowing their expression begged to give her a reasonable explanation for what she'd seen.

"That's right. You wouldn't think it would be necessary for him to have this information if all he's interested in is finding your brothers and sisters, would you?"

She swallowed. "I'm sure Tony thought there was a good reason…"

"Like what, Michelle?"

She couldn't come up with even one possibility. "I don't know."

"He's not the first man to look into the future benefits before making a commitment to you, is he?"

She gasped. "Carter! That's a terrible thing to say!"

His face softened. "I'm sorry, Michelle. Very sorry that I have to handle this in such a manner. But I can't stand back and watch you be hurt again by a fortune hunter."

"Tony's not a fortune hunter," Michelle protested. "He's not interested in my money."

"I understand the two of you have been seeing a great deal of each other during the past few weeks."

"You've been checking up on me?" Michelle asked indignantly.

"I've been keeping an eye on you," he replied without

apology. "Just as I promised your parents I would. I keep my word."

"You're wrong about him, Carter. You don't know Tony, you don't know what he's like."

"What has he told you, Michelle? That he cares for you? That you mean more to him than your money? That he's not like any of the men you've known before?"

She clenched her fingers around the folder, unable to answer.

"Other than that fiasco with Geoff Mansfield, I've never thought you to be a particularly naive young woman. Do you really believe D'Alessandro fell in love with you at first sight? That he didn't ask for this report because he wanted to know the full extent of your worth before making a commitment he couldn't get out of? He even orchestrated your reunion with your sister as a ploy to attach himself to you when you're at your most vulnerable. He *did* hold your hand during your meeting with her, didn't he? And I'm sure you were properly grateful."

"You're wrong about his motives," Michelle repeated dully. "I know you are."

"I hear you spent quite a bit on a man's watch yesterday. Did he turn it down when you gave it to him? Or was he touchingly pleased by the gift?"

Temper exacerbated by pain brought Michelle to her feet. "You overstep yourself, Carter! How dare you have me watched that closely."

He only looked at her without getting up. "I'd say keeping an eye on your recent purchases was relevant to my questions about D'Alessandro's motives. Did he take the watch, Michelle?"

"It was a birthday present," she snapped back, beginning to pace in agitation. "He told me it was too extravagant, but he couldn't graciously refuse the gift."

"I'm sure he had no intention of trying. The man's no fool. Tell me, dear, did you know he was fired from the police department two years ago?"

"Fired?" Michelle whirled to face him, her heart stopping. "No. He quit."

"He told you that?"

"He—" She tried to remember. "No. We haven't really discussed it. But I was sure…"

"You don't have to take my word for this, you know. It's easy enough to check his employment records with police headquarters. Why would I lie to you when I know you can do so?"

Her knees felt weak. She sank back into her chair. "Why was he fired?"

"That I don't know," Carter returned grimly. "Whatever it was was covered up—probably because his father left the force with honors and his mother's a respected attorney with the D.A.'s office. Give me a few more days and I'll find out the whole story."

Desperately needing to be alone to think, Michelle lifted her chin and looked at her attorney, determined to hide her confusion and hurt. For now, anyway. "Was there anything else you wanted to tell me?"

"Your sister, Layla Samples, and her husband have two mortgages on their home. Through sheer stupidity, they got into some financial trouble three years ago and are still trying to bail themselves out. I suggest you keep that in mind should you decide to maintain contact with her."

"You really have done your homework, haven't you, Carter?" Michelle asked dully, bitterly.

He inclined his head. "That's my job. I've always believed in being thorough."

"I'm sure you'll understand that I'd like to think about the things you've told me. I'd like to be alone."

"Very well." Carter rose and straightened his expensively tailored suit, every inch the composed, efficient attorney. "Just keep in mind that I've told you these things for your own good, Michelle. Just as I've always watched out for your best interests, from the time you were a very young girl. Your father trusted me, you know, as did your mother. I never gave them any reason not to do so."

"I know that, Carter." She started to thank him for his concern, but the words wouldn't leave her throat. How could she thank him for breaking her heart?

"We should talk further, but I know you need time. I'll call you early next week. Perhaps we'll have lunch."

She nodded, already lost in her own thoughts. She was hardly aware when Powell left after one long, searching look at her.

Had she really done it again? she asked herself when she was alone, her eyes locked blindly on the now-crumpled folder. Had she fallen again for an attractive face and pretty words? Had she so easily forgotten the hard-earned lessons of her past?

Had Tony been using her?

Everything within her cried out in protest at the thought. Not Tony. Surely not Tony.

And yet…

She was suddenly haunted by some remarks he'd made, comments that had meant little at the time, yet seemed so ominous in retrospect. *"It wouldn't be hard to get used to this,"* he'd said, looking around her dining room the night they'd made love for the first time. And a few days later, after disparaging his apartment, he'd added, *"I've got big plans for moving up someday."*

She'd thought he'd been teasing at the time. But maybe he hadn't been. Maybe those plans of his had something to do with the folder resting so heavily in her lap.

And yet...

She remembered the trembling in his hands when he'd made love to her, the tenderness in his eyes when he'd smiled down at her and assured her that he didn't care about her money. Only about her. Could he have looked at her that way and lied? Could anyone be that skillful at deception? Geoff had never looked so sincere; it had simply taken her a while to notice the duplicity in his handsome face. But Tony had seemed so utterly, honestly trustworthy.

Had he only been telling her what she'd wanted to hear?

Her knuckles went white as her grip tightened on the file. How had he gotten this information? There were details included in the report that even Taylor, her closest friend, had no way of knowing. If he really wasn't interested in her money, why had Tony wanted these figures? As Carter had so coolly, yet accurately pointed out, Tony had no need of this information to find her siblings.

And had he really been fired from the police department? She knew he'd deliberately led her to believe his leaving had been by his own choice. Why hadn't he told her the truth—about that, or about his feelings for her?

"Oh, Tony," she whispered, her throat tightening against the tears she refused to shed just yet. "What have you done?"

Chapter Twelve

Tony knew something was wrong the moment he saw Michelle when she opened her door to him Saturday evening. "What is it?" he demanded, his eyes searching her strained face as he stepped through the door. "What's wrong?"

She stepped back when he would have reached for her, her arms crossing defensively at her waist. "I'd like to talk to you."

His hands fell to his sides. "All right."

What could have gone this wrong since the time he'd left her bed only a matter of hours before?

She turned to lead him into the front parlor in which he'd waited for her the first time he'd visited her home. Not the more comfortable, less formal den, he noted with a frown, sensing some meaning behind her choice of rooms.

What the hell was wrong?

Michelle didn't sit when she entered the parlor, but turned in the middle of the room to face him, still standing in a position that effectively warned him not to get too close to her. "I had a visit from my attorney this afternoon," she began.

Tony muttered an expletive beneath his breath. "So that's what this is about. What did he say to make you look at me like this?"

"Several things, actually," she replied, her beautiful face as coolly expressionless as it had been on that afternoon two months earlier when she'd entered his office to hire him.

As it had before, her attitude made him feel annoyed and defensive. He linked his thumbs in the loops of his jeans, his feet spread in a wary stance.

"All right, let's have it," he ordered. "What did he say? And you'd better have a damned good reason to believe him if that's why you're suddenly treating me as though I've got some sort of contagious disease," he added roughly.

Her chin went even higher at his tone. "Why shouldn't I believe what my attorney tells me?" she asked. "After all, I've known him for twenty-four years."

"And you've only known me for two months," he added smoothly, quietly. "But I'm the one you've been to bed with, aren't I, Michelle? I'm the one who made you go wild in my arms. I thought that meant something pretty damned important to you. It sure as hell did to me."

"Of course it was important to me!" she snapped, her cheeks darkening at his words. "*Too* important, perhaps. I'd hate to think I'd been that much of a fool twice."

"Twice?" His fists clenched as her meaning set in. "You're comparing me to that Geoff guy again? *What did Powell tell you, Michelle?*"

In answer, she snatched a manila folder off a low cherry table, thrusting it into his hands. "He brought me this. And I hope you've got some explanation for it other than the one he suggested, because I sure as hell can't come up with one!"

At least he'd managed to stir her into a temper, Tony thought with grim satisfaction. He'd rather deal with her temper any day than that icy condescension she'd mastered all too well.

Slowly lowering his eyes from her flushed face, he opened the folder. At first glance, he knew exactly what it contained, as well as why Michelle would now be questioning his motives. "Well, hell."

How had Carter Powell gotten his hands on the report Bob had turned in only a few days before?

She laughed shortly, without humor. "Funny. That's pretty much what I said when I saw it."

"This isn't what it looks like, Michelle."

"No?" She cocked her head, her tone sarcastic. "You mean it *isn't* a full, minutely detailed accounting of my financial affairs?"

He winced and cleared his throat. "Well, yes, it is that, but…"

"Then it's exactly what it looks like."

Tony closed the folder and viciously tossed it aside. "Look," he said, trying to keep his tone even and rational. "Let's sit down and I'll explain."

"I don't want to sit down," she refused stubbornly.

He exhaled gustily. "Fine. We'll stand. But the least you could do is hear me out. I assume you gave Powell that courtesy," he added caustically.

Still standing very straight, very stiff, as if holding herself in control by sheer willpower, she made a short, go-ahead gesture with one hand.

Tony ran a hand through his hair in frustration. What the hell was he supposed to say? How could he explain the suspicions he'd harbored when he'd requested this information without the evidence he needed to prove his half-formed theories?

Carter had evidently preyed expertly on Michelle's old insecurities, reminding her how long and how well he'd served her family. In contrast, Tony had nothing but his word—the word of a man she'd known only a few weeks—to convince her of his sincerity.

Part of him was hurt and furious that Michelle didn't automatically trust him, that she'd even consider doubting him after all they'd become to each other. Yet the more rational side of him knew that she'd been hurt too many times in the past for it to be that easy. And he was going to have to ask her to trust him once again. Until he had proof that Carter wasn't the well-intentioned friend he pretended to be, Tony couldn't explain the investigation he was conducting on his own time. For her.

He only hoped he wasn't expecting too much from her.

He wouldn't lose her, damn it. He couldn't.

"Michelle, please," he said, wondering how to begin. "Sit down."

She stood where she was for another long, taut moment, as though torn between pride and logic, and then nodded stiffly and perched on the edge of a chair. Relieved that he'd won even that small victory, Tony chose a seat close to her.

"Do you remember that I told you your money wasn't important to me? That it was you I cared for, not your wealth?"

"I remember everything you told me," she agreed stiffly. *I just don't know if I can believe you,* her eyes added.

"It was true, Michelle. It still is." He took a deep breath before speaking again, knowing he risked everything with his words. "I love you."

A visible tremor coursed through her. Her knuckles went white against the arms of her chair. "Don't say that," she whispered.

"It's true."

She shook her head, refusing to look at him. "I don't want

to hear it. Not now. I want to know about this file. Did you assign one of your employees to get this information for you, Tony?"

"Yes."

Her eyes closed briefly at his stark reply, then opened again though she still stared at her lap rather than at him. "Why?"

He swallowed a groan. "I can't explain exactly. Not yet."

She glanced at him then, suspiciously. "What do you mean, 'not yet'? Why can't you explain?"

"It's part of an investigation," he replied. "But I don't have everything I need yet. Next week, maybe, I can explain everything to you."

"I want to know *now!*" she cried, looking pleadingly at him. "What does this have to do with your search for my brothers and sisters? Why did you need to know these things about me?"

"It doesn't exactly apply to my search for your family. It's…something else. Something I can't really discuss with you yet. I don't have the proof, Michelle."

"Proof?" she repeated, frowning. "Proof of what?"

He remained silent, more frustrated then he could ever remember being in his life. If only he could explain, if only he could hope she'd believe him without any evidence other than his word. *And what if he was wrong?*

She made a choked sound, as though his silence only confirmed her worst suspicions. "Then maybe you can answer this," she said, her voice strained. "Why did you leave the police department, Tony?"

"I quit," he replied, his fists clenching on his knees.

"You quit? Or were you fired?"

His jaw tightened, but he held her gaze evenly. "Does that matter to you?"

"Of course it matters! Don't you think it should?"

"Not if you trust me."

She only looked at him.

Tony sighed heavily. "Yeah, right. That's the real problem, isn't it?"

He rose to pace restlessly around the room, his hands in his pockets. Maybe to keep them from reaching out to her. "I quit the police department, Michelle. My choice."

"Carter said—"

"My choice," he continued as if she hadn't interrupted, "was to quit or be fired. Is that what you wanted to know?"

"What did you do?"

He shot her an angry, fuming look. "You automatically assume it was something I did?"

"Isn't that why most people are given those options?" she whispered, looking as miserable as he felt.

He tried to harden his heart against the look in her eyes, reminding himself that he was the one on trial, the one being unjustly accused of more than one sin, but all he really wanted to do was to take her in his arms and tell her how much he loved her. That he'd never hurt her. Beg her to trust him, whatever the evidence against him. His hands clenched in his pockets.

"It wasn't what I did," he said curtly. "It was what I wouldn't do. At the time, the administration was made up of political game players. There were certain unwritten rules to be followed, certain occasions when we were expected to look the other way rather than to do our jobs. I couldn't go along with that. I didn't cooperate with their games, and I wasn't what they called a 'team player.' I was too impatient to wait for the reforms that were already in the works and I got myself embroiled in an ugly situation. It was best for me to leave when I did, to go into business for myself. To make my own rules."

"Is that the whole truth?"

The quiet question had him whirling furiously on her. "*Dammit,* Michelle!"

"I'm sorry!" she snapped, raising her hands to her temples as though to soothe a vicious pounding there. "I just don't know what to think right now. When Carter showed me that file…"

"You automatically assumed the worst about me," Tony finished bitterly.

She dropped her hands to her lap. "You invaded every corner of my personal life, reduced my entire existence to a series of numbers on a computer printout," she accused him brokenly. "You've told me repeatedly that you don't care about my money, and yet you assigned one of your employees to pry this intensely into my affairs. You've admitted this report has nothing to do with the job I hired you for, yet you refuse to explain why you requested it. What am I supposed to think, Tony?"

Wearily, he closed his eyes. "I know how it looks to you," he admitted reluctantly. "Maybe I expected too much…"

Opening his eyes, he pulled his hands from his pockets and faced her squarely. "I can only tell you again that I love you, Michelle, and that everything I've done was done for a good reason. I'll get the facts I need to make you understand, but it's going to take me a few more days. Now it's up to you. You can fire me…or you can trust me just a little while longer."

"You promised you'd find my family," she whispered.

"Yes. I still intend to do so."

"And this other thing—this 'investigation' that has something to do with me? Will you stop prying into my personal affairs if I ask you to?"

He hesitated, wanting to promise her anything, heavily aware that he couldn't let go of his investigation until he'd proven his suspicions about Carter Powell. "I can't promise that, Michelle. I'm sorry—but please believe I have your best interests at heart."

"I don't know what to believe," she murmured, dropping her eyelashes to hide her expression from him. "I'm really tired, Tony. I'd like you to leave now."

He made a move of protest, vaguely hoping he could convince her of his innocence if she'd only give him a little more time with her. If he could only touch her, hold her.

"Please," she said, her voice barely audible.

He sighed, defeated. "All right. I'll go. I'll call you tomorrow."

"Call me when you have something to show me."

A muscle twitched in his cheek, but he nodded shortly. "Fine. Good night, Michelle."

She didn't answer.

Swallowing a curse, Tony turned and strode out of the room before he did something he'd only regret. Like throw her over his shoulder and carry her to her bedroom, to hold her there until she'd finally learned to trust him. If he thought it would work, he might even try it. But he knew she'd only fight him.

He drove away from her big, walled-in house with a desperate tightness in his chest. She'd hurt him with her lack of faith in him, her willingness to believe that he was only after her money. Hurt him worse than anything had ever hurt him before. But he wouldn't give up on her. He couldn't. He loved her.

He'd provide the proof she needed, he told himself on a sudden surge of reckless determination. And then he'd continue to chip away at those defenses of hers until she finally learned to trust him. To love him the way he loved her. Whatever it took.

For the first time in his stubborn, uncompromising lifetime, Tony D'Alessandro found himself willing to beg, if necessary.

And even though the realization shook him, he knew it was true.

So this was love. Why hadn't anyone warned him how much it could hurt?

Unable to sleep, Michelle prowled around her room long after midnight, her hands tangled in her hair, her thoughts whirling, moods swinging. She couldn't forget the look on Tony's face when she'd implicitly accused him of being more interested in her money than in her. He'd looked so…hurt. Betrayed. Sincere.

I love you, he'd said. And she'd come so very close to melting, holding out her arms to him and begging him to make her understand. Even now, hearing the echo of his deep, rich voice saying those three words, she wanted nothing more than to believe him, to trust that he'd never do anything to hurt her.

She loved him so much. She couldn't imagine losing him now. Never sleeping in his arms again, never spending time with his family, to whom she'd begun to secretly hope to belong someday. He'd seemed so honest when he'd looked into her eyes and promised he wanted only her. She wanted so desperately to believe him.

And then she turned in her pacing and her eyes fell on the crumpled manila folder lying at the foot of her bed.

I love you, he'd said. But other people had said those same words, when it hadn't been her they'd loved at all.

In a sudden surge of anguished frustration, Michelle swung her arm to sweep the file from the bed, its contents scattering across the floor. And then, for the first time since finding Carter Powell waiting for her that afternoon, she wept.

"I don't want to hear excuses, Chuck! I've told you what I suspect about Powell and now I want you to get me the proof!" Tony snapped into the telephone receiver gripped tightly in his fist. "Whatever it takes, whatever you have to do…I want that evidence. If Powell picks up a quarter from the sidewalk, I want to know it, you got that?"

"Tony…"

He gestured curtly at Bonnie, who stood hesitantly in the open doorway to his office, trying to get his attention. "And, Chuck—I want to know where Powell got that report on Michelle. Make that a priority, understand?"

He hung up the phone, then glared at his secretary. "What is it, Bonnie?"

She didn't flinch at his tone—the same one he'd been using all morning, to his regret. He shouldn't be taking his pain out on his employees, he told himself wearily. He owed them more than that.

"I'm sorry," he said, before she could answer his question. "I didn't mean to snap."

"That's okay." Her dark eyes were sympathetic. He hadn't told her what had been eating him today, but she seemed to sense that he was hurting, and to care. "You've got a call on line two."

"Who is it?" he asked without a great deal of interest, rubbing his hands across his face. He'd hardly slept since he'd left Michelle's house Saturday evening—nearly forty hours ago. As tired as he was, he wasn't sure he'd ever sleep soundly again—not without Michelle at his side.

"It's Carter Powell. Want me to take a message?"

Tony's hands fell to the desk, his head snapping up. "Carter Powell?"

"That's what the secretary said."

Tony reached for the phone. "Close the door, will you?"

She nodded, slipping out of the office and closing the door behind her.

"D'Alessandro."

A woman responded. "Just a moment, please."

There was a click and a moment of silence. And then a man's voice. "You don't take advice very well, do you, D'Alessandro?"

"Not without considering its source. Or the motives behind it," Tony murmured. "What do you want, Powell?"

"I want you to leave Michelle Trent alone. She's out of your league, D'Alessandro. You may have turned her head at first, but I'm sure that's about to change."

"Thanks to you?"

"As her attorney, it's my responsibility to protect her from unscrupulous opportunists. She's not quite the unprotected innocent she must have appeared when she showed up in your office looking for her long-lost family."

Knowing he was being deliberately baited, Tony managed not to respond in temper, though it was a wonder the plastic receiver didn't disintegrate within the vicious grip of his fist. "You don't really think she's going to stop looking for her brothers and sisters, do you, Powell? Nor turn her back on the sister she's already found."

"At the moment, you're my primary concern for her welfare," the attorney replied smoothly. "You didn't waste any time romancing her, did you? Some might call your behavior less than ethical—certainly far from professional. Considering your career background, I suppose I shouldn't be surprised."

"My relationship with Michelle has nothing to do with you."

"Relationship? Oh, I think that's rather strong a word. How much is she paying you for your investigation on her behalf, D'Alessandro?"

"That's none of your—"

"Whatever it is, I'll triple it if you'll take yourself off her case. Tell her whatever you like—that you've got too heavy a caseload or find that you've been mistaken in your so-called feelings for her. It's a generous offer, D'Alessandro. I'd suggest you take it."

Tony spoke from between clenched teeth. "I've got a few suggestions for you, Powell. Like exactly what you can do with your 'generous offer.'"

"You're making a mistake if you think you'll have it all. Michelle was almost taken in by a fortune hunter before, but she's no fool. She won't let it happen again. And as a long-time friend and trusted associate of her father, I'll do my best to make sure she's protected from you."

Heated accusations trembled on Tony's lips, so strongly that it was all he could do to hold them back. Instead, he managed to say evenly, "We'll see who's protecting Michelle, won't we, Powell?"

"Don't do anything stupid, boy. You really don't want to take me on. Trust me in that, if nothing else."

"Yeah, right."

"If this is the way you want it—"

"This is the way it's going to be."

"Fine. But when it's over—when your career falls down around your ears for the second time—remember that you were warned, will you?" The subtle threat ended with a click and a dial tone.

"Son of a—" Tony slammed his own receiver down without regard for the condition of his telephone.

He was more convinced than ever now that Carter Powell had something to hide. Though the man was careful with the wording of his threats—a tape of the conversation would most likely have sounded as though Carter was doing nothing more than overzealously protecting a valued client's interests—Tony would have bet it wasn't Michelle whom the attorney was trying to protect. He had his suspicions—his convictions—but he needed the proof. And, whatever it took, he would have it.

He reached for his jacket, threw it over his shoulder and strode toward the door. Jerking it open, he passed through the reception area without pausing, speaking to Bonnie on his way past her desk. "I'll be out most of the day. Use the beeper if you need me."

"All right. I'll see you…"

But Tony didn't wait around to hear the rest. Jaw set in determination, he headed for his Jeep. He was about to begin the task of clearing his name with the woman he loved.

Michelle spent Tuesday afternoon trying to concentrate on problems more important than her own. She was halfway through a letter requesting funds for a charity organization Trent Enterprises had contributed to on previous occasions when her telephone rang. She looked at it for a long moment before answering, both afraid and hopeful that Tony would be on the other end of the line.

She forced herself to pick it up on the third ring. "Hello."

"Michelle, I'm glad I caught you. I need to talk to you."

Though he didn't identify himself, and though she'd talked to him only a handful of times in the past few years, Michelle recognized the voice. "Uncle Richard? What's wrong?"

"I had a call from Carter Powell this morning."

Michelle tensed.

"The man's concerned about you, Michelle, and I'd say he has justification. What in blazes is going on with you?"

"You'll have to be more specific, Uncle Richard. What exactly did Carter tell you about me?"

"That you've begun a reckless and potentially dangerous search for a bunch of strangers you haven't seen in twenty-four years. And that you're having an affair with the private investigator you hired, a man who is quite obviously interested in more than the investigation you hired him to conduct. Carter told me the man had financial information about Trent Enterprises that no one outside the corporation should have access to. You're aware of this?"

Michelle took a deep breath. "Carter showed me the report Tony apparently requested. And I'm looking into it, Uncle Richard. I've given a copy of the report to Charles Major, in case there was any information in it that he considered potentially damaging to the corporation."

The mention of the CEO of Trent Enterprises, Dallas, seemed to mollify Richard Trent only marginally. "I don't like this at all, Michelle. Whatever possessed you to get into this?"

"Mother left me a letter telling me about my brothers and sisters. I wanted to find them, wanted to at least meet them. They're my family, Uncle Richard. Can't you understand that?"

"Frankly, no, I can't. The Trents became your family the day you were adopted. You were raised with affection and financial and social advantages you would never have had otherwise. These other people are strangers to you, raised God only knows how. I'm sure they'll be delighted to claim kinship with an extremely wealthy young woman, but I can't for the life of me understand what you expect to get in return."

Michelle was tempted to reply that her brothers and sisters wouldn't be much more strangers to her than this man she'd been raised to call "Uncle." She bit the words back. "I just want to meet them, Uncle Richard. I assure you I'll be careful."

"As you've been with this private investigator?" he asked skeptically.

Her eyes narrowed. "My relationship with Tony has nothing to do with this. I'm neither a child nor a fool, Uncle

Richard. I'm quite capable of forming my own judgments, once I have all the information in front of me. Believe me, Carter has made sure that I know about Tony's freelance investigation into my financial affairs."

"You should be grateful that your attorney is so dedicated to your welfare. Obviously my brother knew what he was doing by asking Powell to watch out for you."

Again, Michelle had to bite her lip against words that could serve no purpose other than to antagonize Richard.

"Listen, Michelle, it's obvious that you've been lonely since your mother's death," Richard continued, trying to make his tone more conciliatory. "I'm sorry I haven't been more available for you, but you're aware, of course, that Trent Enterprises, California, has been going through a major restructuring and has required a great deal of my time."

"I understand, Uncle Richard." *You were never here for me before—why should I have expected you to be now?* She kept that thought to herself, of course.

"Your Aunt Lydia and cousin Steven would like very much to see you. Why don't you fly out to spend a few weeks with us? Your charity duties can be delegated for a time, and I think it'll do you good to get away from Dallas for a while. Steven has several single friends—men of distinguished backgrounds and impeccable reputations—who'd enjoy meeting you. I'm sure they'd be willing to overlook—well, you know."

"My adoption, Uncle Richard? My less-than-blue-blooded background?"

He sighed audibly at her cutting tone. "Now, Michelle, don't get defensive. You know I think Harrison and Alicia did an admirable job of raising you. You've made a place for yourself in society and in the corporation, and you've conducted yourself quite properly." *Until now,* his tone added.

"You don't need to go out looking for a family, my dear,"

he continued with an unnatural-sounding jocularity. "You have us. I agree that it's certainly time you set up your own household, had some children to occupy your time and affections. That's why I think it would be advisable for you to let us introduce you to some nice young men. I'd be happy to take care of all the travel arrangements. Shall we expect you late next week?"

"No." She forced herself to speak politely. "Thank you very much for the invitation, but I really have too many responsibilities here to take time off just now."

"Michelle, be reasonable. You—"

"Excuse me, Uncle Richard, but I have a meeting this afternoon and I really should be going," she lied without regret. "Thank you for calling. Give my best to Aunt Lydia and to Steven. I'll talk to you again soon."

She hung up, leaving him in midsputter.

She was really getting tired of people trying to tell her what to do, she thought, her temper growing. People who claimed to be acting in her best interests. Carter, Richard— even Tony, who'd tried to convince her that he was looking into her finances for reasons that concerned her, but that he couldn't discuss with her. Even if it were true—and she refused to make that judgment without further evidence—he had no right to treat her as a mindless fool who couldn't take care of herself.

It was true that she'd met him at a time when she was vulnerable, that she'd leaned on him perhaps more than she should have during that traumatic reunion with her sister. But she *was* capable of watching out for her own best interests, dammit, and it was time other people acknowledged it!

She was also fed up with being discouraged from finding her brothers and sisters. They were her flesh and blood, separated only by accidents of fate, and she had a right to know them, to judge for herself whether they'd grown into adults she could respect or even love. Whatever else he may have done, at least Tony had never tried to keep her from finding her family. He and Taylor had been the only ones who'd encouraged her to do so.

Taylor. Michelle sighed as she thought of her friend. She'd be so glad when the photo assignment in Galveston was finished and Taylor home. She needed very badly to talk to someone who'd always been on her side, whose motives were completely open and above suspicion. She needed a friend.

Or a sister.

Michelle pulled her lower lip between her teeth as her gaze turned slowly toward the telephone. She *had* a sister, she thought with a sudden wave of longing. Layla, who'd been so touchingly pleased to find her again, who'd loved her and cared for her as a baby. Who shared her eye color and hair color and the shape of her face. Whose adorable children called her Aunt Michelle.

Nervously moistening her lips, she reached for the telephone and opened her address book. She didn't need Richard's insincere claims of affection, his obligatory efforts to fulfill what he considered to be his duty to his late brother's adopted daughter. And she'd never really belonged to Tony's close-knit clan, no matter how warmly they'd welcomed her among them. She had a family of her own, she thought with renewed determination.

It was long past time to get to know them.

Chapter Thirteen

Michelle looked into the full-length mirror in her dressing room on Wednesday evening, anxiously inspecting her appearance. She wasn't quite sure what was proper for a dinner at home with her sister and brother-in-law, so she'd dressed conservatively in a black silk jumpsuit and simple gold jewelry, her hair swept into a neat chignon.

She checked her makeup, noting that even the skillfully applied cosmetics hadn't completely hidden the effects of four nights of very little sleep. Nor did eye shadow and dark mascara disguise the pain visible in her blue eyes. She could only hope Layla and Kevin wouldn't notice.

She'd been pleased when Layla had accepted her dinner invitation on such short notice. Though the invitation had been extended to the entire family, Layla had insisted on leaving her children with a baby-sitter, explaining that she'd like to have a bit more time with her sister without the distractions of three busy, curious children.

"We still have so much to learn about each other," she'd added, sounding as though she were eagerly anticipating the evening.

Even though Michelle, too, looked forward to being with her sister again, her pleasure would have been much greater if she wasn't still tearing herself up about her feelings for Tony—and her questions about his feelings for her.

If only she could bring herself to accept Carter's assertion—and evidence—that Tony had been using her in the same way Geoff had used her. But, logical though the probability seemed, she simply couldn't believe it. Not entirely. Something inside her—somewhere in the vicinity of her heart—kept trying to convince her that Tony simply wasn't capable of treating her that way. That he couldn't possibly have deceived her so cleverly.

She hadn't heard from him since he'd left Saturday. She'd told him not to call until he had whatever proof he'd claimed to be searching for to justify the report Carter had given her. Obviously he didn't have that proof yet, if it had ever existed at all. But, oh, how she missed him. How she would have loved to have him with her tonight during this dinner with Layla and Kevin.

She heard the doorbell chime downstairs and took one last glance at the mirror. The smile she affected looked natural enough to fool anyone who didn't know her very well— perhaps it would work with her guests. Wishing there was something she could do about the anguish in her heart, she turned and left the bedroom.

Layla and Kevin were waiting in the den, where Betty had been instructed to escort them. The moment she joined them, Michelle could tell that something was bothering them. Kevin wore a sport coat and slacks and tugged uncomfortably at his tie; Layla had on a cotton shirtwaist dress that she smoothed with stiff hands. Holding on to her smile, Michelle held out her hands to her sister. "Layla. I'm so glad you could be here tonight."

Layla's hands were cold. "Thank you for asking us, Michelle."

"Please, sit down. Did Betty offer you drinks?"

"Yes, but we really didn't want anything right now." Layla and Kevin perched side by side on the edge of the oversized couch, looking as though they were being interviewed for a job, Michelle thought in dismay. They hardly looked as though they were comfortable.

Layla cleared her throat. "Your home is lovely."

"Thank you." Michelle wondered if it made her sister uncomfortable to compare the Trent home with her own modest frame house in Fort Worth. "I grew up here," she explained casually. "My parents left the house to me."

"What did your father do?" Kevin asked, looking around the massive den.

"He and his brother were joint owners of Trent Enterprises. Daddy ran the Dallas division while my Uncle Richard handles the California business."

"Do you run the company now?" her brother-in-law asked curiously.

Michelle smiled and shook her head. "I was never really interested in the corporate world, despite my father's encouragement to learn more about it. I handle the charitable contributions for the corporation—budgeting yearly donations, researching and choosing the organizations to benefit from those donations, requesting additional funds from the board of directors when necessary. It's been a very fulfilling job for me, though a demanding one at times."

"You live in this big house all alone?" Layla asked.

"Betty and Arthur, her husband who works for me as general handyman, live in the back wing, but except for them I've lived here alone since my mother died earlier this year."

As though in response to the mention of her name, Betty carried in a tray of fragrant hot appetizers. Relying on signals developed through years of familiarity, Michelle let Betty know that she'd like dinner served very soon. Unfortunately, the evening hadn't started out as well as she'd hoped.

Oh, she wished Tony was there! He'd know what to do to keep the conversation moving.

"How are the children, Layla?" she asked in another desperate attempt to break the ice. She was pleased when Layla's eyes brightened at the question. Like most mothers, she seemed to enjoy talking about her children.

Layla and Kevin had just started to relax a bit when Betty announced dinner. Stepping into the dining room, with its elegant chandelier and exquisite table settings, seemed to make them withdraw even more than before. They sat very stiffly in their chairs, eating the food set in front of them in near silence broken only by Michelle's futile efforts to keep the conversation going.

Fighting an urge to burst into tears, Michelle wistfully compared this awkward family dinner with the D'Alessandro gathering for Tony's birthday. There'd be no embarrassing silences in his family, she thought sadly, no uncomfortable pauses fraught with tension. Tony's family would be more likely to speak their minds about whatever was bothering them, rather than hiding behind polite niceties.

Which suddenly seemed like a very good idea to Michelle.

She set her fork down with a thump, making Layla start and Kevin look up curiously from his dinner. "Layla, is something wrong?" Michelle asked boldly, searching her sister's face across the table. "You seem so uncomfortable. Is it something I've done?"

Layla looked quickly at her husband, then sighed and shook her head. Following Michelle's example, she set her own fork down and folded her hands in her lap. "It's nothing you've done, Michelle."

"Then what's wrong? We talked so easily last week, but tonight we're having to struggle over each word."

"Last week we were in *our* home," Layla explained quietly while Kevin flushed at the words.

"I don't understand," Michelle confessed, looking in bewilderment from Layla to Kevin. "Why should that make a difference?"

"I think what my wife is trying to explain," Kevin began diffidently, "is that we didn't realize when we met you that you were this—well, wealthy."

Not that again. Half-tempted to scream in sheer frustration, Michelle spread her hands beseechingly. "Does that really make a difference? I happened to be adopted and raised by a wealthy couple, but that doesn't change where I came from or who I am. Layla, you're my sister."

"I don't want you to be ashamed of us," Layla admitted. "Or to consider us one of the charity cases you work with all the time. I want us to have things in common—but I'm not sure that we do, considering."

"I am *not* ashamed of you! If I were, would it be so important to me to get to know you both better? And as far as charity, I hardly consider my family as a charity case!"

Kevin reached out to take his distressed wife's hand. "We don't mean to insult you, Michelle. It's just that—well, we don't know many people who live this elegantly. Security fences and servants and houses big enough to hold two or three families. Most of our friends are doing pretty well just to pay their bills."

Michelle's fists clenched in her lap. "I don't have to worry about paying the bills," she admitted, her eyes filling with the tears that had hovered so close since she'd sent Tony away. "But other than that, I'm no different from anyone else. I feel pain and fear and sometimes I get so very lonely. Because of my parents' money, I've been kidnapped and isolated and hurt. I have people guarding me from those who would be tempted to use me to get to the money, and I never really know whom to trust.

"I want to know I have someone who doesn't care about the money, someone who loves me just because of who I am. Someone who remembers me as a little girl who liked horsey rides and jelly sandwiches. Is that so much to ask?" she finished in little more than a broken whisper.

"Oh, Shelley, of course it's not." Layla had left her seat to kneel beside Michelle's chair, her expressive face distressed. "I'm sorry, I didn't mean to hurt you. It just…well, it just took me off guard to see this house and everything. I was being a fool. Can you forgive me?"

Michelle swallowed a sob and tried to smile. "Of course. I'm sorry I unloaded on you like that. I've—I've had a rough week," she admitted.

Kevin pushed back his chair and held out his hand to her. "Think we could start over?" he asked. "We'll try to forgive you for being rich if you can forgive us for being reverse snobs."

Standing beside her sister, Michelle gave a watery chuckle and took Kevin's hand. Then impulsively kissed his cheek. "I'd like to start over," she told him warmly. "I think having a family is worth working for."

"Yeah. So do I. Now can we get back to our dinner? This is the best veal I've ever tasted."

Still smiling, Michelle dashed at her eyes with the corner of her napkin. "I'll be sure to tell Betty you said so. She's very proud of this dish."

Looking far more relaxed than she had earlier, Layla returned to her seat. "Would it help to talk about your rough week, Michelle?" she offered in concern. "Does it have something to do with Tony?"

Michelle's eyes widened. "Why do you ask that?"

"You haven't mentioned him even once this evening," Layla pointed out. "And I could tell when you visited us that there was much more between you than employer and employee."

"Yes," Michelle admitted, "I'm just not sure what at the moment."

"He's not one of the guys who's after your money, is he?" Kevin demanded, looking up from his veal with a scowl that looked suspiciously big-brotherly.

Everything within her wanted to immediately deny that Tony was like that. She made herself answer more cautiously, "I don't know, Kevin. It's…possible."

Frowning, Layla shook her head. "Oh, I find that so hard to believe. He seemed so nice—so concerned about you. Are you sure you aren't misinterpreting something, Shelley?"

As she knew Layla had simply fallen into old habit calling her by her childhood name, Michelle made no effort to correct her. She rather liked it. "My attorney warned me that Tony's been showing undue interest in my finances," she explained when it occurred to her that she would like other opinions. She told Layla and Kevin about the report Carter had brought her.

"How did your attorney get the report?" Kevin asked.

Michelle shrugged. "He wouldn't say."

"You trust him?"

She started to answer that of course she trusted Carter. And found herself hesitating. "He's never given me reason not to trust him," she temporized.

"Sounds like he's going overboard in his responsibilities," Kevin murmured. "Has he made it a practice to keep you from forming outside relationships without his approval?"

"It—hasn't really been an issue before," Michelle answered slowly, thinking back. "My mother was ill for some time before she died and I spent a great deal of my time with her. I have one very close friend that I've known for years and a few other social friends, but I haven't been closely involved with anyone else for some time."

She added carefully, "He did advise me against finding my brothers and sisters. He said he was concerned about me."

Layla made an annoyed sound. "I'm glad you didn't listen to him. I can't imagine you have anything to worry about from our brothers or our little sister. And, trust me, Kevin and I don't expect anything from you but your affection."

"You already have that," Michelle replied with a smile.

Layla returned the smile, then suddenly frowned again. "I just thought of something you said earlier. That you'd been used and hurt and…kidnapped?"

Had she really said that? Michelle bit her lip, surprised at her indiscreet outburst. "It happened a long time ago."

Layla insisted on hearing the whole story. When she'd been told, she sat in white-faced horror, her eyes big and wet. "Oh, Michelle, how horrible for you. No wonder you've learned to be so careful. I don't know how you survived it."

"My parents were wonderful to me afterward," Michelle explained. "Overprotective, perhaps—particularly Mother— but loving and caring and very supportive. It helped, though it was a long time before I stopped having nightmares."

"And no wonder." Kevin's brow was creased with his fierce scowl. "I'd like to have gotten my hands on the guy."

"Actually, Tony's father took care of that," Michelle murmured and then, of course, had to explain the connection.

"I still think you should give Tony a chance to prove he's not after your money," Layla declared afterward. "He's a nice guy from a nice family. And he'd be a fool not to love you for yourself."

"I saw the way he was looking at you at our house," Kevin seconded. "Those weren't dollar signs in the guy's eyes, Michelle. He looked crazy about you."

Michelle wanted to believe them more than she'd ever wanted anything in her life. The very depth of her longing made her even more cautious. "I just need time to be sure," she said. "Time—and something more substantial than words."

Kevin and Layla didn't stay long after dessert, claiming they needed to get home at the time they'd told their baby-sitter. The evening passed much too quickly for Michelle, once they'd gotten past the initial intimidation the couple had felt at the luxury of her home.

"Our place next time," Layla announced as they were leaving. "We'll have a cookout, or something. Let you get to know the kids."

"Lord help you," Kevin murmured, earning himself a laughing punch on the arm from his children's mother.

"That sounds wonderful," Michelle assured them. She kissed Kevin, then hugged and kissed her sister. "Good night, Layla. Call me soon, okay?"

"I will. I promise." Layla followed Kevin out the front door, then hesitated on the walk and looked back over her shoulder at Michelle. "Why don't you call Tony? If you *have* misjudged him, he's got to be hurting as badly as you are."

"I'll think about it," Michelle promised. "Drive carefully."

She closed the door with a tired sigh, relieved the evening hadn't been a total disaster, despite its unpromising beginning. And she was thoroughly intrigued by Layla and Kevin's certainty that she'd misjudged Tony's motives. True, they didn't know him, not even as well as Michelle did...but they'd seemed so convinced that he wasn't the type who'd use her for her wealth.

Oh, how she hoped they were right!

* * *

It was nearly midnight when Michelle finally gave in to an urge that had been plaguing her ever since Layla's parting words. Her hand shaking, she perched on the edge of her bed and picked up the telephone. Even then, she sat for a long time with the receiver in her lap, wondering if she had the nerve to dial the number.

Would Tony be sleeping? Would he be angry with her for sending him away as she had? Had he missed her as desperately as she'd missed him, spent their nights apart remembering what it had been like to lie in each other's arms?

Did he really love her? Or would she be playing right into his hands to give him her trust, when she wasn't entirely sure he'd proven he deserved it?

She closed her eyes and saw his face, heard his deep voice teasing her, laughing with her, murmuring to her as he'd made love to her. She could see him with his family, the warmth and affection that had softened his dark eyes when he'd looked at his mother and his father, his brothers and his dear, elderly aunt. She'd convinced herself she saw that same warmth when he looked at her.

Could she have been so foolishly mistaken?

She loved him. Oh, how she loved him! And right now, in the darkness and silence of her room in the middle of a lonely night, she couldn't seem to convince herself that he had ever lied to her, that he didn't deserve her love.

Taking a deep breath, she punched the numbers quickly, before she changed her mind. She wasn't sure what she intended to say. That she missed him? That she wanted so badly to believe in him? That she trusted him, despite all the evidence to the contrary?

On the fifteenth ring, she finally conceded that Tony wasn't home. It didn't matter what she would have said, he wasn't there to hear it. Her eyes closed, she replaced the receiver on its cradle, wondering where he was at this hour. Who he was with.

And she feared she'd get no more sleep that night than she had during the four long, painful, lonely nights preceding it.

Tony entered his dark apartment and kicked the door closed behind him, so tired he ached all the way down to the heels of his boots. He didn't bother to turn on the living room lights, but headed straight for the bedroom, shedding clothing as he went.

It was two in the morning, he hadn't eaten since breakfast, had been on the run for the past eighteen hours, needed a shave and a shower almost as much as he needed sleep—but his efforts had paid off. He and Chuck had obtained exactly what Tony had expected to find. As well as an unpleasant surprise that had left him with a bitter, dispirited taste in his mouth.

He crawled naked into bed and buried his head in the pillow as though to block out every unpleasant thing that had happened to him in the past few days, from the moment Michelle had confronted him with the file to his more recent firing of an employee he'd trusted.

He'd been tempted to head straight for Michelle's house with the evidence he'd collected, regardless of the hour. Lingering hurt from her lack of faith in him prodded him to shove the facts in her face and demand that she acknowledge how cruelly she'd misjudged him. His piqued ego suggested he make her crawl a little before he forgave her—and he would forgive her, of course, despite his disappointment.

Yet even as those thoughts crossed his weary mind, he knew that all he really wanted to do was take her in his arms and hold her. Bury himself in her softness, her sweetness. Tell her how very much he loved her. Maybe now that he had the proof he'd needed, she'd understand that it was safe to love him in return. That he'd never hurt her, nor would he let anyone else.

Tomorrow. Sinking more deeply into the pillow, he let the first tendril of sleep soothe his troubled mind. Tomorrow he'd be with Michelle again.

Chapter Fourteen

Michelle stepped out of the shower and wrapped herself in a thick terry robe before winding a towel around her dripping hair. On most Thursday mornings, she'd have been up and dressed long before ten o'clock, but today she'd slept late, exhausted from several restless nights and tense, miserable days. She'd awakened to thoughts of Tony this morning—prompted, perhaps, by a night of dreaming of him.

Would she see him today?

She'd just taken an outfit from her closet when a tap on her bedroom door drew her attention. "Yes?"

Betty opened the door just far enough to stick her head inside. "Phone call for you. It's Mr. Tony."

Michelle's stomach knotted, her breathing going shallow. She tried to hide the instinctive reactions from Betty, though she suspected she wasn't entirely successful. "Thanks, Betty. I'll take it in here."

Betty nodded and closed the door, though not without

first giving Michelle a look that all but ordered her to be nice to the man on the telephone. Michelle thought in exasperation that she wished it was as easy for her to give Tony her unconditional trust as it seemed to be for everyone else.

Her hand wasn't quite steady when she picked up the phone. "Hello."

"Hi. Were you busy?"

"No, I was just—" Her left hand tightened on the lapels of her robe, as if he could somehow tell that she wore nothing beneath it. "No."

"I need to see you today, Michelle. I have something to show you. Something important."

"I'll come to your office. What time?"

He paused a moment, then replied. "I'd rather come there, if you don't mind. It's something you'll want to hear in privacy—something you'll have to decide how to handle. Will you be in this afternoon?"

She thought about arguing—it seemed so much safer to meet in his office, rather than her home. And then she told herself she was being foolish. "Yes, I'll be in. Three o'clock?"

"Right." He hesitated again, then asked more softly, "How are you?"

I'm miserable. I miss you. I want to be with you, to burrow into your arms and have you make the pain go away. "I'm fine, Tony."

"Good," he answered, though he sounded oddly disappointed with her answer. "I'll see you this afternoon, then."

"Yes. Goodbye."

He didn't respond, but disconnected without another word.

Staring blankly at nothing, Michelle held her receiver until a persistently annoying beeping reminded her to hang it up.

* * *

Michelle tapped her pencil rhythmically on her desk, echoing the nervous tattoo of her heart. Tony was due to arrive any minute. She'd instructed Betty to usher him to the office she maintained at home, deciding the relative formality of the setting would make it easier for her to listen objectively to whatever he had to tell her.

She'd thought she was prepared to see him, that she had her emotions fully under control. Yet when he stepped into the room, looking dark and handsome and utterly masculine in a black shirt, black denims and black boots, her heart leaped into her throat. The pencil fell from her nerveless fingers. She tried to speak, then found that she couldn't.

Tony cleared his throat, as though he were struggling with the same problem. "Hi, Michelle."

"Hi," she managed in a reasonable semblance of her normal voice. She waved to the leather chair across the desk. "Sit down. Would you like a drink?"

He shook his head, apparently impatient with the formalities. Dropping into the chair, he set a large envelope on her desk.

She looked at it, strangely reluctant to touch it. "What is this?"

"It's what I want to talk to you about. I have something to tell you, Michelle. I'm sorry, but it may be painful for you."

She drew her lower lip between her teeth, waiting for him to explain.

He took a deep breath. "It's about Carter Powell. I assume you'd guessed that."

She nodded, not at all surprised.

"This envelope contains proof that he's been skimming money from your accounts for the past three and a half years—ever since your father died. Powell's been building his own private stash from the trust funds he and your father set up for you. He's been very clever with it. I've had a couple of friends, both accountants, tracing his path through your records. It took them nearly a week, but they found it. The proof is all there, in the envelope."

Michelle swallowed hard. "How did you get my records?"

He hesitated, then sighed. "One of my friends is sort of a computer genius. There's not much he can't find out when he puts his mind to it."

"A hacker."

"Yes."

The thought that not only Tony, but total strangers, had had access to the most intimate details of her private financial affairs made her feel sick. "Why did you do this, Tony?" she whispered.

He frowned. "I told you from the beginning—I don't like being threatened. That first call Powell made to me was a mistake. Had he been genuinely concerned about you, he wouldn't have asked me to lie to you about being unable to find your brothers and sisters. I suspected even then that he had something to hide."

"Why should he have cared about whether I found my family?" Michelle asked in bewilderment. "What would that have mattered to what he was doing?"

"Oh, I'm sure he was genuinely concerned that your family would take advantage of suddenly finding a wealthy sister. He probably realized that his own machinations would come to light if anyone started looking too closely at your finances. You've obviously trusted him to handle things during the past few years, so until now there's been no reason for Powell to worry about being caught.

"Bringing the report to you last weekend was a calculated risk. He probably knew what I was looking for, but he hoped to make you distrust me enough to fire me before I could come up with anything solid. He thought he could easily convince you that I was just another fortune hunter. He didn't expect you to give me a chance to prove I was working in your best interest, rather than my own."

"I just don't understand," Michelle murmured, pressing her fingertips to her temples. "Carter is a wealthy man in his own right. He didn't need to steal from me."

"He's made a good living," Tony corrected, "but it wasn't enough to support both his wife and his mistress in the manner to which they'd become accustomed. Nor would it ensure him the comfortable retirement he was probably planning with your money."

"His mistress," Michelle repeated blankly, thinking of the many times Carter and his wife of many years had dined with her own parents. "You have proof of that, too?"

"Yes."

Though it was a warm day in late June and the temperature in the house was efficiently regulated, Michelle suddenly felt cold. She rubbed her hands slowly up and down her forearms, trying to reduce the chill. "So the financial report Carter brought me was connected to your investigation of him."

"Yes. And by the way, I found out how Carter got his hands on the report. He'd gotten to one of my operatives—Bob O'Brien. Paid him a hell of a lot more than I could to keep him informed about the progress of my work for you. Bob no longer works for me."

Michelle heard the pain of betrayal in his voice, but at the moment she was having too difficult a time struggling with her own similar feelings to offer sympathy. She'd known Carter Powell since she was two years old. She'd trusted him, as her parents had trusted him before her. She hadn't bothered with monitoring his every movement on her behalf, believing him to be one of the few people she could trust with her money, her best interests.

It seemed she'd been wrong again.

"Feel free to look over the evidence I've brought," Tony said, breaking into her dispirited thoughts. "I've brought more than enough to convince you that I'm telling the truth."

"That's not necessary," Michelle replied dully, not meeting his eyes. "I believe you."

"I'm sorry, Michelle. I know this has hurt you."

She took a deep breath, feeling strangely numb. "I must be getting used to it," she mused quietly. And then she reached for her telephone.

"Who are you calling?"

"Carter." She pushed the first familiar button.

Tony's hand covered hers on the telephone, warm against her icy skin. "Michelle...are you sure you want to do that?"

"No," she whispered, without putting down the receiver. "But I think I should let him know I'm going to call the police. It would be less embarrassing for both of us if he quietly turns himself in."

"You're pressing charges?"

"Yes." She met his eyes then, letting her anger show for the first time. "He betrayed me and he betrayed my father. He's not getting away with that."

Tony released her hand. "Good."

Michelle finished dialing the number. "This is Michelle Trent," she said a moment later. "Put me through to Carter. Tell him I strongly advise him to take my call."

Ten unpleasant minutes later, Michelle hung up the phone, her expression stricken. Tony had listened to her side of the conversation, but he wasn't sure what Powell's parting shot had been to turn her face so white. It was all he could do not to reach out to her, to offer comfort he wasn't sure she'd accept from him yet.

"What did he say?" he asked when she continued to sit so

very still and quiet in her chair. "When you asked him why he'd betrayed your father's trust—what did he say?"

"He told me it had never seemed quite fair to him that a girl from a low-class, impoverished family should step into all the Trent wealth and power," she answered in a heart-breakingly flat voice. "It wasn't even as if I'd been born a Trent, he said. He agreed with my Uncle Richard that adoption was hardly the same as pure breeding."

His fists clenching on a surge of pure, primitive fury, Tony fought the urge to leap from his chair and go in search of Carter Powell. How he'd love to shove his fist into that shallow, deceitful, arrogant face!

But to do that, he'd have to leave Michelle. And, judging from her pale, listless appearance, she needed whatever support he could offer at the moment.

"You should have told me," Michelle whispered, her blue eyes big and lost in her colorless face. "You should have let me know what you suspected. I had a right to know."

"I couldn't tell you, Michelle. Not without some evidence to verify my suspicions. I could have been wrong, though my gut feelings all told me I was right. And you wouldn't have believed me, anyway, without proof."

Her eyelashes flicked in reaction to the faint trace of bitterness he couldn't quite keep out of his voice. And then she straightened and lifted her chin, as though dragging her emotions back under rigid control. "I'll pay you for the hours and expenses you've incurred in this investigation, of course, as well as your search for my family. If you'll make up a bill, I'll…"

Tony didn't even try to swallow the vicious curse that leapt to his lips. He slammed his hands down on her desk as he shoved himself to his feet to loom over her. Michelle jumped at his reaction and stared up at him as though he'd lost his mind.

"I know you're hurting and I know you feel betrayed," he

said, his voice low, deadly serious. "But I'll be damned if I'll let you take it out on me."

"I don't know what you mean," she bluffed, her eyes focused somewhere around his Adam's apple. "I simply said—"

"I heard what you said." Deliberately, he rounded the desk. Standing in front of her chair, he reached down to grasp her forearms, pulling her to her feet with a gentle, inexorable pressure. "Now look at me, dammit."

Her wary gaze met his. "I don't appreciate—"

"Tough," he interrupted succinctly. "I haven't appreciated being treated like a money-hungry opportunist during the past week. I haven't appreciated being ordered to provide irrefutable proof that I haven't lied to you or tried to use you. I haven't appreciated sleeping alone the past five nights because the woman I love doesn't trust me enough to believe that I don't give a tinker's damn for her bank accounts! On the whole, I think I've been very patient with you, Michelle. But my patience just ran out."

"I only offered to pay you for your work," she said in a very small voice.

"I didn't do it for pay," he answered gruffly, his pulse reacting to being so close to her again for the first time in so many long days. "I did it because I love you, and because I hated the thought that someone was using you, taking advantage of your trust."

"I did trust him," she whispered, her voice throbbing with pain. "I thought he cared about me. I thought he was a friend. And all the time, he thought...he only..." Her voice broke.

Tony groaned and pulled her roughly against him, his arms going tightly around her. She felt so small, so vulnerable, bringing out every latent protective instinct within him. "I know, Michelle," he murmured. "I know."

Her breath caught on a sob. She stiffened and started to pull away. "I'm sorry. I—"

"No." He held her more tightly. "You're not alone now, Michelle. You don't have to hide your feelings from me."

She resisted only for another moment. And then she burrowed into his shoulder and gave in to the tears she'd been fighting back. Tony bent his head over hers, cradling her to his aching chest. He deeply regretted that in protecting her, he'd had to hurt her. No one, he thought with reckless determination, would ever hurt her like this again.

Michelle didn't cry for long. Swallowing the last of her sobs, she raised her head. He had his handkerchief ready to gently wipe her face.

"Thank you," she murmured.

"Anytime," he replied, smoothing a strand of hair away from her damp, flushed face. "Feel better?"

"Yes," she whispered, her wet eyes darkening as they met his.

His stomach tightened. "Michelle…"

Her arms crept around his neck.

Tony groaned and lowered his head, his mouth covering hers as hungrily as though he'd been starving for her. Probably because he had been. And Michelle returned the kiss with the same desperate intensity, her lips parting in invitation. An invitation he accepted eagerly.

He drew back with a gasp when the kiss strained the boundaries of his willpower. Finding himself dangerously close to taking her right there on her desk, he tried to regain control. It was a close call, but he managed.

"Let's go to your bedroom," he suggested, his voice raw-edged.

Michelle's eyes flew open. "I don't—"

He kissed her again, smothering the words he wasn't sure he wanted to hear. "I want you," he murmured against her lips. "I've missed you."

Her lips moved beneath his, her hands sliding into his hair.

He kissed her deeply, thoroughly, persuasively. "Let's go to your bedroom, Michelle."

She hesitated only another moment before drawing back and offering him her hand.

Feeling as though they'd just avoided a potential crisis, Tony closed his fingers around hers, staying close beside her as she turned and led him toward the stairs to her room. It was going to be all right, he told himself confidently, his blood racing through his veins in anticipation. Michelle was learning to trust him again. He didn't intend to let up until she'd learned to love him as much as he loved her.

Tony noticed that Michelle was unusually quiet as she locked her bedroom door behind them and turned to him. Assuming her silence was a result of the emotional stress she'd been under that afternoon, he spoke soothingly, tenderly to her as he undressed her and then himself. Words of love, of need, of desire. Mostly in English, but occasionally in the so richly expressive Italian language.

He drew her down to the bed, stringing kisses down her throat, caressing her breasts, stroking her silky thighs. "Michelle," he whispered, fitting himself between her legs. "I love you. *Ti amo.*"

Still she said nothing, though her hands were as busy, as avid as his own. She drew him to her, her arms tightly around him, her body arching beneath him. And she cried out in pleasure when he slipped into her, eagerly lifting to his thrusts. When she cried out again, he caught the sound in his mouth, his lips covering hers even as the explosion began for both of them.

When their tremors at last died away, Tony cradled her against his shoulder, unwilling to release her. He stroked her hair with one unsteady hand, his lips against the top of her head.

"I love you," he murmured, closing his eyes to savor the pleasure of having her in his arms again.

* * *

Though he hadn't intended to sleep, Tony woke with a start some time later, realizing that the past few sleepless nights had caught up with him. Judging from the shadows in the bedroom, he'd slept more than an hour. He turned his head on the pillow to see if Michelle was still sleeping—only to find the bed beside him empty.

"Michelle?" he said huskily, immediately pushing himself upright.

She was sitting in a chair across the room, wearing a heavy, dark robe, her legs drawn up within the circle of her arms. She hadn't turned on the lights, but sat in a shadowed corner, looking alone and distant.

"Michelle?" he asked again.

Her head turned in his direction. "Yes?"

"Are you okay?"

"I'm fine."

Watching her closely, he swung his legs over the side of the bed and reached for his pants. He shoved his feet into them. "You're thinking about Powell?"

She shrugged, the motion hardly visible in the shadows. "I was trying not to think at all."

Tony snapped on a light, making her blink. She looked pale and tousled and still sexy enough to make his blood heat in his veins. Wearing only his slacks, he sat on the end of the bed, deciding they needed to talk more than he needed to act on his renewed arousal. "You're being very quiet."

She tightened her arms around her knees, the pose making her look very young and vulnerable. "I didn't want to disturb you. You looked as though you needed your sleep."

"I'm awake now. Ready to talk?"

"About what?" she asked warily.

"About us. I love you, Michelle. I've told you that several times now. You haven't responded."

Her eyelids fell, hiding her expression. "I...don't know what to say."

He fought down the pain. "Do you believe me?"

She didn't respond, other than seeming to curl more tightly into her chair.

"Dammit, Michelle, answer me! Do you believe that I love you? You—and not your money?"

"I—I want to believe it," she said at last, her eyes damp when they slowly lifted back to his.

His fists clenched on his knees. "What more do I have to do to prove it?" he demanded harshly. "How many tests do you have to put me through? I've offered you everything I have. I want to make a life with you, start a family with you, but you have to know you're all I want. I'd sign prenuptial agreements, promise never to touch a penny of your money, whatever I had to do. If I'd met you as Shelley Marie Walker rather than Michelle Culverton Trent, I'd still want to marry you.

"In fact," he added grimly, "I rather wish that's the way it was at the moment. It would be a hell of a lot easier to prove myself to you."

Her hand fluttered weakly in the air, her expression a curious combination of regret and trepidation. "I don't want to hurt you, Tony," she whispered. "I'm not trying to put you through tests. I just...need more time."

He muttered a curse between clenched teeth and abruptly stood, reaching for the rest of his clothes. "Right. More time. More proof. More guarantees."

He thrust his arms into the sleeves of his shirt. "I love you, Michelle," he said flatly. "I'll always love you. But the next move is yours. I won't stop looking for your family, but we can't have a personal relationship if you can't bring yourself to trust me. If you decide what we have is worth taking a few risks, you know where to find me. If I don't hear from you, I'll give you a call whenever I find something on your family."

To his bitter disappointment, she didn't call him back when he turned and left the room.

His revelations about Carter Powell hadn't strengthened Michelle's trust in him, he realized with a sinking feeling in his bruised heart. This latest betrayal had only bolstered her fear of trusting others. And at the moment, he wasn't sure he'd ever be able to break through the protective wall she'd built around herself. Wasn't even sure he had the energy to try.

He climbed into his Jeep, shoved the key into the ignition and turned the wheels toward the massive front gates of the Trent estate. He needed rest, needed time to get over this new hurt she'd inflicted on him. And then he'd probably be back, armed with every emotional weapon he could think of for storming invisible defenses. Because, God help him, he didn't think he could ever walk away from her for good.

Tony had intended to head straight home for about sixteen hours of uninterrupted sleep. He wasn't even sure when he'd changed his mind. But he found himself pulling into the driveway of his parents' home, needing very badly to be with people who loved him and had always believed in him.

He found his father in the den, drinking a beer and watching a baseball game on the cable sports channel. Carla, apparently, was still at work, or Vinnie never would have risked the cigar smoldering in an ashtray at his elbow. "Hi, Dad. Better spray some air freshener before Mom gets home or there'll be hell to pay."

Vinnie nodded at his son and held up a blue spray can. "Got it covered," he said. "I figure I've got a sixty-forty chance of getting away with it this time."

Tony smiled—or tried to.

Vinnie took one look at that weak excuse for a smile and rose to his feet in concern. "Tony? What is it, son?"

"Mind if I get a beer and hang around here awhile?" Tony asked, gesturing toward the television. "We can watch the rest of the game together."

"Of course I don't mind. I'd like that."

Tony nodded and turned toward the small refrigerator installed in a wet bar in one corner of the comfortably furnished room. Vinnie was still standing, still watching him, when he came back with his beer.

"Want to talk about it, Tony?"

Tony shook his head. "Not yet."

Never reticent about showing his feelings toward his family, Vinnie put an arm around his son's shoulders and gave him a bracing hug. "When you're ready, I'm here."

Tony swallowed the lump in his throat. "I know, Dad. Thanks. I may need to take you up on that offer."

"That's what family's for, son. Let's sit down and get comfortable."

"Let me get this straight." Sprawled in an oversized blue leather armchair, Taylor tented her fingers in front of her and looked thoughtful as she spoke for the first time in nearly half an hour of listening to Michelle's garbled rantings.

"Tony says he loves you and wants to marry you. Without being paid or thanked for his efforts, he went to great lengths to expose a man who has been taking advantage of you for years. Tony was even willing to temporarily put up with your suspicions that he may be a calculating gigolo because he didn't want to make accusations against your attorney without evidence, just in case his instincts were wrong. He forgave you for thinking the worst of him and is willing to sign prenuptial agreements promising not to touch your money if you marry him.

"Frankly, Michelle, he sounds like a madman to me. I think he should be shot at sunrise."

Stopping her restless prowling of Taylor's Southwestern-decorated living room, Michelle whirled on her friend in frustration. "I thought you said you'd listen objectively if I'd talk to you about what's been bothering me!"

"I *did* listen objectively," Taylor returned evenly. "I heard every word you babbled. I'm furious with Carter Powell for what he did to you and I think you're entirely right to press charges against him so he doesn't ever try anything like this again. I understand you're hurting and that you think you've been given even more reason not to trust people. What I *don't* understand is why you feel Tony deserves your distrust. Everything he's done has been for your sake."

Michelle moistened her lips and shoved her hands into the pockets of her denim skirt. "I didn't say I don't trust him."

"You didn't say you do trust him, either," Taylor returned.

Michelle couldn't argue with that. She'd spent the past twenty-four hours trying to untangle her feelings about Tony.

"Do you love him?"

Michelle's pulse leaped nervously in response to Taylor's question. "I—"

"Truth, Michelle."

She sighed in surrender. "Yes. I love him."

"So what's the problem?"

"I'm scared," Michelle admitted quietly, looking to Taylor for understanding. "I'm afraid of being hurt again. What if something goes wrong? What if we can't make it work out?"

Still looking deeply thoughtful, Taylor reached up to ruffle her short, dark hair in her habitual gesture. "Remember when you talked me into giving country-and-western music a try, even though I was a hard-core rock-and-roll fan?"

Frowning at the apparent non sequitur, Michelle nodded slowly. "Why?"

"Well, I like it. And I keep thinking of a song that was popular last year…'A Leap of Faith' by Lionel Cartwright. Remember it?"

"Um—yes."

"It seems rather appropriate at the moment. The lyrics point out that you can't always tell what kind of problems you'll encounter in your life, but that real love will always find a way to overcome them. It says that even though your heart's been broken before, you have to take a chance—a 'leap of faith'—and put your trust in someone again."

"It's only a song, Taylor."

"Mmm. But it's true. He says the first step's always the hardest."

"It makes a nice song," Michelle murmured defensively, sinking into a chair that matched the one Taylor sat in, "but real life isn't always so easy. Tony could hurt me, Taylor, worse than Geoff ever could have. That scares me."

Taylor was quiet for a long moment, her eyes curiously blank, as though focused on something Michelle couldn't see. And when she spoke, her voice throbbed with a low, old pain. "The hardest thing I've ever had to face was losing Dylan. Sitting in that hospital waiting room alone, remembering everything we'd found, reliving the moment when that car came out of nowhere and took him away from me—I wasn't sure I'd survive losing him."

Michelle bit her lower lip, distressed by the extent of the suffering Taylor had never revealed so clearly to her before. "Oh, Taylor…"

Taylor drew a deep breath, as though to ward off tears she had no intention of shedding. "For a long time after they told me Dylan had died on the operating table, I was as angry as I was devastated. I was so damned mad that I'd met him only to lose him after only a few short weeks together. I thought it was horribly unfair that those three weeks would haunt me for the rest of my life, that I'd never stop comparing any man I met to the one I couldn't keep. I lay awake nights wishing I'd never turned that corner and walked into him, that he'd never picked up my packages and smiled at me. That I'd turned him down when he offered to buy me a drink. That I'd never fallen in love with him."

And then she shook her head, her expression clearing as she turned her gaze back on her unhappy friend. "You know what helped me then? It was another country song. Garth Brooks's 'The Dance.' It made me think about whether I really would have missed knowing Dylan if given a choice, whether I'd trade my memories of those three perfect weeks with him for anything. And I realized that I wouldn't. Whatever I had to go through afterward was worth having the privilege to know him, be with him, love him and be loved by him. And I wouldn't have missed it for anything."

"But can you ever risk loving again, risking that pain again?" Michelle asked in a tearful whisper, her hands gripped so tightly in her lap that her fingers ached.

"I hope I'll love again someday," Taylor admitted, "if I can ever find anyone who makes me feel the way Dylan did. I don't want to spend the rest of my life alone. I'd like a family someday. Maybe.

"And what about you?" she asked, turning the questioning to Michelle. "Don't you want children, someone to love? Are you going to spend the rest of your life hiding in that big house of yours, guarding your money and your heart? Or are you going to accept the risks that are simply a part of being alive?"

Michelle caught her breath at the wording. She'd taken a chance at finding her family, and she'd found Layla and Kevin and the children. She'd also found Tony and his lovable, close-knit family, who'd welcomed her so warmly among them.

She'd been willing to work at her relationship with her sister…shouldn't she be willing to work even harder at holding on to the man she loved with all her heart?

She'd long since grown tired of guarding the wealth that didn't really matter to her at all. She was tired of being lonely, tired of being afraid. She wasn't a vulnerable eight-year-old now, but a grown woman, competent and experienced and perfectly capable of taking care of herself. Wasn't she also intelligent enough to know when to put her faith in someone else?

"It's your call, Michelle," Taylor said as though she'd read her friend's thoughts. "Is Tony worth the risk?"

Chapter Fifteen

"That's right, Cassie, I've got to pull you off the Jared Walker investigation—temporarily, at least," Tony confirmed into the telephone. "With Bob gone, we're shorthanded until I can find someone to replace him. I need you on the Grayson Industries security report… Yeah, you can follow up any leads you get on Walker in the meantime. But remember that Grayson's a priority right now."

He was already flipping through his Rolodex file for another number when he hung up. He had a stack of calls and responsibilities to get through on this Monday morning. Not that he minded. He'd just as soon work as spend another day moping around his apartment, missing Michelle.

He'd regretted pulling Cassie off the full-time search for Jared Walker. He would have liked to have been able to provide Michelle with her oldest brother's whereabouts as soon as possible. The problem was, he had other cases to handle, other clients to consider. And Cassie had admitted that she wasn't getting anywhere fast finding Walker. Every time she thought she had a lead, the trail grew cold long before she ran it down.

He had gotten more information on Lindsay, but hadn't yet obtained her current whereabouts. As for the twins—he'd come up cold on every angle he'd tried in searching for them.

He'd wanted to give Michelle her family, even if she wouldn't accept anything else he wanted so badly to offer her.

He cursed when he failed to find the number he was looking for in his file. Damned if he could find anything today! Disgruntled, he punched the intercom. "Bonnie—get me Stu Grayson's number, will you? And have you got those letters ready to go out yet?"

"They're almost ready for your signature, Tony."

"Good. Bring them in with Grayson's number. I've got a couple of other calls I can make first." He took his finger off the button and reached for his card file again.

This call didn't take long; he hung up the phone at the same time the door to his office opened. Without looking up from the paperwork littered across his desk, he held out his hand. "You found Grayson's number?"

A slip of paper was placed in his hand. He glanced at it, noting the number printed neatly in Bonnie's familiar handwriting. "Thanks. Got those letters ready for me to sign?"

"Bonnie said she'll have them ready for you in a few minutes. I told her not to hurry. You're going to be busy for a while."

Tony's head jerked up, his eyes rounding. "Michelle!"

With uncharacteristic clumsiness, he nearly fell over his desk when he stood, kicking his chair from beneath him, his eyes locked on the smiling face of the woman he loved. His heart thudded in sudden hope in response to the look in her eyes. He prayed with everything inside him that he wasn't misreading her expression. "What are you doing here?"

Michelle took a deep, bracing breath in response to Tony's question. The expression on his face when he'd looked up to find her standing there had brought a giant lump to her throat. Why, until now, had she allowed her fears to blind her to the love in his eyes? And how could he still look at her that way when she'd treated him so very badly?

"You're busy," she murmured, suddenly shy. "Maybe I should have waited until after business hours."

"I'm never too busy for you," Tony assured her huskily. He walked around the end of the desk, never taking his eyes from her face. He gestured toward the sofa against one wall. "D'you want to sit down?"

"Not yet," she replied, too nervous to sit, her fingers locked tightly around the papers she held in her left hand.

"All right." Stopping close beside her, he crossed his arms and stood at apparent ease, though there were lines of strain at the corners of his mouth. "What is that?" he asked, nodding toward the papers she held. "Something you wanted to discuss with me?"

"Yes." She cleared her throat, then called on every ounce of courage she possessed. "This…this is a prenuptial agreement, Tony. I had my attorney—my new attorney—draw it up. It's legal and binding."

His eyes narrowed. "A prenuptial agreement?" he repeated slowly, looking from the papers to her flushed face. "You're considering my marriage proposal?"

"Does the offer still stand?" she whispered.

His face softened. "Yes," he replied simply. "Nothing's changed about my feelings for you."

The utter sincerity of his words brought tears to her eyes. Her voice trembled. "I don't deserve you, Tony."

"Just tell me you love me," he answered a bit unsteadily, "and I'll sign anything you like. All I've ever wanted is you, Michelle."

In response, she lifted the papers and very calmly ripped them in half. And then in half again. Her fingers opened, allowing the ragged shreds to fall around their feet.

Tony seemed stunned by her actions. "Why did you do that? What are you telling me?" he demanded.

Her tears blurred his face when she looked at him. "I love you, Tony. I trust you. I was a blind, cowardly fool not to trust you from the very beginning. Can you ever forgive me?"

"Michelle. Oh, God." Without hesitation, he reached out to pull her into his arms. "I love you. There's nothing to forgive."

Her arms going tightly around his lean waist, Michelle shook her head against his shoulder, feeling the tears escaping the corners of her eyes despite her efforts to hold them back.

"I should never have doubted you, Tony. You were always on my side, always trying to help me, and I still treated you so badly. I'll spend the rest of my life making it up to you, I promise."

"I understood, you know," he told her quietly, stroking her hair with one unsteady hand. "It hurt, but I always understood. You'd been hurt before, and you kept getting hurt. You had every reason to be cautious."

She lifted her wet face from his shoulder to look up at him. "I've learned that being so cautious is a very lonely way to live. I don't want to be alone anymore, Tony."

He dried her tears with gentle fingers. "You won't ever be lonely again, *tesoro*. I'm going to fill your life with more love, more family than you'll know what to do with. Your brothers and sisters and nieces and nephews. My family, who already love you almost as much as I do. And our own children, however many you'd like. As soon as you want to have them."

"Oh, Tony." She tugged his head down to hers for a long, lingering kiss. "I love you," she said when he finally released her mouth.

"I love you, too, *cara*."

She nibbled at his lower lip. "Tell me in Italian."

He smiled and kissed her. *"Ti amo."*

"Ti amo," she repeated.

"Anch'io ti amo. I love you, too. *Ti adoro.* I adore you. *Ti amo, e ti amero per tutta la vita.* I'll love you for the rest of my life."

He punctuated the impromptu language lesson with progressively longer kisses.

Emerging flushed and breathless from one particularly enthusiastic embrace, Michelle smiled up at him. "I'd like you to teach me Italian. I want to know everything that's being said at your family gatherings."

"Our family gatherings," Tony corrected her. "You'll be a D'Alessandro, too, God help you. And I'd be happy to teach you Italian. In fact, I'd be willing to spend the rest of my life teaching you."

"It may just take that long for me to learn," she murmured, tightening her arms around his neck.

"Does that mean you'll marry me?"

"I thought we had that settled. Of course I'll marry you. It's what I want more than anything in the world."

He kissed her deeply, then drew back just far enough to speak. "About the prenuptial agreement, Michelle. I want you to get another copy for me to sign. I never want you to have cause to doubt me again."

"No." She shook her head stubbornly, utterly determined on that point. "I want *you* to know that I trust you implicitly, that I don't need papers or legalities or anything but your word. I love you, Tony. And I believe in you. Let me prove it to you the only way I know how."

Twin fires flared in his dark eyes. He drew her closer, his hand sliding savoringly down her back. "I'm sure we can come up with some other way for you to show me how much you love me."

She smiled in anticipation. "I'll do that, too," she murmured. "But that will have to wait until we're alone. Your place or mine, but not in your office with your secretary right outside."

"We could lock the door," he suggested, looking absurdly wistful.

She laughed and kissed him, then pulled away. "Later," she said firmly. "I have things to do this afternoon."

"Oh? Like what?" he challenged her.

"I have a wedding to plan," she replied happily. "I have to call Layla and Taylor to help me get started. I'm warning you, my love, it's going to be a major event. I want all your family there."

"*All* of them?" he asked in exaggerated dismay, though he didn't look particularly reluctant.

"All of them," she replied firmly. "Adults, children and babies. All my life I've wanted to belong to a big family. Now you've granted that wish for me."

"You plan our wedding any way you want it," Tony told her recklessly. "Just make sure you don't take more than a month to get it together."

"A month?" she gasped. "But, Tony…"

"Six weeks," he compromised. "That's as long as I intend to wait to make you my wife."

"Then I'd better get started immediately," she said unsteadily, turning toward the door. And then she stopped and turned to throw herself back in his arms for a long, fervent hug. "I love you," she said fiercely. "And I'm going to make you the happiest man alive."

His arms locked around her. "You already have, *tesoro*," he assured her huskily. "Trust me. You already have."

Epilogue

Teresa and Paul D'Alessandro had offered their big backyard as a location for the early afternoon wedding. The acre-and-a-half lawn was filled to capacity with folding chairs, colorful tents, tables of food, masses of flowers. And people. Aunts, uncles, cousins, in-laws, friends.

Taylor served as maid of honor, Layla and another long-time friend of Michelle's were bridesmaids. Vinnie stood as his son's best man, brothers Joe and Mike serving as groomsmen. Layla's son, Keith, proudly carried the rings, while tiny Brittany made an adorable flower girl. Not to be left out, eight-year-old Dawne distributed bags of birdseed to be thrown at the departing bridal couple.

It was a noisy, joyous, haphazardly organized affair. And Michelle wouldn't have changed a minute of it.

"It was the most beautiful wedding anyone's ever had," she enthused, dancing around a plush hotel room much later that evening. "Absolutely, positively, indisputably perfect."

Pouring champagne into two beribboned stem glasses, Tony smiled indulgently at his still-hyper bride. "Perfect?"

"*Perfetto.*"

He managed not to laugh at her accent. "Even when Kevin asked Father Bailey why he had his shirt on backward? Layla nearly melted in embarrassment."

"The kid's been raised Methodist. How would he have known? And Father Bailey thought it was cute."

"Was it perfect when cousin Angelo's two boys got into a fight and spilled the punch bowl all over the skirt of Aunt Lucia's dress?"

"It was an accident," Michelle replied firmly. "Everyone laughed, didn't they?"

"Everyone but Angelo and Aunt Lucia. And the boys weren't laughing when their father got through with them, either."

Michelle made a dismissive gesture with the hand in which he'd just placed a glass of champagne, sending a wave of the expensive, bubbly beverage over the rim to splash at her feet. "Accidents happen."

His eyes laughed at her euphoria. "Is that what you call Teresa going into labor halfway through the reception? An accident?"

"That was a happy coincidence," Michelle replied. "Now we'll always remember little Bianca's birthday—the same day as our wedding anniversary."

"I'm only sorry we couldn't find the rest of your family in time to invite them to our wedding," Tony murmured, setting his half-emptied champagne glass aside.

Michelle shook her head, refusing to let even that dim her pleasure in the day. "Layla and Kevin and the children were there. If we never find the others, I'll always be grateful to you for helping me find my sister."

"I'll find the others," Tony said, his jaw set in determination. "No matter how long it takes."

Suddenly serious, Michelle lifted her free hand to his face, all her love in her eyes. "I know you won't stop trying, Tony," she assured him. "You promised, didn't you? And you always keep your promises, if it's humanly possible to do so."

"You're taking a pretty big chance being so confident in me," he murmured, covering her hand with his own.

"No. I don't think I'm taking a chance at all," she whispered. "I love you, Tony. And I trust you. With all my heart."

His eyes flared. "I love you, too, Michelle. And I'll never do anything to make you regret trusting me."

"I know you won't, darling. Besides," she added with a smile, "you're the one who taught me to swing a baseball bat, aren't you? Just remember that when you're tempted to stray."

"Threats now." He sighed deeply and shook his head, his fingers going to the fastenings at the back of her dress. "I can tell I'm going to have my hands full with you."

Her dress slipped down her shoulders. "In a moment, you certainly will," she agreed, giggling.

"Any complaints, *tesoro?*"

She stepped out of the gown, leaving her clad only in filmy, delectably sexy underthings, and draped her arms around his neck. "Not a one, my love."

He'd caught his breath at the sight of her pale flesh beneath sheer lace and satin. When he spoke, his voice was hoarse, his breathing shallow. "I love you."

She pressed her lips to his, then drew back only far enough to whisper, "Show me how much."

"That's going to take a while," he murmured, lifting her high against his chest and turning toward the bed behind him. "The rest of our lives."

Her smile was blissfully happy. "That's all I could ever ask."

He followed her to the bed, his lean body pressing her deliciously into the mattress, and she lifted her mouth to his, knowing the time for words had passed.

She knew that Tony's love was everything she'd ever longed for. Whatever life brought them from now on would be faced together. Michelle Walker Trent D'Alessandro would never be lonely again.

* * * * *

HARDWORKING MAN

Prologue

"Tony? It's Cassie. I've found him."

"You've found Jared Walker? You're sure you've got the right man? My wife's brother?"

Huddling against the light September morning rain blowing under the eaves of the convenience store outside of which she stood, Cassie Browning tightened her fingers around the pay telephone receiver and turned her back to the impatient teenager waiting in line for the phone. "I'm sure it's the right man, I've got his driver's license photo—he hasn't changed that much from the childhood photograph we have of him."

Cassie's employer, private investigator Tony D'Alessandro, was obviously quite pleased with her report. "Cassie, this is great! I can't wait to tell Michelle. She and Layla have been so anxious to see their brother, especially since I told them how close you were to finding him."

"Um—Tony? You might want to hold up on telling Michelle and Layla that Jared's been located. There's something I haven't told you yet."

Her boss's voice grew sober, wary, as though the gravity of her tone had suddenly gotten through to him. "What is it, Cassie?"

She took a deep breath, then blurted, "Jared Walker's in jail, Tony. He was arrested last night. He's been charged with armed robbery."

Chapter One

Cassie squirmed restlessly in the hard metal chair, folding her hands on the wooden table in front of her as she counted the minutes since she'd been led into the dismal room. She hadn't had a great deal of experience with jail procedures back home in Dallas, but she suspected that the customs in this tiny New Mexico town were somewhat more lax and disorganized than the average. To say the least.

Though the staff she'd dealt with thus far could have stepped straight from a Western version of "Mayberry, RFD," it hadn't been difficult to arrange this interview with Jared Walker, who'd been arrested only nine hours earlier—at 1:00 a.m. on this Thursday morning, to be precise. All she'd had to do was claim to be representing his family, as her employer had instructed her to say.

Tony had been understandably appalled and concerned when Cassie had called him two hours earlier to tell him just where she'd found his wife's long-lost brother. After all, Michelle Trent D'Alessandro was a very wealthy woman who'd been separated from her six siblings since childhood. As much as she wanted to find them now, there was always an awareness that she had to be careful, that the people she was looking for were strangers.

Tony, in particular, was extremely protective of his wife of two months, which explained the instructions he'd given Cassie two hours ago.

"I want to know everything there is to know about this guy," he'd said firmly. "You've got good instincts about people, Cassie. Talk to him. If there's even a possibility he's not guilty, find out what the hell's going on. If you think he's been arrested with good reason, call me back and we'll decide how to take it from there."

He'd added that, whatever prevarications she had to invent, she was not to tell Jared Walker about his sister. Not yet, anyway. Scrupulously honest in his business dealings, Tony wasn't above subterfuge when it came to protecting Michelle. And until they knew more about the man in this tiny New Mexico jail, Tony had no intention of claiming him as his wife's kin.

Something about this whole case bothered Cassie. Though she had found out relatively little about Jared Walker during the past months of investigating, nothing she'd learned had led her to believe he would be involved in an armed robbery. As far as she could tell, he'd led an uneventful, law-abiding life, from high school to service in the U.S. Navy to a series of ranch jobs across the Midwest.

His discharge had been an honorable one, his military record unspectacular but clean, including several meritorious citations. He had no criminal record, had never been charged with even a misdemeanor. His former employers had given him work recommendations, calling him quiet, reserved, very private, but reliable and very hardworking. Would a man like that suddenly turn to crime at thirty-five?

She *would* clear this up, Cassie thought with a surge of determination. She was twenty-six years old and had held more jobs than she could count on both hands, but this was the first one she'd utterly loved from the day she'd started. She'd finally found her niche in private investigation, and though she was only an apprentice now, she fully intended to be a partner someday. And what better way to start than to clear the name of her employer's brother-in-law—assuming, of course, the man was innocent. Cassie crossed her fingers.

And then Deputy William "Slim" Calhoun led in the prisoner—and Cassie's breath caught somewhere in her throat.

She hadn't been prepared for the emotional impact of actually seeing Jared Walker, a man she knew only from an old driver's license photo and a faded family portrait in which he'd been eleven years old. He'd looked innocuous enough in those photos, though he hadn't been smiling in either. But reality was a lean, dangerous-looking man in a regulation orange jumpsuit, his short brown hair disheveled, roughly carved features grim, dark blue eyes holding a wealth of anger, bitterness and a deep-seated pain.

And suddenly Cassie knew that nothing about this case was going to proceed as she'd hoped. This may just prove to be the challenge of her career—her entire life, perhaps.

The first thing Jared noticed about the woman was her shoulder-length mop of carrot red curls glittering like fire in the fluorescent lighting. Her eyes were wide, green, ingenuous, her pert nose scattered with faint freckles. She looked maybe twenty, twenty-one, though he supposed she could be a few years older. Not much.

He'd never seen her before. But, then, he hadn't expected to find anyone he knew waiting in this dingy interrogation room. Slim had told him he had a visitor representing his family. Since Jared Walker had only one family member that he could account for, he'd known from the first that the woman had lied.

He suspected from looking at her that she was an eager cub reporter, hoping for a juicy story for her tiny town newspaper. He didn't particularly care what her angle was as long as he could find some way to use her for his own advantage.

He was innocent of the crime with which these clods had charged him, but proving his innocence would be no easy task in a small town where he had no friends and no alibi. He couldn't even make bail, though he'd already placed a call to the one person who could possibly help him with that.

Jared had one particularly compelling reason to get out of this place as quickly as possible. Not that he intended to share that reason with anyone else—including the young woman watching him so anxiously as he was led in.

The woman gave Calhoun a look that had the paunchy forty-something officer preening in his wrinkled uniform. "Thank you so much, Deputy," she told him, her pleasant voice dripping with gratitude and admiration. "Would you mind if I talk to Jared in private?"

Calhoun frowned. "I don't know, Miz Browning. He could be dangerous. He was armed when he perpetrated the crime."

"*Allegedly* perpetrated the crime," Cassie reminded him gently. "And I assure you I'm in no danger. Am I, Jared?" she asked, looking at him in a manner that dared him to say he'd never laid eyes on her before.

"None at all," he replied, watching as her fair cheeks flushed at his response. Interesting.

"Please, Deputy," Cassie persisted. "This is family business. You could wait right outside the door so I could call if I need you."

Calhoun hesitated, then caved in to the entreaty in those wide, clear eyes. "Okay," he said, nudging Jared to a chair at the other side of the table where Cassie sat. "You behave yourself, Walker," he ordered sternly, scowling in an admirable imitation of Barney Fife at his most ferocious.

"Yeah. Right," Jared muttered, attention still focused on the woman as he took his seat.

"You call out if you need me, Miz Browning. I'll be standing right outside the door," Slim assured her, patting the grip of his .38 and glaring at Jared as he spoke.

"That's…very comforting to know," the woman murmured, only the slightest break in her voice betraying the amusement dancing in her eyes.

Jared felt his interest in her quickening. And then they were alone, the door to the room left open an inch or so despite her request for privacy. The woman clapped a hand over her mouth to stifle a giggle, seeming to need a moment before leaning across the table to speak softly. "Is everyone here like him?"

Jared nodded, his mouth quirking with his first smile since he'd been grabbed in the parking lot of his cheap motel. "Yeah, pretty much. They're all aquiver at having caught themselves a real, live criminal—even though they've got the wrong man."

Her expression sobered abruptly. "*Have* they got the wrong man?" she asked bluntly.

"Yeah." He met her eyes across the table without blinking. "They have."

Cassie searched those penetrating dark blue eyes for a long, taut moment, trying to read the truth in them. So much evidence against him—and yet she simply couldn't imagine this man robbing a fleabag motel office, no matter how hard she tried. She found herself wanting to believe in his innocence—for Michelle's sake, for her career's sake, but mostly because she suddenly had a hunch....

Despite her friends' groaning distrust of her many impulsive hunches, Cassie had rarely been wrong in her instincts about people. Everything she'd learned about Jared Walker in her investigation, everything she saw in his clear blue eyes now, told her he was a man who lived quietly, honestly and carefully. Robbing the very motel where he was staying, leaving the alleged weapon in his room, returning openly and carelessly to the scene of the crime—none of those actions seemed to fit the man who sat across from her now, watching her so intently, so steadily.

"I guess we'll just have to do something about proving your innocence, won't we?" she said evenly, knowing she'd need his full cooperation if she were to find that proof.

His head cocked at her matter-of-fact tone. "Who the hell is 'we'?"

She cleared her throat. "Us. You and me. That's all I meant, of course." She cursed her lifelong inability to lie to anyone she really liked. When necessary in the course of her work, she could lie like a trouper to strangers and people she didn't care for, but she had a very hard time misleading anyone whose opinion mattered to her.

So why couldn't she consider Jared Walker just another stranger?

Don't screw this up, Browning, she warned herself sternly.

"I need some information about last night," she went on quickly. "Everything you were doing, everywhere you went during the time of the robbery. As I see it, our main problem is your lack of an alibi during the hours of eleven and midnight, when the robbery occurred. So what we need to do is—"

"Just wait a minute," Jared broke in shortly, leaning slightly forward so that his low voice was audible only to her. "First I think you'd better tell me who the hell you are, and why you're so all-fired intent on getting me out."

Okay, Browning, watch your step. If you're ever going to be a partner in D'Alessandro Investigations, your career is riding on the next few minutes.

Her fingers clenching in her lap with the pressure she was inflicting on herself, Cassie took a deep breath. "My name is Cassie Browning," she told him softly. "And I'm a private investigator."

He looked startled. "*You?* A P.I.?"

She wasn't flattered by his skepticism. She drew herself up stiffly and nodded. "I could show you my identification, but I don't think this is exactly a good time for that. Slim could walk back in, and he thinks we already know each other."

"Yeah, right. You told him you're representing my 'family.'"

She cleared her throat again. "It was all I could think of on short notice."

"So who are you working for, *Miz* Browning? Who hired you to clear me? Was it Bob Cutter? When I called, I was told he was at his hunting camp and couldn't be reached until Monday."

"I'm sorry," she murmured, making a mental note of the name Bob Cutter. "I can't answer that. I have instructions to keep my client's name confidential for now. I'm sure you understand."

"No, I sure as hell don't," Jared answered roughly. "I have something at stake here. I deserve to know exactly what's going on."

He had a point there. But Cassie had an employer to answer to—an employer who'd been known on occasion to lose his formidable Italian temper when an operative blew a case.

"You'll know soon enough. Right now the important thing is to get you out of here, wouldn't you agree?"

Jared sighed, looking anything but satisfied. "Yeah," he grumbled after a moment. "I want out."

"Good. Then let's get started. Why were you staying in that motel last night? What are you doing in this two-bit town?"

She could have added that she knew he'd left instructions for his last employer to forward his final paycheck to general delivery at the post office in this "two-bit-town"—which was the way she'd located him in the first place—but she kept that to herself, wanting to hear the whole story from Jared.

Jared didn't look as though he appreciated being questioned about his activities. Knowing him to be a loner, she suspected he didn't often find it necessary to explain his actions. But this time it was important. This time his freedom depended on it.

"Jared?" she prodded.

He scowled, but nodded. "I was just on my way through," he explained. "I'm headed for Arizona, where I hope to find ranch work for the winter. I'd worked out my route on a map and told my last employer to forward a check to general delivery here, which I picked up yesterday. So I had some money on me," he added. "I didn't need to rip off the motel office."

Again, she studied the expression in his eyes, analyzed his tone. He sounded very much like an innocent man, she thought soberly. Was she being incredibly naive to find herself wanting to believe him? Despite her characteristic impulsiveness, her habitual snap judgments, the past ten minutes had hardly been long enough for her to get to know Jared—much less to form such sweeping judgments about his character. And yet...

"I'd like to believe that," she said slowly, holding his gaze with her own. "I'd like to help you prove it, if I can."

He crossed his arms on the table and locked his gaze with hers. "Why?"

Flustered by the unblinking intensity of his stare, Cassie squirmed. "Let's just say it's my job."

She quickly changed the subject, becoming all business again. "All right, here's the situation. You checked in to the motel at around 9:00 p.m. The motel owner, Gus Turley, noticed you particularly because there weren't but a few other guests and you didn't look like the usual trucker or weary tourist he generally gets. He also remembered that you paid cash in advance and didn't list a permanent address on your registration card. He said he tried to start a friendly conversation with you but you weren't very polite in response."

Jared grunted. "I was tired. Wasn't in the mood for small talk. So the guy fingered me as an armed robber because I hurt his feelings when I checked in?"

She frowned reprovingly at him. "There's a little more to it than that. The man who robbed him at gunpoint somewhere around 11:30 p.m. wore a ski mask, but he was approximately your size. He had on jeans, boots and a denim jacket, and Turley said he remembered you were wearing a similar outfit when you checked in."

"Me and most of the other guys in town," Jared muttered.

He had a point there. That had been her own instant response when she'd heard the description of the robber's clothing. Jeans and a denim jacket were the norm in this part of the country.

"Anyway," she continued, "the cops went to your room, knocked, didn't get an answer. They went in, found the bathroom window open, your duffel bag still in the room. They didn't find any money, but they found a gun."

"It's not illegal to own a gun," Jared pointed out. "And from what I hear, it wasn't even the same make of handgun Turley claimed the robber had used."

Point two. Cassie had pondered that rather significant error herself. "Yes, well, now he says he was so shaken up he could have been mistaken. It could have been your gun, he says."

"He's wrong."

Cassie nodded and went on with the facts as they'd been presented to her. "The cops staked out the room, caught you coming back at around 1:00 a.m. You resisted arrest."

"Hell, I didn't even know they were cops! They just came out of the shadows and grabbed me the minute I stepped out of my truck. I thought they were muggers. I hit a couple of them, but I think I had good cause."

It didn't surprise Cassie that Jared hadn't been taken easily. She sensed he was the type who'd hit first, ask questions later. Yet, despite her instincts that he was capable of violence, she felt no fear of him. His was a violence kept sternly leashed, she suspected, released only when necessary to protect himself—or someone he cared for. And where the hell had *that* observation come from? she wondered in exasperation.

Immediately distracting herself from that line of thought, she went on. "You said you'd been unable to sleep and had taken a drive. You claimed to have stopped at an all-night diner for a cup of coffee, but the waitress said she didn't remember seeing you."

"She didn't want to get involved, most likely," Jared growled. "They never do."

"Can you describe her for me?"

He shrugged. "Fiftyish. Twenty pounds overweight. Hairstyle twenty years out of date—lots of tight little curls on top of her head. Bleached. Name tag on her pocket said 'Nellie.'"

Cassie lifted an eyebrow. "You told that to the cops?"

He snorted. "Yeah. They said I could have been in anytime yesterday afternoon and seen her."

"Damn."

"They want this conviction, Cassie. I get the impression I'm the most excitement they've had around here in months."

A shiver of awareness coursed through her when he said her name in that rough, deep voice. Why hadn't she noticed right off how sexy he was, despite his scowl?

Whoa, Browning. None of that. Rule number one: Never get involved with the clients.

Not that Jared was a client, exactly.

She avoided his too-knowing gaze as she hesitantly broached the next topic. "Turley thinks you were working with an accomplice, who now has the money you allegedly stole from him. He swears he saw you enter your motel room with someone, though you registered as a single."

"I travel alone."

Jared's expression was shuttered, his voice flat, brooking no argument. It took all her nerve for Cassie to ask, "Did you have any visitors in your room? A—er—woman you'd met in town, perhaps?"

"No."

Unaccountably relieved, she nodded. "So Turley was wrong about that, too. He was probably looking for a way to explain that the money wasn't found on you."

Jared remained silent. She frowned, studying him more closely. "Jared? Is there something you're not telling me? I have to know everything if I'm going to find the proof that you're innocent."

"That's the whole story," he replied flatly. "So what are you going to do now?"

"Talk to Turley, I suppose. And Nellie, of course."

"If you're so convinced of my innocence, how about bailing me out of here? I can help you come up with the proof I need."

Cassie bit her lip, knowing it must have been hard for him

to ask her to bail him out. Jared Walker wasn't a man who'd ask for help easily. She could identify with that. Having always been the stubbornly independent type herself, she knew how hard it was to swallow pride and admit the need for assistance. Why was she beginning to think she and Jared Walker had quite a few things in common? Had the stress of this complicated morning affected her more than she'd thought?

"I'm sorry," she murmured, avoiding his eyes. "Your bail is so high, I don't have enough to cover it. Don't you have anyone to call? A friend? An attorney?"

Was he really so very much alone?

He shrugged. "I've called a friend in Oklahoma, the one I mentioned earlier. He's unavailable for the weekend. As soon as I get in touch with him, I'm sure he'll come through with bail and an attorney—I don't think I want to risk having one appointed for me here. God knows who I'd get, if Deputy Fife out there is anything to judge this town by."

"When do you think you'll be able to reach this friend?"

He shrugged again. "Two, three days."

Distressed, Cassie clenched her hands more tightly in front of her on the table. She hated the thought of Jared spending two or three more days behind bars.

She made a sudden decision to call Tony the moment she left the jailhouse, hoping to persuade him to wire her the money for Jared's bail. After all, Jared was Tony's brother-in-law. And Cassie was here to make sure he didn't jump bail. What could it hurt to get him out of this ridiculous excuse for a jail until he could be brought to a fair trial—or until Cassie found evidence to clear him, which she hoped would be soon.

"I'll do everything I can to get you out of here, Jared," she promised impulsively. "Please believe me."

An Important Message from the Editors

Dear Reader,

Because you've chosen to read one of our fine romance novels, we'd like to say "thank you!" And, as a **special** way to thank you, we've selected <u>two more</u> of the books you love so well **plus** an exciting Mystery Gift to send you — absolutely <u>FREE!</u>

Please enjoy them with our compliments...

Pam Powers

Lift here

How to validate your Editor's
"Thank You"
FREE GIFT

1. Peel off gift seal from front cover. Place it in space provided at right. This automatically entitles you to receive 2 FREE BOOKS and a fabulous mystery gift.

2. Send back this card and you'll get 2 brand-new *Romance* novels. These books have a cover price of $5.99 or more each in the U.S. and $6.99 or more each in Canada, but they are yours to keep absolutely free.

3. There's no catch. You're under no obligation to buy anything. We charge nothing—ZERO—for your first shipment. And you don't have to make any minimum number of purchases— not even one!

4. The fact is, thousands of readers enjoy receiving their books by mail from The Reader Service. They enjoy the convenience of home delivery...they like getting the best new novels at discount prices BEFORE they're available in stores... and they love their Heart to Heart subscriber newsletter featuring author news, special book offers, book reviews and much more!

5. We hope that after receiving your free books you'll want to remain a subscriber. But the choice is yours— to continue or cancel, any time at all! So why not take us up on our invitation, with no risk of any kind. You'll be glad you did!

GET A *Free* MYSTERY GIFT...

SURPRISE MYSTERY GIFT COULD BE YOURS **FREE** AS A SPECIAL "THANK YOU" FROM THE EDITORS

They'd both leaned across the table to carry on their low-voiced conversation, their faces close together, their gazes locked. Now Cassie felt her stomach tightening at their proximity, at the look in Jared's eyes as he looked her over with almost insolent leisure. She couldn't remember any other man looking at her in quite that way before—and her reaction made her breath catch in her throat.

"I suppose I'll have to believe you, won't I?" he murmured finally. "I don't know who you are or what the hell you're doing here, but you're the only hope I've got. Do what you have to do, lady. Just get me out of here."

"I'll try." Her voice came out as little more than a whisper.

He seemed to come to a sudden decision. "Cassie—"

But whatever he might have said—and something told her it had been important—was cut off when the door swung open and Deputy Calhoun swaggered back into the room. "Sorry, Miz Browning, but your time's up. Got some officers out here that have some more questions for the prisoner."

Reluctantly, Cassie stood. "I hope they realize very quickly that you're holding the wrong man," she told the officer curtly, finding it very easy to play the part of offended family friend of the accused. "You're wasting your time questioning Jared while the real criminal is getting away."

"Now, Miz Browning, that's for the law to decide," he told her with an indulgent condescension that set her teeth on edge. "You just run along now and see about getting Mr. Walker an attorney, since he's refused to have one appointed for him."

Cassie paused by the door and looked back at the hard, dark man in the orange jumpsuit, and hated having to leave him like that. He looked so very much alone. "I'll talk to you soon, Jared. Very soon."

He only nodded.

With one last, distressed look back at him, Cassie made herself leave.

She would call Tony the moment she found a telephone that offered privacy. And, for once, she intended to convince her skeptical employer that he should listen to her intuition and wire her the money that would free Jared Walker. And she hoped with everything she had that she wasn't making a huge mistake in believing Jared Walker's declaration of his innocence.

Chapter Two

"But, Tony, we can't just leave him in jail! I'm almost certain he's innocent."

"You can't know that for sure, Cassie. Not without more proof. The cops had probable cause to take him in. Look at the evidence against him. He's the same build as the perp, was wearing almost identical clothing, even had a gun in his room. And all you have is his word that he's innocent. You wouldn't really expect him to tell you if he's not, would you?"

"I just can't believe he's guilty," Cassie repeated stubbornly, frustrated with the unsatisfactory communication offered by a pay phone in a grocery store parking lot. "I've met him, Tony. I've talked to him. I just can't believe he was dumb enough to rob that motel and then get himself caught like that. It doesn't make sense."

Her employer's sigh came quite clearly through the otherwise fuzzy connection. "You've got a hunch, right?"

She made a face she wouldn't have dared had he been able to see her. "Yeah. I've got a hunch."

Tony was silent for several long moments, building Cassie's hopes, but then he dashed them. "Sorry, Cassie. We can't risk it yet. If I wire you the money and he bolts, we've lost the cash and Michelle's brother. Damn, I wish I could get away to join you there this afternoon, but all hell's broken loose here."

Cassie knew Tony would have liked the chance to meet Jared and judge his character for himself, but her ego was still piqued that he didn't quite trust her to handle the case alone. "What's going on there?" she asked somewhat grudgingly.

"Chuck tried to serve a warrant on a father who's delinquent on child-support payments and got two teeth loosened in the process. He's out on sick leave for a couple of days. Michelle's uncle from California's still kicking up a fuss about her looking for her brothers and sisters—says he's going to court if he has to to protect the Trent money from outsiders. He hasn't got a leg to stand on, of course—Michelle's money is hers to do with as she wishes—but he's making her miserable. And Carter Powell has disappeared."

"Disappeared?" Cassie repeated in surprise. "Totally?"

"Yeah. Jumped bail," Tony informed her meaningfully. "It happens."

Cassie thought of the once-prominent attorney who'd been found to be skimming money from several of his clients—Michelle Trent, for one—something Tony had uncovered when he'd begun the search for Michelle's long-separated siblings. "Are you looking for him?"

"No. As long as he stays away from my wife, I don't care where he goes, and I haven't been hired to find him. That's a job for the cops. But I can't get away from here until Monday, at the earliest."

"You're going to make Jared sit in that jail until Monday?" Cassie asked indignantly.

"Unless you come up with more than a hunch to show me he shouldn't be there." Tony's voice softened. "Look, Cassie, I know you've worked hard on finding Jared, and I'm relieved that you think he's been arrested in error. But it won't hurt him to wait a day or two until we've got something more to go on."

"I hate thinking of him there. It's a ridiculous, grubby little jail and he's a man with a lot of pride, Tony. I want to get him out."

"So get busy and find your proof. You're still on the expense account. Since this guy is my brother-in-law, you can consider me your client."

"And if he asks again who I'm working for?"

"We'll talk about that after we clear up this other mess."

She sighed soundlessly. "You're the boss."

"Nice of you to remember that occasionally. Now, do you know what you're going to do next? Need any advice?"

Her chin lifted. "I know the procedure."

He chuckled. "All right. Keep in touch, Cassie. And good luck."

"Thanks, Tony. Talk to you later." She hung up with a muttered curse, not at all satisfied with the outcome of the conversation. Jared was still in jail, and Tony still didn't completely trust Cassie to handle a case alone.

Her stomach growled, making her frown as she glanced at her functional oversize watch. Nearly noon, and she'd skipped breakfast, hoping to arrive in town early enough to verify Jared Walker's identity before he moved on. And then, of course, she'd learned he'd been arrested, and she'd lost her appetite. But now she was hungry again. She decided to have lunch before questioning Gus Turley.

The morning rain had ended hours earlier, leaving the air fresh and clean, the sky clear and deep blue. Cassie hated to think that Jared was spending such a lovely day in jail. The little town wasn't large enough even to merit the familiar golden arches, but she found a passably reputable-looking burger place. She noticed a few odd looks as she entered alone and slid into a booth, but they didn't particularly bother her. She doubted many single women strangers came into this place, which looked as though it were frequented by local regulars.

She ordered a cheeseburger, fries and a large soft drink, to be followed by a slice of cherry pie. The food wasn't bad, though it lost part of its flavor when she found herself wondering what Jared Walker was eating in his cell. That thought had her hurrying through dessert, already anxious to get back to work.

It occurred to her that, even though she'd always taken her work very seriously, she'd become more involved in this case than any of the ones she'd worked on before. She tried to believe that it wasn't because she'd found herself unexpectedly attracted to the man she was working so hard to clear. But she found it all too easy to remember every detail of his rough-hewn face, the sound of his deep, rough voice, the way his dark blue eyes had swept over her so slowly, so very thoroughly.

It was early afternoon when Cassie drove her small car into the parking lot of the motel where Jared had checked in the night before—the motel he'd supposedly robbed during the night. She winced at the name emblazoned on the garishly lettered sign. The Come-On-Inn. *Yuck.*

The place looked clean enough, if in need of paint and new shingles. She couldn't say much for the landscaping, which consisted of a few grubby, thirsty-looking shrubs and a badly rutted asphalt parking lot. Why would Jared have chosen to stay here? Because it was one of the few motels in the area? Because it looked cheap? Or because it was relatively secluded? But then, why would he have cared about that?

Knowing those questions could only be answered by Jared, she shrugged them off and walked into the motel office.

A short, balding man with a heavy paunch bulging over his tooled leather belt looked up at the jingle of the bell over the door. "Help you?"

"Are you Gus Turley?"

His expression turned suspicious. "Yeah. Why?"

She pasted on her brightest smile and leaned comfortably against the blue Formica counter, offering him her business card. "My name is Cassie Browning. I'm a private investigator."

Turley took the card and studied it carefully, then looked back up at her. "This got something to do with that robbery?"

"Yes, sir, it does. I'm trying to determine exactly what happened."

"Yeah? On whose behalf?"

"I'm sorry, my client wishes to remain confidential at this time. Would you mind if I ask you some questions, Mr. Turley?"

Turley glowered, and tapped one blunt, dirty-nailed finger on the paperwork in front of him. "I got things to do. And I already answered plenty of questions for the police. Ask to see their report."

"I've seen the report, Mr. Turley," she answered patiently, still smiling, "but there are just a few things I still need to know. Couldn't you give me just a moment of your time?"

He grumbled beneath his breath, but nodded curtly. "All right. What is it?"

"The man who robbed you—you're sure he was the same size as Jared Walker? Wasn't there anything in particular you noticed about him? The color of his eyes, perhaps? An accent or other unusual speech pattern?"

"He talked a little different—not as deep, I think, but he could have been disguising his voice. Probably would have, since he knew I'd remember him checking in. And the robber was wearing a ski mask," Turley answered. "I didn't see the color of his eyes. All I saw was the barrel of his gun."

"A gun you identified as a 9 mm semiautomatic. Yet the only gun found in Mr. Walker's possession was a .45."

Turley shrugged. "They look a lot alike—especially when you're facing the wrong end of one."

"But you were sure it was a 9 mm. You told the investigating officers it looked like a police issue to you."

"So I might have been wrong," Turley blustered. "Or maybe he gave that gun to the other guy, along with my money."

"What other guy?"

"Whoever it was went into the room with him that evening. Saw them myself, though Walker swears he was alone."

"You're sure it was a man?"

"Could've been a woman. Whoever it was was a lot smaller than Walker, wearing jeans and a jacket, like him. I was here in the office, looking through that window across the parking lot. Hard to tell much from that distance."

Cassie checked the view from the window. As Turley had said, it was a considerable distance. Yet the door of Jared's room—number sixteen—was visible enough for him to have seen whether one person or two had entered. "You never saw the smaller person leave the room?"

"No. I got busy later, watched some TV. Next thing I knew I was being held up. Got nearly five hundred dollars, dammit. I hadn't had a chance to make my deposit yesterday."

"But neither the money nor the mysterious other person were found."

"I'll tell you what I think," Turley confided, leaning heavily on the counter. "The bathroom window was open when the cops went in. I think the little guy took the money—maybe the other gun—and skipped out when the cops knocked on the door."

"So why would Walker have come back so openly?" Cassie inquired, wondering at Turley's apparent conviction that there had, indeed, been someone else with Jared.

She remembered her hunch that Jared had been holding something back when she'd questioned him on that point. "I travel alone" was all he'd said. But *had* he been traveling alone? Was it possible that he was protecting someone by claiming to have been by himself?

Did Jared Walker know more about the robbery than he'd led her to believe?

Was she crazy to still think someone else had committed the robbery, despite all the evidence?

No. Picturing Jared's face, the frustration and pain in his dark blue eyes, she still found it too difficult to believe he had anything to do with this. Turley had to have been mistaken about the second person in Jared's room, just as he'd been mistaken about the gun.

Turley had taken his time answering her question, but finally he shrugged and spoke in an impatient snarl. "Why'd he come back so openly? Hell, I don't know. The guy's just stupid, I guess. It don't take brains to aim a gun and say, 'Give me your money.'"

Cassie would have questioned him more, hoping to shake him on some point of his story, but he brought the conversation to an end, telling her firmly that he had things to do. If she had any other questions, he said, ask the cops.

She sighed. "All right. Thank you for your time, Mr. Turley."

She had her hand on the outside door when he stopped her. "Hey, Miss Browning."

Cassie looked hopefully over her shoulder. "Yes?"

"Tell your buddy Walker that I don't appreciate having my hard-earned money taken from me at gunpoint. He'll find out we don't take kindly to sleazebag crooks around these parts."

Cassie lifted her chin, forcefully swallowing the impulse to tell him that he was all wrong about Jared Walker. But it wouldn't do to antagonize him at this point. He was still the prime witness against Jared. "Thank you again for your time, Mr. Turley. Good day."

She was almost to her car when she spotted movement out of the corner of her eye. She turned her head to find a grubby teenager running away from the motel.

Frowning, she looked back at the window of the motel office. What made her think the boy had been hiding beneath that window, listening to everything she and Turley had said? And why would he have done so?

Impatiently, she shook her coppery head and climbed into her car. Nothing much made sense about this case so far.

"This is *not* the way to get yourself a partnership, Browning," she muttered crossly, starting her engine.

Jared stared blindly at a gray concrete-block wall and tried to ignore a growing urge to slam his fist into its unyielding surface. All that would net him was a fistful of broken knuckles—and he didn't need any more pain at this moment.

A flick of his gaze took in the barred door locking him into the cell. Jail. He'd been down on his luck before, hit plenty of low points in his life, but this was the first time he'd landed quite this low. Sitting in a jail cell, accused of armed robbery,

only two people that he knew of who believed he didn't belong here. A frightened, confused teenage boy, and a mysterious young woman with flame-colored hair and oddly
trusting green eyes.

Cassie Browning. Who was she? Who had hired her? And
why did he instinctively believe she would do her best to help
him, when he'd learned at a very early age that it was foolish
to ever rely on anyone but himself?

He closed his eyes and felt the walls of his cell closing in
on him. His fist clenched on his thigh.

Whatever it is you're doing to clear me, lady, make it fast.

It wasn't hard for Cassie to spot the waitress Jared had described in the twenty-four-hour diner. There were only two
waitresses working the evening shift, one a pretty young Lat-
ino, the other a slightly overweight woman of perhaps fifty
with heavily lacquered bleached hair and the name "Nellie"
embroidered on her pocket.

For the first time since she'd left Gus Turley five hours earlier, Cassie felt her confidence swelling again. In the meantime she'd checked in at a hotel—one with a little more class
than the Come-On-Inn—and made a few calls, biding her
time until she thought Nellie's shift would begin.

Her fingers closed around the photograph in her lap as
the woman approached her table. "What can I get you,
hon?" Nellie asked, her polite smile not quite reaching her
bored eyes.

Cassie thought of the cheeseburger and fries she'd eaten
for lunch. "I'll have the chef's salad, please. And iced tea."

"What kind of dressing?"

Haunted by the memory of the cherry pie that had followed
her cheeseburger, she ordered the diet dressing. Before she
could show Nellie Jared's photograph, the waitress had al-

ready hurried away with Cassie's order, other tables claiming her attention.

Cassie glanced at the grainy driver's license photo she held, and her impatience grew as she thought of this proud-looking man still sitting in a tiny cell. She stared at Jared's roughly attractive face for several long moments before breaking her gaze away with a slight start.

Just a case, Browning. He's just another case. Another step toward that partnership.

Yeah. Right. She sighed imperceptibly and looked up as Nellie bore down on her again with an enormous salad and a quart-size plastic tumbler of iced tea. "Thank you. I…"

But the efficient, no-nonsense Nellie had already moved on, taking an order from a man and woman who'd just been seated in a nearby booth.

Muttering beneath her breath, Cassie picked up her fork and stabbed it into her salad. After all, she had no intention of leaving this diner until she'd asked her questions. Might as well try to enjoy her dinner in the meantime.

She'd finished all she could eat of the salad by the time Nellie returned. "How about some dessert?" the woman offered.

"No, thank you. But I would like to ask you a question if you don't mind."

"What question?" Nellie's face took on the same suspicious expression Turley had worn when Cassie had approached him the same way. It seemed that people in these parts didn't take well to questions from strangers.

Cassie smiled winningly and held up the photograph. "Have you ever seen this man before?"

Nellie exhaled gustily. "That's the guy the cops were asking about, ain't it? The guy who robbed Gus Turley."

"He's only been charged with the robbery, not convicted of the crime," Cassie reminded the woman, trying not to sound too defensive on Jared's part. "He says he was here last night when the robbery took place, having pie and coffee. He described you quite well."

"Look, lady, like I told the police. We get lots of guys in here off the freeway. I can't remember everyone who comes in. And I don't want to get involved. I got problems of my own."

"Please," Cassie said when the woman would have moved away. "Please just look at the photograph. Maybe you'll remember this one."

Nellie hesitated, studying Cassie's face, then nodded shortly and reached for the photo. She frowned at it. "Yeah. I remember him."

"You do?" Cassie's heart leaped into her throat. "You're sure?"

Nellie nodded and returned the print. "Quiet type, but polite enough. Spent a long time over his pie and coffee, like he was thinking about something."

"He was here last night, between the hours of eleven and midnight?"

Cassie was extremely disappointed when Nellie shook her head. "That I can't say. Could've been earlier, maybe later. I get off work at three. I don't keep one eye on the clock while I'm working."

Cassie sighed. "I understand. But you would be willing to tell the police you saw him here last night?"

"I guess," Nellie agreed reluctantly. "I ain't taking off work to do it, but I'll give 'em a call tomorrow. Not that it'll probably do you any good," she added.

"It couldn't hurt," Cassie replied. "Thank you, Nellie. I really appreciate this."

The waitress shrugged. "Can I get you anything else?"

"No, thank you."

"Then you can pay at the register on your way out." In response to a summons from the couple at the other booth, Nellie nodded to Cassie and went back to work.

Cassie left a generous tip. Nellie's identification of Jared's photo wasn't much to go on, she thought as she walked to her car, but at least it was a step in the right direction. One bit of evidence that Jared had been telling the truth.

She'd just put her key into the door lock when she saw the boy again. He was standing in the shadow of the diner, staring hard in her direction. She knew immediately that he was the same teenager she'd spotted at the motel office. She knew, as well, that it was more than just coincidence that he was watching her now.

Who was he? And why was he following her?

Deciding to find out, she started toward him. Only to stop in frustration when he turned and ran, his young legs taking him away too rapidly for her to even hope to catch him.

"Hey, kid!" she yelled after him. "Wait up."

But he didn't stop, of course. Nor had she really expected him to.

"What the *hell* is going on here?" she asked aloud, staring at the spot where the boy had been, ignoring the startled looks she was getting from the couple just exiting the diner.

Damned if she wasn't going to ask for a raise when this case was over.

On that thought, she climbed into her car and started the engine. She had one more stop to make before calling it a day. She wanted to see Jared Walker just one more time before he spent his first full night behind bars.

Cassie was rather surprised to find Deputy Calhoun at the tiny police station. "You're still here?" she asked him. "You're putting in a long day, aren't you?"

"Got two men off with the flu," he replied wearily. "Some

of us are having to pull double shifts. What you doing here, Miz Browning? It's after eight o'clock. Visiting hours are over."

"Couldn't I see him just for a moment?" Cassie begged sweetly, using the same rather awed tone that had gotten her in to see Jared earlier. "I promise I won't stay long."

"I'm sorry, Miz Browning, but it's against the rules. The boss would have my head if I brought Walker out again this late."

"Then maybe I could speak to him in his cell? Please, Deputy Calhoun. I just want to tell him good-night."

The deputy's tired face softened at the entreaty. "Oh, hell, Miz Browning—pardon my language. You're gonna' get me in all kinds of hot water, but…"

"You'll let me see him?" Cassie asked hopefully.

He grunted. "All right. But I'm staying with you this time. And you got five minutes—that's it."

"You're being more than generous," she assured him, trying to look properly grateful.

As she followed the officer down a hallway, Cassie found herself wondering why she was really there, why it had seemed so important to see Jared tonight. Maybe she'd just needed to test her faith again by looking straight into his eyes while he assured her one more time of his innocence. Maybe she needed to convince herself that she hadn't been crazy to believe him the first time, with so little reason to do so.

Yet even as the doubts crossed her mind, she knew she hadn't really changed that hastily formed opinion during the hours since she'd last seen him. Everything within her told her that Jared Walker was innocent. And it was up to her to prove it.

Jared was lying on his cot, still wearing the orange jumpsuit, one arm behind his head as he stared motionlessly at the ceiling. He glanced up when Calhoun said his name, then came to his feet in a hurry when he spotted Cassie.

She regretted having to quell the fleeting look of hope that crossed his hard face. "I haven't arranged bail yet," she said, her fingers closing around the cold, hard bars of the cell door. "I'm sorry."

His expression closed again, he nodded as he approached the door. "Why are you here?"

Cassie glanced at Calhoun, who turned partially away in a small effort at giving them privacy. "I talked to Turley today. And to the waitress, Nellie."

"And?"

"Turley's still convinced you did it, though his identification doesn't stand up very well under heavy questioning. He still insists that you had someone with you when you checked in yesterday. Says he saw you enter the room with someone—either a woman or a small man." She watched him carefully as she spoke, dwelling on this one issue that still bothered her about Jared's story. Turley had seemed so positive, at least about this.

Jared's expression didn't change. "He's wrong."

Making sure Calhoun couldn't hear her, Cassie whispered, "Jared, you're sure you're telling me the truth? You're not trying to protect anyone?"

"Who would I be trying to protect?" he growled, without really answering her question.

"A woman?" she asked reluctantly.

"I told you, there was no woman."

Even more reluctantly, she asked very carefully, "Then is there something else I should know?"

"Like what?"

"Like maybe—you had a guy with you? It's okay if you're—well, you know," she assured him hastily, and not quite truthfully. "I'd understand."

Jared's appalled expression would have been amusing if his

situation hadn't been so very serious. "I am most definitely straight," he told her in a low growl. "I'd be happy to prove that to you if we were alone."

She flushed deeply at his meaningful tone, though she told herself the words were nothing more than a hasty reaction to her implication. Still, she couldn't help wondering what it would have been like to meet him under different circumstances. She was well aware that she was deeply, unreasonably drawn to this angry, complex man, though she wondered if Jared Walker would ever allow anyone to get close to him, even under the best of conditions.

She quickly changed the subject. "I showed Nellie your photograph. She's willing to testify that you were in the diner last night, though she can't be pinned down as to the time."

Jared looked grim. "That's not much."

"No. But it's a start," she reminded him, knowing how bleak his case must look to him at the moment. "They're not going to convict an innocent man, Jared. The system doesn't work that way."

"The 'system' doesn't work at all," Jared answered bitterly. "Believe me, I know. The cops would just as soon lock up an innocent man if they can call the case closed and make themselves look good."

"I can't believe that."

"Yeah, well, that's your problem. If you want to keep on believing in fairy tales, go right ahead. I just hope you don't find out the hard way that you've been wasting your efforts."

The embittered cynicism in his voice hurt her. What must it have taken to make him so hard? Had it begun when he'd lost his mother and then been separated from his younger brothers and sisters when he was only eleven years old?

But, of course, she couldn't tell him she knew about that

without revealing that she'd found him on behalf of his sister, and Tony had strictly forbidden her to do that.

"I won't give up trying to clear you," she could only insist softly.

His hard face softened, so fractionally that she wouldn't have noticed had she not been watching him so closely. "I haven't even thanked you for what you've done today."

Her throat tightened. She knew that expressing gratitude would be as difficult for Jared as asking for help. It touched her that he was making an effort for her. "That isn't necessary."

"Yeah," he said gruffly. "It is. Thanks, Cassie."

"You're welcome," she whispered.

Their gazes held for a long, taut moment, and then Jared moved closer, glancing warily at Calhoun before speaking in a low, private tone. "Cassie, there's something I want you to do for me. I need you to—"

"Sorry, Miz Browning. Time's up," Calhoun broke in, stepping closer.

Jared abruptly stopped speaking, his eyes mirroring the frustration Cassie felt. What had he been going to say? She sensed that it had been very important to him. But, whatever it had been, he'd shut her out again with Calhoun's interruption. She glared at the deputy.

Calhoun cleared his throat forcefully at finding himself pinned between two hard stares. "Uh—sorry," he muttered. "But I really can't let you stay any longer."

Cassie tried to soothe her expression, reminding herself that she might need the deputy's assistance again before Jared was released. "I understand," she assured him. "And I appreciate what you've done."

She turned back for one last look at Jared. "Good night." She knew better than to suggest that he get a good night's sleep. She suspected he wouldn't sleep much at all. She wasn't expecting to get much rest herself, knowing that Jared was spending the night in this dreary cell, and racked with doubts about his innocence and her ability to prove it, one way or another. "I'll see you tomorrow."

He only nodded.

Cassie didn't dare look back as Calhoun escorted her out. She was afraid to risk releasing the tears she felt burning at the back of her eyes at the thought of Jared standing so still and alone, watching her walk away.

You owe me for this, Tony.

Chapter Three

Still wishing she knew what it was Jared wanted to ask her, Cassie crossed the parking lot of the police station toward her car. She was only a couple of feet from the vehicle when she realized that she was being watched again—and she thought she knew who was watching her. But this time, she had no intention of being outsmarted by a grubby kid.

With a noisy exclamation of disgust, she dropped her purse, spilling its contents on the pavement at her feet. "What a klutz!" she complained aloud, kneeling as though to gather her belongings.

In response to a movement out of the corner of her right eye, she launched herself in that direction, calling on all her training as a private investigator. A moment later, she had her hands full of squirming boy, and found herself using all the energy she had to hold him. Not for the first time, she regretted her lack of height. At only five feet four inches, Cassie stood almost eye to eye with the boy, whose fear was lending him strength.

"Either be still or I'm calling for help," she warned him. "I'm sure Deputy Calhoun will come running if I start screaming. Is that what you want?"

The boy froze. "No! Don't call the cops! Please, lady."

"You'll stand still?"

He nodded unwillingly.

"Promise?" she insisted, not quite trusting him.

"You have my word," he answered, and his stiffly dignified tone was strangely familiar.

Frowning, she turned him toward her—only to find herself looking into Jared Walker's dark blue eyes in a weary, defiant, dirt-streaked young face. "Who are you?" she demanded, though she thought she already knew.

"My name is Shane Walker." He looked uneasily at the police station. "Could we get out of here? Please? I don't want them to see me."

"You're Jared's son," she breathed, her knees weakening with the realization. So Jared *had* been protecting someone. But why? Why wouldn't he tell someone that this boy was out on the streets alone while his father fretted in his cell?

Shane froze, his eyes widening in fear. "You're not going to turn me in, are you? Please, don't tell them about me. They'll send me away from him. And I won't go—I *won't!*"

"Hey, take it easy," she said when he struggled in her grasp again. "I'm not going to turn you in. I swear," she added, tightening her grip on his skinny arm. "My name is Cassie Browning. I'm a friend."

He looked at her suspiciously. She wasn't surprised that he didn't trust her yet. Like his father, Shane Walker seemed to be the cautious, reserved type. "If you're a friend of my dad's, how come I've never seen you before?"

She nodded at the logical question. "I only met him this morning," she explained. "I'm a private investigator, and I'm working to clear him of charges. I know he's innocent, and I'm not going to stop asking questions until I've got proof."

"He didn't rob that motel."

"I know." She cautiously loosened her grip. "I know, Shane."

He relaxed marginally. "You're really a P.I.?"

"I've got identification in my—well, it's here somewhere," she said ruefully, glancing at the scattered contents of her purse. "I'd be happy to show you."

He seemed to reach a decision. "All right. I believe you."

She made a face. "Thank you for that magnanimous concession."

"Huh?"

"Never mind. How about helping me pick this stuff up and then let's get out of here before someone sees us."

He hesitated only a moment, looking from her car to the door of the police station. And then he nodded. "All right."

She gave a silent sigh of relief. She still wasn't feeling quite steady. The discovery that Jared Walker had a teenage son had rocked her all the way to her toes, though she couldn't have said exactly why, even if she tried.

"You hungry, Shane?" Cassie asked when they were in her car, leaving the police station—and Jared—behind.

Shane drew his gaze from the rear window, his expression tearing at her heart. "Yeah," he said. "I haven't eaten since dinner yesterday."

She forced herself to speak cheerfully, wanting to ease the pain in his too-old eyes. "Heavens! You must be starving. I remember the way my brother ate when he was your age. Couldn't fill him up."

"You've got a brother?"

"Yes. Cliff's a pilot in Alaska. Delivers freight to the remote areas there."

"Wow. Cool job."

She managed not to laugh at the unintentional pun. "Yeah. He's a cool guy."

But Shane's attention didn't stray long from his father. "I saw you talking to those people today—the motel guy and the lady at the diner. You were asking about my dad?"

"Yes."

"Did it help?"

"Maybe," Cassie replied, not wanting to raise his hopes too greatly at this point. "The waitress remembered seeing him."

"They still think my dad did it, don't they?" Shane asked dispiritedly.

"He's only been charged, Shane. Now they have to prove it. Remember, he's innocent until they've proven guilt without a reasonable doubt. And since he didn't do anything wrong, they're going to have a tough time proving he did."

"My dad says the good guys don't always come out ahead," Shane informed her. "He says you can't always trust the system. That's why he hasn't told anyone about me since he was arrested. He knows they'd stick me in a foster home. My dad hates foster homes."

Knowing Jared had spent seven years in foster care, Cassie bit her lip. Obviously, Jared's experiences had been more difficult than those of the two sisters who'd already been reunited—Michelle, who'd been adopted by a wealthy, prominent family, and Layla, who'd lived with one foster family until her graduation from high school. Again, Cassie was frustrated by her orders not to reveal any information about Jared's family—Shane's family, as well.

"Surely your father doesn't think you should be on the

streets alone," she fretted, not entirely comfortable with Jared's silence despite her understanding of his motives.

Shane cleared his throat. "Well, uh—"

She turned to look at him. "What is it?"

"Dad gave me some money a long time ago, when we started traveling together. Said I was supposed to use it to buy a bus ticket to a friend's house if anything ever happened to him or if we ever got separated—like now. He probably thinks I did what I was told and went to Mr. Cutter. But I couldn't leave him here all alone. I just couldn't."

"I understand." Now Cassie thought she knew what Jared had wanted her to do for him. She thought maybe he'd trusted her enough to tell her about Shane, and to ask her to check on the boy's welfare. She could be wrong—but somehow she knew she wasn't. And it warmed her to think he'd trust her with something this important to him.

"Think you'll be in trouble when your dad finds out you didn't follow orders?" she asked casually.

Shane grimaced. "He's going to be mad as a hornet. But he'll get over it. He always does."

Cassie pulled into the drive-through lane of a fast-food restaurant. "I'll get some food and take you to my hotel to eat it," she explained. "That way we won't risk being seen by anyone who might start asking questions."

Shane gave her suggestion a moment's consideration, then nodded. "That's a good idea," he said approvingly. And then he reached for his pocket. "I'm buying."

"Oh, no. I've got it."

Proudly lifting his chin, the boy pulled out a shabby wallet. "You're working to clear my dad, so that means we already owe you. I'll buy my own food."

Realizing that Shane Walker was every bit as proud—and as stubborn—as his father, Cassie shook her head.

"Look, I'm on an expense account, okay? Everything's taken care of."

Looking as though he wasn't quite sure what an expense account was, Shane eyed her suspiciously. "Yeah?"

"Yeah. Trust me." And darned if she wouldn't turn it in, she thought. Buying the kid's meal was the least Tony could do after refusing to make Jared's bail.

"I've got a bag stashed in a locker at the bus station," Shane told her after she'd purchased enough food to satisfy two starving adults. She'd figured that would be just about enough for one hungry teenager. "Would you mind if we pick it up on the way to your hotel?"

"Of course not. Just tell me how to get there."

"Turn right at the next light."

Cassie looked speculatively at him. "You seem to know your way around pretty well for a stranger in town."

Shane shrugged, sniffing appreciatively at the odors coming from the paper bag in his lap. "I've learned to get by on my own when I have to. I lived on the streets for almost three months once."

Appalled, Cassie stared at him, nearly running a red light before bringing her car to a stop. "When?"

"Two years ago. When I was twelve. My dad found me. I've been with him ever since."

She didn't understand; Shane seemed so devoted to his father. "You ran away from home two years ago?"

"From my stepfather's home. Me and him didn't get along, and my mom stayed too drunk to care. I knew Dad would find me as soon as he came back."

"Came back from where?" Cassie asked, thoroughly confused.

"He was in the navy, stationed on an aircraft carrier. Soon as he could, he got out and came after me. Now he has full custody—my mom and stepfather were really relieved to hand me over to him, I think."

Cassie swallowed hard against words of sympathy she doubted the boy would appreciate. She still wasn't sure exactly what had transpired in Shane's short life, but it was a wonder he'd turned out as levelheaded and well-behaved as he seemed to be. Three months on his own at age twelve! How had he survived?

Shane slipped in and out of the deserted bus station with a stealthy ease that reminded Cassie forcibly of the few homeless youths she'd encountered back home in Dallas. He tossed his bag into the back seat. "We'd better hurry," he said, squirming into his seat belt. "I think my food's getting cold."

Cassie smiled shakily and headed toward her motel. Once there, she settled Shane in her room with his food and a soft drink purchased from the machine outside her door. And then she walked into the office and booked the room adjoining hers, which had fortunately been vacated earlier that day.

Worried about possible inconvenient questions, she'd thought of having Shane stay in her room overnight. But then she'd decided that was an even more potentially awkward situation. She was relieved that the hotel clerk didn't even seem curious as to why she wanted the second room, accepting Cassie's money without hesitation.

Shane had inhaled every bite of the food by the time Cassie returned. She tossed him the key. "You've got the room next door," she said, motioning toward the connecting doorway. "You must be tired."

Shane nodded, his young shoulders slumping a bit. "Yeah. I didn't get much sleep last night."

"Can you tell me what happened last night, Shane?"

His expression grew grim, and he looked so much like his

father that Cassie couldn't help staring. "Me and Dad had been on the road all day—he had a lead on a job in Arizona, just north of Flagstaff," he added, confirming what Jared had told Cassie. "I was tired, so I turned in early. Dad couldn't sleep, so he went out for a while. He does that sometimes to keep from disturbing me when he's feeling restless.

"Anyway, about midnight someone started pounding on the door, yelling that they were the cops and for me to open up. I thought something had happened to Dad and they were there to take me to a foster home," he explained unhappily, once again displaying his fear of the child welfare system his father had taught him to avoid. "I grabbed my stuff and went out the bathroom window. Then I waited in the bushes for Dad. I watched them arrest him."

His tone was so bleak, his eyes so haunted, that Cassie blinked back tears. "Did you hear the reason why?"

"Yeah. Everyone was yelling—and that Turley guy was shouting something about Dad robbing him. I knew they were crazy, of course, but I didn't know how to help him."

"You couldn't have helped him," Cassie assured him gently, her voice husky. "Not then."

"I know. Dad gave me the sign to clear out, so I did. I even went to the bus station—but I couldn't leave him here in jail. I just couldn't, no matter what he'd told me."

"Your dad gave you a sign?" Cassie repeated in surprise. "He saw you?"

Shane nodded. "Yeah. No one else did, but Dad spotted me. That's when he quit fighting them. He jerked his chin and I knew he was telling me to get going. And then they put the cuffs on him and pushed him into the cruiser."

He stopped to clear his throat before continuing. "I hung around the jail for most of the night. I was snooping around the motel, hoping maybe to find some proof that Dad was in-

nocent, when I heard you questioning Turley. Then later I
went over to the diner Dad had said he was going to, thinking maybe I'd have something to eat and ask some questions,
but you were already there. I couldn't figure out who you
were, but I thought maybe you were trying to help."

Cassie smiled at him, her heart already firmly captivated
by the resourceful young man. "You thought right."

Shane returned the smile, making her realize it was the first
time he'd smiled at her all evening. The smile made him look
suddenly younger, like the boy he was rather than the man he
was trying so hard to be.

Again, Cassie felt tears pricking at the back of her eyes.
"You'd better get some rest," she said. "I'll wake you in the
morning for breakfast. We'll decide then what our next move
will be."

But she already knew what her first move would be the next
morning. With or without her employer's permission, she was
bailing Jared Walker out of jail, even if she had to empty her
savings account. Shane Walker needed his father. And Cassie couldn't bear to think of Jared spending even one more
day behind bars.

Shane glanced from the connecting door to the key in his
hand. "You paid for the other room already?"

"Yes. Don't worry about it."

He grinned crookedly. "Expense account, right?"

"Right." She could seriously like this kid.

He paused on his way out, shuffling his feet in awkward
embarrassment. "Uh, Miss Browning—thanks, okay?"

"It's Cassie," she murmured. "And you're welcome. Good
night, Shane."

"'Night." He gave her another of those endearingly sweet
smiles before closing the door behind him.

Cassie sighed and ran her hands through her tangled curls.

"God, Browning. What have you gotten yourself into now?" she asked before reaching wearily for her nightgown.

Shane wasn't the only one in desperate need of rest.

Jared lay wide awake on the hard, lumpy cot, his thoughts torn between worrying about his son and wondering about the woman who was supposedly working to clear him.

He had to believe that Shane had followed orders and headed straight for Bob Cutter's place in Oklahoma when Jared had given him the sign to take off. They'd been through the drill enough for the boy to know what was expected of him, and he was perfectly capable of buying a bus ticket and making the trip alone, though Jared wasn't entirely comfortable with the prospect. Still, it beat being alone on the streets again. And even though Jared knew Cutter was away from home for the weekend, there was an excellent housekeeper who'd take Shane in without a question. The boy would be safe there, though Jared knew Shane would be worrying himself half-sick.

His distrust of the legal system was deeply ingrained, but Jared would have trusted Cassie Browning to check on Shane for him if he'd had a chance to talk to her in certain privacy. He'd been surprised by his own impulse to tell her about the boy. Trust wasn't something he gave easily, and almost never to strangers. But then, few strangers had gone to so much trouble so willingly on his behalf.

Who the hell was she? How did she know of him? Who was she working for? And was she really as honest and trustworthy as she seemed, or was he only being set up yet again?

He *had* to get out of here, he thought, grinding his teeth in frustration. Dammit, he had to. For his son, for himself. And because he was growing increasingly more impatient to find out for himself exactly why Ms. Cassie Browning had suddenly appeared in his life.

* * *

Cassie didn't sleep well. Her disturbing dreams were filled with images of dark blue eyes. Jared's—angry, tortured, wary. And Shane's—frightened, unhappy, heartbreakingly hopeful. Both of them counting on Cassie to help them. And she felt so helpless in response.

When her restless tossing and turning woke her at 1:00 a.m.—twenty-four hours after Jared's arrest, she couldn't help noting—she padded into the tiny bathroom to wash her face and drink some water from a plastic cup.

As she returned to bed, hoping to be more successful with this attempt at sleep, she wondered how she'd managed to become so involved with the two Walker men in such a short time. She'd already lost her heart to Shane—and something told her it wouldn't be too difficult to do the same with his father. And wouldn't *that* be one of the most foolhardy mistakes she'd ever made?

Don't get involved with the cases, Tony had told her over and over again. And yet, Tony had fallen head over heels in love with Jared's sister Michelle the day she'd walked into his office only a few months ago and hired him to find her missing brothers and sisters. Maybe there was something about the Walker siblings that neither Tony nor Cassie had been able to resist.

Deciding she was being silly, trying to blame her emotional fancies on exhaustion, she buried her head in the pillow and ordered herself to sleep. If only she could order herself not to dream….

It was just past 6:00 a.m. when Cassie was abruptly awakened by a heavy pounding on the outer door to her room. She sat up with a gasp, taking a moment to remember where she was and why before reaching for her robe.

"Coming," she called out, assuming it was Shane at her door. He could have knocked on the adjoining door, of course, but who else could it be? Maybe he'd awakened disoriented, too.

It was, indeed, one of the Walkers at her door—but it wasn't Shane.

"*Jared!* How—? When—?"

"The real crook struck again last night. They caught him with Turley's bank bag still under the seat of his pickup and a 9 mm semiautomatic stuck in the waistband of his jeans. I was released with a grudging apology and a warning to 'be more careful in the future.'" Jared's mouth twisted for a moment. "I checked every motel in the area to find you. Why have you registered in two rooms here?"

Cassie was delighted, of course, that Jared had been released. She told herself it was mean and petty of her to be just a bit disappointed that she hadn't been the one to clear him.

"Come in," she urged him, tightening the belt on her robe and smoothing futilely at her wildly tousled curls. "I'll explain as much as I can."

"Yeah, I want you to do that," he assured her, stepping past her into the room. She couldn't help noticing how much more virile and confident he looked in his flannel shirt, skintight jeans and battered boots, rather than the regulation jail jumpsuit she'd seen him in before.

"But first," he said, glancing at the nightstand, "would you mind if I use the phone? I've got to call a friend to check on someone."

"You're checking on Shane? If so, I—"

Jared stiffened, his dark gaze stabbing into hers. Cassie felt a chill slither down her spine. "How do you know about Shane?"

"I—"

The connecting door opened without warning. "Cassie?"

Shane asked, stepping into the room, wearing only a pair of jeans. "I thought I heard my—*Dad!*"

Jared's look of surprise changed quickly to relief. He held out his arms and Shane pelted unselfconsciously into them. Almost unbearably touched by the scene, Cassie had to look away from the expressions on their faces. She was pleased to realize that Jared Walker loved his son as deeply as Shane adored his father.

The embrace didn't last long. Jared held his son away, hands gripped firmly on Shane's thin shoulders. "You're supposed to be in Oklahoma," he said, obviously trying to sound stern. "Why aren't you?"

"I couldn't leave you," Shane answered simply. "I just couldn't, Dad."

Jared sighed. "After all the times we talked about what you should do…" He stopped and shook his head. "You're lucky the welfare services didn't get you."

Shane lifted his head proudly. "They wouldn't have kept me for long."

Jared winced and glanced at Cassie. "They wouldn't have, either."

"No," she agreed with a shaky smile. "I think Shane is very much like his father. The independent type."

Both Shane and Jared looked rather pleased with the comparison, though she hadn't exactly meant it as a compliment.

"Grab a shower and get your things together, son, while Ms. Browning has a chance to get dressed," Jared said, giving Cassie a lingering, all-encompassing glance that had her pulling the lapels of her robe more tightly closed. "I'll be there in a minute," he added, giving Shane a slight shove in the direction of his room without taking his gaze from Cassie.

Glancing speculatively from Cassie to his father, Shane quickly followed instructions, closing the connecting door behind him. Cassie's room seemed suddenly to grow smaller when she found herself alone in it with Jared.

"I don't know how you hooked up with my son," he said, taking a step toward her. "But thanks for watching out for him. And for everything else. It was good to know there was at least one person besides Shane who didn't think I'd robbed that motel. I consider myself in your debt."

She wrapped the tie of her robe around both hands, all too aware of her sleep-tousled appearance and lack of makeup. "You're welcome," she whispered, nervously moistening her lips. "But you really don't owe me anything for what little I did."

"I don't agree," he murmured, his hands settling on her shoulders. "And I don't think what you did was so little. Thank you, Cassie Browning."

While her hands were still tangled in the fabric belt of her robe, he lowered his face to hers, taking her mouth in a long, thorough, heart-stopping kiss. Cassie was trembling by the time it ended, dazed by the intensity of the sensations he'd aroused in her with nothing more than that one kiss.

"I'll be back in fifteen minutes," he told her, stepping away from her just a bit too quickly. "I've got a few questions for you."

Shaking off her lingering bemusement—had she *ever* been kissed like that before?—Cassie dove for the telephone the moment the door to the other room closed behind Jared. Doubting Tony would be at his office so early on a Friday morning, she dialed his home number. The housekeeper answered.

"Hi, Betty, it's Cassie. Is Tony around?"

"Sorry, Miss Cassie. He had a breakfast meeting with a client this morning. Michelle's here, if you'd like to speak to her."

Cassie hesitated, then declined. "I'll try to reach Tony later. Thanks, Betty."

She hung up, wondering if she should have asked Michelle

for permission to disclose her client to Jared. But she couldn't, not when she wasn't sure Tony had let Michelle know Jared had been located.

Stripping out of her robe and nightgown, Cassie dressed rapidly in slacks and a sweater, then hurried into the bathroom to brush her teeth and do what she could with her hair and makeup in the short time Jared had allotted her. Trying to tame her unruly curls with a gold clip at the back of her head, she ran through a list of vague answers to the questions she knew Jared would ask. Questions like who she was working for, why she'd been looking for him, how she'd found him.

She couldn't think about the kiss—had it only been his way of expressing gratitude?—or she'd never be able to function coherently. And she knew she was going to need all her wits about her when he returned.

Dammit, Tony, why'd you tie my hands like this? You don't know how hard it's going to be to tell Jared Walker that I can't answer his questions yet!

Finally satisfied that she'd done the best she could with her appearance, Cassie stepped out of the bathroom, only to find Jared Walker calmly and openly going through the contents of her purse.

"What the—get out of that!" she snapped, making a grab for the leather bag.

He allowed her to take it, seemingly content with her wallet, which he held open. Easily avoiding her snatch at the wallet, he studied her driver's license, then her business card. "D'Alessandro Investigations, Dallas, Texas," he murmured. "That's who you work for?"

"Yes," she answered crossly. "And haven't you ever heard of invasion of privacy?"

"As a matter of fact, I have. I'm trying to figure out if my privacy has been invaded." He looked up at her, and he was no longer the man who'd kissed her until her toes had curled, but a faintly menacing stranger. "Who's your client, Cassie?"

She lifted her chin in a gesture of defiance. "I told you, that's confidential until I have permission to discuss it with you. If you'd wait just a couple of hours until I can contact my boss…"

"I thought maybe my old navy friend Bob Cutter hired you, that he must have sent you as soon as he heard I was in trouble. Though I can't figure why he'd hire someone from Dallas when he lives in Tulsa. Did he?"

"Not as far as I know," Cassie admitted.

"So who are you working for?"

She looked pleadingly at him. "I'm sorry, Jared. I'm under orders. And I don't want to lose my job."

"You've got a copy of my last driver's license photo," he commented, nodding toward the purse she held. "Which means you were looking for me even before I was arrested. Why?"

She remained mute, her fingers clenched around the soft leather.

Sighing his impatience, he tossed her the wallet, which she caught by reflex. "Call your boss. Now. I want some answers. With or without his clearance."

"I just tried to call him," she said, annoyed at the curtness of his command. "He wasn't in."

"Try again."

"Now see here—"

"Fine. I'll call him myself." He displayed the business card he'd kept when he'd returned her other things.

Cassie muttered a curse and snatched up the telephone. "I'll call him," she grumbled, punching in Tony's office number. "But we're wasting our time. He's not… Tony?"

"Yeah," her boss replied, apparently unperturbed by her

surprise at having him answer. "I had an early meeting that didn't last long. Thought I'd come on in and work on some overdue paperwork. What have you got, Cassie?"

"Just a minute." She put a hand over the mouthpiece and looked from Jared to the connecting door. "Maybe you could give me a few minutes to talk to my employer in private?"

"Forget it."

"Dammit, Jared—"

"This concerns me," he replied implacably, crossing his arms over his chest. "I'm staying."

She glared at him, but took her hand away. "Tony?"

"Yeah. What's going on, Cassie?"

"Jared Walker's here, in my room. He's been cleared of all charges—and he wants to know who my client is."

"Immediately," Jared confirmed quite clearly.

Tony obviously heard. "I see. Then I guess you'd better tell him."

Cassie turned her back to Jared in a futile effort to shut him out. "Um—you'll tell Michelle?"

"I've already told her," Tony admitted. "Never could keep anything from her for long. She and Layla will be greatly relieved to hear their brother's been cleared."

"So it's okay now to tell him everything?"

Tony hesitated only a moment. "You trust him, Cass?"

She knew what he was asking. He wanted to know if Jared Walker proved any threat to his wife. "Yes, Tony. I do."

"Then tell him. And ask if he'd like to come to Texas to meet his sisters. If not, I'm sure they'd be delighted to meet him wherever he chooses."

"I'll let you know."

"Do that. Good work, Cassie."

Warmed by his praise, she managed a smile. "Thanks, Tony. I'll talk to you later."

She hung up the telephone and turned to face Jared. She wasn't prepared for his first question.

"Who's this Tony guy?" he demanded. "And what is he to you?"

"He's my boss," she replied in surprise. "And my friend. He also happens to be your brother-in-law," she added, taking small revenge for his arrogance with the blunt statement. "He's married to your sister Michelle. My client."

Chapter Four

Jared shook his head in response to Cassie's disclosure. "Try again. I don't have a sister named Michelle."

"How about Shelley? Shelley Marie? She would have been two years old the last time you saw her."

His eyes widened, then narrowed again. "Shelley?"

Unable to hold on to her irritation with him, Cassie nodded, speaking more professionally. "Next to the youngest of your three sisters—her name was changed to Michelle Culverton Trent when she was adopted soon after you were separated. She and Tony, my boss, were married this summer. She met him when she hired him to find her biological family."

Jared seemed to struggle to understand what she was telling him. "My little sister Shelley has hired you to find the rest of us? After all these years?"

"Yes. She's already found the oldest sister, Layla, the one who's a year younger than you. Layla lives in Ft. Worth, and she and Michelle have become quite close during the past few months."

Jared inhaled sharply. "Layla," he murmured, his eyes focused somewhere in the past. He ran a hand through his crisp brown hair. "Damn."

Cassie tried very hard to read his expression. "You remember them?"

"I was eleven years old when we were separated," he answered. "I remember them."

"I hope you understand why Tony was reluctant for me to tell you at first," she said, nervously clenching her fingers in front of her. "I mean, you were in jail, and even though I believed from the beginning you hadn't done anything wrong, Tony wanted to be careful. I tried to talk him into making your bail, but he—well, he's a really nice guy, but when it comes to Michelle, he's very protective. He wanted to be sure."

Jared inclined his head. "Yeah."

She waited for him to say something else. When he didn't, she offered, "Tony's still coordinating the search for your youngest sister and your two brothers. He hasn't located any of them yet, but—"

"*Two* brothers?" Jared repeated. "There should be three."

"Oh." Cassie bit her lip before explaining. "One of them died in a car accident several years ago."

"Which?" he asked sharply.

"Miles. As far as we know, the twins are still living."

Jared's only reaction was the twitch of a muscle in his jaw. He shoved his hands in his pockets, looking away from her.

Cassie suspected that he was more shaken by the news than he would have her believe. "I'm sorry, Jared. I guess I didn't handle that very well. I'm not very good at breaking bad news."

He flicked her a glance. It wasn't unkind, just...detached,

Cassie decided, wondering if she'd made a mess of everything with her usual lack of tact.

"Jared?"

"I haven't seen them in twenty-four years," he told her. "I didn't know whether any of them were still alive. I'm not so sure this search is such a hot idea."

"How can you say that?" Cassie demanded, perplexed by his attitude. "They're your family. Don't you want to see them again?"

"As far as I'm concerned, Shane is the only family I've got," Jared returned brusquely. "We've gotten along fine, just the two of us. These other people are strangers."

Cassie was stunned by his callousness. Perhaps she'd taken her own loosely knit family for granted at times, but she'd always known they were there for her, should she need them. She couldn't imagine walking away from them for good. "Jared—"

He exhaled through his nose, shaking his head in apparent incredulity at her dismay. "Still living in that fairy-tale world, Cassie?" he murmured. "Believing that every story leads to a happy ending?"

She strongly resented his condescending tone. "You weren't convicted for a crime you didn't commit, were you? Didn't I tell you the system works most of the time?"

"Right. But if the jerk who robbed the motel hadn't been such an idiot and gotten himself caught, I'd still be sitting in that cell and the cops would be quite certain they had their man. It was dumb luck, not the wheels of justice."

She decided it wasn't worth arguing about. "Believe whatever you want."

His mouth twitched in a smile that held little humor. "Thanks. I will."

Cassie thought she'd take almost as much satisfaction from hitting this infuriating man as she had in kissing him. Almost.

She clenched her fists behind her back to keep them away from temptation. "Your sisters really want to see you again, Jared. They've gone to a lot of trouble to track you down."

His faint smile deepened just fractionally. "I can see they put the best investigator on the case."

She scowled. "There's no need to make fun of me," she told him with all the dignity at her command.

"I wasn't," he replied, his tone unexpectedly gentle.

Eyeing him uncertainly, she asked, "Will you come back to Dallas with me to see your sisters?"

He hesitated only a moment. "No. Sorry, but I'd best head on toward Arizona. I need a job for the winter. Got to get Shane back in school. He's already missed a week."

"There are jobs in Texas," Cassie said wistfully, reluctant to let either Jared or Shane leave her life now that she'd found them. "And schools."

He shook his head. Again, his expression wasn't hard or unkind, but he didn't look as though he'd change his mind. "I don't belong there, Cassie. I've been on my own too long now, wouldn't know what to do with a lot of family. Tell my—tell your clients that I appreciate their concern and I send my best regards, but I think I'll pass on a family reunion for now."

"You wouldn't have to go to Dallas," Cassie said, taking one last shot, which she already knew would be futile. "They'd come to Arizona. Or anywhere you like. They only want to see you."

"Maybe some day," Jared replied firmly. "Not now."

He glanced at his watch, a clear indication the conversation was over. "I'd better get moving. Oddly enough, I can't wait to get the hell out of this town."

"A real loner, aren't you?" she grumbled, thoroughly dissatisfied with the outcome of the case on which she'd worked so hard. The case with which she'd become all too deeply involved. "You're walking away without a regret."

"Oh, I don't know," Jared murmured, stepping close and touching the fingertips of his right hand to her cheek. "Maybe one regret."

Cassie looked longingly up at him. Whatever unguarded expression he saw in her eyes made him groan. And then he kissed her again, and Cassie found herself clinging to his shirt as though that tenuous grip would keep him with her.

He took his time, his mouth moving hungrily on hers until neither of them could wait any longer for the kiss to deepen. Cassie parted her lips, and Jared thrust inside with a rough, heated skill that made the blood pound in her veins, bringing every inch of her to tingling awareness. And this time, she didn't even wonder if the kiss was motivated by gratitude. She might not be widely experienced when it came to men, but she knew enough to tell the difference between gratitude and desire.

"Uh—Dad?"

Cassie would have torn herself out of Jared's arms had he not held her where she was. Without the least evidence of embarrassment, he slowly lifted his head and glanced toward the doorway. "Be right with you, Shane."

His dark head cocked to one side, Shane looked from Jared to Cassie with what seemed to her to be amused approval. "Guess there's no need for you to hurry. It's just…"

"You're hungry, right?" Jared spoke with the confidence of parental experience.

Shane grinned. "Yeah."

Jared gave Cassie a rueful glance and released her. "We'll stop for breakfast at the next town," he told his son. "I've had enough of this place."

"I know the feeling," Shane agreed heartily. He turned his attention to Cassie. "Are you going with us?"

Jared answered instead. "Cassie's going back to Dallas. That's the opposite direction from where we're going."

Shane looked disappointed. "Oh."

Jared tossed Cassie's business card on her unmade bed. "I'll put your things back in the truck, Shane. You can take a minute to thank her for all she did for us and tell her goodbye."

"Take my card with you," Cassie said, retrieving it and holding it out to Jared. "My work and home numbers are on it. You could call me—you know, if you change your mind."

He glanced at the card, but didn't take it. "I won't be changing my mind. And I know how to find you. Goodbye, Cassie. Thanks again for all you did for us. Tell your boss you deserve a bonus for this case."

She winced at his mention of her job. Jared and Shane had become much more than just another case to her, though damned if she knew what she was going to do about it.

She turned to find Shane looking indignantly after his father. "He's not always that rude," he seemed to feel obligated to say. "He's just had a bad couple of days."

"I know," she murmured, moved again by Shane's consideration. He really was such a sweet young man.

She pressed the rejected card into his hand. "Keep this, okay, Shane? If you ever need me, you can call anytime."

He studied the card curiously. "Maybe I'll write you sometime?" he suggested rather tentatively. "You know, let you know how we're doing, how things are going in Arizona."

Her smile felt shaky around the edges. "I'd really like that."

"Yeah? Maybe I will, then." He stored her card carefully in his battered wallet, treating it with touching care. And then he slid the wallet into the back pocket of his jeans and looked back up at her. "I'm going to miss you, Cassie. You've been a good friend."

"I'll miss you, too," Cassie whispered. "And we're still friends, okay?"

"You bet." Impulsively, he reached out to hug her, the embrace awkward, but obviously sincere. Cassie blinked back tears as she fervently returned the hug.

A horn honked briefly outside the room. "That's my dad," Shane said, drawing back with his young face rather flushed. "He wants to make it as far as Winslow by tonight. I'd better go."

"Take care of yourself. And your dad."

"I will. 'Bye, Cassie."

"'Bye, Shane."

And then Cassie was left alone, staring wistfully at a closed door.

"Damn," she said aloud, unable, for the moment, to think of anything else to say.

Jared was aware of his son's unblinking regard for a full ten minutes after they'd left the town behind them. He ignored it at first, fiddling with the radio until he found a station that played the contemporary country music Shane preferred. When Shane continued to look at him without saying anything, Jared sighed gustily and slanted the boy a questioning glance.

"All right. Get it said. What's eating you?"

"I liked her, Dad. She worked real hard yesterday to try to clear you, even though she'd just met you. And she didn't talk to me like I was some helpless kid, or call the welfare service or anything. Why'd you have to treat her so bad?"

"I did *not* treat her badly," Jared returned, unaccountably defensive. "I thought I was nice enough. I thanked her for helping us."

"You kissed her off. Literally."

Jared scowled at his son's phrasing, as well as the uncomfortable sensations that coursed through him at the mention of that kiss. He hadn't really wanted to walk away from Cassie Browning—not just yet, anyway—but all her talk of sisters and family ties had made him extremely nervous.

Okay, he'd admit it. He'd sort of panicked. But, hell, he'd been on his own for a long time, responsible for and dependent on no one but himself and his son for the past two years. Maybe it wasn't an ideal life that he and Shane were leading, but they were getting by. Jared didn't see the need to make any radical changes at this point.

He hadn't told Shane about the family who'd initiated Cassie's search. Wasn't sure he wanted to tell him just yet. Not until he decided exactly how he felt about being found by them.

But, damn, the taste of Cassie Browning's pouty mouth had turned him on. Like no other woman had in a very long time.

Spotting a small restaurant ahead, he pointed it out to Shane, knowing only food could distract the boy from thoughts of his new friend at the moment. Now, if only a stack of hotcakes and a cup of coffee could do the same for himself…

But he knew, even as the thought crossed his mind, that he wouldn't be forgetting Cassie Browning anytime soon.

"Look, it's not your fault, Cassie. You did the best you could. You did a hell of a job on this case, actually."

A few days earlier, praise like that from her boss would have had Cassie doing ecstatic time steps across the motel room. Now she could only slump more dejectedly on the side of the bed. "I really tried to talk him into seeing Michelle and Layla. But he's been alone a long time, Tony. I think the idea of family unnerved him."

"I suppose that's understandable. We know he lost both his parents in less than a year, then was separated from his brothers and sisters and thrown into a series of unsuccessful foster homes. He's probably learned not to get close to people, that it's easier not to have personal ties."

"You're right," Cassie admitted regretfully. "Other than Shane, there seems to be no one special in his life except an old navy buddy who apparently lives in Oklahoma."

It had really been foolish of her to fall so hard for a man who'd almost made a career out of being a loner. And yet, she couldn't help remembering the way he'd looked at his son when they'd been reunited. If Jared could love Shane that intensely, couldn't he learn to love someone else? Someone very persistent, very stubborn and very motivated to teach him? Someone just like her?

"Cassie? You still there?"

"Mmm? Oh, sorry, Tony. I was just thinking."

"Uh-oh. I know that tone. What are you planning?"

"Shane mentioned where they'll be staying tonight. I thought maybe I'd follow—try to talk to Jared one more time. Maybe he'll change his mind."

"Cassie. Give it up. You've done all you can do. It's up to Jared to contact us if he wants to be reunited with his family. Neither Michelle nor Layla expect us to force their brother to see them."

Cassie stuck out her lower lip in an expression that her parents could have identified as one of sheer determination. "You know, I'm kind of tired after tracking Jared down for the past few weeks. All the stress and everything. I think I'll take a couple of days off, if you don't mind."

"I *do* mind, as a matter of fact," Tony returned immediately. "Chuck's still out, the guy I hired to replace Bob is still learning the ropes, Michelle's uncle's still raising a fuss. I need you here, Cassie. Come home."

Cassie coughed delicately, not bothering to cover the mouthpiece. "You know, Tony, I'm not feeling very well. I think maybe I'm coming down with something. Probably picked it up in that tacky little jail yesterday."

"Cassie…"

"Just a couple of days, Tony. I swear. And you can take me off the expense account as of now. I'm on my own time."

The word he said was probably illegal over the telephone wires. Since he spoke in idiomatic Italian, Cassie couldn't have said for certain. She winced, waiting with held breath for his decision.

"All right, Browning. You've got a couple more days. But this time, if he says no, you're going to give up. Got that?"

"Thanks, Tony. You won't be sorry. And you know how pleased Michelle will be if I talk her brother into coming there to meet her."

"That's the only reason I'm going along with this," Tony admitted. "Michelle would love to see her older brother—and her nephew. So, you're still on the expense account. But, dammit, Cassie, stay in touch. And don't be gone long."

"I won't. 'Bye, Tony."

She hung up quickly, before her boss could change his mind, and reached for her bag.

Jared Walker was about to find out that Cassie Browning could be as stubborn as he was. That he couldn't look at her the way he had, kiss her silly—twice—then walk out on her without a backward glance.

And she wouldn't turn in her new expenses, she decided, forcefully zipping her bag.

From this moment on, the case was strictly personal.

Though he'd quit smoking two years ago, figuring it was better for his health and a better example for Shane, Jared bought a pack of cigarettes from a vending machine in the corridor of another inexpensive motel, this one in Winslow, Arizona. He carried the pack only as far as a corner of the second-story landing outside the room where Shane slept, then leaned against the wrought-iron balcony and lit up. Jared was having another restless night, but this time he had no intention of wandering very far from his son.

He drew deeply on the cigarette, making a face at the dry, bitter taste. Had he really enjoyed it once? Shrugging, he brought it back to his lips. Might as well finish it now that he'd started.

It wasn't as though he had anything else to do.

Except think. He'd been doing entirely too much thinking today. Too much remembering. Things he hadn't allowed himself to remember in nearly twenty-four years.

The distant sounds of childish voices drifted through his mind. He sighed and gave up on trying to hold them back. His brothers and sisters. God, he'd missed them when they'd been taken away.

As the eldest, Jared had been the one in charge when his alcoholic father was gone and his poor, fragile mother working or resting. Jared had always felt responsible for them all, his mother included, particularly after his father had been killed in an industrial accident, which the insurance hadn't covered because Hank had been drinking that day.

Jared had never quite gotten over the crushing guilt he'd felt when his mother had died less than a year after giving birth to the child she'd been carrying when her husband died. He'd tried so hard to help her, as had Layla, his junior by a year. But their efforts hadn't stopped their delicate, overworked mother from catching pneumonia. Nor had they been able to prevent the siblings from being separated when the social workers decided that no family would be willing to take in seven children, ranging in age from eleven years to eight months.

It would be "best," they'd said, to split the kids up. *Best for whom?* Jared had demanded to know, but he'd never gotten a satisfactory answer.

He'd secretly grieved for his family for years afterward, until he'd finally learned to put them out of his mind so that he could get on with his own life. And he'd learned not to get so attached again. Not until he'd had Shane, whom he'd allowed himself to love more deeply than anyone or anything else in his entire life.

So little Shelley was married now. He held the smoldering cigarette between his fingers and stared blindly at the deserted parking lot below him. Hard to believe. He remembered her as a curly headed toddler, a bright, happy baby who'd loved jelly sandwiches and "horsey-back" rides from her oldest brother, whom she'd called Jerry. She'd been devoted to him, and to Layla, whom she'd clung to, crying when the social workers had come to take her away.

It was nice to know Layla and Shelley had been reunited, that they were growing close again. He was pleased for them, despite his own cautious reluctance to get involved.

Jared had been especially close to Layla, maybe because they'd been so close in age. Together they had made sure the younger ones were fed, bathed, clothed, tucked into bed. A pretty, loving girl, Layla had always been willing to listen, always ready to lend a hand with homework or to take over his chores for a few hours so he could join the neighborhood boys for a game of empty-lot baseball in their hometown of Texarkana, Texas.

And Miles. Eight years old when they'd been separated. Jared could still picture the boy's round, freckled face. Miles could always be counted on to make the others laugh, since he'd usually been laughing himself. A real little clown, with dreams of becoming a stand-up comic or an impersonator like his hero, Rich Little. He'd been pretty good, too, for a kid. Did a great imitation of President Johnson. And now he was dead. Had he ever made it to a stage, basked in the sound of an audience's laughter?

And what had happened to the five-year-old twins, Joey and Bobby? They'd been a handful, always into some sort of mischief. He and Layla had run themselves ragged trying to keep up with them. Jared remembered very clearly telling Bobby that it would be a wonder if he lived to see junior high—it had been a threat, actually. *Had* Bobby seen junior high? Where was he now?

Which left only the baby, Lindsay. She hadn't really had a chance to develop a personality when they'd taken her away, of course. Just a little thing, but she'd been a good baby. Jared still remembered how it had felt to rock her sweetly scented little body in the middle of the night so their mother could catch a few hours' sleep before going in to one of the two jobs she'd worked to feed her kids. Jared and Layla had taken turns looking after the baby, and he'd never really minded doing his part, no matter how much he may have grumbled at the time.

He'd missed them. But he didn't know them now. Why take the chance of an awkward, painful reunion when he had enough to do just taking care of himself and his son?

Shane. Jared scowled. Being arrested for a crime he didn't commit had made Jared all too aware of how very much alone he and Shane really were.

What would become of the boy if anything happened to Jared? He certainly wouldn't go back to his mother and stepfather, neither of whom would want him, anyway. Which left the streets—or foster care, both of which held approximately the same appeal, as far as Jared was concerned.

Should he give Shane the chance to meet these long-lost family members, hoping they would be there for the boy if he ever needed them? Or would he be imposing more stress on Shane by introducing him to these strangers who might have emotional expectations neither Jared nor Shane could satisfy?

"Damn," he muttered, annoyed with his uncharacteristic ambiguity.

It was usually so easy to make decisions, avoid messy entanglements, move on without regrets. Why did he suspect that Cassie Browning had all too much to do with his indecisiveness now?

"Hello, Jared."

Jared looked around sharply to find Cassie standing only a few feet away, watching him with a wary guardedness that showed how uncertain she was of her reception. Had he been the sort of man to believe in the paranormal, he might have wondered if his thoughts had conjured her.

He didn't have to ask why she was here. One of the first impressions he'd gotten of her was that she was the persistent type. Young, eager, reckless, stubborn, idealistic, impetuous. Desirable.

With his abysmal track record with women, he'd thought it best to walk away from this one, feeling he had much too little to offer her. But somehow, even as he'd driven away from her that morning, he'd suspected she wouldn't leave his life so easily. And, no matter how he might try to deny it, he was glad she hadn't.

He ground the cigarette beneath the heel of his boot, deliberately taking his time about it. And then he looped his thumbs in his belt and faced her. "Anyone ever tell you you're a pain in the butt, Cassie Browning?"

Chapter Five

Oddly enough, Cassie relaxed in response to Jared's question—more specifically, to the tone in which he'd asked it. He didn't sound angry that she'd followed him, just resigned. As though he'd really been expecting her all along.

She'd been watching him in tense silence for the past five minutes, working up her nerve to speak. He'd seemed so tough and unapproachable, leaning against the balcony and smoking in the shadows, lost in his own deep thoughts. And he'd looked so virilely sexy that she'd become aroused all over again, just from standing close to him.

She pushed her hands into the pockets of her slacks. "It's been mentioned a time or two," she quipped in response to his only half-joking question.

"Not surprising." He propped both elbows on the railing behind him, one boot resting on the bottom rail as he studied her in the dim artificial lighting. "It's getting late. Took you a while to find me, did it?"

She took offense at the subtle criticism. "I think I did pretty well," she retorted. "Considering that I've had to check the guest registers of twelve different hotels in the past two hours."

"Guess I don't have to ask why you're here."

"I'm sure you know," she replied, hoping his casual tone indicated that he was more receptive now to the idea of meeting his sisters.

"You want my body, right? Want to go to bed with me."

Cassie choked. *"What?"*

"Not so loud. There are people trying to sleep around here, you know. And damned if I intend to be accused of disturbing the peace and spend another night in jail."

She lowered her voice to a sibilant whisper. "You are the most obnoxious, arrogant, conceited—"

"Hey, it's okay. I understand. Those *were* dynamite kisses, weren't they? Can't blame you for wanting to follow up on them. Matter of fact, the same thought crossed my mind a time or two. I'm willing."

Cassie suddenly realized that she'd just been expertly played for a fool. Jared had been baiting her—and she'd swallowed it hook, line and sinker.

"You jerk," she said, more calmly this time.

"You mean you *don't* want to go to bed with me? Well, hell."

She couldn't help giggling, though she suppressed her amusement almost immediately. "You know why I'm really here, Jared," she said, crossing her arms in front of her.

He sighed faintly, abandoning the teasing. "Yeah, I know. Would you mind answering one question?"

"What is it?"

"What's in it for you if I agree to see my sisters? Why are you so determined to talk me into this?"

"Well…" She hesitated, then suggested, "It would look really good to my boss if I pull this off. He still considers me an apprentice, and I'm hoping to make partner someday."

"So I'm just a career opportunity to you, is that it?" Jared asked gruffly.

She dropped her arms to her sides, wishing just this once she could get away with dissimulation to someone she cared about. Knowing Jared would see right through anything but the truth. "That's not the only reason I followed you," she admitted.

"No?"

She gave him a quick, resentful look, annoyed that he was making this so difficult. "No."

He didn't move, though she sensed a change in him, a tension she felt echoed in herself. "Then why?" he asked, his voice a husky murmur.

Dragging both hands through her hair, Cassie attempted a quiet laugh, which came out much too shaky and tentative. "Maybe I just want your body."

When Jared started to move, she hastily held up a hand, palm outward, afraid he'd taken her sadly flat-sounding joke the wrong way.

"No wait. What I really mean is, I'd like to get to know you better. I'm—well, I'm attracted to you, of course, and I think Shane is terrific and—and I think it would be good for both of you to meet your family. Not just because it would be good for my career, but because I think you're both a little lonely and…

"But, anyway," she hurried on when he took another step toward her, "I'd understand if you don't—uh—reciprocate my feelings, but I still think you should see your sisters, for your own—"

Jared put an end to her nervous babbling by smothering the words beneath his mouth.

Cassie didn't even try to resist him. She melted into his embrace like warm chocolate, her arms going around his neck to bring them even closer together. His arms locked around her waist, and for the first time she felt the full length of him against her.

They fit so well. He wasn't overly tall, maybe five-nine, just right for her height. But he was so strong, so lean and hard that she felt utterly, deliciously feminine in contrast. Intensely aware of the exciting differences between them.

The kiss lasted a very long time. As did the one that followed it, and the one after that. Cassie thought she'd be content to stay right here forever, locked in his arms, his mouth moving on hers.

And then he slipped a hand between them to cup her swelling right breast and she knew that it wouldn't be long before she'd need more. Much, much more. And, judging from the hardness she felt pressing against her abdomen, Jared wouldn't be content with kisses for much longer, either.

"You two at it again?" a young, sleepy voice asked cheerfully from behind them.

Dropping his hand, Jared groaned and rested his forehead against Cassie's, giving them both a moment to control their breathing. And then he lifted his head and glared at the grinning teenager standing in the doorway of the motel room. "You're pushing your luck, boy," he said, his voice still rough around the edges.

"Hi, Cassie," Shane said, ignoring his father's warning.

She returned his smile and pulled out of Jared's arms, wondering why she didn't really feel embarrassed this time at being caught kissing his father. "Hi, Shane."

"Good to see you again."

"You, too."

"You're looking well."

She really adored this kid. She nodded in grave acknowledgment of his teasing. "Thanks. So are you."

"Did you have a nice drive?"

"Yes, quite pleasant. And you?"

Jared gave a short laugh, putting an end to the gravely silly conversation. "All right, you two, knock it off. You got a place to stay tonight, Cassie?"

"No, not yet."

"Go back to bed, Shane. I'll be in as soon as I'm sure Cassie's got a room."

"Hey, no problem. Take your time, Dad."

"Shane?"

"Yes, Dad?"

"You want to live to see fifteen?"

Shane's grin deepened. "Yeah. I was kinda hoping to live long enough to get a driver's license."

"Then get back in bed. Now. I'll be in shortly."

"Yes, Dad. 'Night, Cassie. See you in the morning?"

"You bet. Good night, Shane." Cassie bit back a laugh as she looked up at Jared when the door had closed behind his son. "Did I mention that I like your kid, Jared?"

"I'm not surprised. The two of you have a lot in common."

Cassie couldn't help wondering about Shane's mother as Jared escorted her to the motel office. Had Jared ever loved the woman? And how could any mother let go of a wonderful young man like Shane?

She remembered Shane's casual mention of his mother's drinking and, again, she marveled that he'd turned out so well. She thought maybe Jared had a lot to do with that.

Jared waited outside the office while Cassie registered. Fortunately, there were vacancies on this Friday night, since it wasn't exactly the peak of tourist season. She was pleased to be given a room close to the one Jared and Shane shared. She held up the key as she stepped back outside. "All set."

"Good. Where are your bags?"

"In my car." She nodded to the car parked close by the office. "I'll get it."

"I'll help you."

Jared was very quiet as they retrieved her bag from the back seat of the car and headed toward her room. Cassie wished she knew him well enough to guess at his thoughts.

He unlocked her door for her, carried the bag inside and dropped it at the foot of the bed. With what Cassie considered rather touching courtesy, he checked to make sure the utilitarian room was adequate, clean towels available, television functional, an extra blanket in the closet should she need it. "You'll be okay?"

"I'll be fine," she assured him. "I live by myself in Dallas. I'm used to sleeping alone."

His gaze locked with hers. "If it weren't for Shane, you wouldn't be sleeping alone tonight."

Her mouth went dry. She moistened her lips with the tip of her tongue, noting that Jared watched intently as she did so. "I know."

He hesitated, then seemed to force himself to turn toward the door. "Good night, Cassie. Sleep well."

"Thanks. You, too."

He snorted skeptically. "Yeah. Right."

Which meant, of course, that he didn't expect to sleep any better than she did. Sexual frustration wasn't exactly conducive to a good night's rest.

Jared paused with one hand on the doorknob, his back turned to her. She watched him curiously, sensing that he was struggling for words. "What is it, Jared?"

"I'm unemployed," he said, still without looking around at

her. "My track record with women is lousy. I've got a teen-age boy to worry about and a bank account that's a long way from being enough to buy the small ranch I hope to own someday. I'm not exactly a good risk for a relationship. I think you should know that before we—well, before we take this any further."

"Thank you for telling me."

He did glance back then, in response to her wry tone. "You don't look like you're taking me very seriously."

She managed a tremulous smile. "No."

"That reckless streak is going to get you in trouble some-day, Cassie."

"So everyone tells me. It hasn't happened yet."

He exhaled wearily. "Just don't say I didn't warn you."

He was gone before she could respond, had she been able to think of anything to say.

Okay, Browning, you've been warned. The man's not look-ing for a long-term relationship. So, are you going to take his advice and keep your distance?

Her mouth still felt swollen and tingly from his kisses, the deepest feminine parts of her still moist and throbbing with desire for him.

Oh, no, Jared Walker. You're not getting off that easily. Cassie Browning doesn't give up so quickly on something this important.

It wasn't until she was tucked into bed, tossing restlessly on the pillow and trying to think of anything but her physical discomfort, that it occurred to her that Jared had never given her an answer about meeting his sisters.

Cassie was awakened the next morning by the telephone on her nightstand. Expecting to hear Jared's voice, she an-swered with a sleepy smile.

"Cassie? It's Shane. Good morning."

She wasn't really disappointed. "Good morning, Shane. What time is it?"

"Nearly eight. Dad wants to know if you want to join us for breakfast. I'm—"

"—starving," Cassie finished with him, her smile deepening. He laughed self-consciously. "Yeah."

"I'd love to join you for breakfast. Think you can wait another twenty minutes without fainting from hunger?"

"I might last that long—but it'll be close," he returned cheerfully.

"Then I promise to hurry."

"I'd appreciate it," Shane drawled, sounding so much like his father that Cassie's throat tightened.

She jumped out of bed, took a record-breaking quick shower and subdued her wet curls into a French braid. She hadn't brought many clothes with her when she'd left Dallas four days earlier. She pulled a clean pair of jeans and a floral fleece pullover from her bag, trusting that Jared didn't have anyplace fancy in mind for breakfast, judging by the low-budget motels and inexpensive diners he'd frequented thus far.

She had just finished tying her tennis shoes when someone knocked on her door. She pulled it open eagerly, finding Jared and Shane waiting on the other side.

"Good morning." The greeting was meant for both of them, though Cassie looked at Jared as she spoke.

Jared's smile was as intimate as a kiss would have been. His gaze locked with Cassie's. "Good morning."

Shane cleared his throat noisily when several long, silent moments had passed. "So, is anybody hungry? For food?" he added daringly.

Jared cuffed his son's shoulder. "Mind your manners."

Shane grinned. "Yes, sir."

Cassie grabbed her purse and suitcase, knowing there would be no reason for them to return to the motel. Jared took the bag from her, their fingers brushing. Cassie could almost feel the electricity spark between them at the contact.

"Thanks," she said, rather breathlessly.

He looked down at her for another long moment. "Oh, hell," he muttered, then glanced at his son. "Turn around."

Shane laughed, but obliged.

Jared bent to Cassie, giving her a very thorough, quite satisfactory good-morning kiss. Her toes curled inside her tennies at the heat and hunger behind the embrace.

"*Now* we can have breakfast," he said, lifting his head with a rakish smile that made her shiver in response.

"It's about time," Shane proclaimed fervently.

Cassie just hoped she'd remember how to walk to the door. *Wow, could that man kiss!*

With Cassie following in her little car, Jared drove his truck to a small restaurant just down the road from the motel. Shane teased him about his obvious attraction to Cassie until Jared put a stop to it with a firm, "That's enough, Shane."

"Yes, Dad," Shane said, subsiding with a meek tone and a suspicious twinkle in his blue eyes. "But you *do* like her, don't you?"

"I like her," Jared answered, knowing even as he spoke that he wasn't being exactly truthful. He wasn't sure what, exactly, he felt for Cassie Browning, but *like* was far too tepid a word to describe it.

"Table for three?" a plain young hostess inquired when they entered the restaurant. "Smoking or nonsmoking?"

"Nonsmoking," Jared answered for them. He'd given it up again. He hadn't found much pleasure in the one cigarette he'd smoked the night before. He figured he could live without them.

Shane and Cassie kept up a rapid repartee as they ordered their breakfasts and waited to be served, making Jared feel, at times, like a chaperone with a couple of kids. The bond that was forming between Cassie and the boy was almost a visible one. Jared had never seen Shane take to anyone as quickly.

He guessed he could understand that. He felt much the same way.

"You got a boyfriend, Cassie?" Shane asked just a shade too casually, avoiding his father's eyes as he spoke.

"No," Cassie answered in the same tone, and she didn't look at Jared, either. "I guess I've been too busy with my job to have much time for a social life lately."

"Too bad," Shane commented, his expression saying just the opposite. "Did you know Cassie has a brother who's a bush pilot in Alaska, Dad?"

"No, I didn't," Jared replied, realizing with a slight start that he actually knew very little about Cassie's personal life. Odd that he should feel as though he knew her so well in some ways.

"Cliff," Cassie said. "He's a couple of years older than I am. He's a redhead, too, though no one else has been for generations back."

"Your family lives in Dallas?" Jared asked, suddenly wanting to know as much as he could about her.

She shook her head, causing the overhead lights to glisten in the still-damp, dark red braid. "My parents live in Tyler, Texas and Cliff's my only brother. I moved to Dallas because the job market looked better there."

"And you became a P.I.," Jared commented. "You and your brother both seem to be the adventurous types."

Cassie smiled. "Yeah, I guess we are. My parents, who are very sweet, but just a little staid, seem to think we're change-lings, that their real babies were mysteriously replaced by these two redheaded daredevils. They love us, but they don't quite understand our need to constantly challenge ourselves."

Shane laughed, but then defended his new friend. "I think what you do is cool. Your parents ought to be proud of you."

Jared gave Cassie a wry look. "It seems you've won yourself a champion."

Cassie only smiled and turned her attention to the breakfast their waitress had just set in front of her.

Jared waited until Shane had taken the edge off his hunger before bringing up the topic he knew Cassie was waiting anxiously for him to broach. Maybe it would have been better to talk to the boy in private, he thought, but for some reason he wanted Cassie there. He'd already come to value her matter-of-fact comments and her easy way of talking with Shane. And this talk wasn't going to be easy for Jared.

"Son, you remember asking me once if I had any family?"

Jared felt Cassie stiffen, but he kept his gaze on Shane, who looked up curiously from the remains of his huge breakfast. "Yeah, I remember. You said your folks died when you were a kid."

"Right. And I told you that I'd had some brothers and sisters who were separated and sent to different homes. That I assumed most of them had been adopted soon afterward."

Shane nodded, then his eyes widened. He looked across the table at Cassie. "Is that who you're working for? One of Dad's brothers or sisters?"

Damn, the kid was sharp, Jared couldn't help thinking with a touch of pride. Didn't miss a trick.

Cassie glanced at Jared before answering Shane. He nodded.

"Yes, Shane," she said, turning back to the boy. "Your father's sister Michelle is my client. Actually, she's married to my boss."

"Michelle?" Shane looked intrigued. "You remember her, Dad?"

"Yeah. She was just a little thing when we were split up. We called her Shelley."

"She was adopted by a family named Trent from Dallas," Cassie supplied. "She grew up thinking she was an only child, since she was too young to remember her brothers and sisters. She initiated the search for the others when her adoptive mother died earlier this year, leaving a letter telling Michelle about her biological family. Michelle hired my boss for the job, then ended up married to him a few months later."

"And you were assigned to find my dad."

Cassie nodded. "That's right."

"Guess they gave you the best, huh, Dad?"

Jared smiled at Cassie, remembering that he'd said much the same thing only the day before. She'd thought he was mocking her. He hadn't been, any more than Shane was now. "Yeah. Guess they did."

He was relieved that Shane was taking the news so well.

"So I've got an Aunt Michelle," Shane mused.

"And an Aunt Layla," Cassie told him. "And three cousins that we know of so far. Layla has three kids."

"My age?" Shane asked with interest.

"Younger," Cassie replied. "I think the oldest is maybe nine, ten years old."

"Boys or girls?"

"One boy, two girls. I'm sorry, I don't remember their names."

Jared shook his head in wonder at the thought of young Layla with a brood of her own now. Not that it was so hard to picture, really. She'd been a natural at mothering the little ones.

"What about the rest of Dad's brothers and sisters?" Shane asked, still addressing his questions to Cassie. "There were a bunch of them, weren't there?"

Cassie looked again at Jared, who motioned her to answer. He wasn't yet ready to join the discussion he'd initiated.

"Counting your dad, there were seven children. One died in a car accident several years ago, leaving twin boys and a girl still unaccounted for."

"I bet you'll find 'em, won't you, Cassie? You can find anyone."

Cassie flushed at the confidence in Shane's young voice. Jared found the blush sweetly endearing.

She avoided his eyes as she answered, "Tony—my boss— has several operatives on the case, actually, as well as his own efforts. I've spent most of my time just tracking down your dad through military and employment records."

"Operatives," Shane repeated in a murmur, obviously impressed by the term. "Cool."

"So here's the deal, son," Jared said, leaning forward and taking control of the conversation. "My sisters have invited us to Dallas to visit them and get to know the families. They're also willing to visit us here in Arizona, whenever we get settled. They're leaving it up to us to choose."

"Dallas," Shane repeated, looking speculatively at Cassie. "That's where you live, isn't it?"

"Yes."

Shane turned to his father. "I'd like to go to Dallas, Dad."

Jared frowned at the too-quick answer. "We need to discuss it a little more. I don't know if that's the best choice right now. After all, you've already missed a week of school, and I've got to get back to work before our money runs out. Might be better if we head on to Flagstaff and arrange a meeting later."

It never occurred to Jared to make the decision without asking for Shane's opinion. After all, this affected them both, and they'd become a team during the past couple of years.

"Aw, come on, Dad. Another week out of school won't make any difference. I can catch up, you know I can. Didn't I have all A's in Oklahoma?"

"Social studies," Jared reminded him, though he was already weakening at the entreaty in his son's eyes.

"Okay, one B," Shane conceded. "But I'll study real hard when I get back to it, I promise. As for the job, well, you didn't have anything firmed up, anyway. You can always talk to the guy next week rather than this one."

"You really want to go to Dallas? Why, Shane?"

"Well, gosh, Dad. You've got family there. Don't you want to get to know them?"

Jared was staggered by Shane's apparent eagerness to meet this newly discovered family. Had the boy really been so lonely? Had Jared been deluding himself that neither of them needed anyone else in his life? "The question is, do *you* want to get to know them?" he asked, watching his son closely.

"Well, yeah. I think it would be cool to have aunts and cousins and everything," Shane admitted. "Of course, it's been great just the two of us the past couple of years," he assured Jared hastily, as if concerned that he'd hurt his father's feelings.

Jared knew exactly how lonely Shane had been in the years before he had gotten full custody of the boy. Living in a home with an alcoholic mother and a distant, resentful stepfather, Shane had grown up isolated and withdrawn, eager for visits from his seafaring father. For the first time, Jared realized that Shane must have fantasized during those years about having a large family.

Jared's fist clenched beneath the table at the thought of the abuse his son had suffered at the hands of his mother, and the years Jared and Shane had missed together because the courts had denied Jared's repeated attempts to gain custody. The so-called experts had decided the boy would be better off in a home with two parents than with his single, military father, even though those "parents" had proven sadly inadequate for the responsibility they'd been given.

Was that why Shane had taken so quickly to Cassie, why he seemed so pleased that his father was obviously attracted to the friendly young woman? Was the boy starting to fantasize now about a new family, complete with father and mother, aunts, uncles and cousins?

Jared ran a finger beneath the open collar of his flannel shirt, as though it had suddenly grown tight.

Damn. He really didn't need this kind of pressure right now.

"We can't stay long," he warned. "Our money's not going to hold out forever. I've got to get back to work."

Shane shrugged with youthful unconcern. "You could always find something in Texas. Maybe Cassie knows of something," he added.

Jared felt a muscle twitch in his jaw. "I can find my own jobs."

He noted that Cassie was being very quiet, her hands folded in her lap, though she was concentrating intensely on the discussion between Jared and Shane. Just looking at her made his pulse quicken, his loins harden.

He couldn't remember wanting any woman as much as he wanted this one. But damned if he'd find himself married to her just to please his son. He was a long way from ready for a commitment like that.

"You remember what I said last night?" he asked her abruptly, not wanting to clarify his question in front of the boy.

"I remember," she answered evenly, her expression telling him that she remembered every word of warning.

"You willing to risk that it won't work out?"

Her eyes held his without wavering. "I'm willing."

Feeling just a bit cornered, Jared turned to Shane, who watched him hopefully. "You understand that if this doesn't pan out, we'll have to move on? Soon?"

Shane shrugged. "It's what we've always done before," he agreed, sounding suddenly older than his fourteen years.

Jared pushed a hand through his hair. "Okay. We'll give it a shot."

"We're going to Dallas?" Shane asked, eagerly seeking confirmation.

Jared nodded, his gaze still focused on Cassie. "We're going to Dallas."

And he knew, as he suspected the others did, that the decision had little to do with Jared's sisters and a great deal to do with whatever had developed between Cassie and Jared during that first visit in a New Mexico jail only some forty-eight hours earlier.

Chapter Six

"Too bad we can't all ride together to Dallas," Shane lamented as they left the restaurant, headed for their separate vehicles. "That would be lots more fun."

"We'll follow Cassie," Jared replied. "We'll stop and eat lunch together and stay in a motel somewhere tonight. This is a two-day trip."

"Two long days," Cassie agreed, not particularly looking forward to the drive. But at least she'd have their meals together to anticipate along the way. She almost suggested that Shane ride with her for a while, then decided not to deprive Jared of the boy's company.

"If you need to stop for anything, flash your taillights," Jared instructed, seeing Cassie to her car. "I'll flash you if we need to stop."

"I'll be watching," Cassie promised.

"You do that. But watch the cars ahead of you, as well."

"Yes, Jared," she said, making a face at his tone.

"Buckle your seat belt."

"Yes, Jared." She did so, thinking that he certainly was the bossy type. Rather sweetly protective, but bossy.

With a smile in his eyes, he leaned into the open doorway. "Kiss me."

She returned the smile. "Yes, Jared." She lifted her face eagerly to his.

The kiss was brief, a mere promise of better things to come. Cassie thought it just as well. If his earlier kiss had made her forget how to walk, another one like it would probably make her dangerous behind a wheel. But then, there were some people who said she was that, anyway, she thought with a chuckle, and started her engine.

They'd been on the highway for less than an hour when Jared flashed his lights. Cassie obediently pulled over into a roadside rest stop, assuming that was probably the reason, the guys had wanted a break. She rolled down her window as Jared approached her car.

"Lady, you drive like a maniac," he said, scowling as he leaned into the opening. Behind him, she could see Shane slumped in the seat of the pickup, his face buried in his hands.

"What's wrong with the way I drive?" Cassie demanded. She'd been on her best behavior, too!

"For one thing, you've been speeding."

"Only a little."

"And driving too close to the cars in front of you."

"They were going too slowly."

"And changing lanes without even checking the traffic."

"I did not! I always check the traffic before I change lanes."

"And turn down your radio. You're paying more attention to the music than to your driving."

Her jaw dropped. "Now how could you possibly know

how loudly I was playing my radio? And don't tell me you could hear it—I know it wasn't *that* loud."

"I watched you bobbing up and down in time to the music," he returned crossly. "You're supposed to be driving, not bebopping."

"*Bebopping?* Hey, who do you think you are, my mother?"

"I'd just hate to watch you get hurt or killed in a car accident because you weren't paying attention," he said, sounding so virtuous and sermonizing that she could easily have hit him.

His bossiness—and his overprotectiveness—were becoming less endearing by the moment.

"I'll tell you what, Jared," she said sweetly, giving him a smile that showed all her teeth. "You concentrate on getting yourself and Shane safely to Dallas, and I'll do the same for me. Okay?"

He eyed her with sudden wariness. "You're annoyed with me."

"You could say that, yes."

"For caring about your welfare?"

"For not crediting me with enough sense to take care of myself."

He sighed. "Look, I wasn't trying to make you mad. It's just that I—well—"

"You what?" she probed, wanting him to finish what he'd started to say.

"I'm not used to caring."

The stark simplicity of the statement drained all the anger from her, replacing it with a warm, sappy feeling she didn't quite know how to handle. "Oh," was all she could think of to say.

He reached through the window to touch her cheek. "Sorry, Cassie. I shouldn't have chewed you out like that. I won't again."

Her smile was both tremulous and skeptical. "You won't? Ever?"

He returned the smile with a rueful, rather sheepish one of his own. "Well, not until lunch, anyway."

She laughed, wondering how she could have gone so quickly from temper to humor. But then, Jared had been stirring up rapidly changing emotions in her since she'd first laid eyes on him. Something told her she'd always react strongly to this particular male.

"Let's move on," Jared said abruptly, shoving himself upright.

She craned her neck to look up at him. "Don't you and Shane want to—uh—you know?" She motioned toward the public rest rooms at the center of the paved area.

He gave her an incredulous look. "Here? Not hardly. Don't you know the type of weirdos who hang out at these places?"

Her Jared was definitely the prudent type, Cassie thought with a grin as he loped back to the driver's seat of the pickup.

And then her smile faded as she realized how she'd referred to him in her thoughts. *Her* Jared? In her dreams. They were a long way from establishing that sort of relationship.

Still, it was a nice feeling to think of him as hers. For now, at least.

By the time they stopped for lunch, Cassie was a nervous wreck from trying to drive in an exemplary manner, and Shane was a bundle of energy from sitting still for so long. It was a beautiful mid-September Saturday, so they decided in a roadside consultation to get take-out food and eat at a public park Shane had spotted as they entered the midsize town.

The moment they arrived at the park, Shane was off, running as hard as he could down a trail marked for walkers and joggers.

Jared chuckled as he and Cassie followed more sedately,

choosing one of the few empty concrete picnic tables left on such an ideal day for picnics. "He's about tired of traveling. We've been on the road for most of the week."

"I know," Cassie replied with a smile. "I've been right behind you since the day after you left your last job in Oklahoma."

Jared frowned and draped a leg over the bench, reaching for a canned soft drink as he sat down.

Studying his expression, Cassie realized that she was learning to read him. "You don't like the idea of someone tracking you down through your records?"

"Not particularly," he admitted.

"You're a very private person, aren't you?"

He shrugged. "Yeah. I guess."

She sat opposite him, her chin propped in her hands as her elbows rested on the cool concrete table. "If it makes you feel any better, I didn't learn that much about you in my investigation. Only some of the jobs you've held since leaving the navy two years ago. I didn't even know you had a son. I never found a record of your marriage."

"It was a long time ago," Jared replied, his eyes on Shane, who'd been invited to join a game of Frisbee with a couple of boys his age. "I was nineteen and just out of basic training, she was eighteen and ready to get away from a bad home life. Marriage seemed like a good idea at the time, though neither of us tried to pretend we were passionately in love."

"What's her name?" Cassie asked, though she wasn't entirely sure she wanted to hear about Jared's relationship with another woman, even if he hadn't been deeply in love with her. Still, the other woman was Shane's mother—and Shane was a very important part of Jared's life, as the boy would be to Cassie's, should this budding relationship go much further.

"Kay."

"Is she pretty?"

He gave her a rather odd look, but answered, "She was, sixteen years ago when we got married. She hasn't taken very good care of herself since, I'm afraid."

Cassie wondered how to bring up the next question, wondered if she even dared. But she had to know. "Shane said his mother has a drinking problem."

Jared's eyes hardened. "Yeah. That started right after he was born. I tried to tell Kay when we got married that I'd be away a lot—six months at a time on sea duty—but I guess she didn't really understand that she'd be the one left with the responsibilities of the household.

"I was on leave when Shane was born, but had to ship out again when he was only two weeks old. Maybe the next few months were just too tough for her. Anyway, by the time I came back, she'd already started drinking too regularly, though she did a pretty good job of hiding it. I really wasn't aware of the extent of her problem until she'd been at it for a couple of years. We fought a lot about it, but that only made it worse. We were divorced when Shane was five."

Cassie checked to make sure Shane was still involved in the game. "Who took care of him when he was little?"

"I did, on the rare occasions when I was home. I assumed Kay was taking care of him when I was away. I knew she was a lousy wife, but she had me convinced she was a fairly decent mother."

"And was she?" Cassie whispered.

"In her way. He was fed and clothed. And then generally ignored the rest of the time."

Cassie fought down the indignant comment that sprang to her lips. She wanted to know more, wanted to ask why Jared had thought a heavy drinker was a fit mother for his son, was burning with curiosity about Shane's mention of living on the streets for three months until his father had found him. Still…

"This is really none of my business, of course," she said apologetically. "I didn't mean to pry."

Again, Jared shrugged, his expression so distant and shuttered that she wished she'd never brought the subject up. They'd been having such a nice day so far—other than that rest-stop confrontation, of course.

"You may as well know," he said coolly. "I told you I was lousy with relationships. I'm not proud that I didn't even know my own wife was becoming a lush and that my son was being emotionally neglected."

Cassie felt compelled to defend him. "You were young."

"And gone more than I was home. But that's not really an excuse, is it? The real problem was that I had gotten so used to taking care of no one but myself that I just assumed Kay was doing the same for herself and our son. I loved Shane, of course, more than I ever thought it possible to love anyone—but I didn't know how to be a real father to him. My own father was certainly no example. God knows I never saw him much when I was a kid, and he was usually drunk when I did. As far as I knew, the only thing he and my mother ever did together was make babies they couldn't take care of."

Cassie couldn't bear the traces of pain in his voice, a pain he probably thought he concealed from everyone else. And maybe no one else *would* hear it. Maybe Cassie was beginning to understand him better than other people did, or could. She reached across the table to cover his hard, callused hand with her own smaller, softer one. "I'm sorry, Jared. We don't have to talk about this now."

He looked at their joined hands, then slowly back up to her face. Whatever he might have said was cut off when Shane loped up to the table. "You two sure look serious. Something wrong?"

Cassie pulled her hand back to her lap and forced a smile. "Of course not. Are you ready to eat? Our chicken's getting cold."

"It's okay," Shane answered, swinging a leg over the bench in a move very much like his father's. "I like cold chicken."

"Is there any food you *don't* like?" Cassie asked teasingly, distributing paper plates and napkins.

"Yeah. Chinese. Too many little squiggly things I can't recognize."

Cassie laughed, but said, "I happen to love Chinese food. You might just like it, too, if you'd give it a chance."

Shane shuddered dramatically and reached for a drumstick. "No, thanks. I'll stick to the basics. Chicken, cheeseburgers and pizza."

"A fine, healthy diet," Jared agreed gravely, pushing a container of coleslaw toward his son. "Here. Eat your vegetables."

Shane grinned and served himself a heaping portion.

Watching them both, Cassie wondered how any woman could have willingly let these two get away. How could Kay not have known how very lucky she was to have them?

She still wished she knew what, exactly, had happened in their lives two years ago. Whatever it was, it had to have been traumatic. Jared was still eating himself up with guilt. That was something else Cassie was beginning to understand about this multilayered, complex man. How many more layers would she have to uncover to ever know him completely?

And would he ever let her—or anyone—get close enough to really know him?

Sprawled in the shade of an enormous oak tree just starting to don its fall colors, Jared rested back on his elbows and watched indulgently as Cassie and Shane carried on a laughing, dodging, uninhibited game of tag. He found it hard to believe at times that Cassie was twenty-six years old, as her driver's license had said she was. There were moments when she seemed closer to Shane's age than his own.

She was beautiful with her face flushed from exertion, her green eyes lit with laughter, several springy red curls escaping her French braid. Her jeans fit her like a second skin, and she'd pushed the sleeves of her flowered sweatshirt up to expose her lower arms. He wanted her so badly his teeth hurt.

Was he making a mistake to go with her to Dallas, despite Shane's desire to do so? Being an utter fool to think he could ever have the chance at finding with her what he'd been unable to find with anyone else? Didn't she deserve a hell of a lot more than a burned-out, unemployed drifter with more emotional baggage than material possessions?

A hand touched his shoulder, making him realize he'd drifted into his own thoughts and had lost track of time. He blinked and looked up to find Cassie standing only a couple of feet away, breathing rapidly and poised on the balls of her feet as though prepared to run. Shane stood a few yards behind her, grinning broadly.

"You're it," Cassie said, eyeing Jared in open challenge.

He shook his head. "I'm not playing, remember?"

"Tough. I tagged you. You're it."

"Dad's it!" Shane added, his brown hair lifting in the afternoon breeze. Jared realized it was time for a trim—for both of them, actually.

"You two go ahead and play. I'll just watch."

"Being 'it' is too much for you, hmm?" Cassie taunted. "Can't handle it?" She took a step closer, daring him in body language to make a move toward her.

Seeing that she was still ready to run, and sensing that she was quite confident in her ability to evade him, Jared continued to sprawl with apparent laziness, though he felt the muscles in his arms tightening. "If I chose to chase you, you wouldn't get two feet."

Her laughter was ripe with disbelief. "Yeah. Right."

"*If* I were playing, of course," he added, watching from beneath his lashes as she took a tiny step forward.

"You're still it," she reminded him, beginning to relax when he made no move to respond.

He sighed.

Cassie turned her head to look at Shane. "What a wimp," she said. "He won't even—"

Jared was on his feet before she could finish the sentence. He had her pinned to the ground beneath him before she could even think about running. "Want to take back that wimp remark?" he asked, totally unruffled.

Winded and dazed, she blinked up at him, her bangs tangled in her eyes. She reached up to push them out of her face. "We're playing tag, not tackle," she protested indignantly.

He grinned at her disgruntled expression, trying to ignore how very good she felt beneath him. There was nothing he could do to prevent his body from responding to her. Her eyes widened, and he knew she was feeling it, too.

"Take it back," he prodded.

"I—uh—forgot to warn you, Cassie," Shane apologized from nearby, his voice quavering with laughter. "Dad's quick. Sneaky, too."

"So I've discovered," she said, without taking her eyes from Jared's.

"You still haven't taken it back."

"I take it back," she conceded in a rush. "You're not a wimp. You don't play fairly, but you're not a wimp."

"I can live with that." He brushed her mouth with his, very

lightly, resisting the imprudent temptation to deepen the kiss. And then he released her and sat beside her, one knee raised to disguise the condition of his jeans.

Cassie lay where she was, wiping her brow with one hand. "I'm dying."

Shane dropped down beside her, twisted into that boneless position unique to young people. "I'm sure Dad would just love giving you CPR."

Cassie growled. "The boy needs a trip behind the woodshed, Jared. Do your paternal duty."

"I've got better ways of punishing him."

"Yeah? Like what?"

"Hey, Shane. How'd you like me to tell her about you and Penny Bennett?"

"Dad!" Shane flushed crimson, as Jared had known he would. "You wouldn't!"

"Then don't push your luck, boy," Jared answered mildly.

Cassie giggled. "You're right. That's much better than a woodshed any day."

Jared noticed that her top had ridden up to expose an inch of smooth, pale skin above the waistband of her jeans. He cleared his throat and climbed abruptly to his feet. "We'd better get back on the road. Lunch break's over."

"Bossy," Cassie sighed, though she obediently pushed herself upright. "So bossy."

Jared ignored her. Or tried to.

"Want me to ride with you for a while, Cassie?" Shane offered.

Jared noted that she looked to him before giving the boy an answer. She seemed to be taking a great deal of care not to step on his parental toes. "It's okay with me," he assured her.

"Then I'd like that," Cassie said with a smile for Shane.

"Great! I'll get my tapes." Shane loped toward the truck.

Jared grinned at the look on Cassie's face. "Hope you like Garth Brooks and Vince Gill."

"Are they anything like U2 or Guns N' Roses?"

He chuckled and turned toward his truck. "Have fun."

Cassie did have fun with Shane, as a matter of fact. He introduced her to contemporary country music, and she insisted that he listen to one of her classic rock tapes in return.

"Eric Clapton," she breathed at the opening refrains of "Layla." "No one else handles a guitar like that."

"That's what my dad says. But then I'll bet you've never heard Steve Wariner when he really gets wound up."

"Steve who?"

"Oh, man!"

Cassie laughed, thoroughly enjoying herself, though she couldn't help glancing wistfully in the rearview mirror at the lone man in the pickup truck behind her.

They were somewhere in central New Mexico that evening when Jared suggested they stop for the night. "We'll have to make better time tomorrow," he said, looking at his watch, "or this is going to become a three-day trip."

Cassie thought briefly of checking in with Tony, then decided to wait until they arrived in Dallas to call him. As far as she was concerned, she'd been on her own time since taking herself off the expense account the day before. This weekend with Jared and Shane was hers.

They had an early dinner at a cafeteria near their hotel, then took in a seven o'clock showing of a recent comedy film that Shane wanted to see. Cassie sat between the two guys during the movie. Listening to their chuckles—Jared's deep and sexy, Shane's less restrained—she decided she'd never been more content in her life. Especially when, halfway through the film, Jared reached over and took her hand in his.

The three of them were beginning to feel very much like a family. Maybe too much so. But she refused to allow herself to worry about it just yet. Perhaps she would end up brokenhearted, but she had no intention of missing out on this quiet happiness for fear of what might come later.

Jared had driven to the theater, so Cassie climbed into the cab of the truck to sit in the middle again after the movie. Jared slid behind the wheel and started the engine. "It's still early," he said. "I thought maybe you'd like to have a drink with me somewhere."

"Hey, sounds good to me," Shane said cheekily.

Jared gave him a look over Cassie's head. "I was talking to Cassie. *You* can raid the motel vending machines for your usual bedtime snack, watch some TV and then get some rest. We've got a long ride ahead of us tomorrow."

"Can't blame a guy for trying," Shane muttered to Cassie, apparently resigned to a quiet evening.

"Cassie?"

"Yes, Jared. I'd love to have a drink with you," she accepted without hesitation.

He nodded, saying little more during the ride back to the motel. Shane more than made up for his father's silence with his chatter about the movie. And as much as she enjoyed Shane, Cassie looked forward with a mixture of eagerness and a strangely shy nervousness to being alone with Jared.

Though Jared said it wasn't necessary, Cassie insisted on changing out of her jeans before going out again. She slipped on clean slacks and a brightly patterned sweater, pulling the top of her hair back with a gold clip and allowing the rest to tumble to her shoulders in a mass of tight curls. She added small gold earrings and a touch of makeup, the entire process taking less than twenty minutes.

She was running out of clean clothes, she noted, closing her suitcase again. She had one pair of clean jeans and one top left for the trip home tomorrow. If they were delayed any longer on the road, she was going to have to find either a department store or a Laundromat.

Jared was waiting outside her door when she stepped out. He, too, had changed, she noted, into dark twill slacks and a white dress shirt. She tried for a moment to picture him in an Italian suit and a silk tie. The image was mind-boggling. Jared was born to wear jeans and boots.

It was much easier to imagine him in a Western hat and sheepskin-lined jacket, riding the pastures of the small ranch he'd said he hoped to own someday. Carrying the fantasy a bit further, she could imagine Shane riding behind him—and maybe a little girl with long, red braids.

Whoa, Browning. Better not start looking that far ahead. You haven't even got him to Dallas yet.

Jared had spotted a bar close to the hotel. It didn't look too bad from the outside, but they soon realized that the patrons were made up mostly of rednecks spending this Saturday getting drunk and making noise.

Jared cursed beneath his breath when a heavyset bottle-blonde in two-sizes-too-small jeans and a T-shirt that barely stretched over her massive bosom stumbled into the table he had found in a relatively quiet corner. Jared's beer sloshed over the rim of his mug, splattering his slacks.

"Oh, sorry, honey," the blonde said, leaning so close to him that her unbound breasts almost brushed his face. "Guess I've had a few too many, you know?"

Her hands wrapped around the stem of her wineglass, Cassie watched sympathetically as Jared almost reeled from the fumes of the woman's breath. "No problem," he muttered, drawing as far back in his chair as physically possible.

"Hey, you're kinda cute." Ignoring Cassie altogether, the woman threaded her scarlet-taloned fingers through Jared's hair. "Want to dance."

"No." He added belatedly, "Thanks."

She sighed deeply, causing Jared to choke again. "Oh, well. It was worth a shot." And then she staggered away, her attention already focusing on a would-be cowboy at the bar across the room.

Scowling, Jared reached up to smooth his hair by briskly running his own fingers through. "Sorry about this," he said. "Not a very classy place I've brought you to, is it?"

"You couldn't have known," Cassie replied, excusing him with a smile. "And, anyway, that woman was right about one thing."

He eyed her suspiciously. "What?"

"You are kinda cute."

She laughed when he growled something unintelligible and took a long drink of his beer. She would have sworn she saw a tinge of red touch his lean cheeks, though the lighting in the bar was hardly bright. The thought of Jared blushing was so endearing that her throat tightened.

She was really getting in deep this time. And making very little effort to stop herself from falling any farther.

Jared set down his mug and glanced at the crowded, undersize dance floor. "I'm a lousy dancer," he said, sounding as though he were apologizing.

Cassie took a sip of her white wine, wondering what he expected her to say in return. She liked to dance, but she was perfectly happy just to sit in a shadowy corner with Jared, their knees brushing beneath the tiny table.

He cleared his throat. "If you don't mind risking your toes, we could give it a try."

Surprised, she set down her glass. "You're asking me to dance?"

"Yeah. What do you say?"

She smiled and stood. "I say yes."

Jared gave her a rueful look and pushed himself to his feet. "Just don't say I didn't warn you."

The new song was a slow one—fortunately, since it was impossible to do much more than sway in place on the packed dance floor. Cassie had no complaints. Her arms around Jared's neck, his hands at her hips, she felt as though she'd died and gone someplace wonderful, even if that place smelled strongly of beer and tobacco and sweat.

Jared pulled her closer, his head bent to hers. She felt him nuzzling her temple, and her knees went weak, causing her to cling more tightly to him. Their thighs brushed seductively, and she found herself resenting the fabric that separated them. She ached to be pressed this closely against him with absolutely nothing between them. His hands moved at her hips, settling her more snugly, and it was obvious that Jared was as deeply affected by their dancing as Cassie.

His lips brushed her cheek. "Want to get out of here?"

She forced her heavy eyelids open. "Whatever you want."

Jared groaned. "I like the way that sounds."

"Is that right?" Cassie couldn't resist pressing a quick kiss to his firm, stubborn jaw.

"Mmm." He kissed her, his mouth pressing firmly, if all too briefly, to hers. And then he turned with her toward the exit, his arm wrapped securely around Cassie's waist as he guided her through the press of people.

Lost in tingly anticipation of the outcome of the evening, Cassie didn't at first understand why Jared suddenly went tense as they approached his pickup. She looked up to find three disreputable-looking young men in battered cowboy hats and pointed-toe boots leaning against the front fender and passing around a bottle as they laughed uproariously at the off-color jokes they were telling loudly enough for everyone within a block to hear. They quite effectively blocked Jared and Cassie's access to the truck.

Jared stepped slightly in front of Cassie. "Excuse me. That's my truck, and we're ready to leave. Mind moving out of the way?"

All three looked at Jared and then Cassie, obviously weighing his mild tone against the opportunity to flex their macho in front of a woman.

"What if we do mind?" one of them—the biggest, Cassie noted apprehensively—demanded.

"Then I'll have to ask you to move, anyway." Jared's voice was still quiet, but had taken on a steely note that couldn't be mistaken even by cocky young drunks. All three immediately straightened, bracing themselves in response to the subtle challenge.

Cassie looked anxiously from Jared to his potential opponents. They were younger, two of them taller and heavier, made reckless by alcohol. On the other hand, Jared was—well, Jared. She figured that made them almost even, but she wanted to avoid a fight if at all possible.

Another confrontation with the police was the last thing they needed on this trip.

"Please," she said, stepping forward even though Jared moved to hold her back. "We'd really like to leave now, if you'd be so kind as to let us get by."

One of the young toughs whistled. The second leered in what he probably thought was a sexy manner, but really made him look somewhat slow-witted. The third—the big one, again—looked Cassie up and down with insolent leisure. "Hey, red. How about dumping this old loser and having a party?"

Cassie put her hand on Jared's arm when he made a restless move. "Thank you, but no," she said firmly. "Now, if you'll please just…"

"Oh, we can please you, sugar," the big one drawled, eliciting a raucous laugh from his buddies. "We can please you real good. How about if we—"

"How about if you shut up and get out of our way before we call the cops?" Jared growled, stepping forward to face down the young man who'd become the leader of the confrontation. Cassie noted that the other two men fell back a little at the cold, deadly menace suddenly radiating from Jared's narrowed eyes.

Their friend cleared his throat, his hands lifting in what appeared to be capitulation. "Hey, don't get all bent out of shape. If you want past us, all you have to do is start walking."

"Stay close, Cassie," Jared ordered in an undertone, moving cautiously forward.

The big guy attacked without warning, his meaty fist connecting solidly with Jared's chin. Jared staggered back, though he didn't go down.

Cassie saw red. Without hesitation she started forward, fully prepared to do some damage herself. Jared caught her arm and pulled sharply.

"Get back," he ordered, just before the other two, emboldened by their leader's aggression, leaped forward. And then Jared was too busy defending himself to concentrate on keeping Cassie out of his way.

She had no intention of standing back and wringing her hands like some sort of helpless woman in a male-dominated action movie. She hadn't spent five years in self-defense classes for nothing.

She landed a solid kick square in the kidneys of the nearest opponent, making him howl and stagger away from Jared, hands pressed to his back. Without giving him a chance to recover from his surprise, Cassie quite effectively took his mind off that pain with a follow-up kick to the groin. He promptly curled into a whimpering ball on the pavement and lost most of the booze that had given him his foolhardy courage.

Judging him to no longer be a threat, Cassie whirled to help Jared, only to find him watching her in amazement, his hands on his hips, feet spread. The big guy who'd initiated the fight lay on the pavement behind him, moaning and holding a hand to his freely bleeding nose. The third man was nowhere to be seen. Cassie assumed he'd suddenly come to his senses and abandoned his buddies to their fate.

Already other patrons of the bar were approaching, trying to find out what was going on. Jared took Cassie's arm. "Let's get out of here."

She didn't hesitate to climb into the truck with him. Moments later, they'd left the bar and its customers behind them.

Jared didn't say anything for the first few minutes, driving with his right hand as he fingered the darkening bruise on his jaw with his left. When he spoke, it was without looking at her. "How tall are you? Five-three? Five-four?"

"Five-four. And a quarter," she added.

"You weigh—what? A hundred pounds?"

Watching him curiously, she answered, "A hundred ten."

He slanted her a sexy grin that all but melted her into the seat. "You can guard my back any time, tiger."

She looked at that smile, at the bruise on his chin and the lock of dark hair that had tumbled onto his forehead, and she felt herself sliding the rest of the way into love.

Not smart, Browning. Not smart at all.

But it was far too late for her to heed the warnings of her common sense.

Chapter Seven

The motel was quiet, no light showing through the crack in the curtain of the room Jared and Shane shared. "Shane must be asleep," Jared commented, leading Cassie past that door to her own, which was next to it.

"Don't you want to go in and check on him?" she asked, looking back at the other room.

"He's okay." Jared reached over and took her key out of her hand. He slid it into the lock and opened the door, though he made no move to go inside.

Cassie went past him, then looked over her shoulder when he didn't follow. "Aren't you coming in?"

"Is that an invitation?" he asked in return, his voice deeper than usual.

She swallowed hard, knowing exactly what he was asking. "Yes," she whispered through suddenly dry lips. "That's an invitation."

He took a step forward, though he left the door standing open. His gaze held hers captive. "I can't make any promises, Cassie. There are a lot of uncertainties in my life right now. I can't even guarantee what state I'll be living in by this time next week."

"I know." She was pleased at the steadiness of her voice. "I'm not asking for promises. I want this, Jared."

He closed the door very quietly behind him.

She moistened her lips with the tip of her tongue. She'd been completely honest with him. She wanted to make love with him more than she'd ever wanted anything in her entire life. But she was suddenly nervous, unable to pretend this was something she did casually or easily.

Rubbing her open palms against the legs of her slacks, she glanced around the sterile room, which seemed to be filled mostly with bed at the moment. Had she been at home, she'd have offered him a drink or a snack or something. Unfortunately, she had no such diversion available at the moment.

"Cassie." His hands fell lightly on her shoulders. "Relax. We'll take all the time you need. And there's no need to worry about protection. I'll take care of it."

She looked up at him gratefully. "You're a very nice man, Jared Walker."

"Don't start idealizing me," he warned her, his expression suddenly grim. "I'm nobody's hero—not by a long shot."

"I'm not looking for a hero," Cassie answered mistily, touching her fingertips to his battered jaw. "But I think I've been looking for you all my life."

His eyes turned wary at her unguarded words, but she didn't give him a chance to issue any further warnings. All remnants of nervousness vanishing, she went up on tiptoes to press her mouth firmly, hungrily to his.

Jared resisted only a moment. And then he gave a low groan and his arms went around her, crushing her against him.

Cassie couldn't get close enough, couldn't hold him tightly enough, though she tried desperately to do both. In response to her fervor, Jared abandoned all efforts to go slowly or cautiously, his mouth devouring hers, his hands racing over her straining body.

She wanted to touch him, wanted to stroke his chest, taste his skin. She slipped her hands between them and fumbled with the top button of his shirt. His mouth still moving over hers, Jared drew back an inch to give her better access, then grew impatient with her unsteady hands and attacked the buttons himself. Cassie shoved the fabric off his shoulders and down his muscular arms, sighing her pleasure when her hands were free to spread across his broad, hair-roughened chest.

His skin was hot, as if heated from inside, his muscles hard and well-defined. Her thumbs found the pointed nipples buried in the crisp dark curls. She rotated her thumbs and Jared inhaled sharply.

Delighted with his reaction to her, she stroked her hand slowly down his flat stomach to the waistband of his slacks, where she paused. Jared covered her hand with his and moved it lower, so that she found her palm filled with his rigid length, and even through the fabric of his slacks she could feel his pulsing excitement. She moaned in response.

It was a heady, stimulating feeling to be wanted so badly.

Jared twisted, bearing her down to the bed, his hand covering her breast as they fell. Cassie arched into him. He moved his fingers, and she gasped at the waves of sensation that coursed through her.

He parted her legs with one knee, pressing upward until he was wedged firmly in the notch of her thighs. Cassie shuddered. *"Jared."*

"I want to touch you." He tugged impatiently at her clothing, dispensing of buttons and zippers with ruthless haste.

"Yes." She squirmed to assist him.

Her clothes, as well as his slacks, socks and briefs, fell into a tangled heap on the floor beside the bed. Cassie released a long, unsteady breath when she finally felt him pressed full-length against her, nothing between them except their growing desire.

He was warm and vibrant and so very male, making her feel soft and pliant and feminine beneath his hands. She surrendered to the feelings. There were times when the traditional roles suited her quite nicely.

Aware of the need for quiet, Cassie swallowed her cries of delight as Jared took her higher and higher, pushing her precariously close to the edge of ecstasy. She wanted him inside her when she took that leap, but he was relentless. All too soon, she shuddered in waves of pleasure, racked with sensations more glorious, more vividly intense than anything she'd ever known.

He didn't give her time to recover, nor to regret that he hadn't been with her. Instead, he drew her inexorably back to that edge again, and this time when she tumbled over, it was exactly the way she'd fantasized—with Jared buried so deeply inside her that he had become a part of her.

She held him as they both slowly recovered their breath and their senses. She stroked his damp hair, loving the soft, thick feel of it. Loving him.

So long accustomed to blurting her feelings, she found it difficult to hold back the words brimming inside her now. She knew Jared wasn't ready to hear them—at least, not yet.

He'd think she'd lost her mind, of course. After all, they'd known each other only two days. He'd never believe she'd fallen in love with him the moment their eyes had met in that awful jail.

He wanted her, but he didn't love her—at least, not yet, she added with a secret, determinedly optimistic smile.

"What?" Jared said, raising his head to look at her curiously.

She blinked at him. "I beg your pardon?"

"I'm not sure I like that smile," he murmured, brushing a curl away from her eyes. "It looked just a little devious to me."

She chuckled. "Devious? You're imagining things."

"Mmm." He didn't sound entirely convinced.

Cassie stirred against the pillows. "I wonder what Shane found to eat in the vending machines. I'm starving."

He smiled indulgently. "Does great sex always make you hungry?"

She didn't at all like him trivializing the experience they'd just shared to nothing more momentous than great sex. She told herself that maybe he was trying to convince her, as well as himself, that that was all it had been. She believed it had been more. Much more.

For the first time in her impulsive life, she would have to learn to be patient so she didn't drive this frustratingly commitment-shy man away.

Ignoring his question, she reached for the robe she'd left lying on the chair nearby, slipping into it as she climbed from the bed, suddenly restless. "I think I've got some Gummi Bears in my bag. Want some?"

"I'll pass. Cassie?" He raised himself on one elbow to watch her rummage through the bag.

She found the bag of candies and ripped it open to avoid looking at him sprawled nude on her bed. "Yes?"

"What's wrong?"

"Nothing. Why?"

"You're acting funny. Was it something I said?"

"Of course not." She popped a soft red bear into her mouth. "Something I didn't say?"

Her throat tightened, making it difficult to swallow. "No."

"You want me to leave? You've suddenly decided I'm a jerk? You regret going to bed with me? All of the above?"

"I really don't know what you're talking about, Jared." She wished she had a diet soft drink to wash down the candy. She wondered if anyone would see her if she made a dash for the vending machines in her robe.

It was so much easier to think about a late-night snack than to wonder if Jared Walker was going to break her heart.

Or would it be more realistic to wonder when, rather than if?

"Cassie. Come here." He patted the bed beside him.

She stalled. "Think I'll go get a Coke. You want one?"

"No, and neither do you. Now come here."

"You're being bossy again."

He only looked at her. Waiting.

Cassie sighed and sat stiffly on the edge of the bed. "All right, I'm here. What do you—?"

He grabbed her arm and pulled her down beside him, cutting her question off in a whoosh of surprised breath.

"Now," he said, tucking her into the crook of his arm. "Let's talk."

She couldn't quite resist snuggling her cheek more comfortably into the hollow of his shoulder. It felt so good to be held by him. So safe. "What do you want to talk about?"

"Whatever you like. You're not sleepy, are you?"

"No." Far from it. She was so wired with tension and worry and leftover sexual awareness that she wasn't sure she'd sleep at all that night.

"Neither am I. So let's talk. We haven't had much chance to get to know each other, have we?"

Beginning to relax when she realized that he wasn't going

to push her to explain her sudden attack of nerves, she rested a hand on his bare chest and giggled. "Oh, I think we've gotten to know each other fairly well."

"I wasn't talking about biblical knowledge," he replied dryly. "Tell me about your life in Dallas. Do you live in a house, an apartment, a condo?"

"An apartment."

"Any pets?"

She shifted to fit herself more comfortably against him. Jared tightened his arm, willingly accommodating her. "No pets. I like animals, but didn't want to be bothered with finding a sitter or kennel every time Tony sends me out of town."

"Does he do that often?"

"Not really. Most P.I. work these days is done on computer or by telephone. And we specialize in security consultation for local businesses—analyzing their existing security measures, studying loss reports, researching the market for affordable, state-of-the-art security equipment, making recommendations for employee testing, monitoring and incentive programs."

"Incentive programs? What does that have to do with security?"

"A contented, well-treated employee is a much more loyal one," she answered with a smile. "Much less likely to steal."

"How's the search coming for my other sister and brothers?" Jared asked, his voice almost studiously casual. "Any leads?"

"Not on the twins," Cassie replied, trying to match his tone so he wouldn't know that she'd read him again. The question had been much more than casual to him, though it was obvious he wasn't looking for sympathy.

"They went into a series of foster homes after you were separated, were even considered for adoption by one family.

But they kept getting into trouble—nothing serious, just mischievous and annoying—and kept being relocated. When they were nine, a social worker recommended they be split up. She said that would curb their mischievous tendencies."

Jared tensed. "That's the dumbest thing I've ever heard. Didn't she know what that would do to them? They're identical twins, for God's sake!"

"She was a fool," Cassie agreed flatly. "And it wasn't long before her suggestions were vetoed by the child welfare authorities. But the twins had gotten wind of the suggestion. That was the first time they ran away."

"They ran away at nine?"

"Yes. It took over a week for them to be located. From then on, whenever there was the least suggestion they were going to be split, they took off. Their habit of running away kept them in trouble from then until they were sixteen."

"What happened then?"

"They ran off again—and haven't been seen since. At least, not that we've been able to determine so far."

Jared lay quietly for a moment, then asked, "What are the odds that they're still alive?"

"Good," she answered firmly. "They were sixteen. Young, but not helpless. And they had each other to depend on. They're out there somewhere, and we'll find them eventually. Identical twins should be easier to locate than just one person—and we found you, didn't we?"

He shrugged, though he seemed to have taken some encouragement from her confidence. "I never made any effort not to be found."

"That did make it easier," she admitted.

"What about the baby?"

"Lindsay? She's hardly a baby now. She'll soon be twenty-five."

"Damn. I'd forgotten. Any leads on her?"

"Some. We know she was adopted very soon after you were separated. The adoption records were sealed, but Tony has interviewed several social workers who were assigned to your family. Though he hasn't been able to officially verify anything, he thinks he may have the name of the adoptive family, possibly a lead on how to track them down. It will take time, but he's hopeful that we're getting closer."

"And if she's found? Then what?"

"Then, like you, she'll be contacted to find out if she's interested in meeting her biological sisters and brothers."

Jared shook his head. "I can't imagine why she would. We'd all be strangers to her. I remember all of them, of course, but Layla and maybe the twins are the only ones who would've been old enough to share any of my memories. Even Shelley—Michelle—was just a toddler when we split up."

"Yes, but she still wants to see you. You're her brother, Jared. You had the same parents, the same genes—you even look a little alike. That means something to her."

"We look alike?" Jared sounded startled.

"You both have brown hair and blue eyes. And, yes, there's a family resemblance," Cassie acknowledged, lifting her head to study his face. "You'll like her, Jared. She's very nice."

"I think you should know—the main reason I agreed to see her is because of you."

"Because of me?" Cassie repeated, surprised. "Why?"

His hand settled on her robe-covered thigh, kneading gently. "Because you asked me to. If bringing me back with you helps you out with your job, I guess it's the least I can do after you worked so hard to clear me of that robbery charge."

Cassie shook her head, uncomfortable. "Oh, Jared, I didn't want you coming with me out of gratitude. I wanted you to do this for yourself and your sisters, not for me."

"Does it matter why I came?"

She chewed her lip, considering the question. On the one hand, it flattered her that Jared was making the trip on her behalf. On the other, she truly believed he needed this much more than she did.

Jared was more in need of family ties than anyone she'd ever met—if only he'd give his sisters a chance to form them with him.

He'd built such impenetrable walls around his emotions during the lonely years of his youth, walls that only Shane could get past now. Would Michelle and Layla ever be allowed inside? And, more importantly to her, would she? For as close as she and Jared had been only moments before, Cassie knew that there was a part of himself he still held back. A part of himself she longed to know.

"Cassie? You haven't answered me. Does it really matter why I'm going with you to Dallas?"

"No," she answered finally. "It doesn't really matter."

Not as long as you'll give me—give all of us—a chance to really know you while you're there. And maybe a reason to hope that you'll stay.

Jared lay quietly for a few minutes, toying with her hair. He seemed fascinated by the tight copper curls, twisting them around his fingers, watching them spring free when he released them. Cassie could feel her pulse picking up again, increasingly aware that he held her so closely to his nude body that only her thin, loosely tied robe separated them. She buried her fingers in the crisp hair on his chest, her palm pressed just above his heart. She felt it beating rapidly, and was delighted that she wasn't the only one affected by their nearness.

"Cassie?"

She turned her face into his chest, enjoying the spicy, male scent of him. "Mmm?"

"Have you always wanted to be a P.I.?"

She hadn't really expected that question—at least, not now. She tried to forget about sex for the moment and concentrate on the conversation. Not an easy task, especially when Jared slipped a hand beneath the hem of her robe to stroke her thigh.

"Um, no," she managed, her voice coming out rather hoarse. "I changed my major three times in college—from journalism to pre-law to computer sciences. That's what I finally got my degree in. I've had a dozen jobs since leaving college. I took a part-time job with Tony after leaving the last job, just because it sounded interesting and I had bills to pay. I've been hooked ever since. Working part-time gave me a chance to get my training while gaining job experience."

"Are you still part time?"

"No. He put me on full time this summer, after he fired Bob O'Brien."

Jared slipped his hand a bit higher, cupping the curve of her hip. "Why'd he fire the other guy?"

Her eyelids growing heavy, Cassie had to make an effort to remember. "He—uh—he was giving information on Michelle's case to the attorney who had been skimming money from some trust funds he'd helped her father set up for her."

Jared's hand stilled. "Michelle's attorney was stealing from her?"

"Yeah. Tony found the proof. He was really furious with Bob for cooperating with the lawyer, and hurt. He's always expected loyalty from his employees, and he'd always gotten it before."

"I hope they're prosecuting the bastard."

The attorney? Or Bob? Cassie was having a difficult time following the subject. Jared's fingers were unbearably close to a part of her that was beginning to throb heavily in anticipation of his touch. "They had the attorney, Carter Powell, arrested. But Tony told me the guy's disappeared. Jumped bail."

"Is Michelle in any danger?"

"Oh, I'm sure she's not. It turned out she wasn't the only client he was cheating. He's just making a run for it. He'll probably be caught soon. Bail jumpers usually are."

Jared relaxed. He nuzzled the hair at her temple. "Cassie?"

She caught her breath when he slid his thumb into the crease between her leg and her groin, tracing the soft fold with exquisite care. "Y-yes?"

"I think we've talked enough for now. Don't you?"

She twisted to wrap her arms around his neck. "Oh, yes."

His mouth covered hers, his fingers finally moving inward to drive the remaining breath from her body with his skillful pleasuring. Cassie arched helplessly against his hand, relieved that his questions had finally come to an end. At the moment, she couldn't even remember her name.

It was close to 3:00 a.m. by the time Jared forced himself from Cassie's bed. Though he'd never found it hard to leave a woman before, generally preferring to sleep on his own, he found it incredibly difficult to slip out of Cassie's arms.

He stood by the bed for several long, silent moments, just watching her. The faint light coming through the crack in the curtain robbed her of her vibrant coloring, leaving her porcelain pale against the white sheets. Her glorious hair was a dark mass of curls around her face, which looked so sweet and vulnerable in her sleep. It took all his fortitude not to crawl back into the bed with her.

His feelings for her were too strong, his reactions to her too intense. Their lovemaking hadn't been like anything he'd ever experienced before. Something told him he'd never get enough of it, that he'd never find quite the same satisfaction with any other woman.

He wasn't sure what, exactly, he felt for Cassie Browning, but an uncomfortable suspicion niggled at the back of his mind. And damned if he knew what he was going to do about it.

Chapter Eight

Jared had gotten maybe three hours' sleep by the time he finally gave up trying and climbed out of bed Sunday morning. Might as well get an early start, he decided. They still had a long drive ahead of them to Dallas.

He took a quick shower, then stood by the sink and lathered his face before waking his son. "Shane. Time to get up."

Shane stirred, yawned and blinked open his eyes. "What time is it?"

"Little after seven." Jared stroked a razor over his face, wishing he'd shaved before going out to the bar last night. Had his evening beard marked Cassie's delicate skin? There was certainly no part of her he hadn't rubbed it against at one time or another.

"What time did you get in last night? I was up till eleven."

Jared pushed the memories to the back of his mind, before his body embarrassed him in a way it hadn't done since adolescence. "Late. Now get on up and take your shower."

Shane swung his legs over the side of the bed, stretching. He was clad only in a pair of white briefs. Watching in the mirror, Jared was startled to realize that his son was growing rapidly, his arms and chest starting to fill out. At fourteen, his boy was becoming a man—and Jared had missed so much of his childhood. He turned, wiping the remaining lather from his face with a hand towel.

Shane lifted an eyebrow at his father's expression. "You sure look serious this morning. Is— Hey, what happened to your face?"

Jared had forgotten the bruise on his jaw. He glanced back at the mirror, noting ruefully that it had turned a deep purple during the night. That big drunk hadn't had much stamina, but he'd packed a mean right hook. "Nothing serious. A little altercation at the bar last night."

Shane grinned. "I bet Cassie gave it to you. You start bossing her around again?"

Jared couldn't help chuckling, remembering the way Cassie had thrown herself into the fight—and handled herself with impressive skill. "No. And after seeing her in action, I may not try it again."

"This sounds like a story I gotta hear."

"Later. Now take your shower or you might find yourself being left behind."

"Yeah, right." Shane didn't look particularly concerned. He rubbed his stomach as he headed for the shower. "Man, I'm hungry. Hope Cassie'll be ready to go eat soon."

"I'll give her a wake-up call." He could think of a lot of better ways to wake her, of course. He tried not to dwell on any of those possibilities as he lifted the phone and punched in her room number.

Her voice was still husky with sleep when she answered. "H'lo?"

His body reacted immediately and forcefully to the sound of her, and the accompanying image of her still in bed, nude, soft, her hair still tousled from his hands. He was relieved that his son was in the other room. What the hell had happened to his long-cultivated self-control?

Self-annoyance made his tone more curt than he'd intended. "Shane's in the shower. We'll be ready to leave soon."

"Good morning to you, too." The words were spoken just a bit too sweetly. Jared winced.

"Give me twenty minutes," she added. "I'll be ready."

She hung up before he could answer.

"Way to go, Walker," Jared muttered, replacing his own receiver with less force than she'd used. "You haven't even seen her yet today and you've already hacked her off. Real smooth."

What the hell had he gotten himself into by agreeing to this trip?

Seven hours after being rather rudely awakened by her decidedly complex lover, Cassie was still seething with irritation at him. She hadn't really expected him to jump her bones right in front of Shane, she told herself as she drove relentlessly toward Dallas, Jared's truck close on her rear bumper. But did he have to treat her like a passing acquaintance who just happened to be traveling in the same direction he was?

He'd been nothing more than distantly polite when they'd shared breakfast and, later, lunch, which they'd eaten only a half hour ago. Even Shane, who'd ridden with Cassie after breakfast, had looked at his father strangely during lunch, as though sensing for the first time that Jared wasn't being particularly friendly.

She certainly hadn't picked an easy man to fall in love with. How could he take her to paradise so many times during the night, only to treat her like a near stranger the next day? He hadn't even kissed her good morning.

She tried to console herself with the possibility that Jared had been as deeply affected by their lovemaking as she had. And that he was running in sheer panic from the intensity of the experience they'd shared. She liked the idea that his feelings for her weren't casual ones, but what if he succeeded in stifling them before they ever had a chance to fully develop?

Would they ever have another night like that together?

Tense, anxious, annoyed, restless, she twisted the dial on the radio, trying to tune in a decent station. She found a country station and left it on for a while, deciding to give Shane's favorite a try. Three brokenhearted ballads later, she turned it again. She wasn't really in the mood to listen to mournful songs about love gone wrong.

Maybe she could find something mindless and fluffy to take her mind off her troubles. Where were the Bee Gees when she needed them?

Jared cursed beneath his breath when Cassie's little car swerved dangerously close to the center line on the two-lane freeway. She was obviously playing with her radio and not paying enough attention to her driving. Fortunately, there were no cars traveling in the other lane at the moment, but what if there had been?

"She can't drive worth a damn," he muttered, relaxing a little when she straightened in her seat and brought the car back into line.

"Dad, did you and Cassie have a fight last night?"

Jared glanced at his son, who was watching him gravely. "No, we didn't have a fight. Why?"

"Well, you're both acting kind of…I don't know, funny today. Like you're mad or something."

"I'm not mad," Jared denied with a shrug. He was confused, bemused and scared half out of his boots, but he wasn't mad. Not that he expected Shane to understand, even if he should try to explain. Hell, Jared himself didn't understand.

"So you had a good time last night—other than being attacked by those three drunks?" Shane asked, having gotten the story out of Cassie at breakfast.

"Yeah. We had a good time." And that was something else he didn't intend to discuss in detail with his son.

"So what's the problem?"

Jared exhaled gustily at his son's persistence. "Nothing's the problem. We've just got a long trip ahead of us and we're trying not to waste a lot of time today. Okay?"

Shane didn't look particularly satisfied, though he was quiet for a few minutes before asking his next question. "Are you worried about seeing your sisters?"

Jared kept his eyes on Cassie's rear bumper. "Why would I be worried?"

"Well, it has been a long time since you've seen them. I guess I could understand if you were sort of nervous about being around them again."

"Yeah," Jared conceded. "I'm sort of nervous. I'm not sure what I'm going to say to them."

"Did you love 'em—when you were a kid, I mean?"

Jared's jaw twitched convulsively. "Yeah," he said after a moment. "I loved them."

"Do you still?"

Jared had been blessed with a son who was wise beyond his years, bright and funny and amazingly well adjusted, considering his background. He also had a knack for asking questions that could make his father squirm. But Jared had made a real effort during the past two years to be honest with the boy whenever possible and he didn't want to change now, though he wasn't quite ready to discuss his feelings for Cassie—whatever they were.

So, he tried to answer Shane's question candidly. "I don't know, Shane. Right now, I guess I'm just…feeling my way."

About a lot of things. Cassie, for example.

Shane thought about his father's words for a moment, then nodded. "Yeah. I guess I understand that, too. I love you, Dad."

"Love you, too, Shane." They didn't say the words often. But when they did, it meant something special to both of them.

Jared slanted his son a faint smile, warmed, as always, by the affection in the boy's eyes. "Why don't you find another radio station? You know I can take anyone but Willie Nelson."

Shane grinned and reached for the radio knob. "I'll see if I can find any of that prehistoric rock you like."

Jared chuckled. "Smartass."

But already his attention was drifting back to the car ahead of him, his gaze lingering on the back of Cassie's head as she reached up and wearily rubbed her nape.

She was getting tired. They really should stop for a break soon. And maybe this time he'd make an effort to be a little nicer to her. It wasn't her fault that Jared was in such an emotional tangle.

Not entirely, anyway.

They stopped at midafternoon at an ice-cream parlor and arcade Shane had eagerly pointed out to his father. Cassie was rather surprised when Jared slid in next to her in the booth they'd chosen, leaving Shane to sit opposite them.

She tried hard to concentrate on her hot fudge sundae, not an easy task with Jared's thigh pressed to hers. By accident? Or was he deliberately trying to generate enough heat to melt her ice cream? If that was his intention, he was doing a damned good job of it.

Shane wolfed down his supersize banana split with enough speed to give a normal person a major ice-cream headache, then excused himself and headed for the video machines. Jared looked at his son's empty bowl, then at his and Cassie's only half-finished smaller treats and shook his head. "I don't know where he puts it."

"He's a growing boy," Cassie answered with a smile. "He uses up a lot of energy."

"No kidding."

"All this car travel must be difficult for him. He must be getting restless."

"Yeah." Cassie noted that Jared looked a bit guilty with the admission. "He'll be glad when we get settled somewhere."

"Why did you leave Oklahoma?" she asked curiously.

He lifted one shoulder in a shrug. "Job played out. I heard about a job in Arizona, so it seemed like a good place to head."

Cassie bit her lip to keep from pointing out that a life on the road wasn't the most secure upbringing for a boy of fourteen. She didn't say anything, of course. It wasn't really any of her business. And, for that matter, Shane seemed happier than many boys she'd met of his age. He was loved, he was cared for and he was treated with respect. On the whole, Jared probably knew a lot more about raising his son than Cassie could even imagine at this point.

Jared pushed his ice cream away, leaving nearly half uneaten. "Cassie, about this morning…"

She promptly choked on a maraschino cherry. Reaching desperately for her soft drink, she took a bracing sip before trying to speak. "What about this morning?" she asked, realizing Jared was watching her quizzically.

"I just wanted to say I'm sorry. Shane accused me of treating you badly. I didn't mean to."

"You have been rather cool," Cassie admitted, toying with her spoon. "I couldn't help wondering why."

Jared was bending a plastic drinking straw around his fingers, winding it in one direction and then another, as though he, too, was uncomfortable with the direction their conversation had taken.

"I just...didn't know what to say," he said. He glanced quickly toward Shane, who was fighting an enthusiastic battle to save the universe from alien invaders. "Last night was—well, last night was pretty special. But I'm still not making any promises. I can't. Not yet. Maybe not ever."

"I'm still not asking for any promises," Cassie replied evenly, oddly encouraged by his stumbling explanation. He'd admitted last night was special. He seemed even more determined to disclaim any interest in commitment. Was he trying to convince her—or dare she hope that he was trying just as anxiously to convince himself?

She looked at him with a smile, her gaze moving slowly from his so-serious blue eyes beneath a disheveled lock of brown hair to the firmly carved mouth above his poor, bruised chin. "Last night was special for me, too, Jared. Very special. I'll never forget it."

His gaze catching hers, he slid a hand to the back of her neck, pulling her toward him. "Good," he murmured, his mouth hovering above hers. "I don't want you to forget."

And then he kissed her, oblivious of the public setting, the possible audience. Cassie was no more concerned about propriety when she tilted her head to kiss him back, feeling as though it had been days since they'd held each other.

By the time the kiss ended, Shane's galactic battle had ended. He stood beside their booth, grinning in obvious approval. "So, you guys going to sit here and make out or are you ready to get back on the road?"

"Someday, Shane…" But Jared was smiling now, the first real smile Cassie had seen on him all day. She was in a much better mood, herself.

"Hey, Dad. How about if I drive the truck and you ride with Cassie for a while?" Shane suggested, tongue-in-cheek, when they walked back out into the parking lot.

Jared reached out to cuff Shane's shoulder. "Yeah, right. As soon as you produce a valid driver's license."

"How about the fake one I use when I go out with the guys for drinks?" Shane asked, trying without much success to keep a straight face.

Jared shook his head. "Don't even joke about it. Get in the truck, son. I need to have a conference with Cassie."

"A conference? That's what they're calling it these days, huh?" Still grinning, Shane climbed into the pickup.

"Somebody's going to strangle that boy someday," Jared muttered, taking Cassie by the arm as he escorted her to her car.

She smiled at the fond exasperation in his voice. "It won't be you," she teased. "And he knows it."

"He suspects it," Jared corrected her with a quick grin. "He hasn't quite had the nerve to test me yet. He knows just when to back off."

Cassie loved his smile. She only wished she could see it more often. "Why *are* we having a conference?"

"I figure we're about five hours out of Dallas," Jared replied, glancing at his watch. "If we add an hour for dinner somewhere along the way, we should be getting into Dallas at around ten o'clock tonight."

"That sounds about right," Cassie agreed.

"Have you called yet to tell them we're coming?"

"No," she admitted. "I thought I'd call once we were in town."

He nodded. "Good idea. It'll be too late to call tonight. You can talk to them tomorrow and set something up for tomorrow evening, if it's convenient with my sisters."

"I'm sure it will be," Cassie said, knowing both Michelle and Layla would give up just about any plans they could have made to see Jared. She took a deep breath. "You'll stay at my place tonight, of course."

She eyed him as she spoke, wondering if he'd feel it necessary to protest. "I've got a spare bedroom," she added before he could speak. "You and Shane could share it."

"Or Shane could take it and I could share your bed," Jared answered quietly, a hint of a question in the suggestion.

She glanced at the pickup where Shane waited, then back to Jared. "I'd like that," she admitted. "But how would Shane feel about it?"

"In case you haven't noticed, my son is all but pushing us into each other's arms," he replied dryly. "He's been around more than most boys his age. I don't think we're going to shock him if we spend the night together. Unless it bothers you, of course."

"It doesn't bother me." Cassie didn't care if the whole world knew that she and Jared were lovers. She loved him, and she wasn't ashamed of that love. Though she couldn't help wondering what Tony would say when he realized just how deeply, personally involved she'd gotten with this particular case.

She was breaking all of the rules, of course. But Tony didn't have much room to criticize, since he'd done the same with Michelle.

Jared leaned down to brush her mouth with his. "Good," he said, straightening before the kiss could get out of hand—much to Cassie's disappointment. "We'll stop about seven for dinner. In the meantime, drive carefully. And leave your radio alone. You can't watch the road if you're playing with your dial."

Cassie gave him a sweet smile. "Someday someone's going to strangle you, Jared Walker," she said, paraphrasing his comment about his son.

He grinned and flicked her nose with the top of one finger. "But it won't be you," he answered, mocking her reply. And then he turned and headed for the truck, his sexy swagger all but making her mouth water.

Cassie sighed wistfully and climbed into her car, comforting herself with the knowledge that they were only some six hours away from being at her home, at which time she'd finally have him to herself once again.

The only worry dimming her anticipation was the fear that once she had Jared and Shane Walker in her home, she'd never want to let them leave. But would she be able to keep them there?

"Well, you're certainly in a better mood. I take it you and Cassie had a little talk while I was playing video games?"

Startled by Shane's question—as well as the realization that he'd actually been whistling along with the toe-tapping country song playing on the radio—Jared grinned somewhat sheepishly. "Yeah, We talked."

"And…?"

"And—it's none of your business what we said," Jared answered.

Shane wasn't offended. "I'm just glad you settled whatever it was. I like it better when you guys are friends."

Jared concentrated hard on the road ahead, his fingers tightening around the steering wheel. "Cassie's invited us to spend the night at her place tonight. She has an extra bedroom."

"Yeah? Cool. I'm really getting tired of motels."

Jared's fingers flexed. "I—uh—won't be sharing the bedroom with you, Shane."

"I didn't think you would be," Shane answered dryly. "And I don't think you spent most of last night at a bar."

Jared winced. "Son, we've talked about this plenty of times. I don't go in for casual affairs, you know that. What I feel for Cassie—well, it's not casual. But that doesn't mean it's going to lead to anything permanent. I think you're mature enough to understand that by now."

"I understand, Dad. But I still hope it does," Shane added. "I really like her."

Jared couldn't help being pleased, despite his concerns that Shane would be disappointed if he and Cassie couldn't make it work out. "Yeah. So do I."

He hesitated a moment, then said, "She's a nice woman, Shane. This isn't casual for her, either. You know that, don't you?"

"Well, of course!" Shane said, sounding indignant on Cassie's behalf. "Jeez, Dad, I know Cassie's not the easy type. Anybody could tell by looking at her that she's crazy about you."

Which, of course, didn't make Jared feel any better at all. *Was* Cassie getting too deeply involved with him? Was she starting to expect more than he was capable of giving her, despite her assurances to the contrary?

Damn. A week ago he'd just had himself and Shane to worry about. Now there was Cassie, as well as two sisters who'd be expecting some sort of response from him. And he couldn't for the life of him have said whether he was more pleased or dismayed with the twist his path had taken.

"Tell me about the ranch you want to own, Jared," Cassie requested as the three of them lingered over dinner that evening. "How did a navy seaman ever get interested in ranch work?"

"Dad used to ride in the rodeo!" Shane informed her before Jared had a chance to answer.

Cassie lifted a questioning eyebrow. "When was that?"

"My last foster home, from the time I was sixteen until I graduated from high school, was on a ranch not far from Texarkana," Jared replied. "I showed an aptitude for the life then, rode in amateur rodeo competitions whenever I got a chance. My foster father encouraged me to stay on and work for him when I graduated from high school.

"I was tempted—I'd been happier there than at the other places. But I decided it would be best if I struck out on my own for a while. The military looked like a good choice—steady work, free job training, a chance to see some of the world."

Had he left because he'd found himself developing ties again for the first time since he'd been separated from his real family? Cassie couldn't help wondering. "Do you stay in contact with him? Have you seen your foster family since you joined the navy?"

Jared shook his head. "He died of a heart attack six months after I joined up. I never was as close to his wife, so we just lost touch after that."

"I'm sorry." So many people lost to him, she thought sadly. Everyone he'd ever cared about, it seemed—except Shane, of course. And even Shane had been taken from him for several years. No wonder Jared had learned not to get too close.

Jared shrugged, his characteristic response when the conversation turned too personal, too intimate. "Anyway," he went on, his voice expressionless, "when I left the navy, I found work on a ranch in west Texas. Shane and I both enjoy the work, so we've been saving up for our own place for the past two years. Couple more years, and we'll have enough for a down payment on a small ranch. It'll take a while to make a go of it, but we plan on working together at it."

"We're going to call it the Walker Ranch," Shane agreed eagerly. "I kinda like the Double W, but Dad says it's too hard to say in a hurry. We're going to raise champion quarter horses. All we need's one good stud and a couple of fine mares. I want some cattle, too. Polled Herefords, the big red ones. Dad says maybe."

Cassie loved watching the two of them make their plans together. How she wished to see them have their dream come true, to be a part of that future with them!

"My uncle was a rancher in Wyoming," she said. "My parents used to take Cliff and me there to visit for a couple of weeks every summer. Once Cliff and I got to stay six whole weeks, while my parents went to Europe for their first overseas vacation. I loved the ranch."

"Does your uncle still have the place?" Shane asked, his eyes lighting up.

Cassie shook her head. "He passed away, and neither of his sons were interested in carrying on the business. One's a doctor, the other a musician. They sold the ranch right after Uncle Pete died."

"That's a shame."

"I miss him—and the ranch," Cassie agreed. "I understand why you enjoy the life. It's hard work, but it's a challenge."

"The woman likes ranch life and she's good in a fight," Shane said with an exaggeratedly blissful sigh. "Dad, if you don't grab her, damned if I won't. You wouldn't mind waiting a few years for me, would you, Cassie?"

She laughed, her cheeks warming. "I'd be honored to wait for you."

"Last guy who made a pass at my woman ended up with a bloody nose, boy," Jared warned mildly, pushing away his empty dinner plate. "Consider yourself warned."

"Is that right?" Shane asked, his tone sounding so much

like his father's that Cassie couldn't help giggling. "Maybe I'd manage to do more than bruise your jaw if I took you on."

Jared fingered the bruise and eyed his son in challenge, looking rather intimidating to Cassie despite the smile in his eyes. "Think so?" His voice was all the more dangerous because it was so very quiet and polite.

"Or maybe not," Shane backed down hastily, holding both hands palm-up in surrender. "Just making conversation."

"Why don't you just finish your dinner," Jared suggested, turning his head to wink at Cassie.

"Yes, sir," Shane agreed, catching the wink and smiling. "Whatever you say, sir."

"Why couldn't he always be that agreeable?" Jared asked with a wistful sigh.

Her hand over her mouth to muffle her laughter, Cassie resisted the urge to circle the table and hug both of them until their faces turned purple. These two were so very special—and for tonight, at least, they were hers.

She intended to enjoy every minute with them.

They were less than half an hour away from Cassie's apartment when the trip came to an abrupt, terrifying end.

After so many hours on the road without incident, Cassie was relaxed and driving confidently, looking forward to getting home and preparing Shane's usual late-night snack before sending him to bed so she and Jared could be alone. She'd already decided not to even think about her job or Jared's family until the next morning, after another night of his lovemaking to give her the courage to face the future.

She wasn't looking in the rearview window when the accident occurred. She'd just driven beneath a green light, knowing Jared was following close behind. And then she heard the squeal of brakes, the blast of a car horn, followed by the sickening, unmistakable sound of two vehicles colliding behind her.

Slamming on her brakes, she looked back. Her stomach lurched when she realized that another pickup truck had run the red light, slamming at full speed into the passenger's side of Jared's truck. She hadn't even seen it coming, she realized frantically, jerking her car to the side of the road and leaping out the door almost before she brought it to a full stop.

There was no sign of movement from the horribly tangled vehicles in the intersection. The wreckage looked dark and ominous in the artificial glow of the streetlights.

"Call an ambulance!" she screamed to another motorist who'd stopped in response to the accident. Terrified of what she'd find, she ran toward Jared's truck. "*Jared! Shane!* Oh, my God, no!"

Chapter Nine

Cassie reached the driver's side of Jared's truck at the same time as a massively built black man who'd been in the car behind Jared. "Better stand back a minute, lady," he said, holding up an arm to keep her from coming any closer. "Let me look inside first. It might be—well, you know."

She pushed him frantically aside, terror giving her strength even against his muscle. "I know them," she said, her breath catching in a sob. She reached for the door handle. "Jared! Shane!"

Quickly grasping the situation, the man stopped trying to interfere and moved forward to help.

Jared was slumped in his seat, his hands still draped over the steering wheel, the shoulder strap of his seat belt holding him upright. Cassie's heart stopped when she saw the blood. The left side of his face was covered with it.

"Jared?" she whispered, reaching a trembling hand out to him. "Jared, can you hear me?"

She'd never heard a more beautiful sound than his groan. Her knees went weak. She clung helplessly to the doorjamb. "Jared?"

He muttered something and shook his head, as though to clear it. That movement tore another groan from him. His left hand lifted to his head. His eyes opened, bleary and dazed. "Cassie?"

And then his gaze sharpened as full awareness returned. "Shane!"

He twisted frantically in his seat, even as Cassie strained to see around him. "Oh, God. *Shane!*"

Cassie sobbed. She couldn't see the boy, but the agony in Jared's voice spoke volumes.

"Oh, no, please," she heard herself praying, her voice little more than a broken whisper. "Oh, Shane."

Even though it was late—just after 10:00 p.m.—a crowd was beginning to gather. The sound of sirens was already dimly audible. Broad hands fell on Cassie's shoulders, tugging gently. "I've had some experience with this sort of thing," the big man who'd stopped with her said. "Let me see if I can help."

Cassie had always taken such great pride in handling emergencies with clearheaded competence, having never given in to nerves or hysteria in her life. Yet now she found herself trembling uncontrollably, tears streaming down her face as she stared helplessly into the truck.

She'd never faced anything so personally devastating for her.

Oh, God, please let Shane be alive. Don't take him from Jared—or from me. Please.

The first police cruiser pulled close and two officers jumped out, immediately taking charge of the scene, moving back onlookers, clearing a path for the emergency crews on their way. A fire truck rounded a corner, lights and sirens activated.

Again, Cassie felt hands on her arms, drawing her away from the wreckage. She fought them off. "No! I have to know they're all right!"

"Ma'am, we can't help them if you don't give us room," an earnest young officer told her, holding her when she would have pulled away, his hands kind, but firm. "You can stand right here, close, but out of the way. Okay?"

"Please," Cassie whispered, looking up at him through a blinding film of tears. "I love them. Help them."

The young officer searched her face, then tightened his grip on her arms. "Sit down," he urged, tugging downward. "Let's get your head between your knees."

He didn't have to force her downward. Her knees buckled. Had it not been for the officer's support, she would have fallen. Two more hands reached out from her other side, and the familiar deep voice of the black man who'd stopped to help spoke over her head. "I'll stay with her if you need to get back to work."

"Thanks," the officer said gratefully.

People moved around them in the parking lot of the closed-for-the-night business in front of which the accident had happened. The spectators' voices were hushed but avid as they surveyed the scene with a mixture of revulsion and fascination. "That guy looks dead," someone said from nearby.

Cassie lifted her head sharply, gasping when the world spun in response. "I have to go to them," she whispered, placing a hand flat against the pavement to give herself support as she rose.

"Give yourself a minute," her companion urged. "You're still white as a ghost. You try to stand up now, you're just going to pitch back over."

But already the world around her was steadying, her eyes drying as characteristic determination kicked in. "I have to go to them," she repeated. "Please."

The man eyed her cautiously for another moment, then nodded. "Okay. I'll give you a hand up. Take it easy, now. And my name's Frank, by the way."

"Thank you." She clung to his strong, dark hand as she pushed herself to her feet with his help. "What's happening? Where's the ambulance?"

"On the way, ma'am. Steady now."

Cassie craned on tiptoe, trying to see around the officers standing in the open driver's door of Jared's truck. "Is he alive?" she asked, barely able to push the question past the lump in her throat. "Is Shane alive?"

"That the boy?"

She looked up at Frank hopefully, nodding. "Could you see him?"

"I saw him. He's hurt, but he was alive when the officers took over. Hey, you're not going to faint again, are you?"

"I haven't fainted yet," Cassie murmured, though she maintained a grip on his supportive arm.

Just hearing that Shane hadn't died in the accident had sent a wave of knee-weakening relief through her. If only his injuries weren't serious....

Belatedly, she remembered that there had been another vehicle involved in the accident. Looking over the buckled hood of Jared's truck, she saw a group of police and firemen gathered at the second pickup. "Is the other driver hurt badly?"

Frank followed her gaze. "I think he's dead, ma'am."

"Oh, no." Cassie closed her eyes for a moment, then opened them quickly when the wail of a rapidly approaching ambulance caught her attention. It was closely followed by a second ambulance. "Thank God. They're finally here."

"It's only been five or six minutes since they were called."

It had seemed like a lifetime. Cassie watched anxiously as paramedics rushed to the scene, emergency equipment in hand.

Frank's gloomy diagnosis of the other driver's condition was confirmed. The officers gathered around the other vehicle and waved the paramedics toward Jared and Shane, shaking their heads as though to say there was nothing to be done for the other driver.

Cassie started forward when she saw Jared being assisted out of the truck, a bandage being pressed to his head by a woman who was beginning to look harried. Cassie saw at a glance that Jared wasn't being cooperative, particularly when he was urged toward one of the waiting ambulances. He shook off the hands that had reached out to help him.

"He's my son, dammit," Cassie heard him snarl as she took a step closer. "He's my son!"

Evading a police officer who stepped toward her, Cassie slipped closer to Jared, placing her hand on his arm. She searched his face. He was pale, blood-streaked, disheveled, his eyes wild, but at least he didn't look seriously injured. "Jared?"

He looked down at her. She couldn't feel hurt that he blinked as though it took him a moment to remember who she was. She understood that all his concentration, all his emotions were focused on his son.

"Cassie," he said after the briefest hesitation, raising his hand to touch her face. "Are you all right?"

She covered her hand with his. "Of course I'm all right," she assured him, trying to smile. Knowing how miserably she failed. "Are you?"

His eyes turned back to the truck around which so many people were working with what appeared to be feverish haste. "I don't know yet."

A slender young man in a white uniform approached them, his attention focused on the bleeding cut on Jared's left temple. "Here, let me look at that," he offered.

Jared waved him away impatiently. "I'm okay. My son's the one who's hurt."

"Yes, sir, I know, but he's being attended to. At least let me see if I can stop your bleeding. You won't be any help to your son if you pass out, will you?"

"Let him look at you, Jared," Cassie urged, both hands on his arm now. "I'll check on Shane."

Jared nodded reluctantly and allowed the paramedic to lead him toward an ambulance. "I'm not leaving until my son does," he warned the young man.

"No, sir. I don't blame you," the paramedic answered compassionately. "We'll do what we can to treat you here until your son is transported."

Confident that Jared was in good hands, Cassie turned to the truck. "Excuse me," she said to a police officer who was passing here.

"Need to stand back, lady. This ain't a free show," he growled, hurrying toward the intersection where curious motorists were causing a traffic hazard with their rubbernecking.

She sighed and tried again, tapping the shoulder of a man in a fireman's uniform. "Please, can you—?"

"Sorry, ma'am. I've got to fetch a piece of equipment. Talk to an officer," the fireman replied hastily, though not unkindly.

Again, it was Frank, the big man who'd stopped to help after the wreck, who came to Cassie's assistance. He took her elbow and helped her to the young officer who'd drawn her away from Jared the first time.

"I'm Lieutenant Franklin Thompson from the Houston Police Department," he introduced himself, his deep voice carrying just a trace of command, as though he were a man accustomed to being in charge. "The lady wants to know the condition of the boy in the truck. He's a friend of hers."

Responding instinctively to the voice of a fellow officer,

the young policeman cooperated immediately, looking up from the clipboard on which he'd been filling out a report.

"He's trapped in the wreckage by the front quarter panel of the vehicle, ma'am," he explained carefully. "He's alive and stable, I understand, but the full extent of his injuries can't be determined until he's extricated. We're going to have to get the other truck out of the way, then pull him out with special equipment."

"The Jaws of Life?" Cassie asked, having heard the term on the television and read about it in the newspapers.

"That's right, if necessary. In the meantime, it would be best if you and the father stay back. I know you're concerned, but the boy's being assisted by experienced professionals. I don't suppose you can convince Mr. Walker to be taken on to the hospital for treatment of his own injuries, could you?"

Cassie looked back at him. "What would you do if it were your son trapped in that mess?" she asked quietly.

The officer didn't even hesitate. "I'd tear him out with my bare hands if they'd let me."

"Then you know exactly how Jared feels," Cassie replied. She felt very much the same way herself. "He won't leave until he knows Shane's out. Neither will I. But we will stay out of your way."

"I promise I'll keep you both informed about what's going on," the officer assured her.

"Thank you. We'd appreciate that." Cassie turned toward Frank. "And thank *you,* Lieutenant. You've been so much help."

He smiled. "A cop's a cop, even when he's on vacation." And then he led her back to Jared, who was sitting with visible reluctance in the back of an ambulance, one medic taking his blood pressure while the slender young man who'd led him away bandaged his head.

"Here's your friend," the latter said to Jared, looking up with a friendly smile when Cassie and Frank approached. "He's been getting a little impatient," he added for their benefit.

"What's going on out there, Cassie?" Jared demanded.

Cassie repeated what the officer had told her. "They're doing the best they can, Jared."

Jared glared at the paramedic standing over him. "Are you about finished?"

"You're going to need stitches for this cut, but the bleeding has stopped," the young man answered, apparently unconcerned by Jared's curtness. "Your blood pressure's fine, considering the stress you're under, and there's no sign of a concussion. You'll be okay until we can get you to a hospital to be checked out more carefully."

"Not without my son," Jared repeated, already pushing himself off the gurney on which he'd been seated.

"No, sir. Not without your son."

If it hadn't been for the terrible gravity of the situation, Cassie would have smiled at the paramedic's wryly resigned tone. As it was, she could only take Jared's hand when he stepped from the ambulance and reached for her.

She wrapped her fingers tightly around his, both of them turning to watch the painfully slow process of extricating Shane from the mangled cab of Jared's truck.

Jared rode in the ambulance with Shane when the boy was finally transported to the hospital some forty minutes later. Cassie followed in her car, still shaken by the one glimpse she'd had of Shane as he'd been loaded into the ambulance.

He'd been so pale, so still, so vulnerable-looking. What if there were internal injuries? What if he didn't even make it to the hospital?

How would Jared survive if he lost the son he loved so very deeply, after so many other losses in his life?

Her heart wept for both of them.

Shane, still unconscious, was wheeled straight into an emergency examining room upon arrival at the hospital. Though he protested, Jared, too, was led away by hospital staff determined to care for him whether he cooperated or not, followed by a clerk with a stack of admission forms.

Cassie was left to pace the waiting room, her hands wringing in front of her, her head aching from stress and exhaustion. She glanced at her watch. It was almost eleven.

Finding a bank of pay telephones at one end of the emergency lobby, she dialed Tony's home number. Her employer answered.

"Tony, I'm so glad it's you."

"Cassie? Where are you?"

"I'm in Dallas. Oh, Tony." Her voice broke.

"Cassie? Cassie, what is it? What's wrong?" Tony sounded increasingly anxious when it took her a moment to answer.

She drew a steadying breath. "There's been an accident," she said, trying to stay calm and coherent. "Jared and Shane were following me into town and they were broadsided by another vehicle."

"Oh, damn, Cassie, how bad is it? Are *you* okay?"

"I'm fine. My car wasn't involved. Jared seems okay, though he hit his head on the side window. But Shane—" She had to stop again to swallow hard against a rush of tears.

"Jared's son? Cassie, is he—?"

"He's alive," Cassie broke in quickly. "He was trapped in the truck for quite a while until they could pull him out. He's hurt, but I don't know how badly. They're examining him now."

She named the hospital. "Can you come, Tony? I could really use you right now," she added, desperately needing a friend's support.

"We'll be there in fifteen minutes," Tony answered, though

they both knew it was a good twenty-five-minute drive from his home to the hospital. Cassie knew, as well, that Tony would be there in fifteen, if at all possible.

"Drive carefully" was all she said.

It was just under twenty minutes later when Tony and Michelle hurried into the waiting room. Cassie bolted from the hard plastic chair on which she'd been perched.

"I'm so glad you're here," she breathed, taking Tony's outstretched hand in both of hers. "Jared still hasn't come out, and no one's told me anything. I don't know what's going on, and I'm so worried about Shane."

Penetrating black eyes studied her face. "You look awful," Tony said with more concern than tact. "You sure you're okay, Cassie?"

She managed a nod, then almost immediately shook her head. "Not until I know how Shane is," she whispered. "Oh, Tony, he's such a sweet boy. I couldn't bear it if…"

Remembering Michelle, she swallowed the rest and turned to the woman standing quietly behind them. "Michelle. I'm sorry. I didn't mean to ignore you."

"I understand." Michelle D'Alessandro was one of the most beautiful, most elegant women Cassie had ever met. She had been more than a little intimidated the first time she'd met her employer's wealthy, classy wife. But that was before she'd realized that Michelle was kind-hearted, sweet-natured and more than a little shy beneath her polished sophistication. "Thank you for calling us. I wanted to come."

"It's getting so late." Cassie checked her watch again, fretting at the length of time that had passed since she'd seen Jared and Shane. "God, I wish I knew what was happening in there."

Tony turned toward the admissions desk. "I'll see what I can find out."

"Let's sit down," Michelle suggested to Cassie. "You look ready to drop."

"I've been on the road most of the day," Cassie agreed wearily. "And then this…"

"Can I get you some coffee? Vending-machine coffee is usually dreadful, but it might help."

Cassie shook her head. Her stomach was tied into so many knots she was afraid she wouldn't be able to keep anything down. "Thanks, anyway, Michelle."

Ignoring the other people around them in the sterile lobby, Michelle sat beside Cassie on a narrow vinyl bench. "Jared changed his mind about visiting us, I take it."

"Yes." Cassie cleared her throat. "I—I talked him into it. I thought it would be good for both him and Shane to meet their family."

"You can't blame yourself for this, Cassie. You were only doing what Tony and I asked you to do. The accident was just that—an accident."

"A drunk," Cassie corrected bitterly. "I've found out that the other guy was drunk, and that he had a history of drunken driving. He paid for it this time with his life."

She couldn't bear to think that the price might have been even higher.

Tony rejoined them, the frustration on his handsome face indicating that he'd learned little more than Cassie had been able to find out before he'd arrived. He stood beside the bench, his hand resting on his wife's shoulder. "All they'll tell me is that they're being examined and treated and that a doctor will be with us as soon as possible."

Cassie made a sound of disgust. "That's what they kept telling me," she complained. "And I've been here almost an hour. What could be taking so long?"

"Hospital procedures can be very lengthy sometimes," said

Michelle, who had been a hospital volunteer for several years. "Surely it won't be much longer."

Cassie sighed and buried her face in her hands, feeling as though she'd aged decades in the past few hours. Everything had been going so well. How could it have gone this drastically wrong?

"Tell me about Jared and Shane, Cassie," Michelle said, obviously trying to distract her from her worry. "I'd like to know something about them before I meet them."

Cassie straightened, wondering how to explain Jared to this sister who didn't remember him.

"Jared is reserved and rather quiet," she said finally, so easily picturing his usually grave face. Remembering how he'd looked when passion had swept away his reserve.

"He has a great deal of pride," she went on quickly. "He's conservative and a little bossy, but he has a dry sense of humor that comes out when you least expect it. And he absolutely adores his son."

Tony lifted a dark eyebrow, studying Cassie's face. She felt herself flushing beneath the intensity of that regard. "Sounds like you've gotten to know him fairly well in such a short time."

Cassie avoided his eyes. "We have spent quite a bit of time together during the past few days," she concurred.

Michelle interceded, to Cassie's relief. "Is Shane like his father?"

"In some ways they're very much alike, though Shane is more outgoing. He's fourteen—bright, mature, funny. I'm…" She wiped her eyes. "I'm crazy about your nephew, Michelle."

"I'm sure I will be, as well," Michelle said, reaching over to squeeze Cassie's hand. "He's going to be okay, Cassie. If there's one thing Tony's taught me, it's to believe what my heart tells me. And my heart's telling me now that I'm going to have a chance to get to know my nephew."

Cassie had always been an optimist. She tried desperately to cling to that optimism now. "I'm sure you're right, Michelle," she murmured, the words almost a prayer. "I'm sure you're right."

Jared couldn't remember ever feeling more drained than he did when he left the examining room in which he'd finally been allowed to see his son.

Shane was sedated, sleeping deeply, so Jared didn't linger once his questions had been answered to his satisfaction. Having been assured he'd be located as soon as Shane was settled into a hospital room for the night, he headed for the waiting room, knowing Cassie must be frantic by now.

His head ached, though he'd refused the pain pills he'd been offered. He wore eight stitches at his left temple, but that cut and a few bruises were his only injuries from the accident. He fervently wished Shane had been as fortunate.

He wanted Cassie, needed to feel her hand in his, her arms around him. Though he'd spent most of his life on his own, learning not to depend on anyone but himself, just this once he needed the emotional support of someone who cared about him, without strings, without qualifications.

He needed Cassie.

With her copper hair gleaming in the bright fluorescent lighting, she wasn't hard to spot in the emergency waiting area. He had eyes for no one else when he started toward her, his booted stride eating up the distance that separated them.

As though she sensed his approach, she looked up, her eyes meeting his. And then she was on her feet, and a heartbeat later she was in his arms.

He buried his face in her hair and allowed himself the first long, deep breath he'd taken since he'd turned and seen his son's face after the accident. He felt the tremors running through Cassie's slender body and drew her closer, heedless of anyone who might be watching.

"God, Cassie," he muttered, drawing strength from her almost palpable concern for him. "Oh, God."

She drew back only far enough to search his face anxiously. "Jared? Is Shane—is he—?"

"He's going to be okay," he answered quietly, reassuringly, seeing the panic that had sprung into her eyes and chiding himself for causing it. "His right arm is broken and he has a concussion. He's also got a couple of cracked ribs and possible whiplash."

"What about his right leg?" Cassie asked, remembering that the leg had been caught beneath a jagged piece of metal that had come through the cab of the truck with the impact.

"Badly bruised," Jared answered, identifying strongly with her obvious relief that it hadn't been more serious. "Had the metal come through a few inches lower, he might have lost the leg."

"Oh, Jared." Cassie went limp against him, her fingers clutching his badly wrinkled, bloodstained shirt. "I've been so frightened."

"Yeah. Me, too. But he's going to be okay, Cassie. Shane's a tough kid."

"Like his father," she murmured, looking up at him with a trembling attempt at a smile.

"Yeah," he murmured, lost in her tear-filled green eyes. "Like his dad."

And then he kissed her, a long, tender kiss of shared relief, of aching emotion, of a deep, powerful hunger that went far beyond the physical.

He drew back at last to look down at her with a weak smile. "Know where we can get some coffee while Shane's being settled into a room? God knows I could use some."

"Yes, I— Oh!"

Jared was startled by Cassie's squeak, looking at her in question when she suddenly covered her face with one hand and went scarlet behind it. "Cassie? What's wrong?"

"I think she's finally remembered she hasn't been waiting alone," a man's voice answered unexpectedly.

Jared turned his head to find himself face to face with a tall, dark, Italian-looking guy with dark, searching eyes and a quizzical expression. Behind him stood a slender, brown-haired woman in her mid-twenties, her blue eyes locked on Jared's face. He stared back at her, finding so many familiar features that he had no doubt who she was, though he hadn't seen her in twenty-four years. It was like looking at a feminine version of himself, or Shane.

"Shelley?" he asked hesitantly, his hand freezing at Cassie's waist. "Are you Shelley?"

She nodded, her blue eyes filling with tears. "Hello, Jerry. It's so very good to see you."

Shaken to his boots, and still too emotionally drained to conceal it, Jared thrust his free hand through his hair and let out an unsteady breath. He wasn't ready for this, he thought grimly, taking a hard swallow as he tried to think of something to say. He hadn't had a chance to prepare for a family reunion.

But regardless of whether he was ready, he couldn't deny that the woman standing in front of him was his sister and that he had once loved her. Nor was he unaware that his first reaction had been to take her in his arms, even though she was little more than a stranger to him now.

"Damn," he muttered.

He really wasn't ready for this.

Chapter Ten

Realizing what his sister had called him, Jared looked at her in question. "You said Jerry. That's what you called me when you were little."

She nodded, her smile unsteady. "I know."

"You couldn't possibly remember. You weren't even three when we were split up."

"I don't remember very clearly," she replied. "But all my life I've had dreams of playing with a boy named Jerry and a girl named Layla. I didn't know until earlier this year that those dreams were really early memories."

"I answer to Jared these days," he murmured, all but shuddering at the thought of being tagged with "Jerry" again at this point in his life.

Her smile deepened. "And I'm Michelle."

"It must have been unnerving for you to find out you had so many brothers and sisters," Jared commented rather awkwardly, not quite sure what else to say. What were they expecting of him?

She nodded. "It was staggering, to say the least. But exciting, too. I grew up thinking I was an only child, and that I was all alone when my adoptive parents died. I was pleased to learn that I wasn't alone, after all."

"Now you've got more family than you ever imagined," the dark man with her commented with a smile.

Michelle returned his smile. "Jared, this is my husband, Tony D'Alessandro—who happens to come from a huge, extended family himself."

Jared studied the other man closely, deciding he liked what he saw. Looking to be in his early thirties, clean-cut, clear-eyed D'Alessandro was just the opposite of the old movie stereotype of an unshaven, disreputable, somewhat sleazy P.I. On first impression, Michelle seemed to have found herself a good husband. For her sake, Jared was glad.

He extended his hand. "So you're Cassie's boss—the guy who refused to bail me out of jail."

Tony grinned and gripped Jared's hand firmly. "No offense, of course. I'd have bailed you out eventually. Just thought I'd let the New Mexico cops help Cassie keep track of you for a couple of days until I had a chance to check you out for myself."

Jared dropped Tony's hand and draped his arm around Cassie's waist. "Cassie didn't need any help keeping track of me," he said smoothly. "She knows her job. And she's damned good at it. You're lucky to have her working for you."

"Jared..." Cassie murmured uncomfortably, shifting her weight.

Tony's left eyebrow rose, but he nodded. "I'm aware of that."

"Good." Jared glanced at Cassie's flushed face, knowing she wouldn't appreciate his talking her up with her boss. "About that coffee..."

"There's a canteen on the next floor," Michelle volunteered. "It's only a few tables and vending machines—the cafeteria's closed at this hour—but at least it's a place to sit down and have a cup of coffee."

"Sounds good." Jared inhaled deeply, releasing the breath in a long sigh. "I'm wiped out."

"I'll let them know where we'll be if you're needed," Tony offered, turning toward the desk.

Cassie was being unusually quiet, Jared realized. Still keeping her close with the arm he'd wrapped around her waist, he glanced down at her. "Cassie? You okay?"

She nodded, her mouth trembling a bit. "Just tired."

"If you'd like to go on home, Tony and I will stay with Jared until he's reassured that Shane is settled for the night," Michelle suggested, glancing curiously from Cassie to Jared, obviously wondering about their relationship.

Cassie shook her head before Jared could voice the protest that sprang immediately to his lips. He knew she was tired, but he couldn't bring himself to let her go. He needed her with him now.

It was the first time he'd really needed anyone since…well, in longer than he could remember. And he was too damned tired to even worry about that at the moment, he thought wearily.

"I want to stay," Cassie said. "I'd like to make sure for myself that Shane's okay." She managed a smile, though it was a pitiful attempt. "I'll be fine as soon as I get some coffee in me."

Conversation was rather stilted over eight cups of coffee in the all-night canteen. Cassie was still unnaturally subdued, Tony polite but watchful, as though taking his time to judge whether Jared represented any threat to either Michelle or Cassie.

Jared watched Tony with Cassie, a little suspicious at first of the obvious affection between them. He relaxed when he realized that Tony treated Cassie with much the same fond exasperation he might have shown a younger sister. And Cassie responded with affection, respect and just the right touch of impertinence, as though to tell him that he could give orders as her employer, but only to a point.

Jared approved. He didn't like the thought of anyone trying to break Cassie's reckless spirit, despite his own admonitions to her on occasion during the past…damn, had it only been four days since they'd met?

Shaken by the realization that he'd fallen faster and harder for this woman than he'd ever thought possible, Jared didn't hear Michelle speak his name the first time. He blinked when he heard her, realizing she must have spoken before. "I'm sorry, Michelle. What did you say?"

She'd asked a question about his years in the navy. He responded, giving her a brief rundown of the past twenty-four years, leaving out more than he told her, particularly when it came to his unsuccessful marriage. About that, he said only that he'd been married young, divorced a few years later, and had been granted full custody of his son after leaving the navy two years ago.

"Do you think you should call Shane's mother to tell her about the accident?" Michelle asked.

Aware that she couldn't have known better, Jared kept his answer mild, knowing that Cassie was listening intently beside him. "No. She gave up all rights to Shane two years ago. This doesn't concern her."

More than ready to change the subject, he turned the questioning to Michelle, who told him she'd been adopted by a childless couple, raised in a comfortable, secure home, and worked part-time now for her late father's company as administrator of charitable contributions.

Jared wondered why the pleasant, uneventful life she'd described didn't quite mesh with the shadows he occasionally glimpsed in her eyes. Michelle may have been raised in a comfortable, secure home, but she hadn't been completely happy, he decided. Maybe someday she'd tell him why.

Not that it was any of his business, of course, he reminded himself abruptly. It had been twenty-four years since he'd been responsible for this young woman.

"Mr. Walker?"

Jared turned his head in response to his name, finding Shane's doctor behind him. He stood, aware that Cassie did the same. "What is it?"

Dr. O'Reilly lifted a hand to indicate there was no reason to worry. "I just wanted to tell you your son's awake and asking for you. Thought you might want to speak to him a moment before we sedate him again."

"Is that necessary? The sedation, I mean," Jared asked with a frown.

"It will help him sleep more comfortably tonight. He needs the rest."

Jared nodded. "All right. And, thanks. I do want to see him."

Dr. O'Reilly smiled. "I was sure you would. I'll take you to his room."

Jared started after the doctor. Then stopped when he realized he was the only one doing so. He looked over his shoulder. "Cassie?"

She didn't move. "Yes?"

"Come on."

He saw her eyes light up, though she hesitated. "You want me to come with you?"

"Shane will want to see you." Which was only half the truth, of course. Still, Jared spoke confidently, knowing his son well enough to anticipate the request. Shane would know that Cassie would have been worried sick about him.

Cassie glanced at Michelle and Tony, then stepped quickly to Jared's side. "I'd love to see him."

Jared took her hand in his, aware of how right it felt to have her at his side.

He really was going to have to give these complicated feelings some thought. Later.

Her eyes on the boy in the hospital bed, Cassie held back when Jared stepped to Shane's side. Her throat was almost unbearably tight, her eyes burning with the tears she refused to shed in front of Shane. She needed just a moment to recover from the shock of seeing him lying there so still and small in his bandages and cast, his face looking so very young beneath the bruises and traces of blood which hadn't been completely washed away.

"Hi, Dad." Even Shane's voice seemed suddenly younger, higher, less confident than she'd heard it before. "You okay?"

"I'm fine, Shane," Jared answered gruffly, leaning over the bed.

"Your head?"

"Just a cut. A few stitches."

"Does it hurt?"

"Nah." Jared spoke the obvious lie without a blink. "You hurting much?"

"Not too bad," Shane answered, as easily as his father. Cassie couldn't help smiling a little. Neither of them would have admitted if they *had* been in terrible pain. Hopelessly macho, the both of them.

God, how she loved them!

"Where's Cassie?" Shane demanded, trying to look around his father. "Is she okay?"

Touched that the boy would ask about her so soon, Cassie stepped closer to the bed. "I'm right here. And I'm fine."

He looked relieved. "I can't really remember much about what happened," he admitted. "You weren't hit, were you?"

"No. I'd already passed through the intersection by the time the other driver came through and hit your truck."

"I never even saw him until he was right on us," Jared murmured, his expression bleak. "If I'd hit the brakes a little sooner, or had a chance to turn the wheel…"

"I didn't see him, either, Dad," Shane reassured him. "You couldn't have done anything differently. Besides, it turned out okay. Neither of us is hurt bad. A broken arm's no big deal."

Cassie had to blink back tears again at the earnest note in Shane's voice. He was trying so hard to help Jared fight the guilt that was as unfounded as it was inevitable.

A muscle twitched in Jared's hard jaw, but he nodded and managed a faint smile for his son's benefit. "The nurse is waiting outside to give you something to help you sleep tonight."

Shane made a face. "I don't want them to knock me out."

"It'll help you rest, son. Don't give them any trouble, you hear?"

Shane chuckled weakly, his eyelids heavy as he glanced expressively at his bandages and the IV tube running into his left arm. "Not much chance of that," he murmured.

"You could still take on half the staff and win, kid," Jared told him affectionately, gently ruffling the boy's hair. "But maybe you'd better just take it easy tonight. I'll be back in the morning."

"'Kay. You get some rest, too."

"I will."

"Cassie?"

Cassie moved to stand at the opposite side of the bed from

Jared, looking down at the boy with a tremulous smile. "Yes, Shane?"

"I'm expecting to need that guest room tomorrow night, okay?"

"I'll have it ready, just in case," she promised. She leaned over to brush her lips across his cool cheek. "Good night, Shane. See you tomorrow."

He gave her a smile, though she could see the pain in his eyes. "'Night, Cassie."

"We'll send the nurse in now," Jared said, taking Cassie's hand. She knew he was as aware of Shane's discomfort as she was, and that he was suffering with his son. He held her hand in a grip almost tight enough to make her wince, telling her just how hard it was for him to leave.

They rejoined Michelle and Tony in the canteen, finding them waiting patiently for word about Shane.

"He's doing fine," Jared announced, the relief visible in his eyes. "He's hurting, but coherent. Shane's tough. He'll be back on his feet in no time."

"Oh, I'm glad to hear that," Michelle said. "I can't wait to meet him."

"He's looking forward to that, as well," Jared replied. "He was really excited to hear that he has two aunts and some cousins wanting to meet him."

As interested as she was in watching Jared's reactions to his sister, Cassie couldn't quite stifle the yawn that escaped her. It was well past midnight now, and she'd had a very long day after very little sleep the night before.

Jared turned to her immediately. "You're out on your feet. Time for you to get some rest."

"Jared, you'll stay with us tonight, won't you?" Michelle asked politely. "There's no need for you to stay in a hotel when we have plenty of extra bedrooms."

Cassie bit her lower lip, wondering how Jared would respond. She wanted him with her, of course, but didn't quite have the nerve to repeat her invitation in front of her boss and Jared's sister.

What would they think if they knew she and Jared had become lovers so quickly? Would Tony be disappointed with her for losing all sight of professional behavior on this particular case?

Jared seemed to suffer no such qualms. He thanked Michelle for her offer, then added, "But I already have a place to stay tonight."

Both Michelle and Tony looked directly at Cassie, who responded with a fiery blush that must have confirmed all their suspicions.

She cleared her throat noisily. "We knew it would be late when we arrived tonight," she explained. "We'd planned to call tomorrow and make arrangements, then get everyone together."

Tony's eyes glinted, and Cassie tensed, remembering the times she'd teased him during his early involvement with Michelle, wondering if he would fire her now or have the courtesy to do that in private. But all he said was, "No need for you to come in to the office in the morning, Cassie. Get some rest and we'll talk tomorrow, all right?"

"Thanks, Tony."

Cassie glanced cautiously at Michelle, who looked from her to Jared, then back again. And then she smiled with what looked to Cassie like approval before laying a hand on Jared's arm. "As much as I regret the accident, I'm still very glad you're here, Jared," she said softly.

Cassie watched as Jared's face softened fractionally. He covered his sister's hand with his own. "You've grown into a beautiful woman, Michelle. It's good to see you again."

Michelle was obviously touched, her eyes going damp.

"I'll call Layla first thing in the morning. She's so anxious to see you. She's told me dozens of stories about the things you did together when you were younger."

Jared nodded. "I remember." And then he dropped his hand and turned to Cassie. "Let's go."

Knowing Jared had reached an emotional overload of sorts, Cassie nodded and led him briskly to her car. She kept their conversation light and impersonal during the ride to her apartment, giving him a chance to pull his defenses together.

As much as she resented those defenses at times, she knew he needed them tonight. And she wanted to give him enough space that he didn't start feeling cornered before he'd even spent an entire day in Dallas.

Preceding Jared into her functional, two-bedroom apartment in a midpriced complex located in a quiet Dallas neighborhood, Cassie was glad she'd spent a day at housework before leaving town to track Jared down. After a week of sitting empty, the apartment was a bit stuffy, but at least it wasn't cluttered with newspapers, magazines and odd pieces of clothing, as she'd been known to leave it occasionally.

"Can I get you anything?" she offered, leading Jared into the living room, off of which opened the kitchen, dining area and the short hallway leading to the two tiny bedrooms and guest bath.

He shook his head. "I need a shower and sleep more than anything else right now."

She understood. Her own body was so desperately in need of rest that she ached to her toenails. "There's a shower stall in my bath and a tub in the guest bath."

"Where's your bedroom?"

"First door on the right."

He nodded and carried his bag toward the hallway she'd indicated. "I won't be long."

"Take your time." She watched him disappear, wondering if she should prepare the daybed she kept in the spare bedroom, which usually served as her study. Considering how tired they both were, lovemaking seemed unlikely—but would Jared want to sleep with her or alone?

She knew which she'd choose. She couldn't think of any nicer way to rest than curled next to him. But maybe he'd prefer privacy for tonight.

She carried her bag to her bedroom, listening to the shower running in the attached bath as she dropped it at the foot of the bed. And then she moved into the guest room, deciding it was best to be prepared for either eventuality.

She'd just finished smoothing clean sheets onto the daybed when Jared spoke from the doorway behind her. "What are you doing?"

She turned self-consciously, tucking a curl behind her left ear. Her knees went weak at the sight of him, his hair wet, chest still damp, a towel draped around his hips. He wore nothing else.

"I wasn't sure where you wanted to sleep," she explained, dry-mouthed in reaction to him. He looked so very good, even with the bandage at his temple, the day-old bruise on his jaw and the newer bruises marking his ribs and stomach from the abrupt tightening of his seat belt during the accident. The seat belt that may well have saved his life, just as Shane's had probably saved his.

Jared glanced at the daybed and then over his shoulder toward the other bedroom. "Where were you planning to sleep?"

"Why, in my own bed, of course."

"Then that's where I want to sleep. Unless you'd rather I stay in here. If so, just tell me."

How typical of Jared to express his wishes so bluntly, Cassie thought with a weary ripple of amusement. "I would love to share my bed with you, Jared. Though I can't promise anything more energetic than a good-night kiss when we get there."

His grin was endearingly lopsided, his expression understanding. "I don't have the energy to ask for anything more," he assured her. "Come to bed, Cassie. Just let me hold you tonight."

She went to him without hesitation, knowing there was nowhere in the world she'd rather be.

As tired as she was, Cassie wouldn't have been surprised to have slept twenty-four hours without even stirring. But the bedroom was still dark when she woke, the bedside clock letting her know she'd gotten only three hours' sleep. And the bed beside her was empty.

Where was Jared? Had he decided to sleep in the other bedroom, after all? Was his head hurting?

Concerned, she slipped out of the bed, not bothering to don a robe over her thin white cotton nightgown. Her bare feet made no sound on the carpet as she crossed the hallway to look into the spare bedroom. She saw at a glance that the daybed hadn't been disturbed since she'd last seen it.

Knowing Jared had been as tired as she was, if not more so, she grew more anxious, though she tried to reassure herself that perhaps he'd only gone into the kitchen for a glass of water.

She stopped abruptly in the doorway to the living room. Wearing only a pair of jeans, Jared stood at the window overlooking the apartment compound, his back to her as he stared without moving. He obviously hadn't heard her, wasn't aware that she was watching him.

She thought of going back to bed, giving him that space she'd decided he needed. But something in the set of his shoulders drew her forward. She was close enough to touch him when she spoke in little more than a whisper. "Jared? Is something wrong? Is your head hurting?"

He started in response to her voice, his head jerking in her direction. The thin light streaming in from outside glittered in his shadowed eyes—and from a drop of moisture on his cheek. Her chest contracted sharply.

Tears? From Jared? "Oh, Jared, what is it?"

He was still for so long that she thought he wasn't going to answer. And then he released a gust of breath and dashed at his cheek with the heel of his hand—much as Shane would have, she couldn't help thinking.

"I almost lost him," he said, his voice a deep growl. "Dammit, Cassie, I almost lost him. If that truck had hit us one minute later, six inches farther back, Shane wouldn't have made it."

She couldn't bear to see him suffering. She wrapped both hands around his arm, resting her head against his bare shoulder. "Don't, Jared. You're torturing yourself needlessly. Shane's going to be fine."

"I know that. But I can't stop thinking about how close it was."

"Think about how lucky you both were, instead."

"Yeah. I'm trying."

They stood quietly for several long moments, Cassie's head against his shoulder, Jared still staring out the window. Cassie's heart ached for him. She'd never felt closer to anyone else in her life. Though she'd never really been in love before, she'd always known that the true test of the emotion came in the difficult times, not the easy ones.

She and Jared had been through more in four days than some couples experienced in as many years. Perhaps that was why it was so easy for her to love him, Cassie mused. She'd watched him under pressure, at leisure, angry, laughing, distraught. She'd seen him as a father, as a lover, as a fighter. As a man. And she loved every side he'd revealed to her in those days, even knowing that there were aspects of him she still hadn't seen, may never get close enough to see.

But did Jared feel the same way? Did he still see Cassie as a temporary companion, a convenient buffer between himself and his sister while he was in town? Did he really need her as much as she believed he did?

She shivered at the thought that she may have been deluding herself about his feelings, that he could so easily walk away from her as soon as Shane was released from the hospital.

Jared's arm went around her immediately. "You're cold. Let's get you back in bed."

"You need your rest, too," she urged, looking up at him. "Come with me, Jared."

He nodded and walked with her to the bedroom, where he stripped off his jeans. Together they climbed back into the rumpled bed. "C'mere," Jared said, tugging Cassie into his arms.

She slipped a hand behind his neck, feeling the muscles bunched there. She tightened her fingers, kneading a stubborn knot at the juncture of his shoulder. He groaned softly. "That feels good."

"Turn on your side and I'll rub your neck."

"No. You're tired. Get some sleep."

"Jared—" She shoved at him. "Roll over. You're in my bed, so I get to be the bossy one this time."

He made a sound that was very close to a chuckle and finally rolled over as she'd requested, his back to her. Cassie went to work on the knotted muscles in his neck and shoulders, satisfied to feel them slowly easing beneath her ministrations.

If Jared would accept nothing else from her, at least she could pamper him tonight. She tried very hard to convince herself that was enough—for now, at least.

Chapter Eleven

Cassie was rather startled when Jared spoke after lying still beneath her hands for several minutes. She'd thought he was falling asleep, but his voice was fully awake. "I almost lost Shane once before, you know."

Her hands stilled, then resumed their massage. Jared needed to talk. She needed to listen. "When?"

"Two years ago, when he ran away. Kay married a jerk who wasn't openly abusive to Shane, but was totally indifferent to his welfare. He and Kay spent most evenings getting quietly drunk while Shane was left pretty much on his own. I had finally figured out what was going on—" his voice was gritty with self-censure "—and I'd been trying for well over a year to get custody of my son. Kay fought me, more as a way of getting in a few last digs at me than because she really wanted Shane."

"Couldn't the courts see that she wasn't a good mother to him?"

Jared shrugged the shoulder she was rubbing. "No one cared enough to really investigate. Kay did a good job of looking like the loving, concerned mother when she was in public. Hell, she'd kept me fooled for nearly ten years, until Shane finally got old enough to tell me just what was going on. I knew she drank too much, of course, but I thought she put Shane first. I was wrong. I guess I was too involved with my own problems to want to know the real truth."

There was that guilt again. She knew now that he'd never completely defeat it—that it wasn't entirely unfounded, though he'd devoted himself to making up for the mistakes he'd made during Shane's early years.

She didn't insult him by trying to assure him he hadn't made any mistakes. But she did want him to know that he wasn't making them now, not with Shane, anyway. "You're a good father, Jared. Shane's one of the most well-adjusted, levelheaded, brightest boys I've ever met. He didn't achieve those things alone."

Jared rolled to his back and threw an arm over his head, staring at the darkened ceiling. "I've done what I could the past couple of years. God knows there was a lot of damage to undo."

"Why did he run away from Kay and his stepfather? How did you find him?" Cassie asked, sensing he needed to finish his story.

"He'd warned his mother that if she continued to contest me for custody, he'd run away. She didn't believe him—and I thought I'd convinced him to give it up, that I wasn't going to stop fighting for him until I won. But the last time my petition was turned down, Shane lived up to his threats and took off looking for me. Kay didn't tell him I'd just been shipped out for a six-month tour. And she didn't notify me for almost a month that Shane was gone."

"A month!" Cassie gasped. "She let that boy live on the streets for a month before she contacted you?"

"She knew how furious I'd be, how bad it would look for her," Jared confirmed in disgust. "She notified the authorities after about a week, but they were getting nowhere looking for him. Soon as I found out, I arranged for emergency leave and went looking for him.

"It took me almost six weeks to find him after I got back in the States. He'd been living in alleyways and bus stations in Memphis, which was the last place I'd been stationed before shipping out. He would run whenever anyone tried to question him or whenever anyone looked dangerous to him. He spent a couple of dollars a day on food, then swept sidewalks and ran errands in exchange for food when the money he'd taken with him ran out. He's bragged that he never begged for money, never stole anything during that time."

"Oh, God, Jared. A twelve-year-old boy on the streets of Memphis! He could have been—"

She bit the words off abruptly, knowing they'd only make him feel worse. But the images that flashed through her mind were horrifying. She couldn't even imagine how Jared must have felt during those long, desperate weeks, how many sickening possibilities he must have envisioned during his search.

"Yeah." The one grim word spoke volumes. "I'd always loved my son, but it took that to make me realize exactly how much he meant to me. How blind and self-absorbed I'd been before. I was so glad to find him alive and in one piece that I couldn't let go of him for days. Took me two weeks to get around to yelling at him for running off. He sat there grinning while I chewed him out for a good three hours. When I finished, he just said, 'I knew you'd find me, Dad.' I didn't know whether to hug him or take a strap to him."

"You hugged him." Cassie spoke with confidence.

"Yeah. I hugged him. And told him if he ever did anything like that again, I was damned well going to use the strap."

"Kay stopped fighting for custody after that?"

"I didn't give her a hell of a lot of choice. I was granted an honorable discharge from the service to take care of my son, and Kay signed over all claim to him."

Cassie curled her lip. "She's a fool. How anyone could choose a bottle over her own son—especially a wonderful boy like Shane—is beyond my comprehension."

"She's a sick woman, Cassie. She had a rough time of it growing up—an abusive father, a victimized mother. It doesn't excuse her, of course, but—"

"No, it doesn't excuse her," Cassie broke in flatly. "She's an adult now, responsible for her own actions. You didn't have an ideal childhood, either, but you turned out just fine."

Jared's rough laugh held little humor. "Yeah, well, there are plenty of people who'd disagree with you. I'm thirty-five years old, I've got no job and no permanent home. I'm just out of jail and my son's in the hospital—not exactly a fine, upstanding citizen, am I?"

"If you're waiting for me to agree with you, you're wasting your time."

Jared turned his head toward her, his expression tightening at whatever he saw in the faint light. "Don't look at me like that, Cassie."

"Like what?" she whispered, though she thought she knew.

"Like you're seeing something in me that's not there."

She shook her head. "I don't think I'm doing that."

"Dammit, Cassie. I don't want to hurt you."

"Then, don't." She touched a tender fingertip to the corner of his tautly drawn mouth, wanting to ease his mind so he could sleep. She thought she knew just how to do that.

"I don't know if I can help it," he argued. "You expect too much from me."

"I'm not expecting anything more than you're willing or able to give, Jared." She leaned over him, brushing a strand of hair away from the bandage at his temple. "Does your head hurt?"

He frowned. "Not much. Cassie—"

She lowered her head to press a kiss against the bruised skin just below the bandage. Her breasts brushed his chest, the thin cotton of her nightgown the only thing separating them. "Is there anything I can get for you?"

He gripped her forearms, holding her a little away from him. "If you don't stop that you're going to start something you're too tired to want right now," he warned roughly.

She bent her leg upward, over his thighs, her knee coming into gentle contact with his groin. She hid a smile as she dropped another kiss on his bruised jaw. Jared was tired, as she was. But, like her, he wasn't *too* tired.

She rubbed her smooth leg very slowly against his rougher one.

Jared groaned, his fingers tightening on her arms. "Cassie. Go to sleep."

"I will," she murmured, her lips moving against his throat. "Soon." And then she slid a hand down his chest and beneath the sheet that covered them from the waist down.

Jared released her arm to bury his right hand in her hair, cupping the back of her head when she lowered her mouth to one flat brown nipple. She touched her tongue to the hard point, her nose tickled by his chest hairs. She curled her fingers around him, loving the hot, pulsing strength of him.

Jared bit off what sounded suspiciously like a curse, and then moved with stunning speed to flip her onto her back beneath him, his hands going to the hem of her nightgown. "Just don't say I didn't give you a choice," he muttered, sweeping the fabric out of their way.

She smiled and curled her arms around his neck, lifting to welcome him into her body. Jared had shared so much with her tonight. This was something she could share with him, something he needed as badly as she did.

By the time they fell asleep, still wrapped in each other's arms, their bodies heavy with satisfaction, damp and warm from their lovemaking, the problems and questions that awaited them seemed very far away.

Cassie woke several hours later when Jared climbed out of bed. She stretched, aware that full sunlight was streaming through the windows this time. "Good morning."

Jared's smile didn't quite touch his eyes. "Morning. Mind if I take the first shower?"

"Go ahead. I'll make some coffee. I'm sure you'd like to get back to the hospital soon."

"Yeah." He went into the bathroom and closed the door behind him.

Cassie groaned in wry exasperation. She really was going to have to talk to Jared about his morning manners. Did the man never smile before noon?

Or was he only like this on mornings after he'd revealed too much of himself during the night?

Wrapping herself in her robe, she muttered beneath her breath as she headed for the kitchen to put the coffee on. That done, she came to a sudden decision. If she was ever going to teach Jared to love her, she was going to have to start with a course in morning etiquette. And now was as good a time to start as any.

Build all the walls you want, Jared·Walker. I'm not going

to stop trying to get in until you convince me without doubt that you're happier in there all alone.

Jared looked startled when Cassie stepped nude into the shower with him. "What are you doing?"

"I thought we'd save some time and shower together," she replied, taking a bar of soap from the soap dish. "Want me to do your back?"

His eyes narrowed. "Cassie—"

"I was just wondering," she continued blithely, rubbing the soap between her hands. "Do you *ever* smile in the morning?"

"Never before my coffee." Though the words sounded gravely teasing, he continued to watch her warily, as though he wasn't quite sure what to expect from her next.

She slid her soapy hands very slowly from his chest to the tops of his thighs, missing very little along the way. "Then I guess I'll just have to give you a better reason to smile than caffeine, won't I?"

He drew her toward him, a familiar spark lighting his dark blue eyes. "You're a dangerous woman, Cassie Browning."

She smiled and went up on tiptoe. "So I've been told," she murmured against his mouth.

A moment later she found her back pressed against the tiles, her thighs draped over Jared's as he crowded closer. And, as her eyelids grew deliciously heavy, she noted in smug satisfaction that Jared was smiling just before his mouth covered hers.

Shane was awake when Cassie and Jared entered his hospital room an hour and a half after their rather extended shower. He looked up with a smile when they came in. "Hi. They took the IV out."

"You must be feeling better," Jared remarked, noting that his son's eyes were brighter and that he had significantly more color in his face than he had had the night before. Relief coursed through him as he realized that Shane really was going to be all right.

"Yeah. I'm ready to get out of here. You wouldn't believe what they expected me to eat for breakfast."

Cassie laughed and kissed Shane's cheek with an easy affection that Jared watched intently. She really was fond of his son, he thought, warmed by the knowledge even as he worried that both Shane and Cassie would end up hurt.

"I'll bet you ate every bite of whatever they brought you," Cassie accused.

Shane grinned. "Yeah. I did. But it tasted like—"

"Watch the language," Jared interrupted when Shane gave him a teasing look.

"Just get me out of here, okay, Dad? I want to see Cassie's place."

"It's not much to look at," Jared replied, sitting on the edge of the bed and avoiding Cassie's eyes. "Real dump. Broken-down furniture, bullet holes in the walls. Things that move around in the night."

Shane laughed. "Yeah, right. You going to take that without a fight, Cassie?"

"I was just going to tell your father that I hope he finds a warm place to sleep tonight. You and I will get along just fine in my 'dump.'"

"That's assuming the doctor says it's okay for Shane to leave the hospital today," Jared warned, ignoring Cassie's threat. "I haven't talked to anyone yet."

"They'll let me," Shane said confidently. "I've just got a bump on the head and a broken arm. Skinny Mahoney didn't spend the night in the hospital when he got both legs busted by that bull, remember, Dad?"

"Skinny Mahoney got tossed out on his ear for making an

obnoxious pass at the nurse who was trying to take his blood pressure," Jared reminded him with the beginnings of a smile.

"Yeah. He's an obnoxious kind of guy. But he didn't have to stay in the hospital just to let his bones heal up," Shane persisted.

"We'll see," Jared said, not wanting to raise false hopes, though he privately agreed that Shane would recuperate just as quickly at Cassie's place. He wasn't all that sure he should continue to impose on her that way, nor let either her or Shane get too accustomed to being together that much. Or would having Shane and Jared as full-time houseguests for a while make Cassie see that she had been better off before she met them?

And why was he feeling just a little resentful that Shane seemed every bit as pleased to see Cassie this morning as he had his father?

"You going to sign my cast, Cassie?" Shane demanded, looking with some pride at the pristine white plaster. "I'll let you be first, then there's a couple of nurses I'm going to ask."

"You mean you've already been flirting with the nurses?" Cassie demanded in mock surprise. "You haven't even been here twelve hours yet!"

"They said I'm obviously a fast healer," Shane bragged. "I didn't even need a pain pill this morning. I mean, I'm kinda sore all over, but it's not all that bad."

"Just don't get cocky and overdo it, son," Jared warned. "You were pretty banged up in that wreck. There's no reason to rush your recovery, you hear?"

"Yeah, I know." But Shane looked anything but patient. "What about the insurance, Dad? Have you contacted anyone yet?"

"I made some calls from Cassie's place before we left," Jared replied, amused that his son had already thought of the practicalities. "Fortunately, the guy who hit us was well insured, so we'll be covered for everything."

"What *about* the guy who hit us?" Shane asked suddenly. "What happened? How's he doing?"

Jared cleared his throat, aware that Cassie was watching him to see how he'd handle this question. "The guy was drunk, Shane," he said evenly, deciding to handle this as he did all Shane's questions—with total honesty. "He's dead, son."

Shane paled a bit, but didn't look surprised. "I thought he must be. No one would say for sure. I'm really sorry for the guy, you know, Dad?"

Jared nodded, his throat tight. This, too, was typical of his son. Shane held no grudge against the driver who'd come so close to taking his life with his drunken irresponsibility.

It humbled Jared to realize that his boy was a better man than he was.

There was a light tap on the door and Michelle looked in, smiling when her eyes met Jared's. "Hi. Are visitors allowed?"

He stood. "Come on in."

Shane stared at the woman who approached his bed, then looked wide-eyed at his father. "Wow, Dad. She looks just like us! Only prettier."

Jared almost flinched at the observation, feeling the ties of family drawing more tightly around him. "Shane, this is your aunt, Michelle D'Alessandro."

"Hello, Shane. And thank you for the compliment." Michelle smiled sweetly, and just a touch shyly, at her nephew. "It's very nice to meet you."

"It's nice to meet you, too," Shane answered politely, still studying her carefully. "Are you the one with the three kids?"

She laughed and shook her head. "That's your other aunt, Layla. I've only been married a few months."

"So you're the one who's married to Cassie's boss."

Michelle gave Cassie a quick smile. "Yes, that's right."

Shane looked suddenly serious. "I think he should give her a promotion or something for everything she's done for me and my dad. She deserves it."

"Shane…" Cassie murmured, cheeks flaming.

"Shane…" Jared growled in admonition, not wanting Shane to embarrass Cassie further, though Jared had said much the same thing to Tony only the night before. Shane had been on his best behavior for the past few days, but had been known to let his mouth get ahead of his brain at times.

"Well, she does!" Shane insisted.

Michelle didn't seem to be offended. "My husband and I are both very grateful to Cassie for everything she's done," she said.

"She didn't just do it 'cause it was her job," Shane added. "She really likes us, don't you, Cassie? In fact, she and Dad are—"

"Why don't you tell us about Layla's kids, Michelle," Jared broke in ruthlessly, giving his son a frown of warning. "Shane's been curious about his cousins."

Though Michelle's eyes danced with laughter as she looked from her brother to Cassie, she nodded and described Layla's lively children, Dawne, Keith and Brittany, who ranged in age from eight to two.

"Maybe when you find them, some of your other brothers and sisters will have kids my age," Shane suggested rather hopefully.

"Maybe they will," Michelle replied, looking as though she fully understood Shane's desire for the companionship of others his age. "But, in the meantime, my husband has dozens of young cousins your age, and they're a very close family. Maybe someday you can join us at one of their big gatherings for barbecue and a softball game."

"That sounds great," Shane approved. "I like playing softball."

"Then you should fit right in. They're fanatics about the game."

Jared wasn't sure how he felt about Michelle making plans for Shane to be included in her husband's family gatherings. He and Shane had been on their own for so long. Surely he wasn't feeling threatened by this new family who might become important to the boy?

He wasn't proud that so far this morning he'd been jealous of Cassie and now Michelle. It wasn't like him at all.

How the hell had he gotten himself into this situation, anyway?

Cassie was pleased with the remarkable progress Shane was making, though he was already beginning to wilt a bit. She could tell he needed to rest.

Sensing that Jared would want to stay with his son most of the day, she came to a decision. "I think I'll go to the office for an hour or so, if you don't need me for anything," she said. "I really should catch up with Tony about what's been going on while I was out of town."

Jared nodded. "Don't let us keep you from your work."

"I'll see you later this afternoon." She turned to Shane, laying a hand on his shoulder. "I'll sign your cast when I get back. In the meantime, you keep your other hand off the nurses, you hear?"

Shane chuckled, shifting his head restlessly on the pillow in a way that made Cassie suspect sympathetically that his injuries were hurting more than he was willing to admit. "I'm not making any promises," he murmured. "There's one redhead with these incredibly big—"

Cassie giggled and covered his mouth with her hand. "You're terrible, Shane Walker!"

"I was only going to say she has incredibly big syringes,"

Shane said with exaggerated innocence. "Why, Cassie, what did you think I was going to say?"

"Somebody beat this kid while I'm gone, will you?" Cassie asked no one in particular. And then she leaned over to give him a quick, careful hug. "See you in a little while, Shane."

"Don't be long," he replied wistfully, suddenly looking young and uncomfortable again.

"I won't." Cassie glanced at Jared, all too conscious of the eyes on them. "Call the office if you need me, okay?"

He nodded. "We'll be fine," he assured her, his expression carefully shuttered.

Had Michelle not been in the room, Cassie would have planted a kiss on his mouth just to shake that cool composure of his. Instead, she merely nodded and left, knowing she left an important part of herself behind in that small hospital room.

Cassie walked into the tastefully decorated reception area of D'Alessandro Investigations, smiling at the attractive black woman behind the desk. "Hi, Bonnie. Is Tony in?"

Bonnie returned the smile. "Cassie! Good to have you back. I hear you had all kinds of excitement while you were gone."

"Too much excitement," Cassie agreed, wrinkling her nose.

"For a P.I.? There's no such thing. Tony's in his office. Go on in."

"Thanks." Uncharacteristically nervous, Cassie cleared her throat, took a deep breath, and smoothed her hands down the black pleated slacks she wore with a teal-and-black printed shirt.

Bonnie watched her in open curiosity. "Something wrong, Cassie?"

"No. Why?"

"Well, you look—I don't know, like you're going in to have a meeting with the boss or something."

"I *am* going in to see the boss," Cassie reminded her.

"True. But you've never really treated him like a boss before. You're not in trouble or anything, are you?"

Cassie managed a shaky smile. "I'll let you know."

She tapped twice on Tony's office door, waiting until she heard him give permission to enter before turning the knob.

"Come on in, Cassie," he said when he saw her in the doorway. "Close the door behind you," he added.

She swallowed and did so. "I saw Michelle this morning," she said, just to make innocuous conversation. "She was at the hospital, visiting Shane."

Tony waved her to the chair across his desk and leaned back in his seat. "How's the boy this morning?"

"He's doing amazingly well. He was talking and smiling and determined to be released from the hospital today."

"Think he will be?"

"I don't know. Jared hadn't talked to the doctor yet when I left."

Tony looked at the pencil he twisted between his fingers. "Where do you suppose they'll stay tonight?"

Cassie cleared her throat again. "I suppose they'll stay with me."

Tony's left eyebrow rose. "Is that right?"

Her nervousness vanished in a surge of impatience. "All right, let's get it out in the open," she said, leaning forward and planting her hands on her knees as she met her employer's dark eyes. "I got personally involved with this one. I went with a hunch that Jared hadn't done anything wrong and did everything I could to get him out of jail. I was even going to bail him out with my own money if he hadn't been released when he was.

"I adored Shane from the moment I met him, and bought him dinner and got him a room rather than calling the juvenile authorities to report that he was on his own. I followed them to Arizona and kept after Jared until he agreed to change his decision about coming back with me to Dallas—and I wasn't just trying to get him to visit his sister," she finished defiantly.

Though he wasn't smiling, Tony's eyes glinted with amusement by the time she finished. "Is there any rule you didn't break, Cassie?"

"I didn't break any laws, that I know of," she replied carefully, beginning to relax just a bit.

"There's no law against falling in love," Tony commented, setting down the pencil. "And I'd be a real jerk to yell at you for it when I did exactly the same thing, wouldn't I?"

Cassie shifted in her chair. "I never said I was in love with Jared."

"You didn't have to. I recognize the symptoms."

Cassie pushed her hair back with both hands. "Have I been incredibly stupid, Tony?"

He shrugged sympathetically. "There were times when I wondered if I'd ever get past Michelle's lifelong reserve and teach her to trust me. Particularly when her attorney produced evidence to make it look like I was only after her money. We worked our problems out successfully, but Jared's older and harder and he's been kicked around a lot. His defenses have to be firmly in place."

"Except when it comes to Shane, they are," Cassie agreed. "There are times when he almost lets me in—and then he slams a door in my face. It's so frustrating."

"You haven't known him very long. Give it time."

"I just hope I have the time. For all I know, he could take off tomorrow, or next week. I think being faced with family again is making him uncomfortable."

"That's just something he'll have to work out. He *does* have a family, and they care about him, whether he wants them to or not. It's up to him whether he's going to become a part of them or risk losing them again. We knew there were no guarantees when we set out looking for him."

"No guarantees," Cassie repeated. "I knew that. I just didn't know at the time how very much it would come to matter."

"Cassie, if you need to talk, I'm here. I just want you to know that I hope you and Jared work this thing out. I won't get in your way—as your boss or his brother-in-law. Fair enough?"

"More than fair." She smiled shakily at him. "Thanks, Tony. You're a good friend as well as a terrific boss."

"Just call me a sucker for love. Now, I know you'll want to get back to the hospital in a while, but how about giving me a hand with some paperwork for an hour or so? I could really use some help around here."

"Of course. And I promise I'll be back full-time tomorrow. By the way, how are Chuck's teeth?"

Tony grimaced. "Firmly back in place. I had a long talk with him about protecting his face when he takes a punch. He could use some lessons from you on hand-to-hand combat."

Cassie laughed. "Remind me to tell you sometime about the brawl Jared and I got into at a little bar in New Mexico."

Tony groaned and shook his head. "I don't think I want to hear about it."

"Don't worry, boss," she quipped impudently. "I was on my own time. Now, where's that paperwork?"

Cassie had been working for an hour when she finally gave in to an ever-growing urge to place a telephone call. Maybe the need had developed when she'd witnessed Jared's sweet, but rather awkward reunion with his sister, watched as they'd struggled to establish a bond despite the years that had separated them. Knowing Tony wouldn't mind if she took a short break, she punched a series of digits on the telephone dial, charging the long-distance call to her personal calling card.

It was only a moment later when a familiar deep voice answered the low buzz on the other end of the line, so very far away. "Browning Air Freight. What can I do for you?"

"Cliff? Hi, it's Cassie. I'm glad you're in."

"Cassie?" Her brother seemed surprised to hear from her. "Hey, kid, what's wrong? Has something happened at home?"

Cassie bit her lip in a rush of guilt. Had she called her brother so infrequently that he automatically assumed something must be wrong for her to be calling now?

"No, Cliff, nothing's wrong," she assured him hastily. "I just wanted to talk to you for a minute. Are you busy?"

"Of course not. So how have you been, Cass? How's the P.I. racket?"

"Interesting," she answered with a smile, twirling the telephone cord around her finger. "My latest case involves reuniting a family of siblings who've been separated twenty-four years. I guess that's why I suddenly needed to talk to you. I don't want us to end up like that, Cliff."

There was a thoughtful pause from the other end. "I don't want that, either, sis," Cliff said at length, his voice uncharacteristically serious. "Guess we haven't stayed in touch lately, have we?"

"No. But I'd like to try to change that. It's true that we don't get to see each other very often because we live so far apart, but that doesn't mean I don't love you, Cliff."

"I love you, too, Cass. And I'm really glad you called."

She smiled. "Me, too. So, how are you? Is the business going well?"

"Yeah, great. Some months I even come out in the black."

"Good for you. How's your love life?"

Cliff laughed. "I'm in the wilds of Alaska, remember?

Most interesting female I've seen lately was a long-legged moose."

"I hate to tell you this, Cliffie, but you're starting to sound a little kinky. Maybe you'd better spend a few weeks in civilization soon."

"You may be right. What about you? Any interesting prospects on the dating scene? You ready to make Grandma a happy woman yet and change your single status?"

Cassie thought immediately of Jared, of course. But she didn't have the time—or money—to go into a lengthy explanation during this call. "I'll let you know if it happens."

"Does that mean it's a possibility?" Cliff asked, sounding intrigued.

"You know me. Always on the lookout for possibilities," she teased, skillfully evading specifics.

They talked another few minutes, catching up on family gossip, making plans for a Christmas reunion, and then Cassie said she had to get back to work. "It was really good to talk to you, Cliff."

"Yeah. It was. I've got your number. I promise I'll start using it more often."

"You do that. Take care."

"You, too. 'Bye, Cassie."

Her smile was misty when she hung up, but her mood was much lighter. If she'd learned one thing during the past few days, it was the incomparable value of family. She wouldn't take hers for granted again.

Tonight, she'd call her parents. She was definitely overdue for a long, cozy chat with them.

Jared was watching television with Shane that afternoon when Michelle dropped in for a second visit. This time she wasn't alone. The woman who followed her into the room looked very much like her, with only a smattering of gray in her brown hair. Jared came to his feet.

"Layla?"

"Jared." The word was little more than a whisper. Layla stared at him a moment, then threw herself in his arms. "Oh, Jared."

He caught her to him, dozens of memories flashing through his mind, prominent among them the last time they'd seen each other. They'd held each other then, too. And, as she did now, Layla had cried.

He remembered exactly what he'd told her then. "Didn't I promise we'd see each other again, Sissy?"

She gave a watery chuckle and wiped her eyes with her hand. "I thought I'd never hear you call me that again."

"Looks like you were wrong." He held her away from him. "You haven't changed."

Her cheeks pinkened. "I'm thirty-four years old. Not a little girl anymore."

"No. But still as pretty as you were then."

She touched his cheek. "You used to tell me how pretty I was when you wanted me to do your chores so you could go play with your friends. What is it you're after now, Jared Mitchell?"

He chuckled, trying not to show her how touched he was to see her again. Seeing Michelle had affected him, but he and Layla had shared so much in the brief years they were together. More than any of the others, really. "I hear you're a mother now. Still taking care of the little ones, eh?"

"A habit I couldn't break, I guess. I missed my baby brothers and sisters when they took them away."

"Yeah." His smile faded. "Me, too."

"You never looked for us, Jared?" She sounded wistful.

He swallowed and shook his head. "I meant to. But by the

time I was old enough to be out on my own, I decided you were probably all better off without me."

"Looks like you were wrong," she answered quietly, her imitation of him deliberate.

He looked away. "I wasn't sure at first that this was a good idea, Layla. It's been such a damned long time."

"Too long," she agreed. "But you're still my big brother, Jared. And I still love you."

She kissed his cheek, then looked toward the bed before Jared had to come up with a reply. "I want to meet my nephew."

Shane was watching them in fascination, Michelle's hand on his shoulder. He gave Layla a sweet smile. "Hi, Aunt Layla. I'm Shane."

"Oh." Layla approached him slowly, her dark blue eyes—so like the others in the room—devouring his face. "You look just like your father did when I knew him, though of course he was a few years younger. Oh, Shane, it's so nice to meet you."

"Aunt Michelle's been telling me about Dawne and Keith and Brittany. She says Keith's a pistol."

Layla laughed and nodded. "Yes, he is. He'll enjoy meeting his male cousin. My husband only has a couple of nieces."

It occurred to Jared that a lot of plans were being made in this hospital room today. He knew, of course, that Shane would need a few days to recover before they hit the road again. But everyone seemed to be taking for granted that Jared and Shane would be staying in Dallas indefinitely.

The imaginary ropes grew tighter around his chest.

What the hell had he gotten himself into?

Chapter Twelve

After shamelessly begging the doctor to let him go, Shane was released from the hospital late that afternoon. Cassie picked him and Jared up and took them straight to her place, where she pampered Shane so thoroughly that Jared wryly predicted the boy would never want to leave.

Cassie and Shane only smiled at each other. Cassie, for one, would have been quite content for Jared's prediction to come true.

"Would you like some more ice cream, Shane?" she offered. The three of them were sitting in her living room, watching television, and it had been nearly half an hour since his last snack.

"No more snacks," Jared interceded firmly before Shane could answer. "Cassie, he's had enough."

"A glass of milk, then? Or water. Are you thirsty, Shane?"

"I'm fine, Cassie. Really," Shane assured her, then yawned. "Sorry. Guess I'm getting a little tired."

"You should be in bed," Jared said.

Shane frowned. "But, Dad, it's not even ten o'clock yet."

"I know, but you still haven't got all your strength back. Come on, son. I'll give you a hand."

Shane sighed, but conceded, pushing himself out of his chair with his left hand, his right resting in the sling that supported his cast. He limped to the couch where Cassie sat, bent unselfconsciously down to her and gave her a smacking kiss on the cheek. "G'night, Cassie. See you in the morning."

"Good night, Shane. Let me know if you need anything, okay?"

Jared was back in fifteen minutes. He sat beside Cassie on the couch and reached for the lukewarm soft drink he'd been drinking earlier.

"You think he'll be comfortable enough during the night?" Cassie fretted, looking toward the hallway to the guest room. The door was closed, no light coming from beneath it. "He's still so pale and weak-looking."

"He's fine, Cassie. Just needs a few days to take it easy."

"I guess I'm being silly," she conceded with a sheepish smile. "These maternal feelings are all new to me."

Jared stretched one leg out in front of him, studying his boot with apparent concentration as he asked, "You ever think about having kids of your own?"

"Sometimes," she admitted shyly. "I always thought I'd like to have a child before I turn thirty."

The thought of having Jared's child turned her knees to water, though she knew full well he wasn't proposing anything of the sort. He was just curious, most likely.

He gave her a quick glance, his expression still unreadable. "Why haven't you?"

She blinked. "I thought maybe I'd get married first."

"Most women your age are already married."

She couldn't help giggling. "Now you sound like my grandmother. She all but went into mourning on my twenty-fifth birthday. I tried to convince her that lots of women are waiting until after that for marriage and children these days, but she acted like I was already too long on the shelf to ever hope for anything more."

Jared smiled briefly. "How does she feel about what you do for a living?"

"We've told her I'm in computer research. It's close enough to the truth, but it's something she can handle. If she found out I work for a P.I., she'd be convinced I was like those guys on TV—dodging bullets, breaking into secured buildings, sleeping with...er..." Her voice trailed off as she realized what she'd almost said.

"Sleeping with the clients?" Jared finished for her.

"Well—you're not a client, are you? Besides, I was just describing what my grandmother probably thinks a P.I.'s life is like."

Jared grunted something unintelligible and stared for a few minutes at the television, where a moussed-and-pow-dered news anchor was trying to look earnest and intelligent as he read the day's top headlines.

When Jared spoke again, he'd made an abrupt change of subject. "Michelle wants us to have dinner at her house later this week, when Shane's feeling more like getting out. Layla and her family will be there, too."

Cassie tried to look pleased that Jared and Shane would be spending an evening with their family. "You're welcome to borrow my car to get there. Or have you made arrangements with the insurance company for a rental?"

Jared lifted an eyebrow in her direction. "Why would I want to borrow your car? You'll be going with us, won't you?"

"Oh, I—" She twisted her hands in her lap. "Are you sure I'm invited? This sounds to me like a family thing."

"You go, or I don't." Jared spoke with blunt finality.

"But, Jared, you came to Dallas to see your sisters."

"No." He set his glass on a coaster and turned purposefully to face her. "We talked about this before. I came to Dallas because you're here. Dammit, I'm not staying here because of the free lodging, Cassie. You're the woman I'm involved with right now, not my landlady. You have every right to be with me when we join the others."

You're the woman I'm involved with right now. As a declaration of deep feeling, the words left something to be desired. But, from Jared, they were almost a commitment—temporarily, at least, she reminded herself before she could begin to hope for more.

"I'd love to go with you if you want me to, Jared."

He nodded in curt satisfaction. "I want you there."

"Then I'll go."

He nodded again, then changed the subject once more. "Shane and I are both out of clean clothes. Is there a Laundromat around here somewhere?"

"There's one here in the apartment complex," she said. "The small building to the left of the tennis courts."

"Then I'll do some washing in the morning while you're at work. You need me to throw in a couple of loads for you while I'm at it?"

She stared at him in astonishment. "You're offering to do laundry for me?"

He chuckled at the look on her face. "You don't have to look so stunned."

She shook her head and smiled. "For some reason, I find it hard to picture you measuring washing powder and fabric softener."

"You think I buy new clothes once a week? Who do you think's been doing our laundry for the past two years?"

"I hadn't really thought about it. Do you cook, too?" she asked, teasingly.

"I make one hell of a spaghetti sauce. And chili that will curl your eyelashes. Shane's specialty is chicken casserole. He found the recipe in a cookbook."

"Shane cooks, too?"

"We both get tired of eating out sometimes."

Cassie smothered her smile and leaned forward with a mock-grave expression, laying her hand on Jared's knee. "Feel free to stay here as long as you like."

He grinned and pulled her into his arms. "I don't do windows."

"That's okay," she assured him, winding her arms around his neck. "I'm sure you have other talents."

"Several. Want me to demonstrate a few tonight?"

"I would love that." She brought her mouth to his before she could give in to the temptation to tell him that she loved him more with each day she spent with him.

The next three days were among the happiest—and the most insecure—of Cassie's life.

She left each morning for work after having breakfast with Jared and Shane and returned each evening to find the house-work done and dinner on the table. They spent the evenings playing board games, watching television, laughing and teas-ing. And then Shane went to bed, and Cassie and Jared were alone, to talk quietly for a while and then to turn to each other with a hunger that seemed to grow deeper each time they made love.

Shane was rapidly recovering his strength, making Cassie and Jared marvel at the amazing resiliency of youth. He seemed happy with the way things were going, settling comfortably into Cassie's guest room, already scattering enough of his belongings around him to make the room his. When she learned that Shane enjoyed reading, Cassie bought him a stack of Western and adventure books, as well as a couple of excellent novels based on true events in American history. She was beginning to fret about him being out of school for so long.

Shane had even made some friends. While helping his father with the laundry, he'd met the fifteen-year-old twin brother and sister who lived with their mother in the apartment directly across the compound from Cassie's. The three had hit it off immediately, Heather and Scott—the twins—apparently impressed by Shane's slightly battered appearance and experience-based maturity.

Shane spent a couple of hours with them each afternoon when they returned from school, and already he was regaining his color and energy just from the time spent outdoors in the warm autumn weather, to Cassie's delight.

Despite the advice of an attorney Tony recommended, Jared refused to sue the estate of the driver who'd caused the accident, not wanting to cause more grief to the man's widow and three children. He said the settlement offered by the other driver's insurance company—enough to cover all medical expenses and provide him with a new pickup to replace the totalled one—was perfectly adequate, that neither he nor Shane would seek a large profit from the tragedy. Cassie told Tony that the decision served as a perfect illustration of Jared's pride and self-sufficiency.

"So is the guy going to stay in Dallas, or what?" Tony asked as Cassie was preparing to leave the office Friday afternoon."

She sighed. "I wish I knew. He hasn't said a word about his plans. Every time Shane hints that he likes it here and wouldn't mind enrolling in a Dallas school, Jared changes the subject."

She didn't add that Jared's expression always turned shuttered when that particular subject came up, so that she couldn't even begin to guess at his feelings. If he was feeling restless or trapped or even content to be staying with Cassie while Shane recovered, he was doing an excellent job of hiding those emotions.

He was a pleasant, cooperative, considerate houseguest. At night, he was the most giving, passionate lover Cassie had ever even fantasized, but he'd given her no reason to believe he was thinking of making their arrangement permanent.

As careful as she'd been not to push him, not to allow herself to hope for more than he might be willing to give, the uncertainty was driving her crazy. It was so hard not to make plans, not to say things that might sound like she was arranging a future for them. It wasn't in her nature to keep her own wishes hidden for long. Yet she was terrified of doing or saying something that would scare him off.

"I just don't know what he wants," she said with a sigh.

Tony frowned. "It's really not fair of the guy to keep you in limbo like this."

She couldn't help coming to Jared's defense. "He's never made any promises, Tony. Nor have I asked for any. I simply offered him a place to stay while Shane recuperated, and he accepted."

"Something tells me you're giving him a hell of a lot more than a place to stay."

Cassie flushed. "Really, Tony."

"Yeah, I know. None of my business. I just don't want to see you get hurt, Cassie."

"Neither do I," she admitted, pushing a strand of hair out of her face. "But I still can't help hoping…"

It wasn't necessary for her to finish the sentence.

Tony's scowl deepened, but he kept his opinions to himself. "Michelle's looking forward to having everyone for dinner tonight."

"Shane's been talking about it all week. I promised to hurry home so we won't be late."

"Maybe Jared will tell us his plans sometime during the evening."

"Just don't push him, okay, Tony?" Cassie asked carefully. "I don't want to make him feel cornered."

Tony muttered something beneath his breath, then sighed and promised Cassie he'd try not to say anything that would embarrass her in front of Jared. "It's just that I can't help feeling a bit big-brotherly with you," he added.

She smiled and reached up to kiss his cheek, the first time she'd dared such a familiarity with her boss. "Thanks for caring, Tony. See you tonight."

Cassie took great pains with her appearance for the evening, selecting a deep emerald dress that had always been one of her favorites and taming her curls into a more sophisticated style than the casual brushing she usually gave them. She even wore a touch of eyeliner, something she rarely bothered with when she applied her usual light makeup.

Shane whistled when Cassie joined him and Jared in the living room. "Wow, Cassie. You really do have legs, don't you?"

Cassie realized it was the first time he'd seen her in a dress. She tended to wear jeans and sweaters at home, slacks and blazers for work. She ruffled Shane's hair. "Of course I have legs."

"Very nice ones, at that," Jared added, giving Cassie a smile that made her breath catch in her throat.

"Thank you," she managed to reply.

Shane grinned.

Both Jared and Shane wore slacks and oxford-cloth shirts.

They'd been to the doctor that day, and Jared's stitches had been removed, leaving only a thin red scar at his temple. Cassie assured them they looked very handsome, though she knew she was understating. Even with their scars and fading bruises, Jared and Shane were a strikingly attractive pair. Any woman would be proud to be seen with them, she thought with a wistful longing.

"Now that we've all admired each other, I guess we'd better go," Jared announced, his smile fading.

Cassie looked up at him in question. "You don't sound like you're looking forward to the evening."

He shrugged. "Family dinners aren't really my thing."

"How would you know, Dad?" Shane asked logically. "We've never really been to any."

Jared didn't acknowledge that the boy had made a point.

Both Jared and Shane were startled when Cassie drove her car through the gates of what could only be called a Tudor mansion half an hour later.

"What's this place?" Shane asked from the back seat, craning his neck to stare at the massive stone fence surrounding them.

"This is where Michelle and Tony live," Cassie explained, bringing the car to a stop in the circular driveway. A flight of stairs led from the driveway to massive double doors at the entryway of the house, which looked to Jared to be at least fifteen thousand square feet.

He hadn't been prepared for the elegance of his sister's home.

Jared climbed out of the car and glanced around the beautifully lighted and landscaped grounds. "You didn't tell me your boss came from this kind of money," he muttered when Cassie stood beside him.

"He doesn't. This is the home where Michelle grew up. The Trent family home. It's been hers since her parents died."

Jared looked down at her with narrowed eyes. "Michelle's adoptive parents were wealthy?"

"I told you they were quite comfortable," Cassie reminded him.

"You didn't say they were filthy rich," he answered bluntly.

"Not filthy, maybe, but definitely rich," Cassie confirmed. "Trent Enterprises is one of the largest corporations in the area. They're into everything."

"Damn." Jared shoved his hand through his hair, wishing he were anywhere but here. He'd have avoided a hell of a lot of trouble if he'd just gone on to Flagstaff last week instead of following Cassie to Dallas, he thought grimly. He supposed he was paying the price for thinking with his gonads instead of his brains again.

He hadn't seen his sisters since Shane was released from the hospital on Monday, though they'd both called Cassie's place every day to check on the boy. He had begun to feel comfortable with them, but now he was tense again, a touch defensive. What the hell were they expecting from him?

He sensed something was wrong the moment Michelle's housekeeper led them into the enormous wood-panelled den where his family awaited them. Both Michelle and Layla welcomed Jared with strained smiles and troubled eyes.

What had upset them? he wondered, frowning as he studied the other occupants of the room. He recognized Tony, of course. A rounded, pleasant-faced man of his own age was introduced as Layla's husband, Kevin Samples. Jared shook the man's hand, liking the guy right off. He'd already been told Kevin was an accountant. He could tell now that the man was quiet, unassuming, and absolutely adored his wife and three kids.

Layla's children were brought forward next to be introduced. Jared couldn't help smiling when he saw them—eight-year-old Dawne, five-year-old Keith and two-year-old Brittany. They reminded him so much of himself and his own brothers and sisters at the same age.

He gave Layla a smile of approval, noting in amusement that Shane seemed particularly fascinated with the children, who looked at their wounded older cousin with wide-eyed awe.

And then Michelle turned toward an older man standing to one side of the room, and Jared knew that he'd found the source of the tension humming beneath the polite pleasantries.

"Jared, Shane, Cassie, I'd like you to meet my uncle, Richard Trent, who lives in California. Uncle Richard popped in unexpectedly to visit me this afternoon, and I asked him to join us for dinner so he could meet everyone," Michelle explained.

Richard Trent, a tall, distinguished-looking man in his late fifties to early sixties, nodded at Cassie and Shane, then turned to Jared. The suspicion in the older man's eyes had Jared going on the defensive before Trent even spoke. "I understand you've had a run of bad luck since you came to town."

Jared nodded. "A car accident. As you can see, my son was injured, but we were lucky, on the whole."

"Where do you and your son live, Walker?"

Jared crossed his arms, trying to look relaxed. "We spent the past year in Oklahoma, but we're in the process of relocating."

"Oh? To where?"

"We haven't decided," Jared answered smoothly.

Trent lifted an eyebrow. "Just what is it you do?"

Though he would have thoroughly enjoyed telling the man it was none of his business, Jared forced himself to be polite, for his sister's sake. "Ranch work, mostly."

As though sensing the antagonism between Jared and the older man, Shane spoke up quickly. "Dad and me are going to own a ranch someday. Quarter horses and polled Herefords. We're saving up for a down payment."

Jared gave his son a repressive frown. He'd taught the boy not to discuss their business with strangers. This was a hell of a time for Shane to forget that.

"I didn't know you were interested in owning a ranch, Jared," Layla said, her voice just a bit too bright. "But it doesn't surprise me. Even when you were a little boy, you loved horses and cowboy movies."

"I like cowboy movies, too," little Keith piped in, tugging at Shane's leg as he spoke. "Like *Fievel Goes West*. You ever see that one, Shane?"

The adults laughed—all of them except Jared and Richard Trent.

"So, just how were you planning to finance your ranch, Walker?" Trent murmured, glancing meaningfully at the luxury surrounding them. "Bank loan? Or did you have some other scheme in mind?"

Michelle gasped. "Uncle Richard! That's really none of our business."

Trent feigned surprise that she'd be annoyed with him. "I'm a businessman, Michelle. I'm sure your brother understands that businessmen are always interested in hearing the plans of aspiring entrepreneurs."

"Oh, I understand," Jared replied, his narrowed eyes locked with Trent's speculative ones. "I understand completely."

Layla slipped to Jared's side, placing a hand on his arm as though to offer support—or perhaps to hold him back.

"So that's how you've built up these muscles," she said, still a bit too cheerily. "All that hard ranch work. I see you're still living up to your line of the poem, Jared."

He looked at her in question. "What poem?"

"Surely you haven't forgotten," Layla chided. Michelle smiled, obviously understanding the reference. "Don't you remember that all seven of us were born on different days of the week? You were Saturday's child. And Saturday's child has to work for a living."

Jared remembered now. Their mother had been particularly taken with that little poem, quoting it to them often. A wave of sadness went through him as he pictured her, thin and tired, rocking the baby and reciting the verses. He suppressed it immediately, deciding he'd blocked the memory because it had been easier to do that than to live with the old pain.

"What about you, Aunt Layla?" Shane urged, visibly intrigued by this glimpse into his father's childhood. "What day were you born?"

"Monday's child," Jared murmured, still lost in the past. He gave Layla a slight smile. "'Monday's child is fair of face.'"

Layla flushed in pleasure. "You *do* remember."

"Yeah." His smile faded. "I remember."

Shane frowned suddenly. "I thought two of the brothers were twins."

Layla tore her understanding gaze from Jared's. "Strangely enough, Joey was born just before midnight on Thursday, and Bobby just after midnight Friday morning. They have different birthdays."

"Cool!" Shane responded and laughed.

Richard Trent glanced at his watch, quite obviously bored by the reminiscences of a family in which he had no part. "Do you suppose your housekeeper is ready to serve dinner, Michelle?"

Michelle's smile faded. "I'm sure she is. Shall we go into the dining room now?"

As the others left the den, Tony detained Jared with a hand on his arm.

"Try not to let Trent get to you," he muttered. "He thought I was after Michelle for her money, too. He's definitely the suspicious type, but he and his wife and son are the only members left of Michelle's adopted family. It's hard for her to sever all ties to them."

"Yeah," Jared growled. "For her sake, I'll try to ignore him. But what I'd really like to do is knock that smug smile right off his face."

Tony chuckled. "Believe me, I know the feeling. If he weren't Michelle's uncle, I probably would have already tried a time or two."

Feeling rather friendly toward his brother-in-law at the moment, Jared nodded and walked with him into the dining room, his scowl returning when he saw the crystal chandeliers and elegant table settings. He noted that Michelle seemed perfectly comfortable that Layla's three children scrambled into chairs at the long table, apparently as welcome there as the adults, despite the quelling looks Richard Trent gave them.

Thanks to the children, conversation was quite lively while Betty served the meal. Sitting between Shane and Jared, Cassie joined in easily, obviously doing her part to keep the evening pleasant.

Jared found himself unable to participate, except to answer direct questions. His full attention was centered on Richard Trent, who continued to watch Jared with a mixture of suspicion and disapproval. If this was the way Michelle had been treated as she'd grown up, he thought at one point, it was no wonder that there were old shadows behind the present contentment in her eyes.

"I like your house, Aunt Michelle," Shane said, obviously happy with the evening thus far. "It must have been cool growing up here."

"Thank you, Shane. It was a happy home," Michelle replied. Then she added softly, "Though I would have loved to have had my brothers and sisters with me. It was rather lonely at times, being an only child."

"My brother and his wife did their best to give you every-thing you wanted while you were growing up, Michelle," Richard chided her.

"Yes, of course, they did," Michelle answered evenly. "But, like most children, I longed for playmates."

"I'm sure you had your friends," Richard argued. "Your parents hardly kept you a prisoner here. Though they were, of course, careful to screen the people you associated with. When one has attained a certain level of wealth and power, it is always prudent to watch out for those who would take ad-vantage of you. After the unfortunate incident in your child-hood, I would think you'd understand why Harrison and Alicia were rather overprotective afterward."

Jared noted that Michelle paled in reference to the "unfor-tunate incident." He ran his eyes quickly around the table, judging for himself who else understood the reference. Tony looked grim, Cassie annoyed, Layla stricken, Kevin sympa-thetic. Apparently, Jared was the only adult who *didn't* know.

"What unfortunate incident?" he asked bluntly, sensing that whatever it was would explain a great deal about Mi-chelle's occasional haunted looks.

Silence greeted the question, except for little Brittany's babbling from the booster chair next to her mother. Knowing who'd be most likely to give him a direct answer, Jared looked to Tony. "Well?"

Tony glanced at the children, and Layla distracted them by turning their attention to their dinners. "Michelle was kid-napped when she was eight years old," he said quietly. "Her father hired my dad, who was also a P.I. at the time, to find her. He did, and the kidnapper was arrested without incidence."

Kidnapped. Jared set his fork on his plate, losing interest in his food. He looked at Michelle, thinking she suddenly looked very young and vulnerable. "You weren't harmed?"

"No," she answered. "Only horribly frightened. The incident left me wary of trusting people, but Tony helped me get past that." She gave her husband a loving smile, her uncle a quick frown of reproval, and then smoothly changed the subject, asking Shane about his arm.

Shane, whose mouth had fallen open in shock at the story, reassured her that he wasn't in terrible discomfort, then made everyone laugh with his self-directed humor about the difficulties of eating with his left hand. Jared was proud of the boy for sensing that laughter was desperately needed at the moment.

Laughter was the farthest thing from Jared's mind just then. The thought of his younger sister in the hands of a kidnapper made him want to tear someone apart with his bare hands.

Realizing that his feelings were both protective and possessive, he almost sighed. Despite his attempts to maintain his distance from his sisters, he'd already started to care for them again.

A bond had been formed—or maybe it had always been there, only to be rediscovered with their reunion. No matter how far Jared would travel from them now, he'd always know that his family was here—and he'd want to see them occasionally, to know how they were. Just as he found himself wanting to know what had happened to the twins and the baby.

He picked up his fork again and let the conversation flow around him, too deeply lost in his own thoughts to care any longer about whether Michelle's uncle suspected him of being an opportunist who was only after his wealthy sister's money. Jared had more important things to worry about now.

Like what the hell he was going to do with the rest of his life, now that Cassie and his sisters had come into it. And whether those imaginary bonds were suddenly growing so tight that he would never be able to escape them, even if he wanted to do so.

Chapter Thirteen

Cassie excused herself after dinner, visiting the elegantly appointed guest bathroom to touch up her lipstick and give herself a moment to relax in private. Jared's tension had conveyed itself to her, and she'd already been nervous about spending the evening with his family.

She hadn't socialized much with her employer and his wife before. And then, there was the additional pressure of knowing everyone there was aware that she and Jared had become lovers within days of meeting each other. She'd caught more than one speculative glance during the evening and knew the others were wondering where her relationship with Jared was headed.

She only wished she could have given them an answer.

She didn't mean to eavesdrop on Michelle's parting with Richard Trent. Cassie had just approached the foyer through which she'd have to pass to reach the den when she heard their voices. She paused, uncertain whether she should intrude.

"Are you sure you want to make this choice, Michelle?" she heard Richard Trent asking, his tone so stuffy and censorious that Cassie's lip curled involuntarily.

Michelle's voice was sad when she answered. "You're the one who's making the choice, Uncle Richard, by putting it that way. You're the one who can't accept that I needed to find my brothers and sisters, that the Trent money doesn't mean as much to me as having my family with me."

"You know your aunt and I wanted you to come stay with us in California after your mother passed away," Trent reminded her coolly. "You had a family."

"Please, let's be truthful with each other just this once. You never really accepted me as a Trent, Uncle Richard. To you, I was always the mongrel child your brother adopted. You made the offer for me to come live with you only because of some misguided sense of responsibility to my father, not because you love me."

"So, you've chosen this group of strangers over the only family you've known since you were two years old."

"To be honest, Uncle Richard, you're much more of a stranger to me now than anyone else here tonight. I'm sorry, but that's the way I feel."

"Then I wish you joy with them," he replied icily. "And if you really trust that drifter of a brother of yours, then you have less sense than I'd credited you with."

"Please excuse me, Uncle Richard," Michelle said in a voice that shook with anger. "I have to get back to my family now."

"Goodbye, Michelle."

"Goodbye, Uncle Richard. Please give my best to Aunt Lydia and Steven."

Cassie heard the door close with a final-sounding snap. Richard Trent had obviously said all he'd intended to say. Biting her lip anxiously, she stepped into the foyer, concerned about Michelle, furious about Trent's implications regarding Jared.

Michelle looked up when Cassie approached. Her blue eyes, so like Jared's, were dark with pain and regret.

"I'm sorry," Cassie said quickly. "I didn't mean to eavesdrop, but I couldn't help overhearing part of that. Are you all right?"

Michelle sighed faintly and nodded. "I'm fine. I was never close to him, but…well, he was my adoptive father's brother. And I loved my father very much."

"I'm sorry," Cassie repeated.

Michelle tossed her head and forced a smile. "Don't be. I have Layla and her family now and, thanks to you, my brother and my nephew. As well as a husband who loves me almost as much as I adore him. I couldn't possibly ask for more."

Cassie fought down an unbecoming ripple of envy at the obvious love and security Michelle had found with Tony. Would Cassie ever know that contentment with Jared? She knew he'd thoroughly spoiled her for any other man.

Cassie had always suspected that there would be only one great love in her life, and Jared was the one. But did he—*could* he—ever feel the same way about her?

She tried to keep her worry hidden as she accompanied Michelle into the den to rejoin the others.

Cassie could tell that the others were as relieved as she that Richard Trent had departed, taking his suspicions and his disapproval with him. Shane took one long look at Michelle and began to entertain her with a series of silly jokes that soon had his younger cousins squealing with laughter while the adults looked on with indulgent amusement.

Cassie watched Shane with a deep, warm pride, knowing

he was exerting himself to make Michelle smile because he'd sensed his aunt's distress over Richard Trent's behavior. Shane was such a loving, caring, perceptive boy, she mused. It would break her heart for him to leave her life almost as much as it would if Jared chose to do so.

She watched Jared closely during the remainder of the evening, noting that he was pleasant and polite, talking easily enough to Tony and Kevin, reminiscing a bit with Layla. Yet in some way Jared held himself apart from the others, almost like an observer rather than a participant in the activities. He'd relaxed some since Trent's departure, but his eyes were guarded, his smile not quite natural.

Cassie knew him well enough to be aware that something was bothering him. Boredom? Restlessness? Defensiveness?

Unfortunately, she didn't know how to interpret his mood—he'd never allowed her to get quite that close to the darker, deepest part of him.

Close—but not close enough. Would she always feel that way with him? Would he ever learn to open up to her—or even want to try?

She knew she couldn't go on much longer in limbo. Soon she would have to ask Jared about his plans, put an end to her agonizing over the possibilities.

She'd never considered herself a coward, but she was terrified at the thought of initiating a confrontation that could send Jared away from her.

Seemingly oblivious for once to Cassie's tension and Jared's remoteness, Shane chattered contentedly from the back seat on the way back to Cassie's place, pronouncing himself pleased with the evening, on the whole.

"Michelle's uncle is a jerk, isn't he? No wonder she was so happy to find her real family, if that's all she had before.

Everyone else was great—Aunt Layla and Kevin and the kids, I mean. Aren't they?"

"They're very nice," Cassie agreed when Jared didn't say anything. "I met them for the first time at Michelle and Tony's wedding."

"Did you meet Tony's family, too? The Italian ones?"

"Dozens of them," Cassie answered with a slight smile. "I don't remember all the names, but they're a close, boisterous, very friendly clan. Tony's crazy about them."

"Michelle was telling me how much fun they have at family gatherings," Shane explained. "She said they're having a barbecue next weekend and I can go with her and Tony, if I want, to meet some of the cousins my age. I'll still be in this stupid cast, of course, so I can't play softball with them, but it would be fun to meet them. She said some of them even go to the same school that Heather and Scott go to—I'm going to ask if they know any kids named D'Alessandro. It's okay with you if I go to the barbecue, isn't it, Dad?"

Cassie almost held her breath at the question, staring fiercely ahead as she drove, though most of her attention was on Jared.

"I don't think you'd better be making plans for next weekend, son," Jared answered quietly. "The doctor said today that you're up to traveling again if we take it easy. I made a couple of calls this afternoon. The job in Arizona's still open, but it won't be much longer. If I'm going to take it, we need to head that way in a couple of days. We should be able to pick up our new truck Monday afternoon, so we can leave anytime after that."

Cassie's fingers tightened on the steering wheel until her knuckles shone white. She clenched her jaw to keep from begging Jared not to go. She sensed him watching her and made a massive effort to keep her face expressionless.

Shane was quiet for a long, taut moment. And then he

spoke, sounding for the first time since Cassie had known him like a rebellious teenager. "I don't want to go to Arizona."

"Maybe we'd better talk about this later," Jared said, realizing that Cassie's car was hardly the place to conduct such an important discussion.

"Fine," Shane replied flatly. "But I don't want to go to Arizona. I like it here. You've always talked to me before you made decisions like this."

"Dammit, Shane, I have to work!" Jared snapped, making both Cassie and Shane jump at the sudden vehemence of his voice. Almost as though the frustration that had been seething inside him for the past week had suddenly boiled over. "We can't go on sponging off Cassie forever."

"You're not sponging off me," Cassie pointed out carefully. "You've bought groceries and supplies, and helped out a lot around the house. I've enjoyed having you both stay with me."

"We've invaded your home and your privacy," Jared returned. "I'm sure you're ready to get your life back to the way it was before you met us."

"No," she whispered, seeing the road ahead through a thin film of tears. "I'm not ready for that at all."

An uncomfortable silence reigned in the small car during the next ten minutes, until Cassie parked in her assigned space and turned off the engine. Shane opened his door first, flooding the interior with light. Without looking at Jared, Cassie peeled her uncooperative fingers off the steering wheel and reached for her purse.

Jared got out of the car slowly, then stood on the sidewalk staring toward Cassie's apartment without moving.

"Jared?" Cassie asked. "Aren't you coming in?"

He didn't quite meet her eyes. "I think I'll take a walk," he murmured. "I'm not ready to go in just yet."

"I'll walk with you," she offered, moving toward him.

He stopped her with a shake of his head. "If you don't mind, I'd really like some time to myself."

Cassie bit her lip and nodded. "Be careful," she couldn't help saying as she stepped back.

"I won't end up in jail this time," Jared replied, turning away. "Don't wait up."

Cassie and Shane stood side by side on the walkway as Jared strode briskly away, disappearing into the darkness beyond the security lights.

For the boy's sake, Cassie shook herself out of the threatening depression. "We'd better go in. It's getting late."

Shane nodded glumly and turned with her toward the apartment. He'd almost stopped limping during the past day or so; now Cassie noticed that the limp was back. As though he were suddenly too dispirited to master it.

She felt obligated to try to cheer Shane up. Closing the apartment door behind them, she tossed her purse on a chair. "Would you like a soft drink or anything?"

He shook his head, his good hand buried in the pocket of his jeans, his expression as closed as Jared's had been earlier. "No, thanks. I think I'll turn in. I'm kind of tired."

Her heart twisted at his obvious unhappiness. She put a hand on his arm, feeling the tension radiating from his slender body. "Shane, your father didn't mean to hurt you. He's just feeling…pressured, I think. So much has happened to him this past week. Surely you understand that."

Shane nodded reluctantly. "I know. But, jeez, Cassie, why's he still planning on leaving? I mean, I know why he left my mom—they were miserable together and she didn't want him to stay. But his sisters want him here. We don't know anyone in Arizona, don't have anyone who gives a darn about us there. Why would we want to leave here to go there?"

Cassie weighed her words carefully, trying to defend Jared

when what she really wanted to do was agree wholeheartedly with Shane. "Your father is a very proud man, Shane. You know that."

"Yeah. What's that got to do with anything?"

"It bothers him that he doesn't have a job now, that he feels...well...dependent on me. And he's worried about getting you back into school."

"There are jobs here," Shane argued. "And schools. Heather and Scott really like their school. I could go there."

"And maybe you will," Cassie reassured him, though she didn't want to raise false hopes. In either of them. "Your father just needs a little time to sort out his feelings. Maybe you'd better not push him right now, Shane."

"I'll try," Shane conceded with a sigh. "But I'm not just moving to Arizona without telling him the way I feel about it."

"I'm sure he doesn't expect you to."

Shane studied Cassie's face with an intensity that made her rather self-conscious.

"Cassie? Do you want us to go?" he asked hesitantly, as though he worried about her answer, but had to know.

"Oh, Shane." Her eyes filled with tears again, despite her effort to hold them back. She put her hands on his shoulders and held his gaze with her own. "Of course I don't want you to go. I love having you here, both of you."

His eyes sparked with hope. "You do?"

"Yes. I've been very happy these past few days. I would miss you terribly if you leave."

"We've been like a family, you know?" he asked wistfully. "I was kind of hoping to make it permanent."

She almost moaned at hearing her own thoughts put into words. But she had to make him understand that she and Jared had to work out their relationship in their own way, and that in this area at least, Shane didn't really have a vote.

"Shane, I don't know what's going to happen, what your father will choose to do. But you have to know that he loves you more than anything else in the world and that he doesn't want to hurt you. Whatever he decides, it will be because he thinks it's best for both of you. You've always trusted him before, haven't you?"

Shane nodded, chewing his lower lip.

"Then trust him now. He needs to know you're on his side, Shane."

Shane exhaled gustily. "I'll think about what you said."

It wasn't a surrender, and they both knew it. But Cassie told herself she'd done all she could do for now. The rest was between Jared and his son.

She and Jared had their own problems to face.

It took Jared two attempts to fit his key into Cassie's door. Scowling, he let himself in, moving with exaggerated stealth. It was late—after 1:00 a.m.—and he was sure Shane and Cassie were both sleeping. He didn't want to wake them.

He was tempted to stretch out on the living room couch and allow himself the escape of sleep. He was tired of thinking tonight, tired of old memories and frustrating indecisiveness. Tired of remembering the way Cassie and Shane had looked when he'd walked away from them earlier.

Without consciously deciding to do so, he found himself standing outside Shane's room. He opened the door quietly and looked inside. As he'd expected, Shane was sleeping, sprawled bonelessly in the tangled sheets of the daybed, his cast gleaming white in the shadows. Had he gone to sleep still angry with his father?

Jared sighed soundlessly and closed the door. He glanced across the hallway. Even as he told himself not to risk waking Cassie, he found himself walking that way, needing to look at her as he'd needed to see his son.

He hadn't expected to find Cassie's bed empty. He whipped his head around to find her sitting in the big wooden rocker she kept in one corner of the room, her knees pulled up beneath the cotton nightgown that was all she wore as she looked at him from the shadows.

"I thought you'd be asleep," he said awkwardly.

"No."

Jared cleared his throat and shoved a hand through his hair. "It's late. You shouldn't have waited up for me."

"I couldn't sleep."

He wished she wouldn't sit so still, looking so small and vulnerable in the big chair. He was more comfortable with the Cassie who'd jumped fearlessly into a fight with three drunks than with this one, who could so easily be hurt by his clumsiness.

He wasn't sure he'd ever be able to forgive himself if he hurt Cassie.

She represented everything he'd spent the past decade avoiding: commitment, trust, marriage, maybe more children—a lifetime of responsibilities. Making himself vulnerable to someone again, risking the devastating pain of loss through death or disillusionment.

Almost losing Shane in the car accident had all but brought Jared to his knees. Wasn't it enough that there was already one person who meant so damned much to him?

Unable to think of anything to say, Jared took a step forward, cursing beneath his breath when he stumbled over a shoe.

"You've been drinking." Cassie sounded more as though she were making an idle observation than passing judgment.

Jared shrugged. "Yeah. I had a few beers at that yuppie bar a few blocks away from here."

"Did it help?"

"No," he admitted, thinking of his ex-wife's endless quest for peace of mind through alcohol. "It never does."

"Would you like to talk about it?"

"About what?" he asked, knowing as he spoke that he was stalling.

"About whatever is bothering you so badly," she answered patiently.

He dropped to the edge of the bed, his hands clasped loosely between his knees. "I don't know what to say."

"You could start by telling me what you're feeling right now," she suggested, her voice little more than a whisper from the shadows.

Jared stared at his hands. He'd spent so many years repressing his feelings that he wasn't sure he even knew how to identify them now. "I'm not very good at that sort of thing."

"At having feelings, or discussing them?" Cassie asked with just a touch of sympathetic humor.

His mouth twitched in what might almost have been a smile. "Take your pick."

Cassie hesitated a moment, then left the rocker to walk slowly toward him. "Why don't I help you out a little. I'll name some emotions, and you tell me if they apply."

He watched her warily. "I don't think that's—"

"Angry," she said, ignoring his objection.

He shook his head. "I'm not angry."

She came to a stop less than two feet away from him, her bare feet curled into the carpet, her hands clasped loosely in front of her, her glorious hair hanging loose around her shoulders. "Bored."

"No," he murmured, staring at her, at the way the thin light coming through the window made her skin seem as translucent as fine china. "Not bored."

"Depressed."

His body stirred, reacting forcefully to the hint of nipples and the triangle of dark hair just visible through the thin white cotton of her nightgown. "No."

"Frightened?"

He wanted her so badly it scared him to his toes. "Maybe."

She reached out to stroke his hair, her touch so light he hardly felt it. "Trapped."

His throat tightened. "Yeah."

Her hands were cool, soft when she cupped his face between them and leaned toward him. "You know your problem, Jared Walker?"

He knew his problem, all right. He was a hair's breadth away from attacking her, having her on her back beneath him before she could blink twice.

He tried to concentrate on what she was saying. "What do you think my problem is, Cassie?"

"It's been so easy for you to walk away before now," she answered quietly, holding his eyes with her own. "You were taken from your real family when you were eleven, and your one attempt at making a new family seemed to fail when your marriage ended. After that, you made it a habit to leave when things got sticky, to avoid entanglements of any kind. Shane did the same when he ran away from home two years ago.

"Since then, the two of you have had each other, but you've been on the move, never staying anyplace long enough to put down roots. You're feeling trapped now because you know it won't be so easy to leave this time. Shane wants to stay. Your sisters want you to stay. I want you to stay. Now you have to decide what *you* want. And that scares you, because it means making a commitment of some sort. One way or another."

"I'd stick to P.I. work if I were you," Jared said stiffly, his stomach clenching in reaction to her accusations. "You'd never make it as a shrink."

She didn't seem to take offense, at his words or the curt tone in which he'd spoken. "Are you saying I'm wrong?"

"I'm saying you don't know what the hell I'm feeling," he answered roughly.

"So tell me," she dared him. "What are you feeling, Jared?"

Without giving her warning, he tumbled her to the bed, then stretched out on top of her, his hips flexing to make her fully aware of the erection straining against his zipper.

"Now see if you can guess what I'm feeling," he muttered, his hands tangling in her hair.

If he'd thought to intimidate her, he realized immediately that it hadn't worked. Cassie simply twined her arms around his neck, bringing her mouth close to his.

"You want me," she whispered, her breasts brushing his chest, her soft legs shifting to better accommodate him.

"Yes," he growled, lowering his head to hers. "Yes, dammit."

He crushed her mouth beneath his with a hunger that felt too soul-deep to ever be thoroughly satisfied, no matter how many times he might have her. Cassie opened to him with such eager participation that he felt himself tremble in reaction. How could she keep giving so much of herself when both of them knew how easily he could hurt her, how very likely it was that he would?

He counseled himself to go slowly, to keep his touch gentle, his desires reined. But the fires inside him only burned hotter when he tried to bank them, leaving his self-control in ashes. His hands and his mouth raced over her, greedy, desperate, demanding. Cassie made no effort to resist him, responding instead with a sweet passion of her own. He moved, she shifted with him. He took, she gave and then took for herself.

Jared shoved her nightgown out of his way and fastened

his mouth hungrily to her right breast, drawing the distended tip deep into his mouth. Cassie gasped and arched into him, her fingers clenching at his shoulders.

"Jared," she murmured, her voice little more than a broken sigh. "Oh, Jared."

He slid his fingers into the dark red curls between her thighs, finding the soft, swollen, love-damp flesh they protected. Cassie squirmed beneath his stroking, her breath catching, then shuddering out of her. His mouth at her throat, Jared slid two fingers deep inside her, his thumb making a slow, firm rotation.

"That's it, baby," he murmured when she bowed upward in reaction. "Let it happen."

Mindful of Shane sleeping across the hall, Jared covered Cassie's mouth with his own when she would have cried out with the first climax. He briefly regretted the need for quiet, wanting to hear the sounds he drew from her.

He hardly gave her time to catch her breath before he began again, tossing her nightgown aside, tearing at his own clothes until there was nothing left between them. Starting at her earlobe, he nibbled and tasted his way downward, leaving her breasts damp and swollen, her stomach quivering, her knees trembling.

Her toes clenched when he nipped at her ankles, then spread when he tasted the delicate arch of her foot. And then he shifted his attentions higher, making her dig her heels into the sheets and arch helplessly into his mouth as he gave her the most intimate kiss of all.

Cassie was trembling, her soft, supple skin covered in a film of perspiration. She whispered his name, pleaded with him to stop, then in the same breath begged him to go on. Her hands clenched in his hair, alternately tugging him away and then holding him closer. The second climax made her whimper.

Jared surged upward, thrusting inside her before the tiny convulsions ended, groaning when her inner muscles tightened around him. For the first time in over twenty-four years, he felt as though he'd found a place where he belonged. A home.

Cassie gathered him close, welcoming him to that warm, private place with a loving generosity that brought a hard lump to his throat. The last thread of sanity snapped, and he pounded into her again and again with a furious need that left him unable to slow down, unable to hold back anything from her.

Cassie wrapped herself around him and cradled him until the storm was spent, crooning endearments and encouragements, soothing him with her words, her tone, her body. Jared had never felt so deeply loved, so desperately needed. And even as he surrendered himself to a shattering orgasm that all but rendered him unconscious, he knew that he'd never been so humbled, nor so bone-deep scared of his feelings.

It was a very long time before he could make himself move. Even then, the most he could manage was to shift his weight off her, his arms tightening around her as he rolled to hold her against his heaving chest.

He felt the wetness on her cheeks and knew she was crying. He couldn't bring himself to ask her why, though he suspected she'd been as affected as he by the unprecedented intensity of their lovemaking. He was too damned close to tears himself to speak coherently. And, except for a moment of weakness the night Shane was hurt, Jared Walker hadn't cried in twenty-four years.

He knew when Cassie slipped into sleep, her cheek still damp against his shoulder. He cradled her closer, guarding her rest against anything that would hurt her. Himself included.

Nothing had ever been like that for him. The sensations had never been so intense, the need so great. No other woman's pleasure had ever mattered so much to him.

He stared blindly at the ceiling, wondering if he shoul sleep on the couch, after all. Knowing even as the though crossed his mind that he wouldn't be able to force himself to leave the woman who lay in his arms.

You're feeling trapped because you know it won't be s easy to leave this time, she'd said. And though he hadn't tol her, he'd known her words were the truth.

Walking away this time would probably be the hardes thing he'd ever done. But finding the courage to stay coul prove to be the toughest challenge he'd ever faced.

Chapter Fourteen

Cassie had promised Tony she'd work Saturday. She slipped away early, leaving Jared and Shane sleeping. Jared looked as though he'd gotten very little rest during the night. Usually a light sleeper, he didn't even stir when Cassie left.

As she guided her car out of the parking lot, Cassie wondered if she'd be able to accomplish anything at the office when her mind was so occupied with her worries about Jared. She was no closer now to knowing his plans, or believing he would be willing to stay with her. She'd waited up for him last night with a vague idea of confronting him, demanding that he make a decision and end the suspense.

But then he'd tiptoed into her room, looking so sad and lonely and tormented that all she'd wanted to do was hold him, love him, offer him a temporary refuge from the pain. And Jared had responded to her ministrations with such desperate intensity that she still felt dazed in the aftermath, her body pleasantly sore from his relentless lovemaking.

He loved her. Something deep inside her had to believe that he loved her, even as she reminded herself that he might never be able to tell her so. Maybe he'd never even be able to admit it to himself. But his actions had spoken so clearly what he couldn't say in words.

But even believing Jared loved her, Cassie didn't try to convince herself that he would stay with her. He'd spent too many years guarding his emotions, too many years protecting himself from vulnerability to change those habits overnight—or even in the traumatic, eventful nine days since she'd met him.

He needed time to come to terms with his past and his emotions, time to be convinced that his relationships weren't all doomed to failure. Time for Cassie to prove to him how deeply she loved him, that she would love him no matter what they faced in the future. And time was one of the things he didn't seem willing to give.

It wouldn't be easy for him to walk away, not now. But he could do it. Cassie suffered no delusions about the depth of Jared's fortitude. If he decided it would be better for himself and Shane to leave, he'd go with barely a backward glance at the people who loved him here. And he'd leave a hole in Cassie's life that she would never be able to fill, no matter how hard she worked, no matter how many men she might meet in future.

She braked for a red light, automatically taking care with her driving. And then she slammed her fist against the steering wheel.

"Damn you, Jared Walker! Why do you have to be so stubbornly self-sufficient? Why can't you understand how incredibly selfish you're being?"

But Jared wasn't there to hear, of course. Cassie wasn't sure he'd listen even if he were.

Jared was awakened by the sound of a low, hoarse groan. It took him a moment to realize the sound had come from his own dry throat.

Blinking against the full sunlight streaming through the bedroom window, he rolled onto his back, wincing as his body protested the movement. He hurt all over, not just his head, but all his muscles—as though he'd spent the night fighting packs of demons. Which, he supposed, he had.

He looked around the room for Cassie, then, slowly coming out of his disorientation, he remembered that she had to work today. Had she left for the office yet? A glance at the clock brought him fully awake. Hell, it was nearly noon! He hadn't slept that late since…he couldn't even remember the last time.

Scrubbing his hands over his bristled face, he sat nude on the edge of the bed, elbows on his knees.

Great, Walker. You're unshaven, you're hung over, you've lain in bed until noon like some sort of useless bum. Fine example for your son.

He stumbled into the bathroom and turned the shower on full pressure, as hot as he could stand it. He felt himself slowly coming back to life beneath the steaming force of it. He didn't leave the shower until the water ran cold.

The sight of his own face in the steam-fogged mirror over the sink nearly tore another groan from him. He looked like hell. Red-eyed, bearded, haggard. A good ten years older than thirty-five. If this was what a life of leisure did to him, then he'd damned well better get back to work soon. As soon as humanly possible.

He hid the lower half of his face beneath a coating of shaving lather and reached for his razor. He intended to make significant improvements in his appearance before facing his son. Thank God Cassie hadn't been there to see him wake up in the shape he'd been in. He wasn't sure his pride could have taken that.

Cassie. He cursed when just the thought of her made his hand jerk, drawing a scarlet drop of blood from his jaw.

What the hell was he going to do about Cassie? How could he ever forget her sweet generosity during the night? The loving, tender, uncritical way she'd welcomed him back into her bed even after he'd treated her so curtly when he'd left her standing on the sidewalk as he'd walked away.

And how could he ever make himself leave her, even though he had so damned little to offer her if he stayed?

Ignoring the fierce scowl of the reflection in the mirror, Jared finished his shaving, brushed his teeth and stamped into the bedroom to pull on clean clothes. It crossed his mind that the easiest thing to do would be to leave before she came home, be out of her life once and for all with no lingering farewells to torment either of them. But he knew he couldn't do that, either to Cassie or to Shane.

This time, Jared had to think of someone other than himself.

He'd expected to find Shane watching television or reading. Instead, he found a note on the kitchen table, telling him that Shane was having lunch with his friends Scott and Heather and would be staying at their place to watch movies afterward. Jared was alone with his grim thoughts for the next few hours, with no place to go and no way to get there if there had been.

His mood more savage than before, he opened a cabinet and reached for the coffee—the real kind, not the decaf Cassie usually made for herself. Today, he desperately needed the kick of caffeine.

* * *

Cassie looked away from her computer screen when a man's hand waved slowly in front of her eyes. "Tony? What are you doing?"

Her boss set a paper bag on her desk. "It's almost one. I've brought us some lunch."

"Oh. Thank you, but I'm not very hungry. I think I'll keep working on this—"

"Cassie," Tony interrupted firmly. "Did you have breakfast this morning?"

"Well, no," she admitted, "but—"

"Then eat. And that's an order from your employer. You're not going to be a lot of help to me this afternoon if you faint into your keyboard. And we've got a long day ahead of us yet."

She sighed and turned her chair away from the computer. "All right, I'll eat," she grumbled. "But I'm not at all sure this is in my job description."

"Sure it is," Tony answered cheerfully, pulling a chair close to the other side of her desk for himself. "It's right under the clause about catering to your boss's every whim. Fine print, of course."

"*Very* fine print, apparently."

"Right. Here, I brought you a diet cola to go with that."

She accepted the cold can with a nod of grudging gratitude, then unwrapped her sandwich with a marked lack of enthusiasm.

Tony took a big bite of his own sandwich and chewed slowly, his dark eyes never leaving her face. "You look like hell," he pronounced after swallowing.

She glared at him. "Thanks a lot."

"Did you and Jared have a fight?"

"No."

"A quarrel?"

"No."

"Do you want to talk about this?"

"No."

He frowned, looking as though there was something else he wanted to say. But then he relented. "All right. I won't push you. Much. I just want to remind you that I'm here if you need me."

"And I appreciate it," Cassie answered firmly, but with a faint smile. "This time, Tony, I have to handle my problems alone. This is between myself and Jared, and there's nothing you—or anyone else—can do to help. Okay?"

He nodded. "I should point out that you deserve this for breaking the rules and getting personally involved in a case. But since I'm such a good friend, I won't do that."

"Thanks," she answered wryly.

"You're sure you don't want me to go break the guy's arm or anything?"

Cassie was sorely tempted to let him do just that. She'd spent the morning fluctuating between aching sympathy for Jared and resentful anger with him for putting her through this. But, as she'd just told Tony, this was between herself and Jared. Not Tony or Shane or Michelle or Layla or any of the others who cared about them.

And, besides that... "He'd bash your head in," Cassie couldn't resist commenting. "Trust me."

Tony's left eyebrow shot upward. "You don't think I could take him?"

A reluctant smile tilted the corners of her mouth. "I think you'd put up a good effort," she said diplomatically. "But Jared would win. He's learned to fight dirty."

He'd had to, she thought wistfully. For so many years, there'd been no one else to fight for him. No one else who cared enough. And now it might be too late for him to trust that he didn't have to be alone anymore. That all he had to do was find the courage to reach out.

Jared had just finished his first cup of coffee and was pouring a second when the doorbell rang. Cassie wouldn't ring the bell, of course, but maybe Shane had forgotten the key she'd given him. Jared set his cup on the table and went to open the door.

He really hadn't expected to find his sister Michelle standing on the other side.

"Hello, Jared," she said when he only looked at her in surprise.

Annoyed with himself for his uncharacteristically slow reactions today, Jared forced a smile. "Hi. This is a surprise. Come on in."

"Thank you." She walked past him, glancing around the room with a discreet curiosity that let Jared know she'd never been there before.

"Have a seat," he offered, waving toward the couch. "Can I get you some coffee? I was just pouring myself a cup."

"Yes, that would be nice. Thank you."

"You take anything in it?"

"No. Just black, please."

He nodded and turned toward the kitchen, polite pleasantries out of the way. He couldn't help wondering why Michelle had come. Something about her expression had told him she wasn't just making a social call.

"I'm the only one here right now," he explained when he returned with their coffee. "Cassie's working and Shane's hanging out with some kids who live a couple of doors down."

"I knew Cassie was working today," Michelle admitted as Jared took a chair close to where she sat. "I was hoping for a chance to speak to you alone."

He saw the hint of nerves in her eyes and in the fine tremor in her hand when she held her coffee cup. "Relax, Shelley," he murmured, using the old name from half-forgotten habit. "I'm not going to bite."

She smiled, rather sheepishly, and set her cup and saucer on the coffee table. "I know. But I'm not sure how you're going to react to what I want to say."

Jared drained his coffee and set the cup aside. Was Michelle here to ask him to stay in Dallas? Or maybe to find out for herself if her adopted uncle's warnings had been necessary? "Might as well find out," he said bluntly. "What is it, Michelle?"

She took a deep breath. "First, I want to apologize for my uncle's behavior last night."

He shook his head. "That's not necessary."

"But it is. I thought if he met you for himself he'd understand that there was no need to worry about me. That you're too proud and honorable to pose the kind of threat Uncle Richard worried about."

"He couldn't know that," Jared felt compelled to point out. And then he added reluctantly, "You can't really be so sure of that, yourself, Michelle. You don't even know me."

"I know you," she answered evenly, her eyes meeting his without hesitation. "You're my brother, Jared. It's true that I don't remember much, if any, about the short time we had together as children. But I only had to spend a few hours with you to see that you're a good man, that you love your son very much, and that you have maybe too much pride for your own good."

His mouth quirked, but he nodded gravely. "Yeah. Maybe."

"Which is exactly why I'm nervous about the offer I'm about to make," she added quietly.

His eyes narrowed. "What offer?"

She wiped her hands on the legs of her pleated slacks, the

gesture very telling. Jared had spent enough time with her already to know that Michelle was usually utterly calm and composed, her elegant poise developed through years of practice.

"I want to offer you a loan, Jared," she blurted, then bit her lower lip in consternation, as if she regretted speaking so frankly.

"Thanks, but that's not necessary," he answered roughly, making a massive effort not to snap at her. He reminded himself that she was only trying to help, that she couldn't know how precarious his mood was today. "The insurance company is taking care of Shane's medical expenses, we're picking up a new truck on Monday, and I've got a job waiting for me in Arizona. I really don't need a loan."

Michelle made a sound of frustration and pushed a strand of fine brown hair away from her face. "I'm not handling this very well," she admitted. "I didn't mean I think you're in any sort of financial trouble. I know you're not."

She'd probably had her P.I. husband find out to the last penny every detail of his financial standing, Jared thought with a touch of resentment. Even after having over a week to get used to the idea, he still didn't like knowing that Tony and Cassie had methodically tracked him down through his records since childhood. "Right."

"Oh, Jared, please don't get defensive with me," Michelle said, reaching out to lay a hand on his knee. "I guess I'm not very good at this because I've never really had a family. I've been on my own for so long that I'm having to learn how to communicate with other people."

He could certainly identify with that. Had Michelle really been as lonely in her palatial home as he'd been in his far less glamorous surroundings?

He couldn't help softening, remembering the shock he'd felt at hearing about the trauma of her kidnapping. "I know your childhood wasn't an easy one, Michelle."

She shook her head impatiently. "No, that's not what I'm trying to say. I'm no poor little rich girl. Other than a few incidences, my childhood was quite pleasant. It was just that damned money—like a wall between me and my friends, between myself and anyone who could pose a threat to me. Potential boyfriends, employees, strangers. When I learned that I'd been raised in such luxury while my brothers and sisters had been given so little, I felt horribly guilty."

"You shouldn't have," Jared said, trying to keep his tone gentle. "Honey, it wasn't your choice. You were just a baby when we were split up."

"I know that, too. But I'd have traded all the money without hesitation for the chance to grow up with you and Layla and Miles and the twins and the baby."

The mention of Miles made Jared wince. He still hadn't quite accepted that his happy-go-lucky little brother would never be reunited with the rest of them. Would any of the others? "We can't go back and change the past, Michelle."

"No. But we can build a future. We don't have to repeat the mistakes of the past and let those old scars keep us apart now."

"I'm not doing anything to keep us apart," Jared said carefully. "Now that we've found each other again, I'll do my best to keep in touch. For my sake, and for Shane's. But I have to find my own way, Michelle. I have to work, find a place to live, get Shane back in school. The rest of you have lives. You've got to let me have mine."

"Which is why I'm here," Michelle hastened to assure him. "Shane said you and he have plans to own a ranch together."

He nodded warily. "Yeah. We've talked about it. I've been saving, but I don't have enough to make a start yet."

"And when you have enough, you plan to arrange for financing, right?"

"Yeah," he agreed. "But with a bank."

"Fine. Think of me as a bank. I can make you that loan, Jared. With interest and regular payments and legal papers drawn up by an attorney. Or we can arrange a partnership or a cosigning, or whatever you'd find most comfortable. This isn't charity, it's an investment on my part. Tony and I happen to think it's a shrewd one."

His head came up sharply. "You've discussed this with your husband?"

"Of course. Tony and I talk about everything together. When Shane mentioned your desire to own a ranch, Tony thought of one of his father's longtime friends. The man—Mr. McLaughlin—owns a small spread about thirty miles south of here. Mr. McLaughlin hasn't gotten wealthy from his operation, but he has made a good living, and the potential is there to expand and increase the profits.

"The problem is that he's getting older, and would like to retire with his wife to Florida, where their daughter lives. Tony had a cousin who thought about buying the ranch, but then changed his mind when he realized how much hard manual labor would be involved."

Jared was interested despite his reservations. Deeply interested. "I've never minded hard work," he muttered, thinking of how excited Shane would be at the very possibility of having their dream come true. A ranch. A home. No more life on the road.

The very thought of that sort of permanence made Jared break out in a cold sweat. Was that really what he wanted?

"I don't know, Michelle. I don't like the thought of being in debt to you."

She shrugged, a deliberate imitation of his habit. "You'd have to be in debt to someone to own a place like that," she pointed out. "At least in the beginning. I'm not asking for a decision now, Jared. I'd expect you to think about this, of course. Look the place over. Study your options. I just want you to know that this is a legitimate business offer, with no strings, no obligations."

"I don't want you to think I'm not grateful that you made the offer," he replied, covering her hand with his own. "It took a lot of trust for you and Tony to come to this decision. That means a lot to me."

"Does that mean you'll consider it?" she asked eagerly. "You won't turn us down without giving it any thought?"

"I'll think about it. But no promises."

"No," she agreed with a smile. "No promises. And thank you."

He quirked an eyebrow. "For what?"

"For not letting that stiff-necked pride of yours keep you from at least listening to me. I know you were tempted to tell me to butt out of your life."

He couldn't help smiling. "Maybe you are getting to know me fairly well."

"I'd like to get to know you better," she said softly.

"Yeah. Me, too." He squeezed her hand before releasing it. "Cassie told me Tony's making some more headway with the search for Lindsay, that he thinks there's real hope he should be able to contact her within the next few weeks. You think she'll be interested in meeting us, even though she couldn't possibly remember any of us?"

"Oh, I hope so," Michelle said sincerely. "I can't remember her, either, but she's still my little sister. I'd like very much to get to know her."

Relieved at the change of subject, Jared leaned back in his chair and listened with a faint smile as Michelle told him about her emotional reunion with Layla a few months earlier. As interested as he was in hearing the story, part of his mind was still occupied with Michelle's unexpected offer of a loan.

He had to admit that his first instinct had been to turn her down flat, thanking her politely, but firmly refusing to even consider the offer. And then he'd realized he'd been reacting more from pride than logic.

Would he have been so quick to turn her down if she had been nothing more than a banker making the same legitimate offer, rather than the little sister he hadn't seen in so many years? And had her offer really been based on a business decision, or did she think he needed this assistance to support himself and her nephew?

He had a great deal to think about now, some very important decisions to make. But he needed time alone to do so. He just wasn't sure how much time it would take, and whether he had any time to waste. The job in Arizona wouldn't be there indefinitely, and the ranch could be sold at any time if this McLaughlin was serious about retiring and moving away. His head began to ache all over again at this additional bit of pressure.

He was rather relieved that Michelle didn't linger long. Claiming that she had errands to run, she left with one last plea for him to think seriously about her offer before making any final decisions about leaving Dallas. Jared promised again that he would.

He surprised himself almost as much as Michelle when he impulsively kissed her cheek as he saw her out the door. Her eyes were misty when she left, the gesture obviously having touched her.

You're in too deep, Walker, Jared found himself thinking as he stood alone in the room after she left. *With Cassie, with Michelle. With all of them.*

So what the hell was he going to do about it?

Chapter Fifteen

Cassie was exhausted when she arrived home that evening, her weariness resulting from a combination of stress and the hours of hard work she and Tony had put in on a security report to be presented to a client on Monday.

She wasn't sure what to expect from Jared when they saw each other for the first time after the emotional night they'd shared. She certainly hadn't expected him to greet her with a distracted smile and the news that he and Shane were expecting a pizza delivery at any moment.

"Dad's acting a little weird today," Shane murmured, catching Cassie alone in the kitchen for a moment. "Like his mind's a million miles away. He's been that way ever since I got home from Heather and Scott's a few hours ago."

Did that mean Jared was planning to leave? Cassie couldn't help wondering, her stomach clenching in dread. Was he pulling back to prepare her for his departure?

Perhaps she was being paranoid—but she thought she had plenty of reason to be.

Cassie put an arm around Shane's shoulders and gave him a hug—as much for her own comfort as his. "He has a lot on his mind, Shane."

"Yeah," Shane muttered. "Don't we all?"

Cassie sighed. *How very true.*

The pizza arrived, a large-with-everything that they ate in near silence in front of the television, though none of them looked particularly interested in the fluffy sitcom they were watching. Cassie noted that neither Jared nor Shane cracked a smile at the inane jokes—nor, for that matter, did she.

The pizza, usually her favorite fast food, sat like lead in her stomach when she finished. The tension in the room had grown so thick she could almost touch it.

Shane helped Cassie clear away the debris with his one good hand, then shifted restlessly on his feet for a few moments before saying, "I think I'll go to my room and listen to some music."

"No." Jared spoke for the first time in quite a while, glancing up from the chair where he'd sat in brooding silence. "Turn off the television, son. We need to talk."

Cassie shifted in her own chair, glancing toward her bedroom. Did Jared want her to leave them in privacy?

As though reading her thoughts, he looked at her, his expression inscrutable. "This concerns you, too, Cassie."

Oh, God. His tone was so serious, his eyes so shuttered. He was going to tell her he was leaving, she just knew he was.

Oh, Jared, no. Don't leave me. Please.

Struggling to hide her panic, she clenched her hands in her lap and nodded with feigned composure. "All right."

Jared looked from Cassie to Shane, noting the tension that seemed to grip both of them. They sat in almost identical poses, shoulders braced, feet planted, eyes focused unwaveringly on his face. Both of them trying so desperately to look brave, when both were so obviously afraid of what he was going to say.

He swallowed hard, aware of the massive responsibility involved in having two people care so deeply about him.

He drew in a breath. "As Shane pointed out last night, I've gotten into the habit of discussing things with him before making decisions that affect our lives. We need to have one of those discussions now. There are several options open to us, and we need to choose."

"I know what *I* want," Shane muttered.

Jared held up a hand to silence him. "Wait, son. Let me have my say first."

Shane nodded with obvious reluctance.

Satisfied that Shane was listening, Jared continued. "Option number one—the job near Flagstaff is still open, still waiting for me if I choose to take it. It's a big ranch with living quarters, meals and insurance provided. The pay's good and there's a decent school close by."

"It sounds like a good opportunity," Cassie seemed compelled to comment.

Jared looked at her approvingly, pleased that she was trying to be objective. "It *is* a good opportunity," he agreed. "My friend Bob Cutter set it up for me or the ranch owner would never have been this patient about my answer."

"What's option number two?" Shane asked impatiently, the knuckles of his left hand white against the denim covering his thigh.

Jared cleared his throat. "Michelle came by to see me today. Her husband knows a man who owns a small ranch thirty miles south of here, and the guy wants to sell."

Shane's eyes lit up. "A ranch. Really?"

Again, Jared silenced him with an upraised hand. "Wait. I'm not through. I haven't seen the place, don't know anything about it except that Michelle told me it's turning a small profit. Nothing spectacular, apparently, though she thinks it has potential if it's managed right."

"We could make it work, Dad. Couldn't we?"

Jared couldn't quite meet Shane's hopeful eyes. "It's not that easy, son. For one thing, there'd be the investment of getting set up with the place. It would take everything we've got and then some just to get started. Could be several years before we saw any extra money out of the operation."

Cassie's voice was strained when she asked, "Do you— would you be able to make an offer on the place?"

The next part still bothered him, but he knew he had to tell them. "Michelle offered to make a loan for the down payment," he said quietly. "It would be legal and binding, with current interest rates and regular monthly payments, all the papers drawn up by an attorney. She and D'Alessandro are willing to be mortgage holders or partners, whichever we choose."

Both Shane and Cassie were quiet for a moment, as if stunned that Jared would even consider the offer. Cassie finally spoke, tentatively. "Michelle wouldn't have made the offer if she didn't think it was a worthwhile investment, Jared."

He nodded. "I know. At first I thought she was offering a handout, but she set me straight on that pretty quick. It's a legitimate offer."

"Does that mean you're going to take it?" Shane asked, hardly daring to speak out loud.

"There are still a lot of ifs involved," Jared warned. "The ranch may not be what we have in mind, the deal could fall through, the guy could change his mind about selling. And even if we did get the place, we could have a couple of bad years that could wipe us out entirely. We're talking about a big risk here. A lot of hard work. A lot of responsibility. If I sign papers and agree to the conditions of the loan, I can't just walk away from it if either of us gets tired of the work or the routines. You understand that, Shane?"

"I understand," Shane answered quietly, holding his chin at a steady angle that made him look so much older than his years. "We're talking about a total commitment."

"Yeah," Jared agreed. "Total. You'd have to concentrate as hard as ever on your schoolwork, of course, and God knows I'd still want you to have a normal social life, but there'd be chores to do and occasional emergencies to deal with, whatever plans you might have made. I'd still want you to go to college, but maybe by that time we'd be doing well enough to hire extra help to take up the slack while you were gone. I know this is what we've talked about, Shane, but this is reality, not some vague dream for the future. It won't always be fun and it will rarely be easy."

"Yeah, well, neither of us has ever expected life to be easy, have we, Dad?" Shane asked, meeting Jared's eyes as he spoke, fourteen years of difficult memories mirrored in his expression. "I'm willing to give it all I've got. If you are, of course."

Which brought Jared to the one question he had to know the answer to. Aware of Cassie listening so intently from her chair, he leaned forward and faced his son. "Shane, I know this is what you want. But what if it's not what *I* want? What if I tell you that I want to take the job near Flagstaff and that I plan to leave first thing Monday morning?"

Shane didn't even hesitate. "Then I'll start packing to go with you. We're a team, Dad. Where you go, I go."

Jared's breath left him in a soft whoosh as he realized that the bond between himself and his son hadn't been shaken by anything that had happened to them in the past few eventful days. Jared had needed to know that Shane's first loyalty still lay with him.

"What about you, Cassie?" he asked, swiveling his gaze to her. "What are you going to do if I head for Arizona in a couple of days?"

She was pale, but outwardly composed. She met his eyes without flinching. "I'll help you pack," she said. "And I'll kiss you goodbye. And then I'll probably end up following you again…unless, of course, you manage to convince me you don't want to see me anymore."

So this was love. Jared wondered why he'd ever thought it such a painful, frightening emotion.

He spoke past the lump in his throat. "You're taking an awfully big chance, you know."

Her eyes were damp, but steady. "Yes."

Had there ever been any other woman like this one? Jared shook his head in bemusement.

"I've never met anyone like you, never had anyone more willing to take risks for me. From trying to clear me of false charges to being ready to fight a group of drunken rednecks. You nagged me to be reunited with my family, and now you're apparently willing to walk away from your home and your job to be with me. Even with no promises, no guarantees."

Her smile was faint, but genuine. "Yes," she repeated.

"Maybe it's time I start taking a few chances myself," Jared said roughly, getting to his feet. "Come here."

Cassie was in his arms almost before he'd finished saying the words. He held her close, his head bent protectively over hers, his arms locked around her slender waist.

"You won't have to follow me anywhere," he muttered. "Like it or not, you're stuck with me now—with both of us.

So you'd damned well better not change your mind about wanting us."

"No," she whispered through her tears, wrapping her arms around his neck. "Oh, Jared, I'll never change my mind. I love you. Both of you."

He grabbed a handful of hair and tugged, tilting her face to his. "Turn around, Shane," he ordered just before crushing Cassie's mouth beneath his own.

"Yes, Dad," Shane replied, cooperating with a huge grin. Still turned away from them, he asked, "Does this mean we're buying the ranch?"

Jared tore his mouth from Cassie's long enough to answer. "We're a long way from buying the ranch," he warned, lost in the happy glitter of Cassie's brilliant green eyes. "But we're damned well going to take a look at it."

He tilted his head to kiss her from a new angle, unable to get enough of her taste—or the love he felt flowing from her.

"All right!" Shane rocked contentedly on his heels, then asked, still without looking around, "Think maybe we'll have some more kids? I'd kinda like a kid brother."

Jared choked against Cassie's sudden smile. Lifting his head again, he glared at Shane's back. "Don't push it, boy."

Shane's laugh blended with Cassie's. "Whatever you say, Dad," he replied agreeably.

"Go to your room."

"Yes, sir." Shane was whistling when he left. Though the tune was somewhat flat, it was easily recognizable. "The Wedding March."

Jared glared after the boy, then looked back down at Cassie in exasperation. "I do my own proposing," he growled.

She nodded, watching him expectantly.

He sighed. "Oh, hell. I don't have a damned thing to offer you, Cassie, but I'm asking you, anyway. Will you marry me?"

She touched his face with trembling fingers. "Don't you have anything to offer me, Jared?" she asked in an unsteady murmur.

"Only my heart," he answered gruffly, his cheeks warming as he struggled to verbalize his feelings for the first time in so very long. "I love you, Cassie. I have from the first time you visited me in that damned jail. And if you're willing to take one more chance on me, I swear I'll never give you cause to regret it."

"Oh, Jared." The tears that had brimmed in her eyes spilled onto her cheeks. "You've just given me everything I could ever ask of you."

"Does that mean you'll marry me?"

"Yes," she whispered, going up on tiptoe to press her mouth to his. "Yes, yes, ye—"

He smothered the rest with a heartfelt kiss that expressed all the emotion he couldn't put into words.

Epilogue

The third Saturday in October was warm and clear, to the delight of everyone who attended the party Michelle threw that afternoon on the beautifully landscaped lawn of the home she shared with her husband. It was an informal affair, the guests in jeans and sweaters, folding tables set up to hold sandwiches and snacks, canned soft drinks on ice in big barrels. Squealing children dashed around the legs of the adults, who carried on numerous noisy conversations sprinkled with laughter.

It was an interesting group, Cassie noted, standing to one side for a moment to watch the festivities. Most of the guests bore a distinctly Italian look, being members of Tony's huge family, but Layla and Kevin and their children were there, as well as Michelle's closest friend, Taylor Simmons, and of course, Jared and Shane. Yet, despite the disparities of background and interest, the guests mingled freely and easily, thanks in part to Michelle's excellent skills as a hostess.

Cassie smiled when Taylor Simmons approached her. They'd met a time or two before and she'd liked Michelle's dark-haired, smoke-eyed friend from the beginning, admiring Taylor's success as a fashion photographer and appreciating her dry humor.

"Taking a breather?" Taylor asked, leaning against the low brick wall behind Cassie.

Cassie nodded. "This group could wear you out in a hurry."

Taylor laughed and agreed. "Especially Tony's clan. Talk about energy!"

Cassie spotted Shane running across the lawn with two boys and a girl of approximately his age, Layla's smaller children following close behind. Shane had a week to go in his cast yet, but the broken arm wasn't slowing him down much. He'd fallen right in with Tony's young cousins, even seemed to be developing a crush on the pretty girl giggling with him now.

"They certainly know how to have a good time," Cassie remarked, still talking about the D'Alessandro family.

Taylor agreed again, her smile fading to a fond look as she glanced across the lawn to where Michelle chatted with Layla, and Tony's mother, Carla. "I'm so glad Michelle found Tony," Taylor mused. "I've never seen her this happy and outgoing, you know? She was so lonely before. And now that she's finding her own family, she's positively radiant."

Cassie smiled, thinking of the similar changes the past month had wrought in Jared. "Yes. They're all pleased to have found each other again after so many years."

"And speaking of which—that new husband of yours is one fine-looking man, Cassie. You were smart to snap him up so quickly, before the rest of us had a chance at him."

Cassie giggled, proudly twisting the week-old gold band on her left hand. She and Jared were guests of honor at this party, having just returned from a brief, but truly spectacular honeymoon. They'd had a small wedding, attended only by Jared's sisters and their families and Cassie's stunned, but delighted parents and grandmother. She'd only been disappointed that her brother hadn't been able to join them, though he had called and sent an extravagant gift, promising he'd see them at Christmas.

Cassie's family had been delighted with Jared, charmed by Shane, expressing their great relief that Cassie had finally found someone to marry. After meeting them, Shane had teased her mercilessly about her narrow escape from being a poor, lonely "old maid" until Jared had firmly put a stop to the jokes with a reminder that Shane should show respect for his new stepmother.

Shane had spent the past week with Michelle and Tony and, though he'd assured them he'd had fun, he was obviously looking forward to setting up housekeeping with his father and stepmother. He hadn't even complained about the tutor Jared had hired to catch him up on his studies, though he seemed eager to start classes at the school Jared had found for him close to the ranch they were still in the process of buying. The McLaughlin ranch had proven to be exactly what they'd hoped it would be, and all three of them were impatient for the legalities to be out of the way so they could set up housekeeping there.

"Don't expect me to apologize for snapping him up," Cassie teased Taylor, more content than she'd ever been in her life. "I'd have been a fool to let Jared and Shane get away once I found them."

Taylor heaved a deep, exaggerated sigh. "If you and Tony would hurry and find the twin brothers, maybe one of them will turn out to be my prince."

Cassie laughed and assured Taylor she'd do her best, though she felt a bit sorry for the other woman. Michelle had once mentioned that the true love of Taylor's life had died in a car accident just over a year ago. So blissfully in love herself, Cassie could imagine what a devastating experience that must have been for Taylor.

Jared joined his wife only moments after Taylor drifted away to chat with Michelle and Layla. Perceptive as always to Cassie's feelings, he tilted her chin with one finger and looked deeply into her eyes. "You look sad. What's wrong?"

Touched by his concern, Cassie wrapped her arms around his waist and hugged him. "I'm just sorry for anyone who doesn't have what we have. I love you, Jared."

Though he still hadn't quite grown accustomed to Cassie's open, generous affection, Jared willingly returned the hug before settling her within the curve of his arm, where they could watch the party together.

"I love you, too, you know," he commented after a moment, his gaze focused on Shane at play.

Cassie smiled smugly. "I know."

She rested her head on his shoulder. "How does it feel to be surrounded by so much family?" she asked curiously, thinking of what a short time had passed since it had been just Jared and Shane. Now Jared had a wife, in-laws, two sisters and their husbands, two nieces and a nephew, not to mention the missing family members still to be located.

Jared chuckled, obviously following her thoughts. "Different," he replied. And then, after a moment, "Nice."

"I'm glad."

Jared's arm tightened around her. "Cassie?"

"Hmm?"

"I want you to find my brothers. The twins, Joey and Bobby. I want to know what happened to them."

She lifted her head to look at him in surprise. "You know we've been looking for them all along."

"Yeah," he agreed, his expression grave, "but I'm only now coming to realize how much I want to see them again. Lindsay, too, once we find her. Family's important. They all need to know we're here if they want us or need us."

"Does this mean you're not interested in going back to that carefree bachelor life you led before?" Cassie asked, only half-teasingly.

"Not for anything in the world," Jared assured her deeply. "I'm home now, and I plan to stay."

Looking up at him, Cassie realized that for the first time since she'd met him in that New Mexico jail, his eyes were no longer haunted, the old memories and old loneliness having been replaced by a new contentment and purpose. Love glowed where pain had once burned, and she couldn't have been happier for him—or for herself.

She was very, very glad she'd taken a chance on Jared Walker.

* * * * *

Everything you love about romance...
and more!

Please turn the page for Signature Select™
Bonus Features.

ONCE
A FAMILY...

The Writing Life
by Gina Wilkins

For me, at least, there comes a point in every book when the characters suddenly become as real to me as people I have known for years. I know them intimately—their likes, their dislikes, their hopes, their dreams, their fears. Their secrets, flaws, strengths and weaknesses.

When I'm very lucky, this happens early in the process of writing a story—say, chapter three or four. Other times, it takes half a book or more before I really feel like I know the people whose lives are unfolding on the pages. Until that point, they are pretty much strangers to me, and I react to them as I often do to strangers I meet in my real life. A bit shyly, at first. Who are they? What do they want? More specifically, what do they want from *me?*

As I spend more time with my characters, they begin to share more about themselves with me. Often, it's an almost painfully awkward process, taking a great deal more patience than I sometimes believe I possess.

4

If I make the wrong assumptions about them, they freeze up, refusing to cooperate with me, making the writing process sluggish and frustrating. The words seem to ooze in slow, thick droplets onto the page, rather than gush forward in a recklessly glorious torrent, as they do on the best of writing days. Those best days occur only when I take the time to truly listen to my characters.

As I've finally learned from almost twenty years of writing, it isn't a process that can be rushed or forced, even when deadlines loom—and sometimes pass—obligations abound and other projects wait impatiently at the sidelines. And yet I continue to try by sitting in front of a blank computer screen or empty notebook for hours, writing ever so slowly, until that magical moment when at long last the characters open up and let me into their heads.

Once that transition happens, I sometimes have to go back to page one and make a few changes—correcting the inaccuracies I wrote about them before I got to know them. By the time I finish the last page, I feel almost as if I'm parting with good friends—sometimes hating to say goodbye, other times almost gratefully seeing them off, as one does when even cherished guests have stayed a bit too long.

I can give you an example of this process that happened while I was writing WEALTH BEYOND RICHES, my January 2006 Signature Select Saga title. When I began to tell the story,

I thought that hero Ethan Blacklock's mother, Margaret Jacobs, had died of an unexpected heart attack in her sleep. I was well into the book before I finally listened to something he'd been trying to tell me from page one—she had died in a fall down the stairs. This development completely changed the story, of course. How did she fall? I asked him. Was she alone when it happened? Was it no more than a tragic accident—or was there more to the tale that he hadn't yet divulged to me?

My husband happened to wander into my office when I made that startling discovery. "Ethan's mother didn't die of a heart attack!" I exclaimed. "She died in a fall."

6   Being long accustomed to the odd world I inhabit, my husband asked, "How do you know?"

"He told me," I replied. To which he merely nodded, as if that made perfect sense (which is probably why our marriage has lasted for almost thirty years).

Sound a bit strange? I was afraid it might. But this is a development that unfolds for me in every book. Other writers approach characterization and plotting in very different ways, of course. Some highly organized types (for whom I have nothing but admiration and envy) use flow charts, character sketches, diagrams and outlines—they actually know what's going to happen *before* they start to write. But even they have told me that no matter how much plotting and planning they do, they've almost all had characters who took charge of their books and turned the stories in completely different directions than the poor authors intended from the beginning. All we can do when that happens is try to enjoy the ride while we do our best to keep up.

Characterization, for me, is the most important part of a book, movie or television program. I have to truly care about the characters to lose myself in their stories, to be interested in what ultimately happens to them, to cheer for them and worry about them.

It's the same when I write—I need to know the characters and to believe in them in order to make their stories real. I know I've succeeded when I receive notes from readers who tell me how much they enjoy revisiting characters from past stories. What a joy that is for a writer to hear! I even had a fan write to me one time and beg rather sheepishly for me to tell her the gender of the baby one of my heroines was carrying at the end of a book. She knew the happy couple came from my imagination, of course, but she said the story wouldn't be complete for her until I told her whether they had a boy or a girl.

It was an easy question for me to answer; I knew without a doubt that the child was a boy. How did I know? Why, the characters told me so, of course.

Gina Wilkins's
Favorite Recipes

I cook with a distinctly Southern accent, as did
my mother and grandmothers before me. I'm
obsessed with serving "something green" with
every meal, and we all enjoy visiting the local
farmer's market for fresh vegetables in the spring
and summer. My husband likes to grill and
smoke meats, and I've been known to rely heavily
on the slow cooker during deadline crunches.
Even when our three children were attending
three different schools and involved in too many
activities, the family always gathered for dinner
together—even if the main dish came from a
freezer bag and was eaten almost on the run. As
my children move out on their own (only one of
the three still lives at home), I miss those evening
meals most of all, I think. Fortunately, everyone
still lives close enough at this point to come
home often for Mama's cooking.

Here are some of our family's favorite
recipes.

COLORFUL CRUNCH SALAD

4 cups fresh broccoli florets (about 3/4 pound)
4 cups fresh cauliflower
1 medium red onion, chopped
2 cups grape tomatoes

Dressing:
3/4 cup light mayonnaise
1/2 cup light sour cream
1 to 2 tbsp sugar or artificial sweetener
1 tablespoon vinegar
Salt and pepper to taste
Sunflower seeds (optional)

Combine vegetables. Whisk dressing ingredients until smooth, pour over vegetables and toss to coat. Cover and chill for two hours.

SHRIMP ÉTOUFÉE

1/2 stick butter
2 tbsp flour
1 cup chopped onion
1/2 cup chopped celery
1/3 cup chopped bell pepper
1 large clove garlic, mashed
1 tbsp Worcestershire sauce
1 tbsp minced parsley
1 tsp salt
1/8 tsp cayenne pepper
1 cup water
1 1/2 lb shrimp, peeled and deveined

In heavy two-quart saucepan, melt butter. Add
flour and cook over low heat, stirring constantly to
make light brown roux (the color of light caramel).
Add onions, celery, bell pepper and garlic. Cook
until vegetables are soft. Add remaining ingredients
except shrimp. Bring to a boil, then reduce heat
to simmer 15 minutes, stirring occasionally. Add
shrimp and cook until it's done, 3 to 5 minutes.
Serve over hot rice.

CREOLE GUMBO

4 tbsp butter
3 tbsp flour
1/2 cup chopped onion (1 small onion)
1 clove garlic
3 cans (14-1/2 oz size) chopped tomatoes,
do not drain
1/2 cup chopped green pepper
1 bag frozen sliced okra (or fresh sliced okra)
2 bay leaves
1 tsp dried oregano, crushed
1 tsp dried thyme, crushed
1/2 tsp salt
1/4 tsp bottled hot sauce
(I use at least twice this amt)
1-1/2 cups water
1 to 2 lbs shrimp, peeled and deveined
(can use frozen cooked shrimp)
1 lb frozen crawfish tails (optional)

In large saucepan, melt butter, blend in flour.
Cook and stir 7 to 8 minutes until golden brown.

Stir in onion and garlic, cook until onion is tender. Stir in tomatoes, green pepper, bay leaves, spices, okra, pepper sauce and water. Bring to boil. Reduce to simmer, cover, about 20 minutes. Remove bay leaves. Stir in shrimp and crawfish, heat through (if using fresh shrimp, cook until done, 3 to 5 minutes). Serve in soup bowls over rice. May add hot sauce or filé seasoning to taste. I've served this to people who don't like okra, and they still enjoy this dish.

QUICKIE CHICKEN ENCHILADAS

3 chicken breasts, cooked and torn into pieces
(cook in microwave for faster preparation time)
1 can reduced fat cream-of-chicken soup
1 can reduced fat cream-of-mushroom soup
1 (4 oz) can diced green chiles
4 oz light sour cream
2 cups grated cheddar cheese
(or cheddar-jack mix), divided
flour tortillas

Mix soups, chiles, sour cream and chicken pieces. Place some of the mixture in a flour tortilla, sprinkle cheese on top and trifold tortilla. Put in sprayed casserole dish, fold down. Repeat until all of mixture is used (makes approximately nine enchiladas, depending on size). Bake covered at 350° F for 20 to 30 minutes. Uncover, top with remaining cheese, bake uncovered until cheese melts. Great topped with guacamole and sliced black olives and served with Mexican rice or corn.

SWEET POTATO CASSEROLE

3 cups mashed sweet potatoes
(If using fresh, wrap in plastic wrap, poke a couple of
holes in each and microwave five–six minutes per
potato. May also use canned yams.)
1 cup sugar
2 eggs, beaten
1/3 cup milk
1/3 cup melted butter
1 tsp vanilla
cinnamon to taste

Mix together and spread in casserole dish.

Topping:
1 cup brown sugar (packed)
1/3 cup flour
1 cup shredded coconut
1 cup pecans

Sprinkle over potato mix.

Bake at 350° F for 30 minutes.

DIXIE FUDGE CHESS PIE

1-1/2 cup sugar
1 stick butter
3 eggs, slightly beaten
4 tbsp cocoa
1 tsp vanilla
pinch of salt

Mix sugar and butter. Add other ingredients. Pour in uncooked pie shell. Bake at 425° F for 10 minutes. Turn down to 350° F for 30 minutes. Pure sin.

LIGHT MANDARIN ORANGE CAKE

1 yellow cake mix
1/2 cup applesauce
4 eggs
2 cans mandarin oranges (with juice, or drain and use 2/3 cup water)

Mix together. Bake in layers for 25 minutes at 350° F.

Cool completely before frosting.

Frosting:
9 oz light whipped topping
16 oz can crushed pineapple (don't drain)
1 pkg sugar-free vanilla instant pudding

Mix together and frost layers.

Here's a sneak peek...

14

WEALTH BEYOND RICHES
by
Gina Wilkins

Coming in January 2006 from Signature Select

❀

ETHAN BLACKLOCK straightened, leaned against the handle of his shovel and wiped his dripping brow with one deeply tanned forearm. A baseball cap shaded his face, and dark glasses protected his eyes from UV radiation, but he had no particular fear of the sun—even on a hot June afternoon in Dallas, Texas.

Looking around in satisfaction, he noted that he had made quite a bit of progress today. The gardeners employed by his family when he was growing up wouldn't have accomplished as much in twice the time.

Not that there was anyone to take pride in his achievements other than himself. His twice-widowed mother, Margaret Hanvey Blacklock Jacobs, would rather die than admit to her friends that the son she had groomed to become an attorney like her father, then both her husbands after him, had become a mere "gardener," instead.

He snorted at the errant thought and tightened his calloused hands around the shovel grip. Maybe his mother was ashamed of him, but he took great pride in the success he'd had with his fledgling landscape design business. With a grunt of exertion, he plunged the blade into the hard-baked earth, savoring the clean smells of dirt and sweat.

By the time he walked into his kitchen on that Monday evening, he was tired and filthy, but satisfied that the small, but profitable job he had completed that day had been a big success. Well worth the fourteen hard hours he'd put into it. The clients were pleased, the check had already been deposited and he was ready to move on to the next project.

Life was good.

After washing his hands in the sink and drying them on a paper towel, he opened the door to the stainless-steel refrigerator and pulled out a beer. He had just walked into the living room when someone knocked on the front door. With a regretful glance at the armchair in front of the TV, he crossed the room and opened the door without bothering to check who was on the other side.

His caller was dressed in a suit that might as well have been embroidered "hand tailored." A good-looking man in a squarely built way, Sean Jacobs was a year older than Ethan's thirty-one.

His sandy-brown hair was thinning at the temples, but had been styled by an expert. His shoes were Italian leather, and his tie probably cost more than Ethan's entire outfit of denim shirt, jeans and steel-toed work boots.

There had been a time when Ethan had dressed like Sean, himself.

"Sean," he said by way of greeting, stepping aside to allow his stepbrother to enter. "What brings you here?"

Sean's divorced father, Ferrell Jacobs, had married Ethan's widowed mother, Margaret Hanvey Blacklock, almost twenty years earlier. Ferrell died eight years after that. A heart attack— the same thing that had killed Ethan's father, Howard Blacklock, when Ethan was still very young.

Rather than answering Ethan's question, Sean took a moment to study him as they stood in the middle of Ethan's small living room. From the grubby, inexpensive clothes to the dried mud caked on the tops of Ethan's boots, Sean seemed to miss no small detail. "Been working today?" he asked with an awkwardness that was uncharacteristic of the usually glib lawyer.

"Yeah." Ethan made an ironic gesture toward Sean's work "uniform." "You?"

Sean acknowledged the slight dig with a very faint smile. "Yes."

It had been several years since they'd seen each other. Their last meeting had been cool, though not acrimonious. The biggest obstacle between them was that they had absolutely nothing in common, other than having rather briefly been stepbrothers. Because he had nothing particularly against Sean, Ethan tried to inject a reasonable amount of warmth into his voice when he said, "Have a seat. Can I get you a drink?"

"No, thanks." Sean chose a chair.

"I assume there's a reason for this visit? I doubt you were just in the neighborhood and wanted to check out my decorating skills."

The smile faded from Sean's face, leaving him looking so grim that Ethan was now convinced beyond doubt that this was no social visit. "There is a reason, of course. First, I want to express my sincere condolences for your loss. I know you and your mother have been estranged for a number of years, but I'm sure her death has been difficult for you."

Very slowly, Ethan placed his half-empty beer can on a black granite coaster on the nearest end table. "My mother is dead?"

Looking stricken by Ethan's reaction, Sean groaned. "Surely your cousin called this morning to tell you Margaret passed away. He told me he would."

Ethan kept his face impassive. "No. But I haven't checked phone messages yet today. What happened?"

Sean answered quietly, "She fell down the stairs. The housekeeper had gone to her daughter's house in Tulsa for the weekend, and she found Margaret at the foot of the stairs when she returned early this morning—sometime around 6:00 a.m. The police were called, of course, but there was no reason to believe it was anything other than a tragic accident. The doors were all locked, the security system was set and there was no evidence to indicate that anyone else had been in the house. Apparently, your mother made a misstep at the top of the stairs—probably during the night, in the darkness—and broke her neck when she fell. She'd been having balance problems lately. Betty told the police it's the third time Margaret fell in the past few months, though she escaped with nothing more than bruises before. Betty was devastated, having been with Margaret so long. She felt guilty for taking the weekend off, though I assured her no one could possibly blame her. Margaret was always so stubbornly independent."

Ethan hadn't known about the earlier falls,

BONUS FEATURE

but that was no surprise to either of them, since he hadn't been a part of his mother's life in a long time.

"I'm sorry you weren't notified sooner," Sean said, when Ethan remained silent. "As Margaret's attorney, I was the first one Betty called after the police, and then she called your cousin Leland. We tried dialing your number here, but there was no answer. Leland assured everyone he would track you down and let you know. But maybe we simply misunderstood. Maybe Leland assumed I called you, as I thought he had."

20 "I was at the job site by five-thirty this morning. But I had my cell phone with me, as I always do. It wouldn't have been that hard to dig up the number." Ethan wasn't particularly surprised that his cousin hadn't called, since they'd despised each other since childhood.

"I'm sorry, Ethan," Sean said again, awkwardly.

"So, this is a sympathy call?"

"Partly, of course," Sean agreed too quickly. "I am sorry for your loss."

"Right." Since they both knew he hadn't talked to his mother in more than three years, and that conversation had been loud and angry, Ethan figured there had to be more to this visit than simple protocol. "When's the funeral?"

"There won't be one. Your mother left explicit

instructions that she was to be cremated quickly, without ceremony."

Ethan shrugged. "I'm sure Leland will take care of everything quite competently. And if you think he just accidentally forgot to call me today, then you're more naive than I remember you being. Leland and I were never what you would call friends."

Sean grimaced. "I remember. You called him a brownnose and he usually referred to you as 'the Neanderthal.' Those were the more flattering of the nicknames you had for each other, I believe."

Being in no mood for stories about his less-than-idyllic past, Ethan abruptly changed the subject. "You said sympathy was 'partly' the reason for this visit. What's the other part?"

Sean cleared his throat. "You know, of course, that the firm handled all of Margaret's legal affairs."

Ethan resisted the urge to respond with the juvenile and rather dated "Well, duh." After all, his mother's father had started the law firm in which both of her late husbands, and now her stepson, had all practiced. It had been her fondest, and vehemently expressed, desire that Ethan would follow in their footsteps, which had led to their most frequent and most heated arguments.

So this was about the settlement of Margaret's considerable estate. Made sense. And yet, something about the way Sean drew a deep breath before speaking again warned Ethan that his stepbrother did not consider himself to be the bearer of good news. Had Ethan been disinherited? No surprise there.

"I hate to be the one to break all the bad news to you, Ethan, but your mother left almost all of her estate in a testamentary trust. The primary beneficiary is a young woman named Brenda Prentiss."

Ethan wasn't able to hide his reaction to that news. His eyes widened in surprise. "Brenda Prentiss? Who the hell is she?"

"She's a local elementary schoolteacher. Single, twenty-six years old, orphaned with two older siblings, no record of ever having been in trouble with the law."

"What was her connection to my mother?"

"I have no idea. And, apparently, neither does Ms. Prentiss."

Ethan shook his head slowly. "That's crazy."

Sean made a suitably confused gesture with one hand.

"So, you're here to tell me I've been written off with nothing?" Ethan kept his tone light, almost bored, even though he was still reeling from the series of shocks Sean had just given him. "Trust me, that comes as no surprise."

"Actually, that isn't quite accurate. Your

mother did leave you something. Everything inside the house that personally belonged to your father. That was the way she worded it, which is admittedly vague. The house and grounds, themselves—"

"Went to Ms. Prentiss," Ethan recited with him.

"Yes. For the duration of her lifetime, to be passed down to her children, should there be any. If she dies without progeny, the estate passes back to you, if you survive her, or your children, if you do not. If you have no surviving offspring, the remainder of the estate is to be divided between your cousin and several charities."

His throat suddenly, unexpectedly tight, Ethan nodded. There were several of his father's belongings that he wouldn't mind having for sentimental reasons. As for the rest of it—screw it. He wasn't going to fight over a penny of the inheritance he had willingly walked away from years ago. "Will my father's things be delivered to me?"

"Oddly enough, Margaret didn't list any of the items in question. You'll have to make arrangements for a supervised visit to collect what you want."

"Oh, sure. *That* won't be at all awkward."

"I'm sorry, Ethan. Someone should have realized earlier that Margaret didn't include an inventory of your father's belongings with her will. But I'm sure Ms. Prentiss will be accommodating."

"Didn't you just tell me you've never met her?"

"Um. No. I haven't."

"Then she could be the Wicked Witch of the West, for all you know."

Sean shrugged apologetically. "I suppose there's a possibility she could make things difficult for you, though I don't know why she would. After all, she's inherited a great deal from an apparent stranger to her."

"Thanks, Sean." Ethan looked pointedly toward the door.

To be honest, he needed some time alone now. He'd been so busy trying to hide his feelings about his mother's death that he hadn't had a chance to examine them, himself. Once he was alone again, Ethan shut the door, closed his eyes and rested his forehead against the wood.

...NOT THE END...

Look for the continuation of this story in WEALTH BEYOND RICHES by Gina Wilkins, available in January 2006 from Signature Select.

MINISERIES

National bestselling author

Janice Kay Johnson

Patton's Daughters

Featuring the first two novels in her
bestselling miniseries

The people of Elk Springs, Oregon, thought
Ed Patton was a good man, a good cop, a good
father. But his daughters knew the truth, and his
brutality drove them apart for years. Now it was
time for Renee and Meg Patton to reconcile...
and to let love back into their lives.

"Janice Kay Johnson gives readers romance and
intrigue sure to please."—*Romantic Times*

Available in January

Where love comes alive™

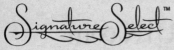

Signature Select™

COMING NEXT MONTH

Signature Select Spotlight
SUNDAYS ARE FOR MURDER by Marie Ferrarella
FBI agent Charlotte "Charley" Dow is on the hunt for her sister's murderer and finds herself frustrated, yet attracted to agent Nick Brannigan. Working together, Charley and Nick must battle the mind of a psychopath, as well as their own personal demons, to put the serial killer away.

Signature Select Collection
WRITE IT UP! by Elizabeth Bevarly, Tracy Kelleher and Mary Leo
In this collection of three new stories, three reporters for a national magazine are given a unique assignment to write about dating practices for the urban set. And when Julie, Samantha and Abby each get to work, love and mayhem result.

Signature Select Showcase
THE QUIET GENTLEMAN by Georgette Heyer
On becoming the new earl of Stanyon, Gervase Frant returns from abroad to take possession of his inheritance. However, he is greeted with open disdain by his half brother and stepmother. When Gervase becomes prey to a series of staged "accidents," it seems someone is intent on ridding the family of him...permanently.

Signature Select Saga
WEALTH BEYOND RICHES by Gina Wilkins
Brenda Prentiss lived a simple life—until she inherited over a million dollars from a stranger! Now several attempts have been made on her life and her benefactor's son, Ethan Blacklock, is the prime suspect. Ethan must prove to Brenda that he's not out to protect his money...he's protecting *her*.

Signature Select Miniseries
PATTON'S DAUGHTERS by Janice Kay Johnson
The people of Elk Springs, Oregon, thought Ed Patton was a good man, a good cop, a good father. But his daughters know the truth. Both police officers themselves, Renee and Meg have been estranged for years. Now the time has come for the Patton sisters to reconcile... and to let love back into their lives.

The Fortunes of Texas: Reunion
THE LAW OF ATTRACTION by Kristi Gold
Alisha Hart can't believe how arrogant fellow lawyers like Daniel Fortune can be, especially when he offers her a bet she can't refuse. Daniel can't wait long for victory, and soon their playful banter turns into passionate nights in the bedroom. But could this relationship with Alisha cost him the promotion to D.A.?